Roland pushed off his ... ... back to the center of the pool. "You can't really mean to ... go such a small pleasure?"

Livy extended one foot and gestured toward it. "My stays don't allow me to unlace my own boots."

He struck out toward her, and Livy simply stood and stared. The water didn't obscure much of his powerful form as it sluiced over him. Wide shoulders, arms finely muscled, and what she couldn't see now she remembered all too well from watching him greedily as he disrobed.

Devere's hand snaked out and wrapped around her ankle. He pulled himself partially out of the pool as he unlaced her boot. Rivulets of water ran down his back, defining every line of muscle and bone.

This was what it felt like to be wanton. She was sure of it. Her skin burned where he touched her. She'd never anticipated her husband's touch the way she did Devere's, had never wanted him to come to her so badly that her hands shook as they did now.

Devere unhooked her garter with a skillful flick of his thumb and slid her stocking down. She lifted her foot, and he pulled the length of silk free. Livy swallowed hard, ignoring the clamor of alarm that sounded dimly inside her. He might be the predator, but she still held the whip. He'd only go as far as she let him...

Praise for

The League of Second Sons Series

Ripe for Scandal

"With her witty dialogue and tender romance, Carr draws readers into her marriage-of-convenience plotline that delves into what happens when the couple falls in love and then struggles to build a strong marriage against the odds. It's a lesson all can savor." —*RT Book Reviews*

"An exciting tale of sensuous romance, seduction, and misunderstandings…An appealing mixture of fun and danger, I was soon caught up in *Ripe for Scandal*…Isobel Carr is an author I will watch for in the future."

—RomRevToday.com

"An enjoyable Georgian romance…With an intelligent marriage of (in) convenience plot, the second League of Second Sons is a fabulous tale."

—GenreGoRoundReviews.blogspot.com

"I really connected with both Beau and Gareth. And I enjoyed their happily ever after. Beau is a strong and sassy heroine who believes in going after what she wants, and Gareth complements her so well. I like the idea of the League of Second Sons, and will be checking out future stories in the series."

—RomanceNovelNews.com

Ripe for Pleasure

"Carr is a born storyteller. She enriches her sensual tale with colorful details, suspense, a treasure hunt, and charming, delightful characters...The fast pace and added humor will have readers eagerly awaiting the next novel in the League of Second Sons series." —*RT Book Reviews*

"With sensual and witty characters, sexy love scenes, a hint of mystery, and evildoers, *Ripe for Pleasure* is simply intoxicating...An exciting start to a wonderful series. I will be eagerly looking forward to the next one."
—TheRomanceReadersConnection.com

"Charming...Filled with adventure, action, a treasure hunt, and romance, *Ripe for Pleasure* is the perfect summer romance book...One of my favorites! A quick read that will have you turning the pages. I cannot wait to read what comes next in the series."
—Renees-Reads.blogspot.com

"Fun and steamy...If you're in the mood to leave the reality of life for a while, you just might want to pick up this book and lose yourself within its pages. I found it a delightful read." —SeducedByABook.com

"Delightful...Tense throughout yet fully 'ripe' with humor. Sub-genre fans will enjoy this charming late-eighteenth-century tale."
—GenreGoRoundReviews.blogspot.com

Ripe
for
Seduction

Also by Isobel Carr

Ripe for Pleasure
Ripe for Scandal

Ripe for Seduction

ISOBEL CARR

FOREVER

NEW YORK   BOSTON

Copyright © 2012 by Isobel Carr

All rights reserved. In accordance with the U.S. Copyright Act of 1976, the scanning, uploading, and electronic sharing of any part of this book without the permission of the publisher is unlawful piracy and theft of the author's intellectual property. If you would like to use material from the book (other than for review purposes), prior written permission must be obtained by contacting the publisher at permissions@hbgusa .com. Thank you for your support of the author's rights.

Forever
Hachette Book Group
237 Park Avenue
New York, NY 10017

HachetteBookGroup.com

Printed in the United States of America

First Edition: December 2012

10 9 8 7 6 5 4 3 2 1

OPM

Forever is an imprint of Grand Central Publishing.
The Forever name and logo are trademarks of Hachette Book Group, Inc.

The Hachette Speakers Bureau provides a wide range of authors for speaking events. To find out more, go to www.hachettespeakersbureau .com or call (866) 376-6591.

The publisher is not responsible for websites (or their content) that are not owned by the publisher.

For Jess, who keeps me sane.

ACKNOWLEDGMENTS

Again, I owe a special debt of gratitude to my friend and plot partner Tracy Grant. Her brain is amazing! I'd like to thank my friends, family, and dog for putting up with the fact that I checked out of the last year and half of our collective lives in order to focus on my writing. Special thanks to my friends Monica McCarty, Jami Alden, Bella Andre, Miranda Neville, Joanna Bourne, and Carolyn Jewel for listening to me whine and helping me celebrate. I'd like to add a new round of thanks to my "tweeps" (especially Sunita, Maili, Growlycub, and SonomaLass), who make the life of a shut-in author bearable and keep it entertaining. Twitter, how did I resist you so long? Last, my agent, Linda Chester, and my editor, Alex Logan: Thanks for being there and helping make this book a reality.

Ripe for Seduction

❧ PROLOGUE ❧

There are three private gentlemen's clubs on St. James's Street in London, each with its own rules and regulations governing membership. They are filled each day with peers who can't be bothered to attend to their duties in the House of Lords, let alone what they owe to their estates and family. Their ranks are frequently swelled by the addition of their firstborn sons, who gamble away their youth and fortunes while waiting for their fathers to die. What's less commonly known is that there is also one secret society, whose membership spans all three: *The League of Second Sons.*

Their charter reads:

We are MPs and Diplomats, Sailors and Curates, Barristers and Explorers, Adventurers and Soldiers. Our Fathers and Brothers may rule the World, but We run it. For this Service to God, Country and Family, We will have Our Due.

Formed this day, 17 May 1755. All Members to Swear to Aid their Fellows in their Endeavors, Accompany them on their Quests, and Promote their Causes where they be Just.

Addendum, 14 April 1756. Any rotter who outlives his elder brother to become heir apparent ~~to a duke~~ is hereby expelled.

Addendum, 15 Sept 1768. All younger brothers to be admitted without prejudice in favor of the second.

❧ CHAPTER 1 ❧

London, April 1785

Bird chatter split the morning air, the sharp cries entering Roland Devere's ears and cracking his head apart. He turned his face away from the sunlight streaming through the window and draped his arm over his eyes.

Never try to out-drink Anthony Thane. Never bet against Lord Leonidas Vaughn. And never fence with Dominic de Moulines. Three rules to live by.

And he'd broken all of them last night, though thankfully not in that order. The evening had begun with a bout of fencing at Angelo's salle and ended in an utter debauch at Lord Leonidas's house on Chapel Street. Vaughn's wife had abandoned them to it with a queenly shake of her head, not even bothering to scold.

The soft tread of someone in some not-too-distant room finally forced his eyes open. It sounded as though whoever it was were tiptoeing about in their stocking feet, but the soft creaks of the floorboards were almost more irritating than the birds. No, they *were* more irritating. Infinitely so, as they spoke to an awareness of his presence and condition.

Roland pushed himself upright, head pounding uncomfortably as he did so. His coat was bound up at the shoulders, nearly swaddling him. He yanked it about. He was still fully dressed save for his shoes, which lolled beneath a chair across from the settee he'd spent the night on. His hair swung into his face, a dark, heavy curtain, and he shoved it back, hooking it behind his ears. A quick search of his pockets and the recesses of the settee failed to produce the black silk ribbon that normally contained his hair.

The last time he'd downed that much port he'd woken upstairs in one of the finer houses of the impure in Florence with a troupe of disgusting little *putti* staring down at him from the bed's canopy, their sly smiles and tiny pricks lurid in the morning light. Vaughn's drawing room was an infinitely more welcoming sight.

His own generation of The League of Second Sons had caroused their way through London, their band growing larger and more raucous as they went. They'd stormed Lady Hallam's ball, invaded the Duke of Devonshire's rout, and been ejected from the coffee house The League had made their own by the elder members who'd retired there for a quiet night. Ultimately, they had finished their evening here in Vaughn's drawing room, or at least he had. No one else appeared to have laid claim to the other settee or the floor.

Roland had a vague memory of Thane flirting with Lady Ligonier in the bow window just before his memory went black. Perhaps Thane had been lucky enough to accompany the lady home. Lucky devil if he had. For the life of him, Roland couldn't remember anyone taking their leave, but he must have been in quite a state if they couldn't even get him up the stairs and into one of the guest chambers.

Roland ran his hands down his chest, yanking them away as a pin dug painfully into his flesh. He glanced down. A thin, brass dress pin, the kind used to hold a lady's gown closed, secured a slip of paper to his coat. Roland tore it free, sending the pin flying.

His own drunken handwriting crawled across the paper:

> *I, Roland Devere, bet Lord Leonidas Vaughn one guinea I can beat Anthony Thane into the bed of Lady Olivia Carlow.*

All three of their signatures were scrawled below the statement, Thane's with an artful flourish that bespoke amusement and sobriety. Roland crumpled the note in his fist. How many witnesses had there been? Who'd been left by the time they'd degenerated into boasts and bets? Good Lord, Lady Olivia was, in to some convoluted way, very nearly a relative of Vaughn's, as his sister was married to Lady Olivia's first husband's brother. What the hell had they been thinking?

A heart-shaped face, brilliant blue eyes under straight pale brows, a jumble of blond curls. Lady Olivia shimmered insubstantially before his eyes. She had been hotly pursued during her time on the marriage mart. An heiress and a beauty. She'd married well...or so it had seemed at the time.

Lady Olivia had been through a lot in the last year. He ought to know, having borne witness to all the most humiliating details of the scandal that had ended her marriage. She didn't need the gentlemen of the *ton* making sport of her, but it was inevitable that she would be pursued like a vixen by a pack of hounds now that she'd returned to town.

Guilt at being one of those selfsame hounds surged before dissipating amid the rush of undeniable anticipation. Lady Olivia Carlow wasn't quite a widow, nor was she ruined in the traditional sense of the word. Her situation was, in a word, *unique.*

Numbness spread through Livy's hands as she read the letter that had arrived on the silver salver with the morning post. The tingling spread up her arms and coalesced into a blinding ball of fury inside her chest. She stared dumbly at the words, raking her eyes over the sentences that sloped haphazardly across the page and ended in a nearly illegible scrawl of a signature.

She'd known returning to town was a mistake. Had known it bone deep. But just when she'd convinced her father that it was a terrible idea for her to accompany him back after the Easter recess, her grandmother had started in, siding with the earl—against her—for the first time since her marriage had ended.

Her marriage. Livy's stomach churned and she tasted bile at the back of her throat. Her marriage had been the great scandal of the *ton* the previous year, eclipsing even the runaway marriage of her former brother-in-law.

Bigamy wasn't a word an earl's daughter was ever

supposed to become familiar with, let alone something she was supposed to experience. It was still nearly impossible to grasp that the man she'd married, the man she and her father had chosen so carefully from her legions of suitors, had already had a wife. Some Scottish cutler's daughter who was, even now, happily remarried and living in Canada.

The crinkle of paper brought her head up from the insulting letter and pulled her out of the spiral of reminiscences. Her father was staring at her over the sagging upper edge of *The Morning Post*. Livy forced herself to pick up her teacup and take a drink. The tea was stone cold, and the sugar lay thick in the bottom, only half dissolved, but it served to settle her roiling stomach all the same.

"Bad news?" the earl asked, brows rising to touch his gaudy silk banyan cap. Livy smiled as her gaze lingered on the cap. It was fussy and old-fashioned. So unlike her father, but her mother had made it just before she'd died and so he persisted in wearing it.

Livy shook her head and refilled her cup. "No, just country gossip from Grandmamma," she said, the lie coming easily to her lips. Lying was a new skill, but it had become a necessary one. She couldn't possibly have been truthful about how she'd felt since her marriage had been invalidated. Not even with her father. Especially not with her father.

The earl smiled, his attention already slipping back to the news of the day. There were ink stains on his fingers. A sure sign that he'd torn himself away from his desk to join her in the breakfast parlor.

Philip Carlow was a man of intellect. A man who waged war in Parliament with verbs and won those battles with synonyms. But it wasn't magic. He wasn't like the bards of old, who could raise blisters with a word or lay waste to an army with a song. And today, she rather wished he were. Surely Mr. Roland Devere deserved some sort of reprimand for having made her such a preposterous proposal?

Livy smoothed the letter on the table and read it over again, sucking the marrow out of every word. Devere's penmanship was atrocious. His quill had stuttered and splattered ink across one corner of the letter. There was a dark ring where a glass of wine had been set down on the sheet of foolscap, making several words run and blur, but his offer—and the insult therein—was unmistakable.

Devere was offering himself as the sacrificial lamb for the pyre of her marriage. Every widow must start somewhere, and he thought, perhaps, she would like to start with him. Arrogant bastard.

Livy toyed with a muffin, breaking off a piece and slathering it with ginger preserves. She chewed thoughtfully. If only she were a widow. Widows were given a great deal of leeway in their behavior. Such an offer might even have been tempting if she were. Roland Devere, dark as a gypsy, handsome as a fallen angel, would have been a very good start for a widow in need of entertainment.

As it was? No. Devere and his ilk were the last thing she needed. And this was just the beginning. Just a warning shot across her bow. She was damaged goods, and men who'd once vied for her smiles would be expecting something more—and offering a great deal less—this time around.

She swallowed and took another bite, letting the heat of the ginger linger on her tongue. Roland Devere was a pompous ass, and he deserved to be punished. No, not just punished. He deserved to be tortured over an extended period of time for his presumption, and he should serve a higher purpose as added penance.

Livy smiled and slipped the letter into her pocket. Not only should Devere do penance, he should serve as a warning to others, and she knew exactly how to go about making him of use.

❦ CHAPTER 2 ❧

There was a pregnant silence about his parents' house in Berkeley Square as Roland entered the front hall. He could feel a chill in the air. The clatter of shutters being thrown open and the distant din of the cook berating the scullery maid stood out distinctly. The words *ruined* and *clumsy* echoing up from the kitchen told the story of some broken piece of crockery or spoiled luncheon dish.

The dim hall was a blessed relief after the god-awful glare of the streets. Roland had retrieved his shoes and escaped from Vaughn's house with no one but an amused-looking maid as witness. His hat, along with the ribbon for his hair, seemed to have disappeared entirely, but his purse had expanded by a good hundred quid, so it seemed more than a fair exchange.

Emerson, his father's butler, greeted him with wide, wild eyes, like those of a cornered dog. The man glanced furtively at the closed door to the drawing room, nodded warningly at a footman in green-and-black livery who stood waiting in the far corner, and held his hand out expectantly.

"My hat seems to have wandered off in the night," Roland said with a shrug. "Fortunes of war, what."

Emerson's hand dropped to his side like a pheasant shot from the air. "Breakfast has been cleared, but I can have something sent up if you're hungry, sir," he said, not taking his eyes from the closed doors. "Ham steak, perhaps?"

Roland's stomach revolted. "No. Thank you, but no," he said. The butler's gaze darted to him but returned to the drawing room doors as if drawn by a lodestone. "Everything all right, Emerson?"

"Her ladyship has a visitor," he replied, using the tone usually reserved for disasters of epic proportions or royal visitations, which were much the same thing in Roland's experience. But that wasn't one of the king's footmen. Nor one of the prince's.

Roland studied the tall, solid double doors. Mysterious footmen aside, the most likely source of disaster was his sister. Margo, newly widowed and returned to England, was ripe for trouble. She'd spent the last decade in the midst of the French court at Versailles, where *liaisons* were an art form and no one played the game better than her husband, the comte de Corbeville.

Well, no one except, perhaps, Margo.

Headache forgot, Roland stepped past Emerson. At his touch, the door swung open without a sound. Silence filled his mother's drawing room. It buffeted him like a cannonade.

His mother looked as though she'd swallowed a toad and couldn't quite choke it down. Her mouth moved, but no words came out. The countess's fashionably grizzled hair trembled, shedding bits of powder that danced in the bright morning sunshine like brilliant motes.

Seated across from her was Lady Olivia Carlow. The object of his wager smiled as she saw him, no hint of anger or reproach on her face. Behind them both, his sister, clothed in unrelenting black, sat in the window seat, sun flooding in behind her. Margo's hands were idle on her needlework, poised as though frozen in time. Her expression was carefully, artfully, blank.

A deep sense of dread flooded through Roland. Lady Olivia smiled again, but there was a brittle edge to her expression, a hint of too many teeth. He knew that expression, having seen it on his sister's face all too often. The lady was out for blood.

His mother finally caught her breath with an audible intake and attempted to gather her wits. "I'm so sorry, my dear. I don't think—I-I-I didn't quite—are you quite sure there isn't some mistake?"

"I don't believe so," Lady Olivia said with alarming good cheer. "But here's your son now. I'm sure he can clear up any *misunderstanding.*"

Dread flared into something closer to outright horror as Lady Olivia emphasized the final word. What the hell had he done last night? What had Thane—damn him—got him into? She couldn't possibly know about the bet, and even if Thane had sought to hobble him by telling her—and had somehow managed to do so this very morning—there'd be no reason for Lady Olivia to run and tell tales to his mother.

Roland glanced at his sister, hoping for a hint as to what was afoot, but Margo merely raised one brow and then pretended to return to her embroidery. However, an amused smile lurking about her mouth was very much in evidence as she bowed her head. Margo was enjoying whatever little drama was underway, which boded ill.

Lady Olivia rose from her seat and stepped toward him. Her eyes pinned him in place, the deep blue a blaze of color in her pale face. One side of her rosy mouth curled up higher than the other as she smiled. She looked entirely too pleased with herself, too sure of herself. Whatever salvo had apprised her of the game they were playing, she was about to return fire.

"Mr. Devere"—her hand slid down into the pocket slit of her gown with an audible rustle and emerged with a small, folded sheet of foolscap—"did you, or did you not, make me this very *charming* offer of marriage just last night?"

She held the letter out, eyes daring him to take it. Roland plucked it from her hand and read it over, growing sicker by the second. He glanced back up to find Lady Olivia watching him, eyes steady and full of power. He'd seen a cobra once, brought all the way from India to dance at a duchess's gala. The creature's gaze had carried less threat than that of the lady who stood before him.

"Perhaps," Lady Olivia said, her eyes never wavering from his, "Lady Moubray would like to read it and judge for herself if I've misunderstood your offer."

Roland swallowed, his mind racing. What the hell was she playing at? She couldn't possibly want to marry him. He was a younger son with a minor sinecure and a matching minuscule income. He hadn't the power or position to wash away the scent of scandal that enveloped her. She needed a lord for that. If it were him, he'd be aiming for a duke. A royal one if at all possible.

"No need," Roland said, refolding the note he'd obviously dashed off at some point after the night had gone dim. It was all he could do not to crumple it in his fist and chuck it into the fire. His friends had let him do it, too, perhaps even instigated it. The bastards. "My offer was unambiguous and quite genuine."

"So I thought." Lady Olivia's smile became a triumphant smirk as she plucked the letter from his grasp and tucked it back into her pocket. "Perhaps when your mother and I have finished our tea you could escort me home."

"Yes, Roland," his mother said uneasily. "You should speak to Lord Arlington at once. It really isn't at all the thing to be making offers to young ladies without speaking to their fathers first."

She sounded as though the affront were to her, not Lady Olivia's father. Perhaps she was hoping the earl would refuse his permission. Save them all from impending scandal.

Lady Olivia clapped her hands over her mouth. Her eyes met his, brimming with amusement at his mother's evident horror. The countess stared at them both, her eyes full of confusion and concern.

"I'm my own mistress," Lady Olivia said as she reclaimed her seat in a flounce of silken petticoats. She looked pleased as Punch after he'd beat Judy into submission. "But I'm sure the earl will feel as your mother does. He does so like to maintain the little formalities that keep us all *civilized*."

• • •

Beneath her hand, Devere's arm tensed and flexed. He reminded her of a grain-high horse being held back when it wanted to run. Livy tipped herself against him, pretending to stumble. He steadied her without missing a step. A gentleman and a rake at the same time, or perhaps his inclinations were mercurial? A gentleman by day and a rake by night?

The idea shouldn't be thrilling, and yet...

"Do you have a key?" she asked, waving one hand at the fenced lawn that made up the private park at the heart of the square.

"Yes," he said, glancing down at her as he fished about in the pocket of his coat.

"My father's house is only around the corner." Livy pulled him to a stop as she eyed the empty square. "And I think this is going to take a few minutes more than the walk there."

Devere nodded stiffly, light winking off the cravat pin set neatly inside the fall of crisp linen. Livy smiled to herself. This was turning out to be far more entertaining than she'd anticipated. Perhaps she was cut out for wickedness after all.

"Peter?" She turned her attention briefly to her father's footman. "Mr. Devere will see me home."

Peter looked skeptical, but he didn't bother to argue with her. He merely nodded and walked briskly off in the direction of Arlington House. Livy took a deep breath. She didn't need a witness, even a chance one, for the conversation they were about to have.

Devere led her carefully across the street, as solicitous as if she actually meant something to him, and let them both into the small park. It was deserted at the moment, not even a solitary nurse with her tiny charges or a footman with his employer's lap dog making use of its oyster-shell paths.

From beneath the shade of the wide brim of her hat, Livy studied Devere's profile. He had a long nose that turned down at the tip, like the ones on so many of the statues in Rome. He was swarthy like a Roman too, the shadow of beard on his jaw still visible even though she could smell his shaving soap.

He'd left her alone with his mother for less than ten minutes, but he'd returned shaved, in a clean suit of clothes, and with his hair neatly tied back rather than tumbling in riotous waves about his shoulders. She rather missed the pirate, which must surely be a very great failing on her part.

In the middle of the open square sat a stone bench, placed at the crossroads of the paths bisecting the immaculate lawn. Devere led her directly to it, dusted it off with his handkerchief, and motioned for her to sit.

He sat down beside her. Long lashes obscured his dark eyes. Devere's hands locked into fists, giving away the simmering anger and uncertainty that he'd otherwise masked. He knew he was caught, and he didn't like it one little bit. Livy bit back a smile.

"I'd like to apologize," Devere began, pitching his voice low even though there was no one but her to hear him. "I honestly don't even remember writing that letter, not that pleading inebriation makes its contents one jot less insulting."

Livy sucked in one cheek and nodded. He sounded

sincere, but she couldn't let him off so easily. Not when his mistake could keep him at her beck and call all season.

"Let us lay our cards on the table, Mr. Devere. You have put yourself entirely at my mercy, and in my present circumstances, I do not find a letter such as the one you sent particularly forgivable."

His head snapped about, and his nostrils flared. He'd only now realized how thoroughly he was trapped, and to how great an extent he'd placed himself in her hands. She almost felt sorry for him. Almost.

"It was, however," she went on, "very much what I expected after the events of last year. My father thinks the world will take pity on me, but you and I both know differently, don't we?"

Devere dropped his gaze to his hands. The seams of his gloves strained. Yes, he knew very well how he and his peers viewed widows and fallen women—game to be stalked, meat for their tables. Her status as something of both would simply add to the frenzy of the hunt. She'd become a singular prize.

"Seeing as the world is what it is," Livy said, "I must formulate a plan of defense. And since you have so obligingly volunteered, I shall allow you to be of use."

"By marrying me?" He glanced up, staring at her, dark eyes seeming to beg for clarification. Livy steeled herself. Those eyes would make a weaker woman reconsider the wisdom of constant exposure. But the woman she was today had been forged in the fire of ruin and quenched in scandal broth. She wasn't likely to succumb to a handsome face and a pair of smoldering eyes.

Her own rising anger sent a jolt of strength through

her. Livy smiled, knowing that her expression was too predatory for a proper female but unable to change it to something more demure. Devere sounded horrified at the idea of marrying her. Good enough to bed, but not good enough to wed. Not anymore, anyway. Her husband had been the one to commit a crime, but she was the one paying for it. If Souttar hadn't died, she'd have been tempted to kill him herself.

"I remain a very good catch, you know," she said, ruthlessly pressing on. "I've complete control of my dowry already, near fifty thousand pounds. And the earl intends to pass only the title and one small, entailed estate to the distant cousin who's his heir. Everything else will come to me, even Holinshed Castle."

Devere nodded, the muscles in his jaw popping out as he ground his teeth. "But," Livy said, allowing her smile to soften, "I shan't hold you to it. Give me the season, serve as my shield, and then we can go our separate ways."

He looked grim, keen intelligence flaring behind his eyes. "A broken engagement will be the final nail in the coffin of your reputation."

Livy nodded. "I'm counting on it. One more soupçon of scandal and my father will never again force me to accompany him to town. I can live out my days as I choose, mistress of my own destiny."

"As long as you understand what you're doing," Devere said, his tone clearly implying that she didn't. "When you give me my marching papers, you'll hand over that damned letter?"

"Of course," Livy said. "You'll have earned it, believe me."

❦ CHAPTER 3 ❧

A long-standing affection?" the Earl of Arlington said, not looking for a moment like he believed a word of it. The man's brow furrowed, eyebrows pinched with doubt and something that looked like the beginning of annoyance.

"Yes, my lord," Roland said, doing his best to appear earnest. It wasn't his most practiced or natural expression, and it didn't come easily. Especially when what he felt was a chaotic mix of excitement, dread, and anticipation. He might have been blackmailed into the role of Lady Olivia's choosing, but it positioned him perfectly to carry out the bet he'd made with Vaughn and Thane. And the beauty of it was, she didn't even see it.

Lady Olivia's father, who couldn't be more than a decade older than Roland was himself, simply stared back at him, looking unconvinced. The man must have married before he'd even reached his majority to have a daughter who was already nearly five-and-twenty.

Roland shook off a niggle of discomfiture. How far

could he push things before the earl's doubts flared into outright disbelief?

"I lost her once," Roland said. "Not being an ideal candidate for the hand of an heiress, I didn't fight for her as I should have, but I don't mean to make such a mistake twice."

"Meaning that you see yourself as more than fit to ask for her hand now that she's damaged goods." Roland held his breath as Arlington's lips pressed into a thin, hard line. The earl wasn't mincing words, and though he was a good deal younger than Roland's own father, he was clearly every bit as used to having his own way. Privilege of being a peer. Their rarefied position in the world lent them all a certain arrogance regardless of their age.

"No, my lord. That's not at all the light in which I see this, though I'll admit that others might." Roland leaned forward, holding his gaze steady, praying his argument was a convincing one. He'd had scant time to formulate it before being thrust into action and his head was starting to pound as last night's debauch once again caught up with him. "Lady Olivia has done nothing wrong. She's the wounded party, and I'd die to defend that fact."

Arlington's grimace softened. "Let's hope it doesn't come to that, Mr. Devere," he said with a bit of a sigh as he settled back into his chair. "I had my way in her first marriage. I take full responsibility for the disaster that ensued. Seeing as I failed so miserably, I'm prepared to let Livy have her way now, and if you are her choice, so be it."

"Thank you, my lord," Roland said. The sensation of a heavy weight pressing down on him grew until he had to force himself to breathe. It was done.

He'd wanted her father to agree, needed the man to do so if he was to keep his side of the bargain, but now that the earl had done so, the responsibility of defending Lady Olivia from the *ton* fell to him. Something that felt almost like guilt washed through him. Roland shook it off. There wasn't any room for guilt in the game he and Lady Olivia were playing.

"Don't thank me yet," Arlington said with a familiar, skeptical look in his eyes. "I think you might both regret your haste a few months hence."

"You mean you think your daughter might come to see that she had better options than a younger son?"

"To be frank, yes, and also, you might find defending her exhausting. It eats at you, you know, watching someone you love being persecuted and knowing that you're powerless to prevent it."

The front door shut with a soft thump that would have gone unnoticed if Livy hadn't been on tenterhooks waiting for her father's summons. She let her breath out and spread her hands over her stomach to keep from being sick. Only the wall of her stays shored her up and kept her from wilting.

Her father had sent Devere away. Panic welled up, choking her as effectively as a pair of hands about her throat. If the earl had said yes, she'd have expected to be fetched down to receive his blessing. Her mouth went dry. Without Devere, she was at *point non plus*. Out of options, save for the unappetizing one of brazening her way through the season on her own, fending off advances—without causing yet another scandal—as best she could.

Livy stood up and forced herself to go downstairs and find her father. If he and Devere hadn't come to blows, she could still salvage things. The earl had never been good at denying her something she really wanted.

She cracked the door to the earl's study open and peeked in. Her father was standing at the window, shoulder braced against the painted sash, gazing out at the street. He turned as she entered, an expression of wry amusement on his face.

The tension drained out of her. Whatever had happened, he wasn't angry.

"What are you up to, pet?" he said, leaning back against the windowsill. "I remember all your suitors, and Roland Devere was never among them."

"A younger son?" Livy said, closing the door behind her. "Of course not. Peers of the Realm, and the heirs thereof. No one lower than heir to an earl made it into the lists, though there were several who would have liked to have done."

The earl shook his head, clearly not appreciating her levity. "I've told Mr. Devere that I'll allow you to have your way, but I wanted to talk to you privately before giving the match my blessing. Are you sure, Olivia? Really sure? There'll be no taking it back once an announcement is made."

Resentment of that simple truth warred with relief. "I'm sure, Papa. I know exactly what I want." Or more to the point, she knew exactly what she didn't want: a life spent paying for the sins of someone else.

For a moment, Livy thought she'd shown too much of her hand, but the earl's expression altered as she watched and the moment passed. "I've no objection to Mr. Devere," her father said, "but I should prefer if you waited a bit before making any kind of public declaration. Let the *ton* at least see him court you publicly for a few weeks at least."

"But privately?"

"Privately, you may consider yourself betrothed," the earl said as he strode toward her, footsteps muffled by the thick Turkey carpets that were layered haphazardly over the floor. He gave her a quick hug and brushed his lips across her forehead. "I hope he makes you happy, darling."

❧ CHAPTER 4 ❧

Roland plucked two glasses of wine from a passing footman's tray and handed one to Lady Olivia with a slight obeisance. Lent was over, Parliament was back in session, and the *ton* had returned to London in force, ready for the Season and a few months of unabashed indulgence. His parents were among the first to throw open their doors, and their soiree was a perfect setting for Lady Olivia to reemerge.

One corner of Lady Olivia's mouth curled into a smile as she accepted the glass. Her fingers slid along his. Desire jolted through him. He wanted to taste that mouth, to drink down every gasp and cry. And he had every intention of doing so at some point before the lady gave him his *congé*. Even if there wasn't a bet to win, bedding Lady Olivia Carlow would have been irresistible.

She tipped her head back, drained the glass, and plucked the full one from his hand without so much as an apologetic glance. Roland chuckled as she took a dainty sip from his glass, batting her eyes at him as she did so.

She knew full well that he truly had meant everything in the letter he'd sent. The game was afoot.

"Moubray House will be filled to the rafters in another hour," she said, her gaze moving out over the crowd as the first strains of the opening minuet momentarily brought the cacophony down to a dull roar.

Lady Olivia's tongue darted out to wet her lips. Roland's pulse leapt as his heartbeat settled into his groin with an almost alarming ferocity. Behind her, the room was a sea of swirling, colorful silks and velvets. The familiar steps of the dance turned chaos into practiced order as if by magic.

"Would you like to join them?" Roland said as a footman took the empty glass from him and disappeared into the crowd. Anything to get his hands on her, even if it was only during the decorous steps of the minuet.

Lady Olivia shook her head, the jeweled pins set into her pale hair winking in the light, bringing life to her powdered coiffure. "Not just now," she said, her intake of breath causing her breasts to swell high above the confines of her bodice. Roland stared at the creamy expanse of skin. How far down would he have to delve to find a nipple? He could almost swear there was a hint of rose areola peeking over the edge of the dark silk with every breath.

A low, throaty chuckle brought his attention up to her face with a snap.

"If you weren't so dark," she said, "I think I might be able to make out a blush."

"Because you caught me taking in the scenery?" He raised his brows dismissively. Magnificent scenery it was, too, a fact of which she seemed all too cognizant.

"Because I caught you considering it as if it were yours, Mr. Devere. It's not," she said with a little shake of her head, "and it never will be. Shall we take a turn about the room?" She slipped her hand into the crook of his arm and pressed her magnificent bosom tightly against him as they wove through the crowd that milled about at the boundary of the dancers.

"Never?" Roland said, a grin pulling at his lips. "Are you quite sure of that, my lady?"

She glanced up at him, the blue of her eyes deepened by the kohl she'd smudged into her lashes. Roland fought the sensation of drowning. She held him there, captive in a private moment in the midst of the throng.

"Did you mistake the terms of our bargain?" Lady Olivia said, a cool hint of warning in her tone. She sipped her wine—his wine—then set the empty glass on a narrow, flower-strewn commode as they drifted past it.

"I don't believe so." Roland forced himself to look away and study the crowd as he led her toward some imaginary destination. "But I also don't believe the terms are so cut and dried."

The laugh that escaped before Livy could stop it turned heads all around them. The crowd seemed to step back, leaving the two of them on display in their own little tableau. Devere seemed oblivious to the room's collective attention battering them like the waves of a storm. The air of anticipation made Livy's head swim.

With an elegant bow, Devere settled her on one of the long, padded chaises that lined the walls of his parents' ballroom. He claimed the seat beside her, flicking out the skirts of his coat with practiced ease. The sensation of dizziness grew stronger, and Livy took a deep breath, trying to shake it off. He was just a man. A man like any other.

"You believe there's room for negotiation?" Livy said. Let him flirt all he liked. Truth be told, it was a pleasant change from the quiet life she'd led at her grandmother's and the strained unpleasantness of her former husband's house.

Devere smiled in response to her taunt, and Livy tapped her left cheek with her fan. His smile widened, and she could feel a responding flush rising on her cheeks. It would be so very easy to succumb.

"That's a *no* that means *yes*, my lady."

"That's a *no* that means *fetch me a drink*, Mr. Devere," she replied as she flicked her fan open. Dizzy, faint, flushed, she felt as though her skin might burn right through the layers of linen and silk that encased her. He looked at her as though she were a morsel on a plate. As though he could eat her in one bite. Swallow her whole.

"Your wish is my command," Devere said. "I shall return momentarily."

He stood and slipped into the crowd. Livy plied her fan a little more rapidly. Tonight he was every inch the gentleman, at least on the outside: hair formally dressed, its usual curl almost entirely tamed, wide shoulders encased in dark, subtly striped tobine, gloves and evening shoes lending him a polished air. But that smile was all pirate. Or all djinn, if she was to stick with the theme suggested by his quoting *The Arabian Night's Entertainment*.

Devere glanced back over his shoulder, dark eyes filled

with promise. Heat pooled in her belly and a sudden wave of longing coursed through her. Livy crammed it down, crushing it ruthlessly.

Roland Devere was a rake who'd made a reprehensible overture. Giving in to his blandishments and seductive glances was madness. Playing the jilt at Season's end was going to put her beyond the pale as it was. Falling pregnant or being caught *in flagrante delicto*, however, would be mortifying to her father and would transform her false engagement into a real one instantly.

Scheherazade had woven tales to preserve her virtue from the sultan. Livy suddenly realized the comparison was not as apt as she might like. She was more likely to spend the Season concocting reasons to keep herself from presenting her virtue to Devere like a present on Boxing Day. The thrill that skittered up her spine when he touched her, however decorously, was dangerous. And even knowing the danger, she couldn't prevent herself from glorying in the sensation.

Livy kept her chin up as several gentlemen eyed her as they passed. She knew them all. Mr. Gleeson. Lord William. Lord Medways. Their looks of open appraisement were exactly why she'd forced Devere into this charade.

Give any one of them so much as a smile and they'd interpret it as an open invitation. Deny them what they expected, what they wanted, and she risked them claiming to have enjoyed her favors out of spite. There was no way to win the game, only to refuse to play at all. And no way to refuse to play except to out-maneuver them from the beginning.

Devere stepped out of the crowd, wide shoulders

blocking her from the three men's view. Relief washed over her, the feeling almost more dangerous than simple lust. He wasn't protecting her out of the goodness of his heart. She'd be wise to remember that.

Devere reclaimed his seat and handed her another glass of peppery burgundy. When she looked up, the men were gone, doves fleeing before a hawk.

"Let us return to the subject of negotiations." Devere's voice curled around her, seductive as a caress.

Livy sipped her wine, steeling herself for battle, and watched Devere over the rim of her glass. The terms were hers, and they were firm. They had to be.

Devere leaned in, close enough that she could feel his breath whisper hotly across her skin. Livy resisted the urge to retreat. If he thought for a moment he had her on the run, she'd never regain the ground she'd lost.

"Perhaps what I'm speaking of isn't really a matter of negotiations," he said, the words barely discernible above the din of the room. "It's more a matter of a confession. I promised to defend you, to protect you, to squire you about and spend my days at your beck and call, but I never promised to behave like a eunuch while doing so."

A thrill shot through her, and the wineglass tumbled out of Livy's grasp, sending a shower of crimson liquid down her skirts. It wicked into the silk even as Devere cursed and yanked his handkerchief from his pocket.

"Rolly?" Devere's sister, the comtesse de Corbeville, appeared before them, her mourning gown stark but fashionable in every small detail. "What kind of dolt gives a woman red wine to drink in a squeeze like this? I could swear I taught you better." She sounded half disgusted but looked entirely amused, her dark eyes brimming with laughter.

"You did, dearest," he said apologetically, ceasing to dab at the ruin of Livy's skirts.

"Come along, Lady Olivia," the comtesse said, a sly smile hovering about her lips. "Let us see what can be done to remedy the situation."

Livy rose and Devere's sister bore her off, pushing her way through the crowd as though her mother's guests were nothing but chickens loose in the garden. She clearly expected them to make way, and they did, though the entire room seemed to follow their every step with rapt attention.

"Don't worry," the comtesse said as they ascended the stairs. "Paxton was with me at Versailles. She's got worse than wine out of silk over the years, believe me."

They reached the quiet refuge of the comtesse's suite of rooms, and Livy found herself thrust down into a chair while a maid of indeterminate years frowned over the damage to her gown and then set to work with powders and brushes and chamois cloth.

Devere's sister strolled over to her dressing table to fuss with her hair. She toyed with the curls of her fringe, primping them into place, and then turned her attention to adjusting the small silhouette that adorned her bodice. She caught Livy watching her, and her eyes sought Livy's in the reflection. "Are you really going to marry my brother?"

Livy glanced at the maid, and the comtesse burst into laughter. "Paxton doesn't speak a word of English." Devere's sister turned about and sat down on the delicate gilded bench beside the dressing table. "You and my brother put on quite the little show the other morning, but whatever was in that letter, it wasn't a proposal. Rolly looked as sick as a horse when you handed it to him."

Livy bit her lip and studied the comtesse. She was beautiful, but there was something almost brittle about her, and it wasn't merely the severity of her mourning clothes. If anything, black suited her. It made her look like a Spanish noblewoman, darkly intriguing.

"Is it so hard to believe that your brother would ask me to be his wife?"

"It's *impossible* to believe," the comtesse said, though her tone wasn't unkind. "Just as it's impossible to believe you'd say yes if he did." Devere's sister held her tongue for a moment, waiting for an answer. When Livy remained silent, the comtesse smiled and shook her head. "Not going to admit it's a sham? That's fine, too. I wouldn't either if I were playing a deep game." She picked up a small glass bottle and applied the stopper to her throat. The faint scent of orange blossoms wafted across the room. "I shall simply have to watch and speculate. It should make for an interesting Season at the very least."

The maid finished with her ministrations, and Devere's sister came over to examine the results. "*Bon!*" she said. "Good as new. And now I shall return you to the ballroom, but not, I think, to Rolly. Let's give him something—someone—to be jealous of, *non*?"

❦ CHAPTER 5 ❧

M aking headway, are we?"
Roland turned to find Anthony Thane had appeared silently beside him, the sound of his approach masked by the din of the music and chatter that filled the room. The big man had a wry look of amusement on his face.

"More so than you." Devere sipped his wine and continued to study the crowd, waiting for his sister and Lady Olivia to return. They'd been gone entirely too long for his liking. Lord only knew what Margo might say. His sister had always verged on the outrageous, and a decade at the French court certainly hadn't done anything to change that. She'd been dubbed *la folle Anglaise* at Versailles— the mad Englishwoman—and she was still very much the same madcap.

Thane chuckled. "Should I cut you out, popinjay?"

Roland fought back the urge to warn his friend off. He'd find out soon enough that Lady Olivia wasn't inclined toward a turn as a wanton widow. In the meantime, it might be entertaining to watch him try his luck.

"Feel free to make a fool of yourself, mountain. In fact, I'll take myself off to the card room, leaving you a clear field, if you'll promise to come and fetch me when you can no longer stand the pain of rejection."

Thane's brows rose, but he didn't lose one iota of his smug confidence. And under normal circumstances, he might have stood a chance.

Roland's mouth curled into a grin as he made his way to the card room. It almost felt like cheating, but Thane was more than overdue for a set-down. Bastard had the devil's own luck with women and cards. Women tended to be impressed with Thane's impressive height and his elegant demeanor. A tame beast. That was what his last ladybird had called him.

Inside the room the countess had dedicated to gentlemanly pursuits such as cards and smoking, Roland found a handful of his friends gathered round one table, some of them playing hazard while the others merely looked on.

"Mamma would have apoplexy if she knew you were dicing in her house."

Dominic de Moulines grinned at him with boyish abandon, his teeth blindingly white against the dusky skin he'd inherited from his African mother. He rattled the dice in their box. "Then it is a good thing *la chère comtesse* won't be coming in to verify that we're playing decorously at whist, *non*?"

Roland shook his head at the Frenchman and claimed a spot beside him. De Moulines sent the dice tumbling down the table and there was a collective groan of annoyance as he won yet again.

Lord Leonidas Vaughn caught Roland's eye. "I'll bet

you a guinea our *chevalier* can't keep hold of the dice for another three goes."

Roland met Vaughn's gaze. There was a disreputable glint in his green one, and Roland had learned long ago to never trust the sincerity of the blue one.

"I think I've had enough of one-guinea bets this week," Roland said, reaching for the decanter on the table and refilling his glass.

There was a collective, silent pause at the table before his friends burst into guffaws of laughter. One of the tables of whist players grumbled loudly while glaring at them.

"How are you progressing?" Lord Malcolm Reeves said when he'd regained the ability to speak. "You appear to have all your limbs intact, so I assume she didn't show the letter to her father."

Roland glared at his friends. "How could you have let me send such a letter?"

"You were unstoppable," Vaughn replied.

"Dead-set," Lord Malcolm added.

"I believe the phrase you used at the time was *a slave to your muse*," de Moulines said, twisting the knife with obvious glee. "You were adamant that your poesy be sent immediately. There was no deterring you."

"You could have stopped me," Roland protested.

Vaughn smiled, pleasure and amusement leaking out of every pore. "Isn't our pledge to aid and abet one another in our endeavors?"

Margo propelled Lady Olivia back into the ballroom with one hand at the small of her back. They were nearly of a height, but there was something about the girl that made

Margo think of her as delicate, as younger than she actually was. With her big blue eyes and heart-shaped face, she looked like a child, or, more accurately, like a child's expensive doll.

If Lady Olivia wanted to survive the season and whatever game she and Rolly were playing, then Lady Olivia was going to have to set the tune. If the girl let Rolly get away with doing so, it would be disastrous. Margo sighed as the girl's expression hardened when the swirl of guests swallowed them up. What was her family thinking? She wasn't ready to face down the *ton*. Not by a long shot.

"Let me see," Margo said, surveying the room, one finger at her lips. She needed just the right candidate. Her perusal stopped as Anthony Thane nodded to her. Margo smiled back, but shook her head *no*. Thane was tall, imperious, handsome in a rough sort of way, but he wouldn't make Rolly the least bit jealous. They were too good friends for that.

Thane put his hand over his heart as though shot, and Margo burst into laughter. The man she'd known when she made her come-out hadn't had a humorous bone in his body. He'd changed while she'd been gone. Well, if the truth be told, so had she.

"Come away, my dear," Margo commanded, pushing her charge forward into the crowd. "Mr. Thane won't do at all for our purposes. Well," she added, glancing back at him through the crowd, "he might do for mine, but not for yours. We need someone a little grander than Thane to torture Rolly with."

Lady Olivia stared at her, looking slightly thunderstruck.

"Have I've shocked you?" Margo said with a sigh, cursing her blithe tongue. "Sometimes I forget how *English* the English can be."

"But—but *you're* English," Lady Olivia said, a hesitant smile that looked to be half confusion pulling at her lips.

Margo made a dismissive gesture with one hand. "I was English," she said, steering the girl firmly past one of her own hopeful-looking swains. "Stay away from Lord Omsbatch."

"You just smiled at him."

Margo stopped and turned to face her brother's supposed bride. "What I might do is very different from what you should do, Lady Olivia. After the life I led in France, and the *roué* I married, no one really expects me to play the grieving, saintly widow. Etienne's death is generally thought to have been a relief, though most people aren't rude enough to say so to my face. *You*, on the other hand, are balanced upon a knife's edge. Smile at Lord Omsbatch, and you'll fall one way. Turn up your nose, and you'll at least maintain your precarious position."

Lady Olivia opened her mouth to protest, but nothing came out. She licked her lips. "And if I marry your brother?"

Margo broke into a grin of pure amusement. "If I thought for a moment that you were going to commit such folly, I'd throw you at Lord Omsbatch without hesitation. He's not a very nice man, but at least he has the title and fortune to resurrect your standing in society."

"And you think that's what I want?" Lady Olivia sucked in a sharp breath and caught her lips between her teeth.

Margo stared the girl down. "No, I'm fairly certain that it isn't. That's what worries me—"

"Livy, dear, there you are." The Earl of Arlington's greeting cut Margo off, and his daughter sighed with obvious relief. "Hello, Papa." Lady Olivia offered her cheek to her father, and the earl kissed it. "Done fleecing your friends at cards?"

"Impudent brat," the earl said with an indulgent smile. "Madame de Corbeville, isn't it? I think you were younger than my daughter when I last saw you."

"I think you must be right, my lord. Though it makes me feel ancient to own it." Margo found herself staring at the man. She certainly had been much younger, so much so, in fact, that she remembered Lord Arlington as being *old*, and he was nothing of the kind. Chagrin flooded through her.

"Fishing for compliments?" the earl responded with a lively, teasing look. Instead of lines of dissipation, Arlington had laugh lines etched into his face, and his eyes were every bit as blue as his daughter's. Ridiculously, Margo's heartbeat wavered and then ticked upward.

"Were you ready to go, Papa?" Lady Olivia said, a proprietary hand on her father's arm.

"So early?" Margo said, even as the earl said, "No, darling, I just couldn't seem to find you earlier."

"Nothing to worry about," Lady Olivia said, glancing uneasily between them. "Just a little mishap with a glass of wine."

The sudden awkwardness of the moment was shattered by the appearance of Anthony Thane. He greeted them all with a very elegant bow. "Lady Olivia, I was hoping for the honor of a dance. My lord, with your permission?"

Lord Arlington nodded and waved them off. Thane swept Lady Olivia out into the sea of dancers. "And you, my lady," the earl said, holding out his hand to her, "perhaps we could—not dance, obviously—take a turn about the room, and you could tell me the latest news from Versailles."

❧ CHAPTER 6 ❧

Livy glanced back over her shoulder. Her father and Devere's sister were flirting. And at the moment, they looked as though they were unaware anyone else in the room even existed. She'd never seen her father look at a woman that way. In fact, she'd never seen her father look at a woman period. Somehow, it had never occurred to her that he might.

Livy swiveled her head about again as she and Thane slid into the set that was already underway. Her father and the comtesse were gone, lost in the crowd. Feeling a bit at sea, Livy forced her attention back to her partner and the dance.

A woman several couples up the line glared down at Livy, her face pinched and haughty. Lady Pearson. They'd been friends before and during Livy's marriage, or so Livy had thought. After a whispered conversation and a long, pointed stare, Lady Pearson and her partner stepped out of the set.

Anger snapped through Livy, bringing her chin up.

Her head began to throb, a sharp stab behind her left eye. Livy shook off the pain. She had every right to be here. She'd been invited just as they had, and she'd not done anything wrong. Not once in her life had she taken a misstep that was worthy of even mild reproach, let alone banishment. At least not until a couple of days ago...

She circled palm to palm with Thane, and he bent to whisper, "Don't pay them any mind."

Livy forced herself to smile and pretend that such a snub didn't smart, that having her partner notice didn't make it infinitely worse. This was only the beginning. Engaged to Devere or not, there were surely plenty more slights to come in the next few months. He could keep the gentlemen at bay, but nothing could prevent the ladies of the *ton* from treating her poorly. And clearly previous friendship wasn't going to save her either. Did Lady Pearson think Livy's disgrace was catching?

"Thank you, sir, I won't," she said on the next pass, forcing the words out as she pinned a smile to her face.

Thane led her through the steps with surprising grace. She'd expected a certain roughness based on his size alone. There didn't appear to be an ounce of fat on him, but he was almost intimidatingly large. Devere topped her by a good six inches. She barely reached Thane's shoulder.

They were only halfway up the line when the music came to an end, the violins stretching out the final notes long after the other instruments had fallen silent. As Livy rose from the prescribed curtsy, Thane retained her hand, placing it securely on his arm. "Would you like a drink, my lady?"

Livy nodded. "More than anything," she said with a laugh. "Is there champagne?"

"If we can't find a footman with champagne, we can form a raiding party and procure some. I happen to be more than familiar with the cellars." He stood to his full height and glanced about the room. "I don't see a single suit of Moubray livery in circulation. Let's try our luck in the drawing room. They wouldn't dare leave the dowagers unattended."

Thane reappeared in the card room looking entirely too pleased for Roland's liking. "I left her with your mother in the drawing room," Thane said as he filled a glass of brandy for himself and cast a jaded eye over the table.

With the same self-satisfied expression still plastered on his face, Thane strolled away to join a knot of older Whigs who were in heated discussion beside the fireplace.

Roland tossed back the contents of his own glass and nodded to the table. His friends grinned back. Bastards, every one. They were enjoying this far too much. If they discovered that he was firmly under Lady Olivia's thumb, there'd be no living it down.

He discovered the supper dance underway as he went in search of Lady Olivia. Hungry guests were already heading toward the dining room. Roland pushed past them, feeling like a salmon heading upstream.

Lady Olivia was exactly where Thane had left her, sitting on a settee beside Lady Moubray, with the Duchess of Devonshire, the duchess's sister Lady Duncannon, and Lady Melbourne finishing out the circle. A beautiful trio, composed of some of the most scandalous—and powerful—women in the *ton*.

The duchess saw him first, a wide smile lighting up her face. "Mr. Devere, have you come to steal Lady Olivia back? Thane warned us that you might try."

The entire room went quiet, all eyes on him. Roland bowed. This was what he, what they, wanted after all. For the *ton* to take notice. "The supper dance has already begun, and Lady Olivia was kind enough to promise it to me."

Lady Melbourne and Lady Duncannon shared an amused glance. The duchess simply raised one supercilious brow. "That is kind, isn't it?" she said pointedly, looking at him as though she could see right through him.

"Very," Roland said through gritted teeth.

"Olivia," the Duchess of Devonshire said as Lady Olivia rose from the settee and shook out her skirts, "do come to my at home tomorrow."

"Yes," Lady Duncannon drawled. "We clearly have more than just what you've been up to in the country this past year to catch up on."

Lady Olivia accepted the invitation, bobbed a quick curtsy, and excused herself. Roland forced his shoulders to relax. He could keep the gentlemen at bay, but she was on her own when it came to the ladies.

Lady Olivia squeezed his arm, wrapping both hands about his biceps. She looked up, blue eyes gleaming with excitement. She looked like a gleeful child. Beautiful and full of wonder.

"I wasn't sure what my reception would be," she said. "Though my father and the Devonshires are great friends."

"One never knows about the wives," Roland said with a chuckle.

She shook her head, eyes clouding over for a moment. "No, one never does."

They entered the ballroom just as the music died, the final strains of the violins sharp before they were drowned out by the sudden surge of conversation.

The room began to empty, and Roland tugged Lady Olivia to a stop. "Are you hungry?"

She shook her head. Roland clenched his jaw to keep from grinning. He could think of several more entertaining ways to spend the next hour, but he didn't want to risk spooking her.

A few people lingered on the outskirts of the room, most of them in deep conversation. Roland put a hand over Olivia's and led her back toward the drawing room. The corridor was empty now, only a faint murmur giving a hint to the presence of guests somewhere deeper in the house. He plucked a key from his pocket and opened the door to his father's library. He pushed Olivia inside and shut the door firmly behind them.

The room was dark. Only the bit of moonlight leaking in through the windows made it possible to navigate around the chairs and desk. Roland locked the door, and Olivia spun back to face him as the bolt *snicked*.

"Why does your father keep the library locked? Most gentlemen would want to show off such a magnificent room."

Roland smiled. "When Margo made her come-out, a group of drunken guests wandered in and spent the better part of the evening drinking Father's best brandy and rearranging his books."

Olivia crossed the room to the bookcase closest to the

first set of windows and ran her fingers lightly over the spines of the books as though she could read the titles that way. Roland trailed behind her, stalking her.

If he rushed his fence, she'd run. He could see the line of tension in her shoulders, in the way she held her head. She was considering her next move, anticipating his, weighing her options.

"The earl just about had apoplexy in the morning when the mischief was discovered," he added, taking another step toward her. "Especially when he found someone had taken it upon themselves to illustrate his copy of the *Iliad*. So now we keep it locked tight whenever there's a party of any kind."

Olivia glanced warily over her shoulder. She turned about, back to the bookcase, eyes locked to him, almost daring him to come any closer. Outright rejection would have led him to escort her promptly down to the supper room. But this wasn't rejection, this was uncertainty, with a strong current of curiosity.

She nodded, golden curls a silver halo in the moonlight. "Making it a perfect room for trysting."

"Well, yes," Roland said. He closed the distance between them in two long strides and reached for her.

Olivia leaned back, one hand coming up to check his progress. She pushed back against his chest, fingers splayed wide. She shook her head, but her lips were parted and her nostrils flared as she breathed in. "But we're not trysting."

"No?" Roland stepped closer, legs tangling in her skirts.

"No," she said, her breath hitching so that she could

barely get the word out. Her hand trembled, the tension of the arm holding him back going slack.

Roland leaned in. "Why ever not?"

Livy's lungs seized as Devere's words slid across her skin. He hadn't touched her, but he was close enough that it felt as though he had. His lips were beside her ear. His hands were on the bookcase, hemming her in. Desire flared inside her, making it impossible to catch her breath.

Why not? She'd known the answer a moment ago. She could still remember that there was one, but it had become elusive, evaporating under the heat of his gaze like a puddle on the walk after a summer shower.

"Because." She forced the word out as his lips grazed the lobe of her ear.

His mouth moved to her jaw, tracing it in a series of feather-light kisses, lips soft and warm against her skin. She tipped her head back, and Devere kissed her hard, tongue sweeping inside, tangling with hers, demanding a response. Livy's hand tightened on his waistcoat, pulling him closer.

Why not? Livy gave up searching for the answer and kissed him back. Trysts, seductions, lovers, none had come her way before or during her marriage. Why not have them now?

Devere's gloved hand delved into her bodice, kidskin fingers brushing over her ruched nipple, sending a jolt of pure desire through her entire body. The rattle of the door handle brought her back to her senses. Livy came up for air with a gasp, the back of her head pressed hard to the books behind her as she pushed Devere back.

Devere leaned in. His soft *shhhhh* whispered across her cheek. "They can't get in."

Livy shoved, hard enough to rock him back a step. Flustered, annoyed with herself more than with him, she stepped past him, shaking out her skirts with both hands. "We're not trysting, Mr. Devere, because I've no desire to do so." Because it was too dangerous to do so. Too easy to lose her head, to lose the hold she had over him and become just another conquest.

"No?" He sounded utterly unconvinced, and there was little wonder. She'd kissed him with an abandon that had matched his own. Her knees still felt watery with the need to sink to the carpet and drag him down with her. Her own desire, her own lack of control was why they wouldn't— couldn't—play such games with each other.

Devere strode toward her. Livy stood her ground, though she felt decidedly faint. He smiled, gaze raking confidently over her.

"No," Livy replied, grateful that her voice came out steady and sure. It was the only thing about her that was.

"If I lifted your skirts, I'd find you wet and ready, wouldn't I?"

"But not willing," Livy said, trying to hide her chagrin at the fact that he was right. She could feel the slick heat between her thighs and the throbbing ache shooting from breast to groin. And a part of her wanted to goad him into doing just that.

She could deny that she wanted him, but the truth was painfully evident. It was possible she'd made a fatal error in judgment when she'd thought to run him in harness for the season.

"Willing is only a matter of degrees." Devere caught her by the waist and pulled her to him. "You're already approaching the tipping point…" His voice trailed off as though he expected her to sink into his embrace at that very moment.

"I'm not fool enough to tumble into your bed, Devere." Livy laced her voice with steel, more to bolster her resolve than because she believed it would bring him to heel like a well-trained hound.

He nuzzled into her hair, mouth hot over the pulse point below her ear. Livy shivered, fighting hard to maintain some shred of dignity and self-control.

"Pity," he said, blowing over the wet mark on her skin. "If good, honest lust is not enough, I could make you fall in love with me."

"And I could make you wish you were dead," Livy ground out from between clenched teeth.

Devere's answering laugh skittered up her spine, raising gooseflesh as it went. "That's a dare if I've ever heard one."

❧ CHAPTER 7 ❧

The Duchess of Devonshire's at-home was really more of a political assembly. A great number of the Whig grandees were gathered together under her roof. Some of them managed to confine their visit to the prescribed fifteen minutes and their conversation to mere social pleasantries, but the majority of them had settled in for the afternoon and were loudly discussing a vote to remove the prime minister from office.

A few of the female guests took one look at Livy and hastily decamped. The duchess scowled at their retreating backs and waved Livy over to her side. "Ignore them," the duchess said. "I'd take you upstairs for a comfortable coze, but we'd risk the wrath of Nurse if we woke the babies from their nap."

"Little Gee was just a newborn when I saw you last," Livy said, a sharp pang slicing through her. "She must be walking by now."

A child of her own would have been disastrous given the circumstances that had led to the dissolution of her marriage, but she'd wanted one. Badly. Hell, she'd wanted a dozen. The idea that she might never have one now was enough to make her wish she'd had one anyway. Bastard or not, the child would have been her heir.

The duchess looked as if she had no trouble following the train of Livy's thought. "A reminder of just how long it's been," the duchess said, reaching out to give Livy's hand a sympathetic squeeze. "Why on earth didn't you write? You must have known miring yourself away in the country wouldn't solve anything."

Livy nodded. "At first I meant to, but then it just seemed impossible. A widow who isn't really a widow? Was I supposed to put on a show of mourning? Was I supposed to suffer through the stories in the paper, the inevitable cartoons in the print shops?"

The duchess shrugged one elegant shoulder, a hint of a sad smile lurking in the corner of her lips. "I've put up with worse."

"Yes, Your Grace, but you are, when everything is said and done, *still* a duchess, with a powerful husband and a secure place in the *ton*. I'm just the ruined daughter of an earl."

"Which is still quite something," the duchess replied almost tartly, her expression hardening. "You're not some country squire's daughter seduced by a handsome captain in the local militia."

Livy found herself smiling, chagrined. "So stop acting as though I were?"

"Stop expecting people to treat you as such and give them a colossal set-down if they dare to even try. Be brazen, an unconquerable colossus."

"Wise advice," the Viscountess of Duncannon said as she joined them, her little King Charles's spaniel frolicking about her feet until she sat and it settled in her lap with a possessive air. "And should you need help with that, I imagine there are plenty of semifallen wives in Town ready to assist."

Shouting broke out across the room, followed by the sound of a fist being banged on a table and the high-pitched rattling of china. The duchess frowned.

"Gentlemen," she said, not shouting, but loud enough that the room froze. "Fisticuffs must go outside."

A few mumbled apologizes were followed by a swift, if quiet, return to the argument. The duchess shook her head. "Men, children, and dogs. The same rules apply when trying to tame them. And now, my dear, please explain just what you're doing with Mr. Devere in your pocket?"

"Mr. Devere has made me an offer of marriage," Livy said, throwing caution to the wind. As a tidbit of gossip, the news would spread quickly through the *ton*. "And I've accepted, though my father asked us to wait a bit before making a public announcement."

The duchess's brows shot up, disappearing behind the curls of her fringe. Her sister burst into a loud bray of unladylike laughter that startled the spaniel in her lap, causing it to leap to the floor and slink beneath the settee.

"Well, that is brazen." The duchess's mouth quirked into a sly smile.

"A magnificent choice," the Viscountess of Duncannon said with such appreciative warmth Livy was left in no doubt of just what the countess thought magnificent.

• • •

Henry Carlow shivered and eyed the overcast skies of London with disgust. He turned his collar up and tugged at his gloves, attempting to edge out the chilling breeze that had whipped up to welcome him home. Damp, soot-stained, crowded, the greatest city of Europe or not, London was a far cry from the golden shores of Italy, where he'd spent the past several years as an aide to the ambassador to the court of Naples.

He scowled at the ever-increasing clouds and pulled his muffler up to cover his chin. His blood had thinned during his time in Italy. It was the only explanation for the fact that his bones ached with the chill and his ears felt as though he could snap them right off. What would it mean to spend a winter in England again?

The gulls were a raucous chorus overhead, their cries mingling with those of the street vendors hawking oranges and meat pies and gin out of innumerable barrows and baskets. The fishwives were every bit as lively, cursing one another with a vigor that could only be admired.

Bird shit splattered across the shoulder of his coat, and Henry cursed his family under his breath as he wiped it away with his handkerchief. What the devil was Arlington thinking?

He'd left behind sunny Italy and the charms of the most accomplished courtesan he'd ever encountered after receiving the alarming news that Arlington intended to bring Olivia to London for the Season. After the humiliation and scandal of her bigamous marriage, Olivia's stated plan of living quietly in the country with her grandmother had been eminently sensible. And it had meant she'd be waiting there, securely, like Sleeping Beauty, until the day he swept in to rescue her from a life of shame and exile.

It had become a lazy dream to idle away the hot afternoon hours when everything in Naples ground to a halt. He'd always liked Olivia—it was hard not to—even if he'd resented the drain her dowry had put on the estate he was to someday inherit. Really, she was an earl's daughter. There was no reason her dowry had needed to be so excessive. Her bloodlines were more than enough to have guaranteed a good match. Fifty thousand pounds was a fortune. The kind of dowry a banker's daughter needed to secure a gentleman.

When Olivia's marriage had ended so precipitously, Henry had written to express his condolences and to offer his support. It had been politic to take her side. He would be the next Earl of Arlington. It made perfect sense to marry the current titleholder's daughter and secure the fortune along with the title. Society would understand the practicality of their arrangement. They might even applaud his gallantry.

And Olivia? Well, Olivia would be indebted to him. He'd be a hero. He'd make her a countess, just as her first husband would have done eventually. How could she be anything other than grateful?

Henry motioned to his valet and handed the man his sullied handkerchief. "See that the bags are secured, Perkins."

Trusting his man to see to it, Henry stepped into one of the hackneys that waited to carry passengers away from the coaching inn and settled onto the sagging seat. The stench of old straw and rotting leather enveloped him. A sharp, foul note lay underneath it, a clear sign of someone's late night of overindulgence and a hasty cleaning job.

"Perkins, get me an orange," Henry yelled out the still-open door. He kept it propped open with his foot as he waited.

His valet appeared a moment later, orange in hand. Henry took it with a nod as Perkins climbed onto the rear-facing seat and shut the door behind him with a snap.

Henry put the orange up to his nose and inhaled gratefully. It was strange to be surrounded by the babble of his native tongue once again. The twang of the jarvie's low accent as he urged his nag into motion was almost dear. Henry swallowed hard, the annoyance of the damp, gray skies dissolving under a sudden upswing of nostalgia.

It might be freezing, but it was still England. Still home. The cold was nothing a good English ale, a hearty steak and kidney pie, and a hot quaking pudding couldn't make infinitely better. Once he'd had those, he'd be ready to run his Olivia to earth and see just what bout of madness had prompted her to return to London so soon.

❧ CHAPTER 8 ❧

Come along, sister-of-mine."

Margo's head snapped up, and she felt her cheeks flush. Rolly was standing in the doorway of her room, clothed in tobacco-brown superfine with a sherry-colored waistcoat embroidered with a palm trees and monkeys. She hadn't heard him open the door, busy as she was trying to calm her nerves and settle her stomach. She felt like a blasted girl about to make her debut.

"Father sent me to fetch you," Rolly said, pushing away from the door frame. The floor creaked as he stepped toward her, his shoes and buckles shiny against the dull wool of the carpet. "You know how he hates to keep the horses waiting."

"You mean how *he* hates to be kept waiting," Margo replied as she dabbed on a bit of perfume. She put the stopper back and set the bottle down, the glass clicking against the Japanned tray that held all the various pots and vials of paint and powder and scent that she had brought home with her from France.

She hadn't used most of them since returning to England. The current fashion in London was for a more natural appearance than was favored at the French court. The lightest dusting of powder on the skin, the barest hint of rouge on the cheek, and a smudge of kohl about the eyes was all the English considered *de rigueur*. She felt naked.

Margo took a deep breath, smoothing her hands over her waist and down over her full skirts. "Am I presentable?"

Rolly grinned, one side of his mouth sliding up higher than the other as it was wont to do when he was feeling mischievous. "For a widow in deepest mourning?" he said offhandedly as she stepped past him. "Eminently."

"Wretch," Margo shot back as she hurried down the corridor. Trust her roguish brother to point out that she wasn't supposed to care only six months into her widowhood. She was supposed to be distraught, bereft, grief-stricken. She'd been none of those things since her husband's death, as he well knew.

Rolly's answering laugh and the tread of his heels chased after her. Margo pushed aside her failings as a widow. She missed Etienne, but that was all. Missed him the way one did a friend who'd gone away. For that's what her husband had been in the end, a friend she saw on occasion as they both went about their separate pursuits and affairs. It had been his mistress, Madame D'Arbly, who'd been inconsolable at Etienne's passing, and Margo who'd had to console her.

Rolly caught Margo at the bottom of the stairs. He took her silk opera cloak from the waiting footman and held it out. She stood still while he shook it out and draped it over her shoulders.

"You look lovely, Margo," he said, squeezing her shoulders before letting go. "Good enough for Arlington to want to take a bite."

Margo inhaled sharply and spun about. Rolly danced backward, but she caught him a glancing blow with her fist all the same. Sometimes she couldn't help wishing she were an only child.

"Very ladylike," Rolly said as he clapped his hat onto his head, toggling it to make sure it was secure.

Margo glared, turned about on her heel, and headed out to join her parents in the coach. Arlington had invited them all to Drury Lane tonight. Whispers of a betrothal between her brother and Lady Olivia had already begun to circulate.

On the surface, tonight was merely another step in the slow unveiling of that relationship. A demonstration that both families supported it. But behind the invitation, Margo could sense other forces at work. There was something there, a connection between Arlington and herself that was nearly irresistible.

The damp night air kissed her skin as the footman handed her up into the waiting coach. Margo took the rear-facing seat across from her mother. Her father glanced impatiently at the door as Rolly crammed his way in, his long legs crushing Margo's skirts as he twisted about to fit into the narrow space.

Margo yanked the yards of black watered silk aside as they got underway. She wanted to look perfect tonight. As perfect as she could anyway, decked out in widow's weeds. The eager burn of excitement she remembered from her first Season licked through her, warming her from the inside out. She'd had more than one lover over the years—it would have been strange had she not, given that *affaires de coeur* were almost as important as politics in the corridors of Versailles—but she couldn't remember the last time a man had left her feeling breathless with anticipation.

She and Arlington had crossed paths several times over the past few days. The first time was purely by chance. It had to have been. She'd accompanied her father to hear a scientific lecture at the British Museum. Short of bribing her parents' servants, Arlington couldn't have known she'd be there.

Afterward, she and Arlington had strolled through the marble halls, discussing commonplaces about the Season, but she had let slip that she preferred to end her late nights with a dawn ride before falling into bed. The next morning she'd encountered the earl on a natty black with one white stocking up over its knee, shuffling down the sandy track in Hyde Park in the predawn glow. Rolly had given her a decidedly amused glance, but he hadn't said anything as the earl fell in with them as if this encounter was purely serendipitous.

They'd crossed paths again at Negri's, where he'd treated her and her mother to tea. It was there that he'd proposed tonight's outing. But Arlington had been looking at her, his vivid blue eyes intent, waiting to see her reaction, not that of Lady Moubray.

Yes, the Earl of Arlington was most certainly pursuing her, but she wasn't entirely sure he knew what he would do if he caught her. Nor was she sure what she would do. He was intriguing, but his pursuit was almost decorous.

Taking a lover was something she had every intention of doing, when the right circumstances and the right man presented themselves. Marrying again wasn't. And even though she could feel the tug of attraction building between them, Arlington seemed too honorable a man to do anything so improper as seduce the sister of his daughter's betrothed.

He'd done nothing more than kiss her hand the night of the ball, hadn't done even that on any of their subsequent meetings. His reticence was unnerving, not at all what she was used to dealing with from the men of her acquaintance. At Versailles, her husband's friends had begun propositioning her within days of their marriage, and their pursuit had only intensified in the weeks after his death.

Margo fiddled with one of the pins that held the bodice of her gown to the jet-encrusted stomacher. This wasn't Versailles, and Arlington wasn't some French courtier whose romantic intrigues were nothing but political showmanship or pleasure seeking.

And there was Rolly to consider as well. Margo didn't believe for a moment that whatever he and Lady Olivia were up to could be taken at face value, but all the same, she didn't want to spike his wheels unnecessarily, and Lord love her, she didn't want to cause a scandal here on her own shores. She'd done enough of that in France.

Roland took in the expression on Lord Arlington's face as the earl set eyes on Margo with an amused shake of his head. The man was utterly infatuated, though he was doing his best to hide it. It was impossible to mistake

Arlington's fleeting smile and the way his eyes returned to Margo again and again as he waved them into the box.

Poor devil. Margo would eat him alive.

Roland glanced at his sister as she took a seat beside their host in the front row of the box. Margo nodded to the earl, but immediately turned her attention to the boxes on the other side of the theatre, putting on quite the show of ease as she nodded to friends across the abyss of the pit.

Lord Omsbatch nodded back, light flashing off his quizzing glass. Roland frowned. Yes, Omsbatch seemed a more likely swain for Margo than Arlington, though it wasn't a connection he'd choose for her.

Roland forgot about his sister's romantic intrigues the moment Lady Olivia turned to study him over her shoulder. She was seated alone in the back row, just behind his parents. A gown of scarlet silk set off her skin as though she were a pearl in a setting of rubies. She looked every inch the confident young society matron she should have been.

Standing beside her was a stranger who could have been her brother. He had the same blond hair and the angles of his face were a younger version of Lord Arlington's. The man frowned as Roland stepped toward them, his expression changing to polite indifference as Olivia turned to look at him.

The man dropped a hand to rest casually on Olivia's shoulder, two fingers touching the naked slope of her neck. Roland fought back the urge to pitch the man over the rail and into the pit.

"Mr. Devere, do you know my father's heir, Mr. Carlow?" Olivia said, glancing between them.

"I've never had the pleasure."

Carlow's mouth crooked into a somewhat disdainful smile. Clearly his presence wasn't any more welcome to Carlow than Carlow's was to him.

"Mr. Devere," Carlow said with a nod, his thumb moving in a lazy circle on Olivia's shoulder. *This is mine*, he was saying none too subtly. *Don't get any ideas. Don't touch.* Roland felt the same way.

"Henry's come all the way from Italy to support me in my return to the social fray," Olivia said with genuine, guile-free pleasure.

Roland looked pointedly at Henry's encroaching hand and then back to the man's face. Carlow fell back a step, his hand falling to his side. For the briefest moment, the man's eyes snapped with fury. Whether it was at being challenged or at his own blunder of giving ground, Roland couldn't tell. What was perfectly clear, however, was that Mr. Henry Carlow wasn't at all pleased with Olivia's betrothal.

"I see Lady Robert trying to gain your attention, my lady," Roland said, enjoying the way Carlow's eyes narrowed in annoyance. "Shall I take you to her?"

Roland held out his hand, and after the slightest pause, Olivia allowed him to help her up and escort her out of her father's box. Roland shot Carlow a triumphant look, and the man glared back darkly. He'd just nipped her out from under the man's nose, and there wasn't a damn thing Henry could do about it.

The corridor that ringed the theatre was nearly empty, just a few pages and footmen dashing by on errands and the occasional late arrival making haste for their seat.

Roland tucked Olivia's hand tightly into the crook of his arm and set off slowly toward the boxes on the far side.

"Did you really see Lady Robert beckoning?" Olivia said, her tone clearly implying that she knew he was lying.

Roland shrugged ever so slightly. "I may have been mistaken. It may have been Mrs. Staniland waving to my mother. The theatre is damned dark in places."

"Or it may have been Mrs. Hahn trying to attract your attention," she said with an artful little sigh. "Don't think I didn't notice her chagrin at being ignored at your parents' ball. Past conquest?"

Roland stopped dead in his tracks, pique and horror at war within him. "Almeria Hahn? If you think for a minute—"

"How am I to know whom you've dallied with over the years?" she said with a show of faux indignation. Olivia batted her eyes, clearly waiting for an answer.

"Well, you can start by assuming that Bishops' wives—especially those with a squint and a mole that a witch would be proud of—are unlikely to be counted among their ranks."

"Really?" Olivia dropped his arm and took a step away from him. She leaned back against the paneled wall, hands tucked behind her. Her exact expression was impossible to decipher, but there was a definite hint of exasperation in it, perhaps even annoyance. "I've heard it said that one woman is very much like another in the dark."

"Only by a man who's touched in the head," Roland responded with feeling.

"So not Mrs. Hahn? What about Mrs. Pipkin and Lady Mossiker? They've both been glaring at me like gorgons, and I can't imagine it's merely because I carry the stench of scandal."

A harried matron with three girls in tow skirted past them. Roland held his tongue until they were out of earshot. "Whatever I may have done, and whomever I may have done it with, I'm gentleman enough not to speak of it."

"You mean it's none of my business," Olivia said, her tone verging on arctic. "While my entire history is an open book, not only to you, but to the world. I imagine you've bandied your conquests' names about with your friends. But I'm to have no warning?"

Roland grasped her arm and propelled her back into motion. He should have thought of this, should have dealt with it. For she was right; there were certainly past lovers who might be very angry indeed to find he'd suddenly given up his claim to bachelorhood, and not in their favor.

Olivia's hand balled into a fist and she tried to pull away. The roar of applause from inside the theatre washed over them. Roland swung Olivia about to face him, keeping a tight grip on her arms to prevent her from storming off.

"You're right, my dear. I'm not gentleman enough not to have done my share of bragging over cards and wine, but then you already have proof of that." He held her in place, wanting to shake her almost as much as he wanted to kiss her.

A small, black page dashed past them, a note clutched in his hand, the peacock feathers on the front of his turban streaking back like a flag being carried into battle.

"Do you want the laundry list," Roland finally said

when they were alone again, "or only the names of those whose noses might be out of joint at the moment?"

"I fear we don't have time for a full accounting." Olivia tipped her head back to stare up at him.

Roland let his breath out slowly. "Just now realizing that your choice of pawn might not be as ideal as you thought?"

Olivia swallowed hard, looking as though she were preparing to take a beating. Almost as though she wanted whatever he said to be hurtful.

Roland loosened his grip. "Mrs. Pipkin's antipathy I can't explain, so you'll have to put her glares down to offended sensibilities," he said. "But yes, you're right about Lady Mossiker."

Olivia nodded. "But not now?"

"Not since autumn."

"Good," Olivia said firmly. "And now, I believe we're missing the play."

"Lord Arlington?"

Philip realized with a start that he hadn't the slightest idea what Madame de Corbeville had just said. He'd been too busy watching her saying it. Her two front teeth were ever so slightly crooked, and her upper lip was a work of art. It was bowed and fuller than her lower lip. And just now both lips were parted in a grin, the lower one caught almost guiltily between her teeth.

"Worried about my scapegrace brother alone with Lady Olivia in the deserted byways of the theatre?" she said.

"No," Philip said, leaning forward in his seat until

the orange blossom scent of her perfume filled his head. "Livy is more than capable of managing your brother."

Madame de Corbeville's grin widened, and Philip swallowed hard. She was ridiculously beautiful, but it was the devilish glint in her eye that was truly enchanting. He recognized the rush of infatuation for what it was, but that didn't make the heady feeling any less intense or one whit more appropriate.

"She does seem to have rather taken him in hand, doesn't she?" the comtesse said.

Philip nodded, and the babble of the crowd washed over him. There might be a few stray theatregoers who were there to watch the performance, but most were there to see and be seen. The true show was taking place on their side of the stage, not on it.

The din abated a tad as the orchestra's opening notes announced the imminent arrival of the performers. The comtesse didn't so much as turn her head. She just stared back at him, dark eyes large and knowing, very much like a cat deciding if it would deign to let you pet it.

Philip forced himself to turn his attention to the stage while every fiber of his being wished this wasn't a family party. He was aware of the Moubrays to his left and his heir at the far edge of the box, leaning out over the pit to speak with the people in the next box. But they were somehow nothing more than set dressing, no more real than the painted canvas backdrop behind the actors.

Madame de Corbeville's father had let drop that she was accompanying him to a lecture at the British Museum, and though Philip had told himself he wouldn't go, he'd found himself lurking in the back of the room,

listening with half an ear to a lecture on the artificial production of cold air and guiltily staring at his daughter's
future sister-in-law like an apprentice mooning over a
milkmaid.

Just as he'd found himself riding at dawn every morning in the hopes of seeing her, and rushing down the street
when he spied her entering Negri's. In idle moments
he found himself picturing her smile. His dreams were
filled with her: naked, writhing atop him like Lilith in the
Garden.

He'd lost his wife when Livy was still in the nursery,
and though he certainly hadn't taken a vow of celibacy
during the intervening years, his occasional affairs had
always been fleeting, and his partners every bit as desir-
ous of discretion as he was. Margaret, comtesse de Corbeville, however, had a reputation for being anything but
discreet.

❧ CHAPTER 9 ❧

A heavy fog, almost like the mist that sometimes covered the moors at home, had settled over the city sometime in the wee hours of the morning. The air stank of coal and brine. Livy felt almost as though she were drowning as she drew a deep breath and flexed her hands, fingers fighting the stiff leather of her gloves. Usually once the leather warmed, they were as pliable as her own skin, but at the moment, they felt almost like mittens around her cold fingers.

"Did you want to go back?" Devere said, reining in his own mount and watching her with dark, all too inquisitive eyes. "You needn't indulge Margo and me in our insanity."

Livy shook her head as her mount danced beneath her, eager to be off. Devere and his sister had invited her to join them on their ride before they turned in to sleep the morning away, and before Livy could decline, her father had accepted. And he'd accepted in such a way that it was clear that he'd met them here before. Livy had never paid much attention to her father's coming and goings, but it was blindingly clear that something highly unusual—for him at least—was unfolding.

"I'm curious about this tradition of yours," Livy said with perfect truthfulness. "Besides, Triton's been eating his head off all week. If he doesn't get some exercise, he'll knock down the stall."

Devere laughed, the sound warm and inviting. Livy slanted a glance at him through the fog. Only a few paces away, he was insubstantial around the edges. She could very well imagine him a djinn come to spirit her away. The idea of it was tantalizing in a way that had become impossible to ignore.

She wanted him. Her blood fired with every touch. If she'd been a widow with a house of her own, she might already have invited him to her bed. It was a mortifying realization and an impossible situation.

A steady pattern of iron-shod hooves on stone reminded her that her father and Devere's sister were close at hand. Livy concentrated on the noise and the low hum of their conversation. She could catch only snatches. A word here, a phrase there, the comtesse's throaty chuckle.

A sudden flash of jealousy coursed through her. Was Devere's sister already her father's lover? It didn't seem fair that the comtesse had so much freedom while she herself had none. That so many women had such freedom, she corrected herself as Devere's confession regarding Lady Mossiker flashed through her head.

Half the women of the *ton* seemed to have taken a lover at one point or another, and so long as they were careful and their husbands indulgently turned a blind eye, life went on as though they were as chaste as nuns. The unfairness of it all burnt in her chest like a live coal.

As they reached the entrance to Rotten Row, Livy glanced back over her shoulder. Her father and the comtesse were riding as close as a harnessed pair. Her father's knee was lost in the folds of Madame de Corbeville's habit. There was something intimate about it, something that spoke of an easy companionship that seemed more disturbing than the possibility of her father taking a lover like any other man.

The fog was lighter here in the park than between the buildings, but that could have been merely due to the ever-growing light as the sun struggled to come up. The sandy track was, unsurprisingly, deserted, with the exception of a fox that slunk out of sight as soon as it spotted them, nothing but a blur of fiery fur.

"Shall we risk a canter?" Devere said as his bay tossed its head and minced in place, ready to be off.

Livy responded by touching Triton's shoulder with her crop and his side with her heel. The gelding sprang into motion, the sudden demonstration of what muscle and bone could do utterly thrilling. Speed and cold damp air chased away her blue devils.

Devere's startled oath chased after her, and Livy grinned into the fog, imagining his face. She wasn't the most graceful dancer, her needlework was barely passable, and she had no delusions about her skill on the pianoforte, but she could ride.

Fog whipped past her, water beading on her lashes. Olivia blinked it away. Devere and his big bay nearly caught her at the end of the track. She could hear Devere's low whistle of appreciation and the soft thunder of his mount's hooves on the dirt.

Livy slowed Triton to a canter, allowing Devere to catch up, and they reached the end of the track neck and neck. He looked at her appraisingly.

"Good seat."

Livy bowed her head, accepting the compliment. She turned Triton about, her heart pounding. Devere and his bay circled, the bay's bit jangling as he tossed his head, still eager to run.

"Again?" Devere said, his grin showing an expanse of straight, white teeth. His beard was growing in already, the dark shadow on his cheeks and chin lending him a disreputable glamour.

Livy smiled back at him, and he shot off down the Row, the bay's long tail streaming out behind him. She set off in pursuit, letting Triton have his head. The bay was larger, but his rider was heavier, making the contest somewhat even.

Devere grinned back at her, inviting her to try and catch him. A sudden rush of attraction swamped her. Livy sat back in the saddle, and Triton slowed to a walk. She let her breath out in a huff, watching the thin trails mingle with the fog. The mist was burning off. Her father's black gelding blended with the comtesse's black habit and her own dark mount as the pair ambled slowly toward her.

Devere swung around them and trotted back toward her. Lady Duncannon's *magnificent* echoed in Livy's head, and her breath caught in her chest. This was how women got themselves into trouble. How young matrons seduced themselves into liaisons they would otherwise have never even have contemplated.

He was hers for the asking. That simple truth seemed fantastical. The urge to discover if Devere deserved the reputation her friends so clearly intimated itched beneath her skin.

Devere plucked her out of the saddle, his hands wrapped about her waist, squeezing in. Livy's pulse sped, and her head swam. He didn't merely assist as she slid down as most gentlemen did. He lifted her and set her on her feet. And he did it without the slightest sign of effort. His hands didn't slip. His arms didn't shake.

Livy nodded as she got her feet under her, and Devere stepped back, his hands lingering for a moment longer than necessary, fingertips whispering over her ribs before releasing her. Her father's groom harrumphed like an offended dowager as he led her horse away. Devere smiled conspiratorially, inviting her to share his amusement at the man's disapproval.

Livy shut her eyes, shut him out, and shook her head. She couldn't afford to indulge him at this exact moment. She was too close to forgetting that it was all a ruse. Too close to wanting it not to be, or making the irreversible choice to allow it to become something more.

Devere's sister was still mounted. Livy's father stood beside her, running one hand absently over her mount's neck as they spoke.

Livy covered her mouth with her hand as she yawned. "Do you really always end your nights this way?"

"*Always* would be stretching the truth," Devere said.

"But yes, it's something of a tradition when we're in town. In the country, we always rose early for a morning ride, but with the late hours we all keep here in London, that becomes impractical, if not impossible. This is our compromise."

"You'll have to come to Holinshed when Parliament takes its next break," Livy's father said, his invitation clearly including both Devere siblings. "I'm sure Livy would love to show it to you both. I'll send round an invitation to your father later today."

Livy glanced at her father with horror. The last thing she wanted was Devere at Holinshed. It was hard enough to manage him here. In the country, she'd be at her wit's end trying to keep him in line and trying to keep herself from being swept up, swept away.

Devere bent over her hand with a flourish and then swung up into the saddle with a quick motion that clearly indicated he wasn't anywhere near as exhausted as Livy. After the theatre, a series of balls and routs, and their dawn ride, she felt as if her flesh was about to melt from her bones. He looked ready to start his day, not end it.

The earl slapped the comtesse's mount on the haunch and walked back to wrap an arm around Livy as the siblings rode out of the mews. As they reached the passageway from the mews to the street, both of them looked back, smiling. Dark hair, dark eyes, and the similarity of features made them look almost like twins, though Livy knew Devere's sister was several years older than he was. The comtesse gave a jaunty little wave and then settled her hat more firmly on her head before trotting out of view.

• • •

Roland wandered into The Red Lion in the late afternoon and claimed a place at the table where Thane and Vaughn were sprawled. They both looked flush with health and well rested, and at the moment, Roland cordially loathed them. He captured the pot of coffee that sat waiting on the table and emptied it into a cup whose owner had apparently already been and gone. He inhaled the decadent scent of it as he waited for it to cool enough to drink.

He'd taken Margo home, but he'd been unable to sleep. He'd crawled into bed expecting to pass into the arms of Morpheus instantaneously, only to be kept awake by the rumble of wheels, the distant clatter from the kitchen, and the sound of the neighbor's maid singing as she scrubbed the front steps. After several restless hours, he'd given up and rung for a bath. A hot soak wasn't exactly a replacement for sleep, but it served to make him feel marginally alive again.

"Well, well," Vaughn said with a chuckle as he looked up from the house of cards he was constructing on the table. "Chasing Lady Olivia till dawn, were we?"

Roland blew on his coffee and took an exploratory sip. Sweeping Lord Leonidas's precarious creation onto the floor would be a petty response, but he was still sorely tempted.

"Your plan is never going to work, you know," Thane said, settling back in his chair until the wood squealed in protest. "The lady in question is, well, a *lady*."

Roland eyed his friends over the brim of his cup and continued to blow on it. They could think what they liked. He could sense Olivia weakening, could almost feel her curiosity building like a static charge before a storm.

Roland swallowed a mouthful of coffee, the bitter liquid reviving him as it spread its heat to his toes and fingers and sparked his brain into a simulation of life.

"And you're implying what?" Roland said with a growl. "That my sister, or any number of your own paramours I could name, isn't?"

Vaughn gave a choked-off laugh and his house of cards collapsed, sending cards cascading across the worn table top and onto the floor. Thane harrumphed and added another lump of sugar to his own steaming cup. Before Roland could insist Thane answer the question, Malcolm Reeves dropped into the seat beside Vaughn and tossed a letter onto the table. The folded sheet of paper with its broken wax seal revolved in a full circle before coming to a somewhat ominous stop.

"Blakely wants us to check up on Miss Bence-Jones," Reeves said, a hard, bitter note coloring his voice. "Says something's amiss, but he's not sure what."

"Is her brother throwing up yet more obstacles to their marriage?" Thane said, reaching for the letter.

"Not that Blakely knows of." Reeves swept up the cards nearest him and shuffled them absently. "At least not specifically. He says he hasn't received a letter from her in several months, which is unusual. Though her mother and brother forced them to put off the marriage while they were in mourning for Sir Thomas, they'd been allowed to correspond, so long as Lady Bence-Jones read their letters. Blakely just wants to make sure she's all right."

"The newly minted Sir Christopher does seem the kind not to bother telling his sister's betrothed if something happened to her, doesn't he?" Vaughn said, and

Roland found himself nodding in agreement. He'd known Christopher Bence-Jones since they were at Harrow. The man had always been an untrustworthy scoundrel. The kind of boy who broke something and then ran to point the finger at someone smaller, poorer, or even less popular than himself.

Thane's expression darkened as he read the letter. He might have a wicked sense of humor when it came to his friends, but he was also loyal as a hound, and the circle of people he felt to be under his protection extended to his friends' dependents as well to themselves. Roland had always surmised it was down to his size. When you were as large as Thane, people naturally looked to you for assistance.

Thane finished the letter and carefully refolded it, his fingers crimping every fold as though it were somehow important to preserve the letter in perfect form. "Has anyone seen Miss Bence-Jones since the Season started?"

"Saw her in the park a few weeks back," Vaughn said. "Still decked out in black and white from head to toe."

"Well, if the Bence-Joneses are in town, someone can pay a call and see if Blakely has any real reason for concern," Reeves said, his brow relaxing. "I was dreading coming up with a reason for going all the way to Wales to check up on her. Blakely's a friend—"

"But it's *Wales*," Roland cut in with a derisive snort.

"Exactly," Reeves replied with feeling. "Nothing but rain, hills, and a series of unpronounceable places. Got lost once and crossed over accidently on my way to a house party near Three Ashes. When I found the first road sign, I thought perhaps I'd gone mad and lost the ability to read."

⚞ CHAPTER 10 ⚟

The door to the shop opened and an elegant, turbaned matron with a trio of girls rushed in. They were followed by a gust of wind that smelled strongly of rain. The door came to a stop half open, fighting the wind, and Livy's footman kicked it shut behind them.

Livy glanced away from the gloves she was considering to study the gray sky outside. It had been clouding up when she'd set out on this expedition, but clearly rain was now imminent.

Her father had warned her to take an umbrella, but if it began to rain in earnest, she'd still be soaked by the time she reached Arlington House. A spatter of drops hit the window, and out of the corner of her eye, she saw her footman wince. "Peter, run and fetch a hackney now, before it gets any worse," Livy said, knowing he was already mentally calculating where the closest stand was.

Peter nodded with obvious relief, set down the packages he'd been minding, and dashed out into the oncoming storm. Livy turned back to the gloves. She laid the swatch of fabric for her new gown across them and studied them intently. The pink was a very close match for the flowers, but all things considered, she preferred the blue, to match the penciling. The blue would likely wear better, too. The pink was so pale it was sure to show every mark, and there was also the white pair with floral bracelets printed on them to consider.

Livy plucked all three pairs off the counter and handed them to the shopkeeper. "I can't decide, so I'll be extravagant and take all three."

The woman smiled and began to carefully wrap them up. The younger shopkeeper helping the trio of ladies at the other counter was also busy wrapping up a great quantity of gloves and handkerchiefs and shoe rosettes. The weather clearly wasn't going to ruin the shop's day. Livy's day, however, was looking bleaker by the second.

A flash of lightning illuminated the growing gloom and a distant rumble of thunder came tumbling after it. The youngest of the girls let out a squeal, her eyes huge and round. "Beth," the woman in the turban said without taking her eyes off the pair of chicken skin gloves she was examining. "You will be pleased *not* to react to a little thunder as though you were the heroine of a gothic romance or you will stay in the nursery with your brother the next time we venture out."

"Yes, Mamma," the girl responded, her attention riveted on the rain now lashing against the shop windows.

Another round of thunder and the audible increase in the strength of the rain caused Beth's mother to look outside with a grimace. "I told your father we should have taken the carriage," she said, her voice frosty with annoyance.

Peter's liveried form appeared through the rain. He cracked open the door, but didn't step inside. "I got one, my lady. Had to fight off Lord Colchester's footman," he said with a self-satisfied grin, "but I got it."

Livy smiled her thanks, but found herself glancing back uncertainly at the shivering and clearly frightened girl. In this downpour, they'd never find a hackney of their own, especially as they didn't appear to have any kind of servant in tow to send in search of one. Beth looked as though she were one more clap of thunder away from dissolving into tears.

It wasn't a reaction Livy understood, but she'd certainly encountered it before. There was a maid at Holinshed who came positively undone at the first clap of thunder. The housekeeper had actually had to slap her once to stop her having hysterics.

Beth sucked in a shuddering breath, and Livy began to consider just how wet she'd get walking back to Arlington House. She brushed her hands over her skirts. Silk really had been a poor choice for such a day.

"Pardon me, ma'am," Livy said, her decision made. "Perhaps you and your girls stand in more dire need of a hackney than I? I brought my umbrella, and it's only a few streets to my house." Poor Peter was already soaked through; it wouldn't make a spot of difference to him if they walked.

"Thank you," the woman said a bit uncertainly. "That's very kind. But we couldn't."

"Peter," Livy said, "could you help the ladies into the hackney?"

Her footman managed to keep the look of surprise from his face as he held Livy's umbrella and carefully escorted first the mother and then each of the girls to the waiting hackney.

"Can I leave all this here until I can send someone to fetch it?" Livy waved one hand at the pile of packages and bandboxes she'd collected as she and Peter roamed Pall Mall.

The proprietress nodded, the lacy frills on her cap flapping about her face. "No need to send anyone, my lady. I'll have them delivered as soon as my grandson returns from his last errand."

Peter retuned, wet and bedraggled, and held out her umbrella. "Coming down cats and dogs, my lady," he said, his expression clearly telling her he thought her mad to have given the hackney to what appeared to be the family of some Old Bailey solicitor.

Livy let her breath out in a long huff as she braced herself. She'd never much liked this gown anyway. Jonquil was not her best color.

She stepped out onto the walk, and the wind pushed her down the street, whipping her skirts about her legs until she nearly stumbled and fell. Livy gave a nervous titter of laughter and clutched at her umbrella. It felt as though it might lift her off the walk at any moment.

By the time she reached the corner, Livy was beginning to regret her largesse with the hackney. "I deserve to be sainted," she mumbled under her breath as she waited for a coach to pass before she braved the street. The coachman hunched on the box like a gargoyle, his hat pulled down and the collar of his greatcoat flipped up.

A sudden strong gust turned her umbrella inside out and snatched away her wail of protest. Within seconds, she was as wet as if she'd been tossed into the Thames. Without a word, Peter took her umbrella. He sheltered it from the wind with his body as he attempted to restore it to usefulness. It sprang back to its original shape just as a howling gust ripped away Livy's hat and sent both hat and umbrella tumbling down the street.

The indignant expression on her footman's face nearly sent Livy into whoops. "And the dish ran away with the spoon," she said with a laugh that verged on tears. "Never mind, Peter. It's not as though it would actually help at this point."

The coach stopped a few feet past them, and the door flew open. The comtesse de Corbeville leaned out. "Get inside, my dear!" she yelled over the wind, beckoning frantically. Livy ran for the coach, the soles of her shoes slipping and sliding over the wet cobbles. Peter all but tossed her into the waiting carriage. The door slammed shut behind her with a resounding thud that was almost as loud as the clap of thunder that followed it. Livy collapsed back onto the squabs. The coach swayed as her footman joined the driver on the box.

Livy twisted her wet hair back from her face and tied it into a knot. A rivulet of water snaked down her neck, making her shiver.

"You have impeccable timing, Madame."

Devere's sister grinned back at her, looking even more like her brother than usual with that impish expression lighting up her face. "Happy to be of service," the comtesse said, pulling a large, lace-edged handkerchief from her pocket and holding it out. "Let us get you home and dry before you catch your death."

"I'm not such a delicate flower, I assure you," Livy insisted, taking the proffered handkerchief.

The comtesse pushed the hot brick warming her own feet toward Livy. Livy toed off her wet shoes and put her stocking-clad feet on the brick with a sigh of contentment. "Besides," Livy said, peeling off her wet gloves, "it would take more than a little rain to make me miss the regatta tomorrow."

"It would be a shame if you had to travel to Ranelagh with your father and me in the coach rather than joining Rolly and his team in the shallop," the comtesse said, her tone lively and filled with innuendo.

"A shame for whom?" Livy said from behind the handkerchief as she mopped her face dry. The coach rocked, buffeted by the wind, and Livy dropped the embroidered scrap of linen onto the seat beside her gloves and braced herself, not entirely sure it wouldn't careen over like a beached ship ready to be scraped clean of barnacles.

"For us both, I think," Devere's sister replied with perfect aplomb, dark eyes dancing with mischief.

Livy realized with a start that her mouth was hanging open. She shut it with a snap, and the comtesse let loose a long trill of laughter.

"Forgive me," the comtesse said as the coach lumbered to a halt. "Eventually I'll remember how to school my tongue like an Englishwoman again. But one of the magnificent things about being a widow—English or French—is the freedom it accords you. *N'est-ce pas?*"

Livy nodded, feeling gauche and provincial and incredibly envious in the face of the comtesse's bald declaration. The coach door opened, exposing them to the tumult of the storm, and the steps fell with a reverberant clang.

"*Au revoir*," Devere's sister called after her as the wind battered them both and Livy bolted for the house.

The coal in the grate crackled, and Livy stretched out her feet to get them incrementally closer to its heat, wishing for a good, roaring wood fire such as she was used to having at Holinshed. Try as she might, she couldn't seem to get warm with just a tiny brazier full of coal, and she couldn't stop thinking about her encounter with Devere's sister.

Livy cradled her cup of tea and brandy, sipping at it as she attempted to warm herself from the inside, too. She had been her father's de facto hostess since before she was out of the schoolroom. She'd had the male half of the *ton* at her feet while she took her sweet time deciding whom to marry. And in all those years, she'd never felt at a loss.

Even when the news of the ruin of her marriage had struck, she'd known exactly what to do. And not that she could ever admit to it, but her first response, her first emotion, had been a profound sense of relief.

Souttar had been a mistake. A handsome, wealthy, titled mistake. She'd been miraculously set free, and that freedom was worth every snub, every witticism, and every insult. It was even worth the guilt she'd felt after his death.

It was certainly worth the risks inherent in the gamble she was taking now with Devere. Keeping him close and yet under control was rather like playing keeper at the Tower menagerie: If the leopard wasn't stealing umbrellas and hats, the monkeys were biting people, or the bear had slipped his chain and swum off up the Thames to harass the fishwives at Billingsgate.

And the comtesse was no easier to predict or contain.

The Devere siblings simply didn't play by the same rules as everyone else, even the rest of the *ton*. It was as if they'd been given some other rule book than the one she'd been privy to her whole life.

One that was decidedly more interesting.

Livy pushed the thought away. More interesting or not, if she joined in, she'd lose. It would be like attempting to join a cricket match if one had only ever played rounders on the village green. Both games required a bat and ball, but there the similarities ended.

And the day after tomorrow, assuming the rain let up, was the regatta, and afterward, a grand supper with fireworks and dancing at Ranelagh Gardens. She was committed to spending the entire day with her press-ganged swain.

A shiver of anticipation ran through Livy. She wasn't as immune to Devere's charms as she would like to be, as she should be. She knew him for exactly who and what he was—rogue, rake, seducer—but there was still a kindling spark when he touched her, and a flare of curiosity that was becoming almost irresistible.

No. Livy bit her lip and sat up to add more brandy to her tea. Devere didn't even need to touch her. A look was enough to set her pulse racing and make her body ache and throb, wanton as a mare in season. And he knew it.

That was the true problem. Not that he wanted her. A man's ardor cooled quickly enough if one gave him no encouragement. Nor was the fact that she wanted him impossible to overcome, if she were left with the distance and time to master herself. The simple fact that he knew she wanted him, however, was dangerous in the extreme.

~ CHAPTER 11 ~

Roland employed the brass knocker on the Bence-Jones's front door with rather more force than necessary. He'd attempted to call on the ladies of the house the previous day, in the driving rain, but had found them not at home. He'd tracked Sir Christopher to Tattersall's, where the man had taken one look at him and all but disappeared in a puff of smoke.

What did Sir Christopher think he was going to do to him? And more importantly, what had the man been up to that he thought might elicit a wrathful response? Roland had a very bad feeling about the situation, and Blakely was clearly right to be suspicious.

After an interminable wait, the door finally opened. "Are the ladies at home?" Roland said, holding out his card.

"I'm very sorry, sir," the butler said, the phrase sounding rote, as if it had been employed time and time again, "but the family is not receiving visitors today."

Over the man's shoulder, Roland could clearly see Miss Bence-Jones peeking out of a doorway. She looked poised for flight, as though she might throw caution to the winds and admit him in spite of whatever orders her brother or mother had given.

Roland met her gaze and waited silently, willing her to take action. Blakely deserved a woman who was willing to take a chance for him, who was willing to fight for him. Miss Bence-Jones bit her lip and shook her head, her expression not just pained but frightened.

What the hell had Sir Christopher done? Miss Bence-Jones had always been too sweetly ladylike to appeal to Roland, but she'd certainly had enough spirit that he had understood why his friend had asked for her hand. The stricken girl frozen in the doorway was a ghost of the lively one he'd last seen before her father's death.

"Could you please tell them I called," Roland said, pitching his voice to carry to her, "and that I hope to see them at Ranelagh tomorrow night? Or failing that, perhaps at my mother's at-home next Tuesday?"

Miss Bence-Jones nodded, glanced furtively over her shoulder into the room behind her, and disappeared from sight. Roland reclaimed his calling card and took his leave. Her family had clearly made a prisoner of her, which meant that Reeves and Blakely were right to be worried, and whatever was going on, it wasn't a simple illness or a change of heart on Miss Bence-Jones's part.

The previous day's storm had blown through, leaving behind just a few scattered clouds. As the sun slid behind one, Roland turned up the collar of his greatcoat and quickened his pace. He skirted a puddle as he crossed the street and turned south toward St. James's Street and The Red Lion.

Damn Sir Christopher. Roland swung at a rotting apple in the street with his sword stick and sent it bouncing down the gutter. Blakely couldn't possibly ask to come home at the moment, which meant that it fell to his friends to sort it out, to The League.

Thane would want to go slowly and keep things quiet. Reeves and de Moulines—fire-eaters, the both of them—would act first and repent at their leisure, more than likely causing a huge scandal in the process. Blakely's career wouldn't stand up to that sort of thing. The diplomatic corps frowned upon scandals, at least among their junior aides. The ambassadors themselves always seemed to be embroiled in one imbroglio or another: political, financial, amorous, or some combination thereof.

Roland's best allies for such an undertaking were Vaughn and Sandison, who'd come at it sideways with all the skills and deception they'd learned at their fathers' knees. Except Vaughn had raced home to Dyrham because one of his prize mares was due to foal any day and Sandison was mired in Kent with Vaughn's sister, who was in much the same condition as the mare.

Roland sidestepped a pile of horse dung, swung at the apple again, and came to an abrupt halt as his gaze came to rest on the sight of Lady Olivia being driven in a curricle by Carlow. All thought of Blakely and Miss Bence-Jones fled, burnt away by a flash of anger that set Roland's blood boiling.

Olivia had skipped their morning ride, sending word with her father that she was too unwell to join them. She'd also begged to be excused from their plans to meet at Lady Picford's ridotto that evening. Supposedly she was spending the day abed, attempting to ward off a chill she'd taken when caught in yesterday's storm. Except there she was, clearly doing nothing of the sort.

Roland watched the curricle roll merrily down New Pye Street and turn up into Mayfair. He knew damn well that Carlow wished him at Jericho, but having his place usurped by the likes of Henry Carlow was more than Roland was willing to stand for. Olivia had demanded a show of fidelity for the farce they were enacting, and she'd damn well better be offering him the same. It was going to be bad enough being publically jilted in a few months' time; having anyone think that he'd been thrown over in favor of Carlow, that was asking too much.

What would Olivia say if he called to check on her? If he caught her in her habit, clearly just come in from her drive? Would she beg his pardon, make some excuse, or merely stare him down as though he'd no right at all to lay claim to her?

Indignation and anger fueling every motion, Roland lengthened his stride. If he hurried and cut through the mews, he could reach Arlington House before they'd even had time to climb down from the box.

Livy clambered down from Henry's curricle without assistance, sweeping her skirts clear of the step with a practiced twist. She'd hung herself up once, as a girl of twelve, and the humiliation had been enough to set her practicing the maneuver until she had it down to an art.

Henry handed the reins of his curricle to one of her father's grooms, signaling his intention to stay at least long enough to see her inside. She hadn't intended to go out at all today. She'd been huddled near the fire in her bedroom, still trying to thaw her bones after yesterday's dousing, when Henry had burst in and demanded that she accompany him to look at a small suite of rooms he was thinking of letting for the remainder of the Season.

He'd been so excited about it that she hadn't the heart to say no. So even though the last thing she wanted to do was set forth into the blustery day, she'd dutifully pulled on her redingote and gone with him. The hot brick inside her swansdown muff had gone cold while they were debating furnishings and making lists of warehouses. It was merely a heavy weight in her arms now.

When Henry had first arrived in London, he'd thrown out hints that he'd like to be invited to stay at Arlington House, but the earl had proved remarkably deaf. It had been almost comical to watch Henry drop hints about the mean size of the rooms and the uncomfortable nature of the beds at Ibottson's Hotel while her father commiserated and pretended not to understand the purpose of Henry's comments.

Henry was too proud to ask outright and risk a rebuff, and her father was too polite to simply tell him to go to the devil. It wasn't that her father disliked Henry per se, but the earl had certainly never encouraged his presumptive heir to act like a true son of the household. Henry had never run tame about the estate or been given an allowance by the earl as some presumptive heirs were.

Livy studied Henry in the dappled light thrown by the fast-moving clouds. It was hard to imagine him in her father's place, even if he did have the Carlow coloring and the Carlow nose.

Would she feel the same if Henry were her brother rather than a somewhat distant cousin? Livy turned the question over in her mind while worrying her lip with her teeth. Yes. She'd known all her life that Henry would inherit, so in that way he was very much like a brother, but it still seemed impossible that someday people would address him as *Arlington*.

"When they're cool enough, give them a drink," Henry said, patting the closest horse on the shoulder. "I'll be back for them after I've seen Lady Olivia in." Henry held out his arm, and Livy allowed him to escort her out of the mews.

Did he know that her father meant to leave Holinshed Castle and Arlington House to her? That he'd inherit the title but very little else? The most recent entail had been broken by her grandfather, and the estate that had been conferred with the title was little more than a rocky hundred acres on the Welsh border.

Livy shifted the muff from one arm to the other and shook her arm to get the blood flowing freely again. Henry obligingly held out his hand.

"Give it here, cousin," he said, sliding the muff from her arm and tucking it under his elbow like a package. "So what do you think of Chapel Street? It's not the most fashionable address..."

"But is such a thing really all that important when it's only for the Season?"

"I suppose not," Henry replied with a shrug that clearly implied that it was but he was resistant to admitting to such a prejudice.

Livy held her tongue. She'd nearly forgot how important

appearances were to Henry. He always wanted to do the right thing. And by *right*, he meant that which would be most favorably looked upon by Society, that which would garner him the most praise, the most prestige. It was why he'd gone to Italy with Sir William, rather than take holy orders as his father had wished.

The *ton* might like him more for his supposed love of king and country. Livy did not. She'd seen his father's face when Henry had announced that his calling lay outside the church. He'd been devastated. They'd both known what Henry had meant was that life as a vicar wasn't grand enough for him.

She and Henry emerged from the narrow alley that led from the mews to the street to find Devere waiting on the steps, looking as though he'd been stationed there some time. His expression was one of benign patience, but Livy could clearly make out the faint signs of annoyance. His lips were ever so slightly clamped and one brow quivered as though it would fly up at the slightest provocation.

Good. He shouldn't place the slightest confidence in his right to monopolize her time or control her movements. It would serve as a useful lesson to him not to try.

Devere pushed away from the area's iron railing, and Livy felt her bravado falter. She'd canceled their plans today—twice—and now she'd been caught abroad, the picture of health. She knew precisely how it looked. The question was, how best to respond?

An explanation and apology would imply that he had a right to one, which under normal circumstances—which these clearly weren't—he would. Brazening her way through it would likely enrage him, but it would leave her in a stronger position. And maintaining the upper hand had come to feel vital.

"Mr. Devere." Livy pasted a bright smile on her face and moved toward him with both hands extended. "As you can see, I'm feeling better."

"Clearly," Devere said, bending over her hand after casting her a look that put her immediately on her guard.

Livy fought back the rising urge to explain. How did his sister and the other masterful women of the *ton* manage to restrain themselves? To always remain cool and calculating? To make flirtation seem effortless? It was galling to find herself constantly having to remember that she and this charming man were essentially at war.

The door opened on well-oiled hinges, and Devere dropped her hand and motioned her inward. Henry shoved past him to lead her into the house. Livy glanced back and nearly burst into laughter at the look of disdain on Devere's face. He might be annoyed by her outing with Henry, but he didn't consider him a threat of any kind. He caught her gaze as he followed in Henry's wake, idly swinging his swordstick.

Livy took a deep breath and ducked her head as she removed her hat. She'd chosen her path, best to stick to it. If she gave ground, she'd never make it up.

"I thought a bit of air would do her good," Henry said as he handed her muff to a waiting footman and shrugged out of his greatcoat. His intention to put Devere in his place was unmistakable. "And as you can see, I was right."

Livy bit back a groan. Devere's gaze slid past her and settled on Henry. Devere's eyes glinted with sudden amusement, but his smile had a hard edge to it. He was clearly relishing the opportunity to take his annoyance out on someone, even if it wasn't her.

Devere circled behind her, quiet, waiting, towering over Henry. In response, Henry pulled himself up to his full height, which was still a good four to five inches less than Devere's. Livy stifled an unkind giggle. Poor Henry was like a bantam facing off with a fighting cock. Or like Apollo standing beside Ares. Fair, handsome, romantic, but utterly eclipsed.

"So, Mr. Carlow," Devere said, his tone lazy and dismissive, designed to enrage, "you've adopted the role of nursemaid? Will we see you in skirts soon, like an actor ready for a production of *Romeo and Juliet*?"

Henry sputtered, his response nearly choking him. His face turned an unbecoming shade of puce and his eyes bulged. Livy took Devere by the arm and propelled him into the drawing room. He came along without the slightest protest, merely quizzing her with dark, dancing eyes that invited her to join the fun.

"Stop," she hissed under her breath. "My cousin was merely—bah! You're at *my* beck and call for the Season, not the other way round. So you'd best swallow your pride and learn to run in harness."

For a moment, she thought she'd gone too far, but then Devere burst into laughter. He bowed before her, leg extended and hat sweeping the floor. "Yes, my queen."

❧ CHAPTER 12 ❧

Mare tails were all that was left of the morning cloud cover by the time Roland spied Lady Olivia descending the Westminster Bridge stairs. He'd been on his family's shallop since first light, making sure everything was ready for the race and their day on the Thames.

A loud and raucous crowd had formed on and above the steps and stretched along the Thames for as far as Roland could see. And though the race was due to start shortly, the royal barge had yet to arrive. Until the king was there to see them all off, nothing could happen.

Margo waved cheerfully as Arlington shouldered his way through the throng and helped Olivia into one of the waiting wherries. Roland nodded back at his sister, unsurprised to see that she'd accompanied the earl to see his daughter off. Gossip had already begun to swirl about the two of them, as it was wont to do whenever Margo set up a new flirt. The fact that she was barely six months into her mourning period only added fuel to the fire. And the fact that his own name was being linked with that of Arlington's daughter added just the right touch of scandal.

The earl gave the small boat a push with his foot to help it move clear from the steps, and the waterman heaved mightily against the current as he rowed Olivia out to the Moubray shallop.

When Roland glanced up from the swiftly approaching wherry, Margo and Arlington had already disappeared from sight. The calls of street hawkers offering hot meat pies and nosegays and gin punctured the dull murmur of the crowd and mingled with the music floating over the Thames from a large barge anchored some distance away. The Duke of Devonshire had hired it so that he and his friends might enjoy following the race and arrive at the festivities at Ranelagh without the inconveniences of traveling there by coach. Inconveniences Roland rather suspected his sister was looking forward to.

As the wherry approached, Olivia looked rather as if she were being rowed to the Tower for an appointment with the executioner: chin up, back stiff, hands folded in her lap, one clutching the other. The breeze kicked up, pulling hard at her cloak, and Olivia snatched at it, dragging it down and wrapping it securely around her.

She met his gaze across the water, and her eyes appeared to widen with apprehension. As well they should. They'd left the battle only half fought the day before, interrupted by Henry and the arrival of tea and a plate of warm-from-the-oven rout cakes.

Roland smiled back at Olivia, well aware that she'd already learned to mistrust what others might interpret as a friendly gesture. She wasn't stupid. In fact, she was proving to be an entertaining and skilled combatant. Just when he thought capitulation was at hand, she'd slip from his grasp. When he expected apologies or excuses, she went on the attack.

She was more than merely intriguing. She was a worthy opponent, which made her something dangerously close to fascinating.

The waterman's wherry bumped up against the side of the shallop, and Roland stepped forward to assist Olivia as she attempted the dangerous crossing from one boat to the other. She put her hands up, her cloak flapping out behind her like a set of wings. The wherry rocked as Roland half lifted her into the shallop, and the waterman grinned at the flash of legs and the tangle of skirts. A cheer went up from the Devonshire barge as Roland set her on her feet and gave them all a bow.

One of Roland's oarsmen gave the wherry a shove with his oar, setting it spinning away. Devere tossed the retreating waterman a coin. The man snatched it from the air with one hand, barely missing a stroke.

The shallop swayed slightly as he stepped back from Olivia. She threw out one hand for balance and looked wildly about.

"Never been on a shallop?" Roland led her carefully toward the low canopy erected between the coxswain's position and the oarsmen's benches.

Olivia shook her head and ducked under the rippling fabric, taking her hand from his as she did so. She lifted her petticoats as she stepped inside and settled down among the pillows he'd piled deep all around the inside of the small structure. Roland had gone to great lengths to see that Olivia would travel ensconced in comfort.

"No," she said as she unclasped her cloak and let it fall from her shoulders. "I've only ever ridden on some of the larger pleasure barges, such as the one the Devonshires are on today."

"There aren't too many families that still maintain shallops." Roland looped one arm over the finial of a support post and studied their competition. "Seems like there's fewer every year. When I was a boy, there must have been fifty or sixty of them out here for the race. Last year there were only twenty-two. Today I count only seventeen. Eighteen, including ours."

The river seemed almost empty compared to what he remembered when he was a boy, though the shallops and barges were no less beautiful today than they had been then. Brightly painted, some with gilded details, almost all with colorful canopies and a crew of liveried oarsmen, the shallops were something special, something utterly different from the mean wherries of the watermen and the large pleasure barges such as the king used. They were a gentleman's conveyance. London's answer to the gondolas of Venice.

"So your family's seat is on the water?" Olivia said, leaning forward so she could see his face, giving him a rather expansive show of bosom as she did so.

Roland nodded, dragging his attention from Olivia's charms to the wider view of the river. "It's up near Syon Park." He sucked in a lungful of brackish air. Today was one of his favorite days of the year, and this rendition of the traditional race between the families owning estates along the Thames was set to be particularly memorable. He'd have Olivia alone for the better part of the afternoon. Well, as alone as you could be on an open boat with a crew of nine. "Too far to comfortably use as a base when Parliament is in session but close enough for country house parties to be a reasonable part of entertaining during the Season. In fact, my grandmother's—" Roland broke off as the sound of trumpets announced the arrival of the king. No doubt Margo would see to it that Olivia and her father were invited to the house party his parents were planning for the next Parliamentary recess.

The music on the Devonshires' pleasure barge likewise came to an abrupt halt and all heads turned to watch the royal barge as it moved ponderously up the river. King George looked a bit hipped, but the queen was wreathed in smiles. She nodded to Roland as the Moubray shallop bobbed unsteadily in the wake left by the larger boat's passing. Roland bowed in return, feet braced carefully to keep himself upright.

"What happens next?" Olivia asked *sotto voce* as she leaned past him so she could see the royal barge.

"The king will give a short speech, and then at his signal, we'll be off. I need to stand at the bow and appear attentive. You're welcome to join me."

Olivia responded with a wide, open smile that somehow felt like a caress. Roland helped her to her feet and carefully shepherded her up the narrow walkway, past the oarsmen who were busy keeping them from drifting, to the small, open area at the shallop's bow.

She gripped the rail, giving him her back. The breeze lifted her hair, sending curls tumbling about her shoulders.

Roland tugged on one, wrapping it about his finger. In the sunlight, her hair was nothing short of amazing. Not just blond, but burnished gold, like that of a princess in the fairy tales Margo had read to him when he was young. It blazed, molten, against the blue of her gown and the deep blue-gray of the water. Roland let the curl go and put his hand on Olivia's waist to steady her. At her sharp intake of breath, something sinful unfurled in his chest.

The crowd on the banks cheered as the king rose from his throne. Snatches of his speech drifted over the water, but most of it was lost to the hubbub on shore and the lapping of the water. Olivia leaned back, pressing against Roland's chest. His heartbeat lurched, blood flowing past his ears so loudly that he barely heard her as she asked over her shoulder, "Can you hear him?"

"No," Roland said softly, as all around them oarsmen dropped their long oars into the water in anticipation. "But it's much the same every year: honor, what-what. A noble race, what-what. Striving against the unconquerable river, what-what. You know how he sounds."

Olivia laughed softly as she nodded in response and returned her gaze to the king. "Your impression is almost unkind."

"What's unkind is half the world adding that dismal punctuation to their own speech. Sycophantic lapdogs." The last came out with more of a growl than he intended, but the king's oft-repeated phrase had spread to half the *ton* and infected every mushroom in England with social ambitions.

Olivia's head fell forward as she clapped her hand over her mouth, stifling a giggle. Unable to stop himself,

Roland dropped a kiss on her exposed nape. She smelled of lemons today. Lemons and the barest hint of rosemary.

She turned to give him a haughty, appraising look. Roland wrinkled his nose at her, refusing to pretend to be chastised or repentant when he was neither, when he had plans to do far worse today than merely kiss her bare neck.

When he finished his proclamation, the king reached into a gilded cage held by one of the young princesses and tossed a small dove into the sky. As the bird darted away, the coxswains' shouts filled the air and across the river the oarsmen collectively put their backs into the race.

The first few strokes made the boat lurch and shiver as though it might fly apart. Olivia swayed and laughed as she clung to the bulwark. After a moment, the oarsmen found their rhythm and the boat steadied, moving forward with a slightly undulating swiftness.

"Shall we sit?" Roland waved one hand toward the canopy.

Olivia didn't respond. She simply stood and watched as all around them the shallops jockeyed for position and the coxswains hurtled insults at each other with the same foul talent employed by the fishwives of Billingsgate.

Lord Brownlow watched with narrowed eyes as his shallop pulled past them, chasing the lead boat. He dabbed at his jaw with a large handkerchief before stuffing it up the sleeve of his coat with an impatient gesture. Brownlow had won the last three years in a row, and several times before that. He and his father both had eschewed a place in town in favor of their main estate and made frequent use of the river as they came and went from town. They had, perhaps, the most practiced team on the water.

"My lady?" Roland stepped back from Olivia, and she turned about as though surprised to suddenly find herself unsupported.

"Sorry, yes," she said, one hand still holding fast to the bulwark while the other attempted to keep her hair out of her eyes. After a moment, she shook her head ruefully and tottered carefully toward the canopy, her petticoats brushing the oarsmen's elbows when her step occasionally faltered. Roland marched swiftly after her, catching her as she nearly fell.

"No sea legs," he said, settling her down among the pillows once again.

"You try it in heels and skirts," she shot back, her brows pinched with indignation.

"*Touché.*" Roland crouched down and flipped open the hamper he'd had cook prepare and pack for them. "Would you like a glass of wine?" he said as he pulled a bottle of claret from the basket and attacked the wax seal with a penknife.

"By all means." Olivia arranged herself more comfortably among the pillows and bolsters, draping herself over one of them, one knee drawn up and the other stretched out, the lacquered heel of her shoe glinting in the sunlight.

Roland grinned at her and pulled the cork from the bottle with a satisfying *pop.* "You look like an odalisque in a seraglio."

"I was thinking granddame of Venice."

"Not courtesan?" he said, pouring her a glass of wine and leaning forward on one knee to offer it to her.

"No," Olivia said with a superior little smirk as she took the glass. "*Not* courtesan."

Roland shrugged, filled his own glass, and sprawled out beside her on the carpeted platform. "Courtesan certainly sounds more *enticing* than granddame, don't you think?"

Olivia took a sip of wine and sank farther into the pillows. "To a man like you? Certainly."

"A man like me? You mean one who's breathing?"

She shook her head, but one side of her mouth was quirked up with amusement. "Very well," she said after taking another sip. "I look like a courtesan in a gondola in Venice. You do remind me a bit of Casanova."

"You've met Casanova?" Roland slid closer to her as his question hung in the air. He worked his free hand out of its glove and eased it stealthily under the hem of her petticoats.

Olivia, still oblivious to his maneuver, shot him a look brimming with mischief. "When I was very little girl, he came to England. He called himself the Chevalier de Seingalt at the time, but the maids couldn't help whispering about who he really was. They were giddy with it. I should like to see Venice," she added with a somewhat mournful sigh.

"Why don't you?" Roland said as his fingers grazed the back of her knee, trailed over the silk of her stocking, and traced the line of her garter. Olivia's eyes widened and she nudged him away with her foot.

"Maybe someday I shall," Olivia said in the same tone one might say *maybe someday I'll see a unicorn*.

"No, really?" Roland scooted a tad closer, the movement of his hand on her thigh hidden from the busy oarsmen by her skirts and the pillows and the angle at which they lay. "As you told me yourself, you're a woman of independent means. You're of age. There's nothing to stop you going."

"I've never been farther afield than Yorkshire," Olivia said. She froze, like a grouse about to take flight, as his hand crept higher, skimming along the silken skin of her inner thigh. "I've never even crossed the channel. I wouldn't know the first thing about orchestrating a trip to Venice."

"Then you'd certainly end up being taken prisoner by Barbary pirates off Gibraltar and would live out your days in some Mohammedan pasha's harem."

"With my luck? Yes." Olivia glared at him as he grazed her skin with his nails. She drained her cup in one long, decisive draught. "Would you please pour me another glass?"

Roland smiled, thoroughly enjoying her flustered response and the heightened color creeping up her cheeks. "Take mine," he said as his hand reached the apex of her thighs, and she inhaled sharply.

"They can see us," she hissed, gesturing with her chin toward the oarsmen who were hewing hard to their labor.

"Then best not make a fuss and attract their attention." Roland took one last sip from his glass and held it out to her. The dark liquid sloshed with the gentle rocking of the boat. "If we were in Venice," he said, "there'd only be the gondolier, standing where the coxswain is now. Think of the possibilities."

Olivia took the glass from him and tossed half of it back with a defiant air. "*You* are not invited to Venice."

"No? What a shame." Roland slid his thumb along slick, soft folds. His middle finger found the swollen peak concealed within them and circled slowly. "For I'm quite skillful with the gondoliers." He pushed his thumb inside her, and Olivia shuddered slightly, her thighs clamping down on his hand. "You might find me useful."

Olivia took another sip of his wine and stared steadfastly at some distant point out on the water, as though ignoring him would change the location of his hand or her body's reaction to his touch. She was hot as a furnace and wet as a woodland spring. Bedding her was going to be magnificent.

"I'm not some whore who'll lift her skirts simply because you desire her to do so," Olivia said softly, still refusing to look at him.

Roland crooked his finger around her clitoris so that each contraction of his hand milked the tiny bud and pushed his thumb deeper within her. "I'd rather you lifted them because you desire to, because you desire me."

Olivia took a long, shaky breath, right on the edge of her release. She turned her head to look at him finally, pupils wide, nothing but a ring of aqua left to show their color. "I really should like that drink now," she said, her voice as wavering and unsteady as the hand that held out his now-empty glass.

"Then tell me outright to stop."

"Stop."

Roland obligingly slid his hand away, and Olivia made a small, involuntary sound of protest. Chuckling, Roland reached for the bottle and refilled both their glasses.

Roland toasted her before drinking. "You really should have let me finish."

She glared at him over the rim of her own glass. "Because it would have helped you along on the lust to love part of our dare?"

"That, and it would have kept you from a long night of wondering what I might have done next."

❧ CHAPTER 13 ❧

Livy choked on her wine and spit it inelegantly back into her glass. Devere gave a great bray of laughter in response before finishing his own glass in one long draught and getting up to wander back to the shallop's bow, tugging on his glove as he went.

He was right, the devil. Her body thrummed with frustration. Ached with it. She could still feel his hand on her, inside her. Her skin was flushed. Her nipples were almost painfully tight, and she was sticky and damp where he'd stroked and teased her.

He glanced back at her, a wide grin splitting his face. He knew exactly what she was thinking, what she was feeling, and he was going to be insufferable. The wind whipped his hair about his face, tugging curls loose from his queue, making him again the pirate of his mother's drawing room.

With a huff of annoyance, Livy poured the last of the wine into her glass and settled back against the padded bolster. The raucous cry of gulls overhead and the distant sight of them whirling against the sky made an impressive backdrop for Devere as he stood at the bow. It was like a scene out of a painting. A Canaletto or a Tillemans.

Devere's gaze slid away from her as they caught up to a competitor with oarsmen decked out in the devil's own gold-and-black livery. Shouting ensued between the two coxswains, a conversation composed of words she only half understood. They were cut off by a stout man wearing a bagwig and an embroidered coat more suited to an evening at St. James's Palace than a day on the river.

"A hundred pounds, Mr. Devere," the man shouted over the water. "A hundred pounds that I'm standing on dry land before you."

Livy pushed herself up and stepped out from under the canopy. It wasn't so much the outrageous sum as it was the man's tone that set Livy's back up.

The boats were close enough now for her to make out more than the ostentatious embroidery on the man's coat. Lord Brownlow. A thoroughly unpleasant man in her thankfully limited experience. His wife and daughters always had a cowed air about them, always looking to him before answering even the most commonplace question, as though seeking permission to speak at all.

As a younger son, Devere didn't have a fortune to throw around. A fact that Lord Brownlow clearly knew. He was enjoying the fact that Devere was caught between declining a bet he couldn't afford to lose and accepting one he couldn't afford to pay.

"My lord," Livy shouted as she walked to join Devere in the bow. Her blood hummed with wine, frustrated desire, and the anticipation of a skirmish. "I think that in honor of my very first shallop race, we should make it more interesting than mere money."

Both men watched her warily, but she could see that Devere was more than curious to hear what she was about to say. Lord Brownlow looked decidedly displeased to have been interrupted. Devere flicked a pitying glance at him, as though he knew the man was out of his depth.

"And what would be more interesting than money, my lady?" his lordship said as the Moubray shallop drew even with his own.

"Personal dignity?" Livy suggested with a patently false smile. Devere sucked in a sharp breath, clearly understanding where she was going. That ability to read her mind, to anticipate her actions, was one of the things she both liked and distrusted about him.

Lord Brownlow stared back at her, frowning, clearly waiting to hear her suggestion.

"I heard from Madame de Corbeville that there's a tradition of dunking the winning coxswain in the river," Livy said, watching him closely.

"Yes..." Lord Brownlow said, his expression darkening as he caught on.

Livy's smile widened. Brownlow's elaborate coat and wig would look all the more ridiculous sopping wet. "I propose the reverse," she shouted. "First one of you there gets to knock the other into the Thames."

"Is this your way of attempting to be shot of me?" Devere asked quietly. Livy met his gaze fleetingly, but didn't answer. She hadn't thought of that particular silver lining to losing.

"Very well," Devere said more loudly. "What say you, Brownlow?"

The baron stared at them both with a disgusted expression. "Sims!" he shouted, his face starting to mottle with annoyance.

"Yes, my lord?" his coxswain responded.

"If I end up in the river, you'll be looking for work without a reference. I shall see you at Ranelagh, Devere. Lady Olivia." He nodded and retired to his own canopied haven. His coxswain shot them a dirty look and urged his crew on with a promise of his own share of the prize money.

"A one-pound bonus each," Devere said to his oarsmen, "if we beat those bastards to the finish." In response, they leaned into their oars, expressions hardening. Devere leaned casually against the railing. He'd lost his hair tie again, and his dark curls were loose and running riot in the wind. "What have you got me into?" Devere said with a bemused shake of his head.

"You won't melt."

The road from London to Ranelagh was choked with carriages of every description. Margo had been sad to begin the trip inside a closed carriage rather than being free to enjoy the air in a curricle or phaeton, but the swirls of dust blowing by the windows as the dry road was churned by hoof and wheel made her grateful that Arlington had chosen as he had.

The earl's coach had been appointed to address every comfort or need. There was wine and an array of savories and sweets. He'd brought cards, books, and a traveling chess and backgammon set. There were pillows and traveling blankets and bricks that would be heated for the trip home if the night turned out to be unseasonably cold.

Margo was used to a more Spartan existence: cold rooms, drafty halls, fireplaces that did little more than smoke, and a husband who cared only for his own comfort, never for hers. Arlington seemed to care for little else and had prepared for their short excursion as though they were setting off for a grand tour.

The distinct sound of the coachman coughing from the box broke in upon them, and the coach momentarily darkened as a severe cloud of dust blocked out the light. Margo watched it swirl by like a brown fog. "How did you know?" she said as she returned to studying the backgammon board that lay between them on the small table that folded down from the door.

"That we should be eating dust all afternoon?" the earl said as he slid his pieces down the board and claimed two of hers. "Simple. It's not raining, eliminating mud from the two options, and half the *ton* is off to Ranelagh today. Dust was inevitable." He smiled as he said it, laugh lines crinkling from his eyes down across his cheeks.

Margo's chest tightened, and she barely held herself back from reaching across the table that separated them to touch his face. It was ridiculous to be seduced by something as simple—as sweet—as a man's sunny disposition, but she couldn't seem to help herself. Lord knew she'd been seduced by less on more than one occasion.

And for all that he'd become a devoted swain, the earl remained maddeningly respectful. Any other man would have thrown up her skirts and had his way with her before they'd reached the first turnpike.

Margo squirmed on her seat. If she couldn't will him into action, could she provoke him into it? If she slid her foot between his legs would she find his cock straining for release? Would he thrust the table out of the way, sending the backgammon board and the ivory and ebony disks flying? Or would his expression change from admiration to disgust?

Margo rolled the dice and moved her pieces to capture one of Arlington's. The earl raised one brow and shook his head, not looking at all as if ravishment was on his mind. "I fear you're not paying attention, Madame. You could have had three."

"I told you at the outset that games of strategy were not where my talents lay," Margo replied with a shaky laugh. She was wanton, and Arlington was a gentleman in every sense of the word. How on earth had she allowed her fancy to fall upon a man so unsuited to her purposes?

The earl collected the dice, his long-fingered hands brushing across the board in a way that made Margo's pulse leap. He dropped them into the dice box with a rattle and gave her an appraising look as he shook them. "A gentleman should never call a lady a liar, so I'll merely note that I believe you to be pandering to my vanity."

Margo cocked her head and did her best to look innocent. "Why on earth would you think that, my lord?"

He shot her a look of pure disbelief before sending the dice rolling down the board. "I know what life at court is like," he said, handing her the leather dice box, fingers sliding along her hand as he did so. Was his touch purposeful, or was it only wishful thinking on her part?

"Whether that court is at Versailles, St. James's, or St. Petersburg makes no difference," he continued. "And whether you call it intrigue or strategy, it amounts to the same thing. One is either good at it, or one isn't."

"So my ability to survive life at court—"

"Not just survive, Madame," Arlington interjected as she turned the dice box in her fingers. "Be honest. You flourished by all accounts."

Margo twisted uncomfortably on the seat, suddenly aware of every point where her clothing pinched or bound. Arlington was staring at her with clear, blue eyes. Not in an accusatory fashion but with uncomfortable penetration and insight all the same. He saw her. Knew her. And still he acted the gentleman.

His happy disposition didn't diminish his intellect one iota. In fact, it made him dangerous in a way she'd never encountered before. It was hard to remember that behind that handsome face and ready smile was a mind every bit as devious as her own, or so gossip made out. Arlington was a power to be reckoned with in the Lords, according to her father. A man of presence and persuasion.

"My skill as a courtier somehow means I should be better at backgammon than I am?" she said, shaking the dice vigorously. He smiled again, and the tension between them dissipated like a soap bubble bursting.

"No," he said settling back against the squabs and stretching out one leg so that his foot was braced on the bottom of her seat. "Your talent as a courtier means that if you actually applied yourself, you'd be giving me a much better game than you are. Hence my conclusion that being bad at backgammon is a sop to my vanity. I assure you, though, being bested by a woman won't leave me bruised and battered. Shall we begin again?"

Margo nodded. She hadn't been purposefully allowing him to win, but she hadn't been invested in the outcome either. Backgammon was merely a way to distract herself from turning idle daydreams of seduction into action.

Arlington reset the board, and Margo found herself almost shaking with the desire to slide across the narrow space and climb into his lap. He glanced up from the board when he was done, his expression almost hungry before he schooled it into something milder. Margo swallowed hard, heat licking through her. That slight slip of control left her almost dizzy. She hadn't been imagining the attraction that seemed to pull between them like a taut rope. It was right there below the surface, carefully leashed.

"If you really want to see me at my best," she said, reveling in the feeling of being sure of herself once more, "we should play chess."

~ CHAPTER 14 ~

Lord Brownlow came sputtering to the surface of the Thames with a curse, and Livy bit back an unkind laugh. His wig was clutched in one hand, leaving his balding pate exposed to the full glare of the sun. With his slightly protruding eyes, he looked like a seal dismayed at finding itself so far up river.

The sound of the Moubray oarsmen cheering was almost loud enough to drown out the whistles and hoots from the shore. Devere leapt from the shallop to the steps and bent to help the baron from the water. Brownlow stared at Devere's extended hand for one long, pregnant moment. He grabbed hold of Devere's wrist and heaved, his legs kicking away from the short pier.

The unexpected attempt to drag him down caused Devere to lurch forward. He caught himself and hauled the baron up. Devere dangled the smaller man a foot or so above the ground before dropping him unceremoniously to his feet. "That's ungentlemanly, my lord," Devere said. "You made the bet, and you lost."

The dripping baron pitched his ruined wig into the Thames with an angry growl. It sank swiftly, disappearing from sight like some monstrous sea creature startled into flight. "Call me ungentlemanly again and you'll be naming your second," the baron ground out.

Livy clapped her hand over her mouth, not quite catching the laugh before it escaped. Devere tossed her a repressive glance, and Livy grinned into her hand, daring him to remonstrate with her. The idea of a duel between the two men was ludicrous. Devere was half his age and twice his size. Win or lose, he'd be a laughingstock, but the scene unfolding between them was attracting a good deal of attention.

"Your estate's not far, my lord. Change and dry off," Devere said, far more kindly than Livy would have. "If you still feel the need to run me through after that, I'll be dining with Lord Arlington under the rotunda."

The baron shook as he attempted to get his temper under control. His face was mottled pink and puce. Making a desperate bid for dignity, he turned on one heel and clambered back into his shallop. The crowd renewed its riotous celebration and spilled down the steps until she and Devere were completely engulfed.

Livy shook her head and went to fetch her cloak from under the canopy. You'd think he'd won the race the way people were carrying on, but there were several shallops already tied up. They'd done no better than fourth at best.

By the time she'd shaken out her cloak and clasped it around her neck, Devere had cleared enough space on the quay for her to alight. One hand held firmly in his, the other clutching her skirts, Livy jumped across the small gap between boat and solid ground.

When she was clear of the boat, Devere nodded dismissal to the coxswain. "Buy the men some supper and a drink or two," he said, tossing the man a small purse, "but keep them sober enough to row us back to town. I'll send a footman to fetch you back when you're needed."

The man nodded, and the oarsmen immediately set about mooring up the boat. Devere wrapped an arm about Livy's waist and drew her up the steps. The heat of the afternoon coalesced in his hand, burning through the layers of leather, silk, and linen between the skin of his hand and that of her back. Livy nearly stumbled on the stairs as a wave of indecent longing swept through her.

She should have clouted Devere over the head with a pillow—or better yet, the wine bottle—the moment she felt his hand on her knee. The last thing she needed was to be desperately, painfully, aware of what she was striving to resist.

At the top of the stairs, the stone gave way to a long oyster-shell walk that led to the imposing edifice of the Royal Hospital and then turned right toward the pleasure garden.

The crowd swelled as they made their way past the hospital and the entrance to Ranelagh came into view. On the lawn outside the Corinthian archway, tents and booths were set up as though a fair were taking place. Oarsmen in their colorful livery were scattered about, but most of them were under one large awning toasting the winning coxswain. The man was every bit as wet as Lord Brownlow, but he wore his dripping coat and wig like badges of honor.

At the gates, Devere showed the doorkeeper a small brass token and they were ushered inside with a bow. "Box five," the doorkeeper said, sweeping his hand out dramatically toward the hive-like rotunda. A colorful swarm of guests moved in and out, rotating into the garden and returning from their perambulations in a constant flow.

"Shall we see if your father and Margo have arrived?" Devere said, straightening to his full height and surveying the milling guests. A shiver of attraction ran down Livy's spine, making her hands and feet tingle. She'd never thought of height as a particularly attractive quality, but the feeling of daintiness Devere's size gave her was an attraction all its own.

"I thought the entire point of the shallops was that they were faster?" Livy let her breath out in a sigh. If only he had some fatal flaw. Or rather one that showed on the surface, for he was—like all libertines—flawed at the core. His sins should have been branded on his cheek like those of a common criminal.

"Shallops are faster—plenty of races on the various betting books about town to prove it, but there's no telling when they set out. We waited for the king for some time. They could have had a half an hour or more head start. At the very least we can find the supper box your father reserved and get a drink before exploring the gardens," he said, a wicked grin sliding across his face. "Since someone drank nearly all my wine, I'm rather parched."

Heat licked through Livy anew. "Well then, let's see to your needs." Devere's smile grew at the double entrendre, and Livy batted her eyes as though unaware of what she'd said. He deserved a little teasing, a little frustration.

"Let's," Devere agreed as they wove their way toward the massive rotunda that was the main feature of the gardens. It was two stories tall, with boxes all the way around on both floors and a large center tower that was built to hold a fire. At the moment, the fireplace was merely stacked high with logs, ready to be lit when needed. All around it were tables and benches, which Livy knew would be cleared away after supper so the dancing could begin. She hadn't been to Ranelagh since the year she'd made her come-out, but very little had changed.

The elegant steward who oversaw the rotunda showed them to one of the large boxes on the ground floor. "Lord Arlington bespoke a cold nuncheon upon your arrival," the man said. "If you'll please be seated, I'll direct its delivery immediately. There's claret, champagne, and shrub waiting in the wine cooler. If you desire anything else, you have merely to ask."

Livy took a seat on one of the red velvet benches while Devere pulled a cold bottle of champagne from the large wine cooler hidden in the corner and set about opening it. By the time he'd poured them each a glass and topped it with a bit of the lemon shrub, footmen had arrived with trays of savory buns, finely sliced ham, a cold roast chicken, a salad of peas and mint and cucumber, and a plate of assorted kickshaws.

Livy took a macaroon from the plate of kickshaws and ate it while Devere carved the chicken. She licked crumbs from her fingers and reached for a second biscuit.

"Starting with dessert?" Devere said as he made up a plate for her.

Livy shrugged. "I'm famished. Eating dessert first doesn't seem to be the crime today that my nurse made it out to be."

"Plenty of worse crimes to commit," a female voice announced from just outside the box.

Livy turned to find her father assisting the comtesse up the low steps. "Exactly," Devere said as his sister took a seat beside him and snagged his wineglass. "Like stealing a man's drink."

The comtesse merely grinned and took a sip. Livy nearly choked as her mind flashed back to her own recent commandeering of his glass and just what he'd—they'd—been doing at the time. Devere's sister cocked one eyebrow as though she knew exactly what Livy and her brother had been up to on their journey.

A powerful wave of jealousy swept through Livy and she set down her glass, afraid she'd snap the stem. If she were a widow like the comtesse, she could allow herself to succumb to Devere's advances and the world would hardly bat an eyelash.

Her husband wasn't here for the *ton* to scorn and slight, and society didn't like being cheated of their entertainment any more than the ancient Romans had liked gladiators who refused to fight. Without Souttar to satisfy their bloodlust, the *ton* would happily make do with her.

"Did you enjoy your first trip in a shallop?" the comtesse said, a knowing smile still lingering about her eyes.

When there was nothing left of their meal but bones and crumbs, Philip waved Livy and Mr. Devere off into the oncoming dusk to watch the lanterns being lit. Madame de Corbeville smiled up at him conspiratorially and held out her empty glass.

Philip paused, stunned in that instant by just how

appealing that smile was. Sweet and sinful at the same time. After a moment, he shook off the feeling of being a fly trapped in amber and grinned back at her.

Though she was ostensibly dressed in mourning, the subtle pattern of the black silk of her gown was picked out with sequins, giving the center of each tiny flower a magical glint. The whole thing shimmered in the candle-light, making the comtesse appear like a dark jewel in a red velvet box.

The great fire at the center of the rotunda was being stoked, and the tables cleared away from what would shortly become the dance floor. The boxes around them were overflowing with merrymakers. The din of their conversations created a low burble, not unlike that of the rushing Thames a short distance away.

Madame de Corbeville worried her lower lip between her teeth, watching him with an assessing look he was hard-pressed to interpret. She'd been eyeing him all day as though she were on the verge of taking a step of which she was unsure. Such reticence didn't seem natural to her at all.

The comtesse had beaten him at a game of chess, and it had been clear—at least to him—that she was well on her way to winning the second game that was interrupted by their arrival at Ranelagh. No, beaten wasn't the right word. She'd routed him fully, almost effortlessly.

He honestly couldn't remember the last time anyone had given him a good game, let alone beaten him. Nor could he remember enjoying the sensation of losing before. But there was something about the almost embarrassed little smile that lit her face as she checkmated him that was disarm-ingly charming.

And charming wasn't a word that normally sprang to mind when he thought of Madame de Corbeville. Vivid, alluring, beautiful; she was a siren. But that smile wasn't the smile of a siren; it was the smile of a flesh and blood woman. One who wasn't entirely certain of herself. That flash of vulnerability was a glimpse behind the mask she wore, and that sight was possibly the most riveting thing he'd witnessed yet.

That smile made her real.

Philip twirled her empty glass between his fingers. "Lemon or strawberry shrub? Or perhaps claret?"

"Lemon shrub," she said, ceasing to chew on her lip and smiling back at him instead. "If Rolly didn't consume all of it, that is. I think my brother drank the better part of two bottles of champagne."

Philip fished an unopened bottle of shrub from the wine cooler along with another bottle of champagne and made short work of removing the cork. "I rather imagine managing Livy is enough to drive most men to drink."

The comtesse's mouth sagged open for a moment, and she blinked at him as though she were at a loss for words. After a moment, she gave a girlish twitter of laugher and reached for her newly filled glass.

"The challenge will do Rolly good," she said as she swirled the glass about, mixing the lemon-infused brandy with the champagne. "He's far too used to having women fall into his lap like ripe fruit."

Philip felt a moment of uneasiness. He'd been joking, but he could see that Devere's sister wasn't. Livy had never given him a moment's worry. At least not until the day she'd fled her bigamous husband's house and put herself under her grandmother's protection. He'd never imagined a day when he wasn't the one she turned to, and it still smarted when he let himself dwell upon it. He'd wanted the best for her, wanted her to be sure of the facts, of the law, but he could see now that she'd taken his advice to stand her ground as a betrayal.

He *wanted* to believe the story of flouted love his daughter and Devere had regaled him with, but his gut knew better. The ever-present doubt flared into something close to anger, and he damped it down.

He knew his daughter. If she'd been in love, she'd have never agreed to marry someone else. No, there was some other game afoot. He'd lost Livy's trust, and so she'd chosen her own champion. All he could do was trust in her judgment.

How she had got Devere under her thumb was the real question. The other one, of course, was how did she plan on keeping him there?

❧ CHAPTER 15 ❧

The last pink edge of dusk disappeared behind the first volley of fireworks. The air filled with the acrid scent of gunpowder. Margo pulled Arlington up the exterior stairs of the rotunda for a better vantage point. She leaned against the railing that encircled the walkway leading to the first-floor boxes and stood silently watching the rockets burst from the barges on the Thames and explode overhead.

Each burst of color was followed by cheers and shrieks and laughter, as if the audience filling the garden were made up of nothing but children. Arlington's face was bathed in colored light from the lanterns, making the shadows and hollows appear purple and blue while the planes of his face were red like a devil.

The earl turned to look at her, and Margo's chest nearly seized. She wrapped both hands around one of his wrists and slowly drew him along the walkway.

Arlington followed along unresisting, a quizzical expression causing his brows to rise. The doorways leading to the numerous small boxes that were accessed from the walkway were filled with people. At several points, they had to work their way through the standing crowd that was eagerly gathered to watch the display.

"Don't want to watch the show?" he said as they circled and the rotunda began to block their view. The walkway beyond, offering no view of the fireworks, was completely deserted.

Margo shrugged and sped up. "I'm betting that everyone unlucky enough to have been assigned a box on this side will have gone out by now."

Arlington's expression changed from mild confusion to sudden comprehension. The hungry look from the carriage returned as Margo laughed and pulled him through a door that had been left ajar on a darkened box.

This one was perfect. No one would blow out the lanterns if they intended to return anytime soon. Light filtered in from the chandeliers hung all about the dome of the rotunda, providing just enough illumination for her to make out the small table and chairs pushed up to the edge of the balcony overlooking the rotunda floor. The soft sounds of the musicians testing their instruments drifted in between the steady boom of the fireworks.

Arlington kicked the door shut behind them and grabbed one of the ornate chairs. "What are you—oh," Margo said as he wedged it under the knob and turned back to face her, mischief plain on his face even in the dim light.

"This is foolishness," he said, taking a step toward her, hands poised as if he were almost afraid to touch her.

"No, foolishness was wasting our trip playing chess," Margo replied. She took a step toward him, splayed her hands on his chest, and thrust him down into one of the small chairs.

Low, throbbing heat flooded through her, making her limbs heavy. Her heartbeat plummeted from her chest to lodge between her thighs. She hadn't been touched by a man in more than six months. In all the years of her marriage, Margo didn't think she'd ever gone six days without a man in her bed. Not always her husband, true, but then Etienne had been busy elsewhere as well...

Arlington pulled her to him by her skirts, nearly yanking her off her feet. He pushed her petticoats aside, dragging her into his lap. Margo straddled him, shivering as the metallic trim on his coat scraped coldly across the skin of her inner thighs.

The earl gripped her hips as she settled in his lap, thumbs circling on her hip bones. His mouth traced the line where neck and shoulder met, hot and predatory. Any doubts she'd had vanished. He wasn't the least bit disgusted, and he wanted her every bit as much as she wanted him.

Margo fought her way down past the froth of petticoats between them, fingers tracing the lean line of Arlington's chest and stomach until she found the buttons that secured his breeches. The earl's breath hissed out of him as she freed his cock, wrapped her hand about it, and gave it one long, hard stroke.

"Jesus," Arlington mumbled against her neck, his hands sliding around her hips, tugging her toward him.

His breath shuddered in and out, warm on her damp skin. His cock hardened in her hand, swelling until her fingers could no longer encircle it. Margo held him fast as she mounted, greedily taking as much of him as she could on the first down stroke. The sharp, hollow ache that had been building all day burst into the first hint of climax as he guided her up and brought her back down.

Arlington's hands slid out from under her skirts, moved up her back, and hooked over her shoulders. He drew her down as he thrust into her, his cock riding hard against the mouth of her womb with every stroke.

Margo clutched his coat, set her forehead against his, and stared directly into his eyes. He gazed steadily back, unblinking. She felt more than saw him smile and his cheek brushed hers, ever so slightly rough with the promise of beard. Margo shut her eyes and gave herself over to the purely physical joy of racing toward her release.

The earl came with a growl and buried his head in her breasts. He flexed up, arching against her, as the first tingling wave of climax hit, and then, with a sudden splintering crescendo that echoed off the walls, the chair beneath them broke.

They landed in a heap atop the ruins of faux-gilt wood, and Margo burst into peals of laughter. Arlington stared up her, shock turning slowly to amusement as he too began to laugh.

The earl set her gently to one side and wiped his streaming eyes. He scrambled up, the skirts of his coat entangled in the remnants of the chair. Margo sat on the floor, trying to get control of her breathing and rein in her frustration. She'd been so close, so damn close.

Arlington dusted off his coat, freeing it from the shards of wood, buttoned up the placket of his breeches, and shot his cuffs. A quick tug settled his coat smoothly across his shoulders, and he was once again the consummate gentleman. No one would ever know that moments before he'd been fornicating like a satyr.

He reached down and helped her up, lifting her to her feet with one powerful motion. He was stronger than he appeared. Whipcord-hard under a deceptive layer of silk.

Margo smiled with covetous wonder as she shook out her skirts. She'd expected elegance and civility, a courtly lover, not a display of raw physical prowess. He was magnificent.

She tugged the bodice of her gown into place, running her hands over it to make sure it wasn't gaping open and that she hadn't lost any pins. Arlington kicked the broken chair aside, sending it flying across the box, and crossed the small space to remove the blockade from the door.

He smiled guiltily as they slipped out onto the walkway, his fingers intertwined with hers. A deafening boom washed over them as what appeared to be the finale of the fireworks display erupted overhead, raining down showering, glowing sparks.

Margo leaned back against the wall of the rotunda, still trying to catch her breath, heart hammering with excitement and exertion. "Do you realize you still haven't kissed me?"

Philip chuckled at the absurdity of the comtesse's comment. Her face lit up as he stepped closer, pinning her to the wall, chest to chest, hip to hip. He captured her mouth with his own, kissing her hard, with all the frustrated urgency still rushing through his veins.

Why the devil had they sent the carriage back when they'd arrived? If ever there was an evening not to share a conveyance home with his daughter, this was it. A long carriage ride home would be the perfect place to finish what that damn chair had so rudely interrupted.

The comtesse—Margo—softened in his arms, wilted almost, her hands trapped between them, lying quiescent against his chest. Philip broke off the kiss and turned them both about so they were staring out over the brightly lit garden, her back to his chest, his arms about her waist. He rested his cheek on top of her head and simply held her there, not quite ready to return to being Lord Arlington and Madame de Corbeville just yet.

Margo leaned back into him, clearly no more eager than he to reenter the fray. The sky darkened as the last motes of the fireworks winked out and the strains of a minuet seeped out into the night, calling the crowd back to the rotunda. The first wave of guests returning to their boxes broke them apart.

"Shall we go and watch the dancing?" Philip said as they reached the bottom of the stairs.

Margo wrapped her hands about his biceps with a sigh. "If this were a masquerade, I could have worn scarlet and danced until I wore through the soles of my shoes."

"The Dorringtons are giving a masquerade in a few weeks' time," Philip said with a grin as they made their way back toward one of the entrances to the rotunda.

Margo shook her head ruefully, setting her dark curls bouncing. "I'm afraid I haven't been invited."

Philip's grin widened as he tucked a stray curl back behind her ear. "Neither have I."

The sight of Lord Arlington brushing Madame de Corbeville's hair back from her face brought Henry Carlow up short. His heartbeat redoubled in his ears, a staccato panicked drumbeat. What the devil was going on?

He'd come to Ranelagh with a party of friends and had spent the better part of the evening grinding his teeth as he continually stumbled across Olivia and her damn swain. The idea that Livy intended to marry that useless oaf, to hand over her fortune and her person to a man with nothing to recommended him but the skills of a hedgebird— cards, horses, and pugilism—was enough to make him wish that Protestants had maintained the nunneries and the tradition of locking unruly females within their walls.

He kept waiting for Livy to come to her senses. Eventually she must realize that Devere was little better than a gazetted fortune hunter. The man would never be able to offer her what he could: a title, respectability, and consolidation of the Carlow lands and fortune.

Livy had always been quick-witted. It was one of the things he genuinely liked about her. Surely the obvious solution would occur to her. Or it would if only he could send Devere packing. But maybe there were more dire machinations afoot.

Madame de Corbeville said something to the earl as they approached the Chinese Pavilion where his cronies were ensconced at cards, and Arlington's answering bark of laughter set Henry's pulse racing even harder. His hands curled into fists. He took a rage-induced step toward them before getting himself back under control.

He knew what an infatuated man looked like. Lord knew he spent enough time watching the ambassador make a fool of himself over every Italian woman who so much as glanced at him. The earl looked thoroughly besotted. He kept one hand on the comtesse at all times, as though unable to stop touching her.

Henry stalked back into the rotunda, his stomach churning with horrid possibilities. He sank into a seat in the box his friends had rented and reached for the open bottle of brandy. One of the demireps they'd brought with them slid into his lap, and the overwhelming scent of roses pushed into his nostrils until he could actually taste it. He gestured for her to pour and then slugged the full glass of brandy back in one go, letting the burn quiet his nerves.

The whore in his lap batted her eyelashes at him and refilled his glass, her free hand pushing down to splay over the fall of his breeches. Henry pushed her hand away and her expression hardened before she could force a smile. Henry knocked back the second glass and nodded toward the bottle.

"Again, Suzette."

"Rachel," she said with a pout. "Suzy is dancing with Lord Harry."

"Rachel," Henry said, trying to sound conciliatory. "Pour me another brandy, and then perhaps we'll join Lord Harry and your friend in the next set."

Rachel smiled and complied. Out on the floor, Olivia whirled by, hair and skirts flying as Devere swung her through the steps of the gallant. Henry grimaced, staring until they disappeared in the sea of dancers.

Losing Livy and her fortune would be disastrous, but if Lord Arlington were to remarry and produce an heir of his own? There would be no recovery.

❧ CHAPTER 16 ❧

The mingled scents of dust and horse and leather grew stronger as Roland strolled across the yard at Tattersall's and turned into the entrance of the barn. His friends were at the far end, gathered in a lively semicircle around Lord Leonidas Vaughn.

It was Monday, settling day, and it had been a very good week, and not just because Lady Olivia was one step closer to capitulation. Thane owed him fifty guineas, Reeves owed him thirty, and he didn't owe anyone so much as a groat. That eighty ought to be more than enough to buy the gelding Lord Leonidas was selling today. Dyrham-bred or not, it was hard to imagine anyone offering more than that for the animal.

Roland wandered down the wide aisle between the stalls, stopping to give the once-over to a chestnut mare from Lord Dandridge's stable before moving on to the cluster of men standing outside the stall of an eighteen-hand black gelding with a blaze so wide it might almost have been called piebald. The chestnut was a beautiful animal, but the black was nothing short of magnificent. It looked like it ought to be carrying an armored knight into battle with a pennant waving overhead.

Roland nodded to his friends and ran a gloved hand up the gelding's beautifully arched neck. He dug in and scratched behind one swiveling ear. The horse exhaled loudly through its nose and dipped its head to lip at Roland's pocket. It caught the flap with its teeth and tugged.

"Greedy beast," Roland said, freeing his coat from the animal's grip and fishing for the lump of sugar that Reiver knew was there. He fed it to the horse and then dusted his gloves off.

"Still intent on buying him?" Thane asked as he unfolded his Bargello work pocketbook and counted out a stack of banknotes.

Roland nodded, tucking the banknotes into his pocket. "I was at Dyrham the last time the duke took him out, God rest his soul. I wanted him then, but His Grace wouldn't part with him."

"He was Grandfather's favorite," Vaughn said with a slightly sad smile. He rubbed his knuckles fondly between the gelding's eyes. "And though I'm loath to part with him, that's pure sentimentality. I need the space for breeding stock."

"How's the new foal?" Reeves said.

Vaughn's face lit up. "He's a right devil, just like his sire. Up on his feet in record time and running across the pasture like he has the wind in his blood before the week was out."

Roland chuckled at his friend's nearly paternal enthusiasm while Thane rolled his eyes. Reeves ran a knowing eye over the gelding and nodded. "The new colt is a Godolphin descendant, just like Reiver here, isn't he?" Reeves said as he pulled a snuffbox from his pocket.

"Yes." Vaughn put a shoulder against the wall and wrinkled his nose as Reeves inhaled a pinch of snuff and immediately sneezed. "They're both out of Skyscraper."

Thane let out a low whistle. "The grand stallion of Dyrham. He must be going on twenty now."

Vaughn nodded. "He's twenty-four. Born the same year as Beau. I doubt there will be too many more foals for him, making the new one all the more precious."

"And how's our termagant?" Roland said. "Still enjoying the pleasures of Kent, is she?"

"Safely delivered of a daughter and busy planning the christening by all accounts. She and Sandison will be up as soon as the babe can travel." Vaughn slapped the gelding on the neck, and the animal shook its head, mane flying out. "Are you going to make me an offer, Devere?" he said. "Or did you want to wait and end up bidding against Squire Watt for him?"

"Watt wants him?" Roland suppressed a surge of annoyance. The hunting squire had a large fortune to draw upon and was well known for paying outrageous sums for horseflesh.

"Offered me sixty pounds," Vaughn said with an amused smile, "but I told him I'd already promised you the right of first refusal if I sold him. Besides, it wouldn't seem right to sell him outside the family, so to speak."

"Will Thane's sixty guineas get it done?" Roland pulled the notes Thane had just given him from his pocket and held them out. "Or should I make Reeves here produce what he owes me as well?"

"You are possibly the worst negotiator ever born," Thane said with undisguised disgust. "It's no wonder you're perpetually in the basket. You don't up your own offer. You wait for the other party to do so and then you never offer all of what they ask."

"Sixty guineas is more than fair," Vaughn said, cutting off Thane's lecture. "Did you want him delivered to the mews at Moubray House or to Croughton Abbey?"

"To Croughton if it's not a bother," Roland said after Vaughn had tucked the banknotes into the commodious pocket of his greatcoat. "There's to be a party there next week, and Reiver will save me having to ride one of Frocester's slugs."

"Your brother does have execrable taste when it comes to horses," Reeves said with a shake of his head. "The flea-bitten gray he was on when last I saw him would have been better suited for a country parson's gig than a viscount's stable. If it wasn't within an inch of being a damn pony, I'll eat my boot."

"It's not Frocester's fault," Roland said with a twinge of conscience. "You know he has a lame hip. He picks his mounts for comfort and smooth gaits."

"Why doesn't he just take a chair when in Town?" Thane said as they all wandered out to the yard to watch as the pretty little chestnut mare was put through her paces. They stopped in the shade of the colonnade, letting those actually interested in purchasing the dashing little mare occupy the yard itself.

"Father once called it an embarrassingly womanish means of conveyance, and it was more than clear that he meant Frocester to hear him say it. My brother took the slight to heart. How could he not?"

"How many of our fathers can't stand their heirs?" Reeves said before taking another pinch of snuff. He shut the little porcelain box with a click and dropped it back into his pocket amid the collective nods.

"And vice versa," Thane added. "Look at the prince and the king. They'd gladly murder one another if given half a chance."

"It can't be comfortable, for father or son, to know that the one can only come into his own by the death of the other," Vaughn said as he dusted off his hat and settled it on his head.

"Almost makes one glad to be a younger son," Roland said.

"No, it doesn't," Reeves said, giving voice to what Roland was sure was a communal sentiment. "Though I'm damn glad it was my brother, not me, who's to be sacrificed on the altar of dynastic marriage. Have you seen the rabbit-faced heiress my father is backing?" Reeves gave a dramatic shudder. "But for the grace of God and five minutes tardiness on my part, that could be my fate. Good Lord!" Reeves broke off, his attention riveted to a group of men on the other side of the yard. "Isn't that Sir Christopher?"

"It is," Roland said darkly. "I've been trying to run him to ground for days. He's never *at home* when I call, and his sister appears to be a virtual prisoner. When Margo called, Lady Bence-Jones admitted her but claimed her daughter was too unwell to join them."

"Shall we corner him now and get to the bottom of Blakely's missing letters?" Reeves cracked his knuckles, his eyes lighting up in anticipation.

"Drawing Sir Christopher's cork won't get us any-where," Thane said as he put a restraining hand on Reeves's shoulder. Reeves cast him a dark look but didn't shake him off.

"Has Miss Bence-Jones changed her mind?" Vaughn said, eyeing them all with a furrowed brow. "I thought the matter settled."

"As did Blakely," Reeves said, his dander clearly up about his closest friend's dilemma. "And then Sir Thomas had the temerity to up and die, and his son insisted they postpone the wedding for a proper period of mourning."

"I see," Vaughn said. He blew out an impatient breath, and his mismatched eyes narrowed as he watched their quarry bid on the chestnut mare. "Have any of you thought to bribe a servant?"

The note that was returned via the Bence-Jones's maid, who was only too happy to play go-between for a few paltry crowns, was written in an elegant copperplate hand but obviously dashed off in a hurry given the splatter of ink that marred the page. It said only: *Yard. Eleven o'clock. Tonight.*

Roland tossed it onto the scarred wood of the prime table at The Red Lion and dropped into a seat. "Which-ever of us goes, we'll be lucky not to be arrested for housebreaking."

~≪ CHAPTER 17 ≫~

Roland pushed away from the wall as Reeves emerged from the card room at the Hughes's ball. Livy was dancing with Carlow and promised to Lord Gregory for the following set, so she was unlikely to notice his absence.

He and Reeves set off on foot for the Bence-Jones's residence, bypassing the long line of standing carriages and idle, dozing teams. They skirted past a huddle of coachmen dicing by the light of a linkboy's flambeaux and were roundly cursed as their shadows allowed one of the dice to disappear into the gutter.

Reeves yanked his watch from his pocket and snapped it open as they passed beneath one of the infrequent oil lamps that attempted to push back the night in Mayfair. "We'd best hurry, or we'll leave the poor girl cowering in the dark."

Roland lengthened his stride as Reeves tucked his watch away. His sword knocked against his leg, and he steadied it with his hand. The only sounds in the streets were the scrape of their shoes on the pavement and the yapping of a small dog who took offense at their passing too close to his domain.

The Bence-Jones house was dark as they approached it, not even a light left on on the porch. Roland narrowed his eyes. Yes, the knocker was still there. Sir Christopher hadn't somehow discerned their purpose and spirited his sister out of town.

The mews were deserted. No dog or stable lad to raise the alarm as they counted gates, pushed the third one open, and slipped into the yard. Like most of the houses in town, the Bence-Jones's terrace didn't boast an actual garden, just a small courtyard that was taken up almost entirely by coal and ash bins and a large water butt.

"Hello?" Miss Bence-Jones's greeting came out in a tenuous warble.

"Miss Bence-Jones," Roland said quietly, putting out a reassuring hand.

Her teeth chattered, and she clutched her cloak more tightly about her. Reeves shut the gate silently behind them. "We brought the packet of letters Blakely sent. Copies of the ones he's sent since your father's death."

She reached for them, revealing what appeared to be her nightclothes beneath the cloak. "Thank you. I thought—I thought he'd..." She paused, clutching the fascicle of letters to her chest and took a deep, shuddering breath. "I didn't know what to think."

"Neither did Blakely," Roland said as kindly as he could. The anger thrumming through him was for her brother, not her. It was important to remember that, to keep it at the forefront of his mind.

"Kit wants me to marry his friend, Mr. Price," Miss Bence-Jones said. "He's been encouraging me to believe myself jilted. Harping on the issue until I'm ready to scream. But I had no idea he was keeping my letters from me. I assume my letters to John have also been interfered with?"

Reeves nodded grimly. "And Lady Bence-Jones?"

"My mother says I should be grateful to have a brother who cares so very much for my welfare," she said, not sounding at all as if she agreed with her mother's opinion.

⊰ CHAPTER 18 ⊱

"W hich do you like better?" Henry said as he leaned over the pattern book at Stone and North's. "The shield back or the lyre?"

Livy glanced over his shoulder, casting her eye over the page of chair designs. "I thought the rooms you rented were furnished."

"The chairs all creak and the drawers of the desk stick," he said as he turned the page. "And the carpets are worn through in spots. And it's best not to even discuss the state of the mattress. Considering what I'm paying, you'd think they wouldn't be such a shambles."

Livy hid a yawn behind her hand. The furnishings had seemed fine to her when they'd toured the rooms, but Henry always had been more fastidious than she about such things. He positively loathed most of the furniture at Holinshed. Livy couldn't help but be glad her father had decided not to leave it to him. Holinshed deserved to belong to someone who loved it. Someone who thought it was special and appreciated its eccentricities and oddities.

"Well, cousin?" he prompted.

"The shield back," Livy said, tapping it with one finger. "It has a more masculine look to it. The lyre back belongs in a lady's boudoir or a drawing room."

"I agree," Henry said a bit too brightly, as though he were trying to turn her up sweet.

Livy had a sudden vision of Holinshed filled with little gilt chairs. She repressed a shudder and turned to stroll across the room. The shop smelled of wood, orange oil, and beeswax. Small tables were set beside both windows to take advantage of the light. Each was stacked high with pattern books. Henry had insisted she accompany him. Acting as though it would be a treat for her. She couldn't imagine why. Her maid was standing outside, waiting patiently for them to finish, playing with the ribbons of her hat.

Henry made his selection known to the proprietor and led her back out to the pavement. A phaeton, glossy black with its wheels and details picked out in gold and green, rolled toward them, Devere's sister deftly steering the pair of high-stepping bays. Beside her, Lord Sudbury lounged at his ease, his arm stretched out across the back of the seat, looking very much like the cat who'd caught the canary.

The comtesse smiled when she saw Livy and touched the brim of her hat with her whip as she passed, very much as a gentleman would have done. Livy waved. Beside her, Henry made a stammering sound that was clearly part shock and part disapproval.

"I'm glad to see *that woman* has moved on from attempting to entrap your father," he said, his upper lip curled with disdain. "Sudbury is a much more appropriate object for her schemes."

"Whatever do you mean?" Livy said, unable to keep the annoyance from her voice. Henry had no right to speak of her father, or Devere's sister, that way. Her hand must have tightened on his arm because he tugged it away from her.

"Have you really not noticed? The *comtesse*"— he stressed the French title as though it were somehow damning in and of itself—"has been pursuing your father relentlessly. It's the joke of the season: the Monk and the Laïs of Versailles."

"Don't call my father that," Livy snapped. "And don't speak of Madame de Corbeville that way either."

"I wasn't saying *I* find it funny," Henry said. "Quite the contrary. Imagine if she were to succeed in seducing him. Your father is a *gentleman*. Circumstances might arise under which Lord Arlington might feel compelled to marry the creature. And then where would any of us be?"

"You mean where would *you* be?" Livy said, her temper rising.

Henry gave her a pitying look. "That's right," he said. "You're going to marry Devere. So I guess it won't matter if you're displaced as mistress of Holinshed."

Henry took his leave at the front steps of Arlington House and went off whistling between his teeth. Livy stalked inside, her maid trailing after her, and went directly to her room. She peeled off her gloves and washed her hands in the tepid water in the stand by her dressing table. She felt unclean.

If it was the lady's day at the Bagnio near St. James's, she'd have been tempted to drag Frith back out. But it wasn't. Women got access only one day a week. At the moment, the baths were undoubtedly overrun with whores and the gentlemen who sought to combine the pleasures of a shampoo with other, less respectable indulgences.

Livy rubbed the back of her neck, massaging away the tension. Of course she'd noticed her father and the comtesse's flirtation. She wasn't blind. But it hadn't occurred to her that anything serious might come of it. Given the comtesse's well-known predilection for dalliance, it seemed far-fetched and fantastical to suggest such a thing, but trust Henry to have an eye toward the prize. If her father remarried, Henry could lose everything.

Her maid had retreated to the chair beside the window to reattach a flounce on the gown Livy had worn to Ranelagh. Frith's needle and thimble winked in the sunlight. Livy checked her hair in the mirror, twisted a curl back into place, and went downstairs in search of a few moments' solitude.

She'd left the copy of *Dangerous Connections* she was reading in the drawing room the previous afternoon. She found it lying just where she'd left it, but one of the maids had closed it, marking Livy's place with a length of ribbon. Livy threw herself down on the settee closest to the window and flipped the book open, but after several attempts to lose herself in the story, she set it aside and went out into the garden instead. The original, *Les Liaisons Dangereuses,* had been better. It was somehow milder in translation.

Small stone benches were set under arbors all down both brick walls that separated their garden from those of their neighbors. Espaliered apple and pear trees were set between them, their profusion of blossoms humming with bees.

Livy wove her way past the neatly trimmed herbal borders and then sat down on the very last arbor, ignoring the chill of the stone that crept through the layers of her petticoats. The soft scent of fruit blossoms enveloped her, with a cloying hint of jasmine lurking underneath.

She couldn't imagine her father remarrying. If he'd had any inclination to do so, wouldn't he have done it long ago? It would have made perfect sense for him to take a new wife when he was a young widower. Doing so now seemed almost preposterous. Her father hated for anything to disturb his peace. He liked his routines, to have everything in its place. New servants annoyed him, for heaven's sake. A new wife, especially one with Continental ideas of how to run a house, would drive him mad.

A trio of wrens flittered through the garden, stalked by the small cat who ruled the kitchen with an iron paw. The birds chattered loudly to one another as they hopped across the small lawn and dove through the bushes, always staying just out of reach of the tortoiseshell queen. The cat gave Livy a baleful glance as it slunk past and disappeared in the direction of the mews.

A soft whine and an ear-splitting hiss alerted Livy to the presence of the earl's hound. The pack stayed at Holinshed, but her father rarely left Hastings behind with the rest. Hastings was as much pet as working dog. The giant, rough-coated deerhound came trotting up from the back of the garden, looking entirely pleased with himself. No doubt he'd scared the cat out of one of her lives.

He wormed his way into the arbor, making the bower

of jasmine shake, and dropped his head into Livy's lap. He dragged his damp whiskers across her skirts and stared up at her with large, brown eyes. Livy ran a hand down his back and gave the dog several hearty thumps.

The comtesse didn't seem like the kind of woman who'd like life at Holinshed. It was all muddy dogs, ancient plumbing, and constant maintenance of the old castle walls. The only parties they ever gave were the balls that accompanied the annual stag hunts, where the guests were as likely as not to arrive muddied to the brow and windblown from the hunt.

And Hastings and the pack were constantly underfoot, even though they had their own quarters in one of the abandoned towers. The maids were forever complaining about the dirt the dogs tracked in. Her father had finally hired a scrub woman whose only job was to clean up in the pack's wake.

It was an elegant, if unusual, solution, and so very like her father. He always said the pack had been there before he was born and would be there when he was gone. They were a fixture, every bit as important to him as the deer park and the library.

What would Devere's sister make of Holinshed? Her life up until now had been court politics and dancing attendance upon a queen. She'd said so herself. And if the comtesse hadn't spelled out which of the gentlemen in her stories had been her lovers, it was well known that some of them—many of them—had been. There was a certain softening about her eyes when she spoke of the French queen's favorite, Axel von Fersen, for example, that told its own story.

How would Devere's sister feel about swapping that for nightly discussions of the latest translation of Virgil and taking tea with the vicar's wife? It was impossible to even imagine her in such a setting. It was even more impossible imagining her father being made happy by the kind of life that the comtesse de Corbeville relished.

Worse still, how would the comtesse react when she found out that Livy had no intention of marrying her brother, but instead meant to stay on at Holinshed? It would be untenable for them both.

Selfish. Ungrateful. She was a horrible daughter to even think of putting her own desires above her father's. Livy blinked back tears and rose from the bench, snapping her fingers to bring Hastings to heel.

The giant hound whined softly and licked her hand. Livy scratched his head absently, her mind racing in three directions at once. If Henry was right, if the comtesse was what her father wanted, she'd have to return to her grandmother's house and be content to visit Holinshed only as a guest.

～ CHAPTER 19 ～

The door of The Red Lion opened to reveal a slip of a girl clutching a red stuff cloak tightly about herself. The doorman moved to eject her, and her wail of protest cut through every conversation in the room. Any man who hadn't already been watching the drama unfold, while silently praying he wasn't the man she was about to accuse of some un-Christian act of barbarity, had his attention dragged to the door whether he wanted to become involved or not.

"You can't be here, miss," the club's doorman said, as Roland shot to his feet.

"It's all right," Marcus Reeves said, releasing the room from the grip of silent, stupefied horror. "Leave her be."

Roland stepped past the men playing whist near the door and took Miss Bence-Jones by the elbow. She left the hood of her cloak firmly in place as he steered her back out onto the street. She was shaking so hard she could barely stand. He caught the first hint of a sob and cursed under his breath. They should have acted sooner.

Should have taken her away instead of merely delivering Blakely's letters.

Reeves, with whom Roland had been drinking and discussing plans for the upcoming Epsom Derby, hurried after them, both their coats and hats in his arms. "Get her away," he said, nodding toward the dilapidated coaches waiting at the hackney stand just down the street, "while they all still think she's some girl you've led to ruin and nothing more."

Roland half led, half carried Miss Bence-Jones to the nearest hackney coach and bundled her inside while Reeves spoke a quick word to the driver. His friend jumped in behind them and shut the door with a hollow snap. As the coach began to move, the girl took a deep, shuddering breath.

"Dry your eyes," Reeves said, shoving his handkerchief into her hand. Roland glared at him. Bullying her wouldn't help things.

"What direction did you give the coachman?" Roland asked.

"None," Reeves said with an exasperated sigh. "I simply told him to drive until we told him different. By the sly wink he gave me, I assume he thinks we're two drunks sharing a whore."

Miss Bence-Jones finished drying her eyes and pushed back the hood of her cloak. Even in the dim interior of the coach, her swollen eye and split lip were impossible to miss. Reeves sat up straighter as he studied her, his expression hardening.

"Your brother," Roland said, "or your would-be suitor?" The urge to do likewise to the guilty party shot through him with a strength that almost frightened him.

"My brother," the girl said. She twisted Reeves's handkerchief in her hands, her head bowed. "He found John's letters. I should have burnt them, I know," she added bitterly, "but I couldn't bring myself to do so. They were all I had."

"And what are we to do with you now?" Reeves's question cut through the air, making the poor girl flinch. Roland shook his head at him. Though he knew his friend well enough to know his anger was directed at her brother and not at Miss Bence-Jones, she didn't.

The girl swallowed audibly. "You said you'd help me. I'll be of age in couple of months. And when I am, there's nothing my brother can do to stop me marrying Blakely."

"As well your brother knows." Roland dragged his fingers over his scalp, pushing roughly through his hair, trying to force a plan to rise from the depths of his brain.

"Christopher said as much tonight when he confronted me about the letters. He said perhaps I'd look upon his friend's offer more kindly when I'd been bedded and ruined. When John would no longer want me."

"And you told him to go to the devil." Reeves's statement was accompanied by a chuckle that clearly implied admiration.

The girl flicked her glance over him. "Not in those words, but yes. That's what earned me this." She gestured to her swollen eye. "And then he locked me in my room and left the house. I assume he intended to return with his friend and secure my consent to the match one way or another."

Her tone was surprisingly matter of fact. Roland's previous acquaintance with Miss Bence-Jones would have led him to believe hysterics would be a more likely response.

"Escape out the window?" he said. "Or did your maid smuggle you out?"

"My maid is the one who gave my letters to Christopher." Fury, pure and simple, vibrated through every word. "But you have to be a fool not to have a key to your own room. Once I knew my brother was gone, I slipped out through the yard and ran to the one place I knew I might find John's friends."

"So we need to hide you away until you come of age?" Roland mulled over the options in his head.

"We could send her to Blakely's family," Reeves said. "They must have a stake in this, seeing as the settlements were already drawn up and signed."

Roland shook his head. "I thought of that weeks ago. His mother has gone to Spa for her health, escorted by both Blakely's brother and his wife. There's only the youngest at home, and I can't see a boy of fourteen holding off Sir Christopher should he come looking for her. Sadly, it would be easier to transport her to Blakely in Paris." Roland glanced at Reeves, hoping his friend would have some grand scheme in mind. "Though pointless until she's of age."

"And equally pointless if we can't locate an English clergyman to marry them—not the easiest thing to do in France—for you know a priest isn't going to officiate at a wedding between two English Protestants."

Roland nodded again. Trust Reeves to have moved on to future hurdles when the question at hand was what the hell to do with her now. Tonight. She was hurt, penniless, a runaway without anything but the clothes on her back, and her brother would undoubtedly be looking for her at every inn and hotel in London.

They needed someplace quiet, someplace no one would come looking, and that no one was likely to connect in any way with Miss Bence-Jones. Roland suddenly smiled. "We can take her to Lord Leonidas's house. He and Lady Leonidas are in the country. The house is shut up, but the servants are still in residence, and no one would think to look for her there."

Lord Leonidas's housekeeper, Mrs. Draper, looked somewhat shocked when she opened the door to Roland's incessant pounding. She was wearing an ugly flannel wrapper and an enormous, floppy nightcap over her grizzled hair. She was also armed with a poker.

"Mr. Devere?" She lowered the poker. "His lordship's not in Town."

"I know, Mrs. Draper, and I hate to impose, but it's something of an emergency." He stepped aside and pushed Miss Bence-Jones past the still-blinking housekeeper and into the hall. He thought she might just eject them, but then her expression changed as she took in Miss Bence-Jones's injuries.

"I can see that, sir."

Reeves cleared his throat from behind him to urge him inside. "Don't want to be seen dawdling on the steps of a closed house. Defeats the purpose."

The housekeeper ran a jaundiced eye over them all. "If we're aiming for secrecy, you'd best go back to his lordship's study," she said, waving them toward the corridor that led directly to the back of the house. "Everything's under Holland covers at the moment, but don't mind that."

Roland made his way carefully through the dark house. He knew this one almost as well as he knew his parents' house. Lord knew he'd spent enough time here over the past couple of years. The library was a good choice. Its windows were on the backside of the house so no one would be alerted to their presence when they lit a candle.

The door swung inward with the softest of creaks. Where he was used to carpet, there was only a smooth expanse of wood. Miss Bence-Jones stepped past him and stopped in the middle of the room looking lost. Reeves threw himself down into one of the ghostly, cloth-covered chairs before the cold fireplace.

Mrs. Draper appeared with a lit candle, and the light flickered, flowing eerily over the people and furniture in the otherwise dark room. She set the candlestick on the mantel and then her hands fluttered down over her dressing gown. She stared at him expectantly.

"I'll write to Lord Leonidas in the morning, Mrs. Draper," Roland said. "But I assure you, he'd want to help under the circumstances."

The housekeeper's mouth pursed. "I'm afraid to ask just what those circumstances might be, but so long as I won't have the constabulary breaking down the door, I'll wait to hear from Lord or Lady Leonidas before disagreeing with you, Mr. Devere."

"Miss Bence-Jones's family would have no earthly reason to look for her here. If she stays inside and away from the windows, I think we can consider her, and the house, safe. Just pretend she's not here, at least as far as such a pretense is practicable."

"The less I know, the better, sir," Mrs. Draper said. "For now, you can leave the lady in my hands. Come along, my dear." The housekeeper retrieved the candlestick and motioned toward the door. "We'd best get a compress on that eye."

Roland nodded reassuringly when the girl looked to him for confirmation. "Go along. Reeves or I will be back tomorrow to check on you."

With an uncertain glance, Miss Bence-Jones nodded and allowed the housekeeper to escort her out of the library. The room plunged back into darkness. Roland forced himself to relax, to ignore the urge inside to find something, someone, to pound on.

Reeves let out a low whistle. "That's a good night's work," he said as he stood. He yanked his coat down and smoothed the lapels. "And I for one think we deserve to get stinking drunk."

❦ CHAPTER 20 ❧

The shore slid past with surprising speed. The last vestige of London had disappeared some time ago, giving way to verdant fields, stands of ancient oaks, and immense willow trees that trailed their branches into the water. Livy sipped her wine and watched as a large heron took flight from among the reeds. Laughter from under the canopy drew her attention, and Livy sucked in a sharp breath, remembering with vivid clarity her recent trip aboard this same shallop.

Her father was ensconced beneath the flapping canvas with Lord Moubray and the comtesse. Today, chairs had been provided, along with a small table upon which her father and Devere's sister were playing cards.

Devere leaned in, his breath a warm caress on her skin. The scent of sandalwood pushed away the slightly briny air of the Thames. "Do you think your father is prepared to lose his phaeton?"

"His phaeton?" Livy glanced quickly at the trio under the canopy. Lord Moubray looked to have nodded off, his chin sunk deep into the lacy frill of his cravat, while her father and the comtesse appeared oblivious to anything but the game and each other.

"He just bet it against Margo's promise to attend a house party at Holinshed."

Devere was still standing close, too close, his hip firm against her own. The hollow ache of desire flooded through her. She'd been reliving the sensation of Devere's wicked hands under her skirts whenever she had a moment's peace. And not because she wanted to; she simply couldn't seem to stop herself.

"Does your sister want a phaeton?" Livy said, forcing herself to resist the urge to sway into him, to press closer, to replace the warmth of the sun with the warmth of his skin.

Devere's smile widened into a grin and she felt her knees go weak. "She won the Earl of Sudbury's pair of matched bays at silver loo of all things, and knowing Margo, I'm sure she'd love a phaeton to hitch them to, rather than the somewhat staid whiskey she has the use of now."

"Surely someone in your family has a sporting vehicle suitable for such a pair?"

He shook his head. "I can't afford such a luxury, my brother Frocester has no interest in anything so dashing, and father will be damned before any woman, even his daughter—maybe especially his daughter—is seen driving his curricle."

"Look," Livy said, pointing toward shore. "An otter. I can't remember the last time I saw one."

"You should spend more time on the water," Devere

said, his voice soft and low, as though he too were remembering their recent trip. Livy felt her face flush and kept her head turned firmly toward the shore.

The otter slipped out of sight with a splash, and Livy sighed. Devere squeezed her arm, and she tipped her head back to rest on his shoulder, letting herself pretend for a moment that he was something other than a rogue who'd sent her a rude and impertinent letter with no goal other than aggrandizing himself by climbing into her bed.

"We're almost there," Devere said. "Just around this next bend the river narrows, and then you'll see Croughton as it was meant to be seen."

The house wasn't at all what she expected. She'd been picturing a half-timbered Tudor manse. The kind of thing one of Henry VIII's advisors might have retreated to when he fell out of favor with the volatile king. Instead, Croughton Abbey was a Baroque palace of pale yellow stone that shone in the bright afternoon light as if lit from within.

"Cromwell pulled the original house down around the ears of the fourth earl and burnt the remains," Devere said. "When the monarchy was restored, his widow rebuilt on the very same spot, but on a much grander scale."

"A woman to be reckoned with, eh?"

"All the best ones are."

Olivia smiled as the compliment sank in, a faint, rosy blush coloring her cheeks. Roland felt the full strength of it cut right through him. She smiled often, but rarely at him, or more to the point, rarely with such perfect ease.

If both their fathers weren't a few feet away, he'd have stolen a kiss. As it was, he had to content himself with the more subtle delights of shoulders and hips brushing as he pointed out the sights.

"The bank has been left wild for the swans, but after that low stone fence, you enter the formal gardens, which continue up to the house."

"And that?" Livy pointed to a giant green dome in the distance.

"The yew arbor. Perfect for the adventures of derring-do—"

"Or hiding from one's tutor," Margo said from under the canopy.

"Or governess, as I remember." Roland grinned at the memories of the hours he and his siblings had spent inside their private forest.

"I taught you all the best hiding spots," his sister said.

"That she did," Roland said to Olivia. "The yew arbor, the dovecote, the hayloft."

"The attics," Margo said with a laugh. "The dairy. The ice house."

"Holy terrors, were you?" Olivia said, eyeing him as though she knew every fit and start of his childhood.

"I'd say no, but lightning might strike me down."

Olivia raised one hand to lift the hair from her neck, sighing as the breeze blew across her damp skin. "I was fond of The Raven Tower for hiding when I was small."

"Holinshed sounds positively medieval."

She tipped her head back so she could look up at him over her shoulder. "You have no idea. There's even a dungeon."

"That's been a wine cellar for the last hundred years or more," Lord Arlington said as he studied his cards.

"It was still a magnificent place to hide from Nurse, who was convinced it was haunted," Olivia said softly enough that it wouldn't carry to their nearby family members.

"No whispering," Margo yelled, slapping down her cards with a chagrined expression. Their father awoke with a snort, and Roland hid a grin. "Rolly?" Margo stared out at him from under the canopy. "It seems Lord Arlington's phaeton is safe, for now," she added darkly. "But you'll have to escort me to Holinshed in a few weeks."

Roland rolled his eyes. "What a trial you are, sister of mine."

Margo scrunched up her nose at him, and Roland turned his back to her. "Frocester is waiting for us," he said as they slipped past one of the immense willow trees and the stone jetty and steps came into view.

"Good, good," Lord Moubray said, seemingly fully awake now. "Is your mother with him?"

"Not that I can see, Father." Roland raised a hand in greeting, and Frocester thrust his chin up once in acknowledgment. He was dressed as he preferred, for comfort, in buckskins and a loose nankeen shooting coat. Roland could practically feel their father's glare of disapproval.

The shallop scraped the small dock, and the coxswain jumped out to secure it. Roland leapt out after him, and Frocester greeted him with a wide smile, stepping toward him with the rolling gait his bad hip created.

"No Mamma?" Roland said, glancing up to see if she was waiting in the garden.

Frocester shook his head slightly. "Mrs. Verney and

the vicar's wife called just as we were setting out. Poor Mamma is undoubtedly trapped in a verbal fugue."

"Well then, we shall have to go and rescue her," Roland said as he helped Olivia out of the boat. "Frocester, I don't think you know Lady Olivia Carlow? Olivia, my brother, Lord Frocester."

"My lord," Olivia said, extending her hand.

Frocester took it, looking as though he'd been struck dumb. After a brief pause in which he practically goggled, Frocester recollected himself and bowed over her hand. "Welcome to Croughton, Lady Olivia. I-I trust you had a pleasant journey?"

"Very," Olivia said with a smile that seemed to leave his poor brother dazzled.

Roland chuckled to himself as he helped Margo onto the dock. Frocester had never been in the petticoat line, nor was he comfortable with strangers. He'd married a girl they'd known all their lives and settled into quiet domesticity here at the Abbey without a single romantic adventure to speak of. It was almost as if Frocester were a different species than he and Margo, whose peccadilloes were both numerous and notorious.

"Margaret," Frocester said, giving their sister a swift, hard hug. "It's good to have you home." He remained with his arm about her for a moment before she drew him over to Lord Arlington for an introduction.

Their father followed Arlington out of the shallop with a spry leap that belied his sixty-three years and offered his arm to Olivia. "Come along, my dear," Lord Moubray said, tucking her hand into the crook of his elbow. "It's a lovely walk up to the house on a day like today."

A huge swan came hissing out of the tall weeds as they made their way up toward the river gate. It shook its feathers, rattling them loudly, puffing itself up. Olivia shooed it off with a flap of her skirts and a laugh. It circled back, head snaking about, eyeing them darkly.

"The cygnets will be hatching out any day now," his father said. "Can't blame the poor thing for being demented."

Olivia glanced back at Roland, eyes alight with amusement. He grinned back at her. Somehow he'd never expected his father to fall victim to her charms, but the old man had clearly done so.

Lord Arlington partnered Margo, the two of them carefully skirting past the still-disgruntled swan, leaving Roland and Frocester to bring up the rear. His brother's slower pace meant that the two couples quickly outstripped them.

"You're really going to marry that girl, Roland?" Frocester gave him a questioning stare, his brows puckered with what looked like disbelief or maybe concern.

Roland gave a bark of laughter. Trust Frocester to be even more incredulous than Margo when it came to his settling down. He saw Olivia glance back again as she and his father reached the gated archway that led to the gardens. Roland waved her on. No doubt his father would expound upon every detail of the garden as they went. The earl knew every plant, every stone, every vista. The garden, more than the house itself, was his beloved hobbyhorse.

"I've pledged to do so," Roland said obscurely. His brother would be scandalized if he knew the truth.

Frocester's gaze followed his. "Mamma is horrified," his brother said as though betraying a confidence. Roland sighed. Of course his mother was horrified. Lady Moubray had a talent for turning a blind eye to her own family's foibles, but she was unforgiving when it came to anyone else's.

Their father stopped and cut several lilies with his pen knife, handing them to Olivia with a courtly flourish. She held them to her nose, flirting shamelessly. Roland breathed a sigh of relief. His mother's opinion would give way to her husband's in the end, and the earl was clearly more than ready to welcome Lady Olivia and her fifty thousand pounds into the family. Sham or not, having his family's backing for the season would make everything smoother. As his father led Olivia on toward the house, he stopped frequently to add to her bouquet.

"Well," Frocester said, his boots crunching loudly on the oyster-shell path, "she certainly seems to have captivated Father. Can you imagine what he'd say if you or I raided his garden to make a posy?"

❧ CHAPTER 21 ❧

The latent scents of beeswax and lapsang greeted Margo as she led the way into the The Little Parlor. Sunlight filled the room, charging the golden damask walls and gilded furniture with warmth that actually seemed tangible. The room's welcoming reception was entirely at odds with that of its occupants.

Margo forced a smile as the three women currently ensconced over tea all turned to stare at her as though she were the leader of some barbarian horde. "Hello, Mamma. Mrs. Verney. Lady George." Margo nodded to the squire's ancient widow and the vicar's wife. Both women gazed back at her with silent disapproval.

Margo felt her lip begin to curl. They hadn't approved of her when she'd been nothing but a headstrong girl, and now that she was a widow with a distinctly wild reputation, their dislike was palpable, and frankly, mutual.

Philip stiffened beside her. She could almost feel him donning his role as *the earl*, ready to defend her. Margo gave his arm a grateful squeeze and moved to kiss her mother's cheek. The rest of the party flooded in behind her, loud and raucous. Her father was laughing, Lady Olivia still on his arm. Her small posy had grown into an enormous bouquet. She looked a bit startled as she too earned a frosty glare.

Lady Olivia's chin went up, just as her father's had. Disturbing, the little tics that ran in families. Philip went forward to bend over Lady Moubray's hand, and the countess filled the growing breach with introductions. Her dour callers seemed to settle farther into their chairs like ticks burrowing their heads into a dog. Mrs. Verney reached for a ratafia biscuit while Lady George held out her cup to be refreshed.

"Why don't I show our guests to their rooms, Mamma," Margo said, filching a biscuit for herself. "That way you and the ladies can continue your coze."

Her mother gave her a slightly indignant look, eyes flaring wide for the briefest of moments, but the countess was too good-mannered to say anything more than "Thank you, dearest." Poor thing. She'd clearly been hoping their arrival would drive her visitors out.

"Lord Arlington, Lady Olivia, come with me if you please," Margo said, already heading for the door. Her father took a seat beside her mother and motioned for a cup of tea. Rolly and Frocester both excused themselves and followed them out.

"I'll see you all at dinner," Frocester said with a nod before he turned and headed into the library.

"We've made good our escape," Margo said with a laugh.

"Escape is right," Lady Olivia said, blinking her eyes

as though stunned. "I could feel my blood freezing in my veins. It was like facing down basilisks."

"It's not you, I assure you," Rolly said.

"No," Margo said. "It's you. Mrs. Verney still has hopes for Rolly and her granddaughter. I'm sure news of your courtship has flooded the county. You're an interloper and a thief. As for Lady George, as the vicar's wife, she believes she has the right—"

"The responsibility," Rolly interjected.

"—to censure anyone and everyone who fails to meet her exacting moral standards. And she does so with bludgeoning silences and sniffing disapproval. Don't pay either of them any mind. Let's get the both of you settled so you can rest and change before dinner. What do you think, Rolly? The Chinese Bedroom for Lady Olivia and The Argory for Lord Arlington?"

Her brother smiled, clearly having a different plan in mind. "You don't think Lady Olivia might be more comfortable in The Palm Room?" he said, naming the bedchamber closest to his.

Margo glanced at him over her shoulder as they all ascended the main staircase. "I'm afraid I've been using The Palm Room. It's a big house, but somewhat short of bedchambers," she added, glancing at Philip. "Frocester's wife claimed my old suite when she came to live here."

"Holinshed is much the same," Lady Olivia said as they reached the landing. "During last year's stag hunt, we had gentlemen sleeping in the library as well as in several of the closets."

"I like an overflowing house," Philip said with a chuckle. "It's more convivial than a quiet one."

Margo smiled at him, and he grinned back. "The Chinese Bedroom is here," Margo said, pushing open the first door. Lady Olivia stepped past her, turning about slowly as she took in the Oriental splendor of the Chinese-papered walls and the matching embroidered silk furnishings. She stepped over to the window and cocked her head.

"It overlooks the gardens," Rolly said.

"And the river," Lady Olivia said. "What a magnificent view."

"Rolly, can you find Mrs. Patterson and have their servants and trunks sent up? Have them send up a vase as well."

Her brother shot her a disdainful look, swept them all a profound leg, and left to do her bidding. "Don't be afraid to open the windows," Margo said. "Lord Arlington, shall we?"

"The Argory?" Philip said as he followed her down the corridor.

"It was originally built as a study," Margo said as they circled back past the stairs and crossed through The Grand Saloon. "It's in the other wing of the house." The Saloon's far doors opened to a corridor with a much smaller staircase in the middle. "It's the first door, there."

The room was dark, in a comforting, restful kind of way. The walls were lined with bookshelves and above them was a pale blue-and-white frieze depicting the adventures of Jason and the Argonauts.

"Are there books even behind the bed?" Philip asked, leaning in to better see what should have been the headboard.

"Yes," Margo said. "These are the sixth earl's personal collection. When his grandson, the seventh earl, decided to build a grand library, he left this room as it was."

"Except of course for swapping the desk for a bed," Philip said with a deceptively casual air.

"Except for that, yes," Margo replied as the earl reached for her. She ducked his hand, moving backward toward the door. "Your valet will be here at any moment."

"All the more reason for you to come here, now." He took a step toward her.

Margo bit her lip and shook her head. Her hand closed on the doorknob. "As much as I'd like to tumble into bed with you, my lord, this isn't Versailles, where the servants are used to turning a blind eye to whatever mischief their betters might be up to."

Philip burst into laughter. "I never supposed it was. I wasn't planning on anything more scandalous than stealing a kiss."

The knob rattled in her hand, and she stepped aside as the earl's valet arrived, followed closely by two footmen with his lordship's trunk. Philip leaned against one of the posts of the bed, eyes hot with frustrated desire.

"That's a shame," Margo said from the doorway, "for I was."

Dinner had been interminable. Margo had chafed and fidgeted through the entire meal. Up until now, being reduced to near childhood status in her parents' home hadn't seemed like such a burden. It was becoming rapidly clear, however, that she was going to need an establishment of her own.

Her means were more than sufficient to support a small house in Town, but her mother had been adamantly against it. It was enough to make returning to Paris, where she had a house, and friends, and a life of sorts, seem more appealing than it had been just after Etienne's death.

When the meal was over, the gentlemen had remained at table with their port while she and the other women had retreated to The Little Parlor. She'd pleaded a headache after the first glass of sherry and excused herself.

It was several hours before Margo heard the telltale sounds of someone moving about in the room above hers. She'd hadn't put Philip in The Argory merely because she thought he'd enjoy the room.

She curled up in the window seat and listened. She followed the earl's clear tread as he crossed the room. The lighter patter of his valet's steps sounded as the man moved into the small closet and then back into the bed-chamber. The scrape of the bookcase that hid the entrance to the closet was followed by the low murmur of voices and then the muffled sound of the door closing.

Margo took a deep breath and slipped out of her room. The house was quiet and dark. Not even the distant sound of the servants moving about the kitchen was apparent. Just outside her door was the small, circular staircase that connected the two main floors of the house in this block.

Her slippers were silent on the stone staircase, but she stepped carefully when she reached the corridor and ducked into The Argory. The earl was in bed, reading by the light of a branch of candles. He shut his book with a snap and tossed it aside. The light licked over his naked chest, playing off of muscle and sinew.

"I wasn't sure you were coming."

"Really?" Margo said, flicking her eyes over him. She slipped off her dressing gown and tossed it onto the chair beside the bed.

"It never pays to be too certain of anything," he said carefully.

"I suppose not," Margo said, pulling her nightgown over her head. Philip sucked in a harsh breath as she dropped it atop her dressing gown.

He smiled, eyes roaming over every curve with hungry appreciation. Margo raised a challenging brow, and the earl's smile widened into an outright grin. With sudden decision, Philip threw back the covers and reached out to yank her into the bed.

He rolled her beneath him and brought his mouth down over hers. There was nothing sweet or courtly about his kiss. It matched her own burning sense of urgency perfectly. His tongue tangled with hers, and their teeth clashed.

His hand slid between her thighs, and Margo gasped, arching up to meet the stroke of his fingers. The earl's mouth found her breast. He caught her nipple between his teeth and bit down hard enough to make her gasp.

Margo tightened her thighs around his hand, on the verge of climax. A hollow, ravenous ache flooded through her. She slid her hand down the hard plane of his stomach to find his cock.

"Now, Philip." Her voice came out in a breathy whine. "Please."

The earl's mouth left her breast. He blew across her wet skin, causing her nipple to bud tightly. His thumb continued to circle. Her thighs began to shake.

"I was thinking of lingering a bit." Philip pushed her hand away from his cock and found the pulse point beneath her ear and sucked lightly. "Savoring the moment."

Margo hooked one leg over his hip, skin sliding sensuously over skin. "Later, my lord."

His answering chuckle vibrated through her sternum. "We did this your way once, frantic, with no finesse, and I don't think either of us found it particularly satisfying."

Trapped beneath him, Margo huffed indignantly. Philip caught her wrists and pinned her hands above her head, holding her in place one-handed. If she wrapped her hand around his cock again, the game would be up, and he wasn't ready to cede control to Margo. Not yet, anyway. He delved into her with the hand that was still between her thighs. Her body contracted around his fingers.

Margo stared up at him, plans for retaliation clearly flitting behind her dark eyes. Philip kissed her again, lingering over her mouth. He sucked on her lip, traced the edge with his tongue, and then plunged in and devoured her.

"I swear to God, Philip," she said when he moved on to explore her neck. Her voice rose on his name as his teeth scraped over the skin where neck met shoulder.

"Swear to any gods you like," he said, sliding a third finger into her and pushing down hard on her clitoris with his thumb. "Just do it quietly."

Margo's breathing hitched and she went suddenly rigid, trembling from head to toe. Philip kissed her hard, cutting off her keening cry of climax. Before the last ripple faded, he fitted his body to hers and thrust in.

Wet heat welcomed him. Margo's body yielded to the invasion of his own and her thighs tightened around him, soft flesh cupping his hips. She arched, gasped, and ground against him as though searching for more. Philip let go of her wrists, and she braced herself against one of the rows of books that made up the headboard.

Each hard thrust was met with one of her own. Margo strained beneath him, knees rising to grasp his ribs. Every small sound he wrung from her spurred him on, narrowing his world: this room, this bed, this body. Damp skin and ragged breath, nothing else existed.

This was what he'd missed all these years as a widower. True physical communion. Something not to be found in fleeting trysts, the expensive *serails* of London, or within the circle of his own hand.

The satisfaction of giving pleasure was a delight of its own, and one he'd been denied at Ranelagh. Margo's release crashed over him, and he spilled himself into her. The room flickered to black, and he came to lying atop her, while Margo's hands moved lightly up and down his spine and her quim pulsed in time with the heartbeat that sounded loudly in his ear.

"That, my lord, was splendid," she said with a languorous purr.

Philip rolled off her and threw himself down beside her on the bed. He pulled her over to him, curling his body around hers, not wanting to give up touching her for even a moment. He buried his face in her hair, his head swimming with the sweet scent of her perfume.

"Marry me," he said.

Margo stirred in his arms, adjusting the arrangement

of her limbs. Philip's fingers idly circled one of her nipples. The softness of a woman's skin was always a marvel, something that never grew old, never failed to enchant.

She caught his hand, trapping it. One of the candles guttered in its socket, hissing before going out.

"I mean it, Margo." He nuzzled the back of her neck, arm tightening about her. "Marry me."

Margo took a shaky breath and pushed herself up, one hand braced on the bed beside him. Philip forced his gaze from the sway of her breasts to her face.

She smiled, but shook her head. "No."

Philip flopped onto his back, trying not to scowl. Annoyance, with himself and with her, flooded through him. He'd made a tactical error. He should have waited to bring the topic up.

Margo leaned over him. She kissed him softly. Philip dragged her down, gripping her arms so hard she winced. He let go. Still sprawled atop him, Margo smoothed one of his brows with her thumb and then propped her chin on her fist and simply stared at him.

"No?" Philip said, unable to let the topic go. "Nothing more? Just no?"

Margo sighed, rolled away from him, and reached for her dressing gown. Philip caught her and pulled her back to the center of the bed.

"I'm barely seven months into my widowhood."

"Which you wouldn't let stop you for a moment if you wanted—"

Margo stopped him with two fingers pressed to his lips. Her dark eyes glittered in the candlelight. "You really don't want to marry me," she said. "I was a horrible wife."

Philip kissed her fingers and removed her hand from his mouth. "I don't believe you." He tugged her closer.

"Of course you don't," Margo said with a sad shake of her head. "Which is why I can't marry you."

"Afraid you'll disappoint me?" he said bluntly. "That I'll bore you? That we'll both regret marrying in haste?"

"All of that and more, you lovely, deluded man. I'm fickle, inconstant—"

"Do you love me?"

She made an inarticulate sound of annoyance, her brows pinching into a frown. "At the moment? Yes." Her hands smacked down on the bed. "But who's to say I'll still do so in a month?"

Philip stared at her. She was being ridiculous. The silence stretched, broken only by the distant, plaintive call of a peacock. Margo's eyes searched his face, begging for understanding, for capitulation.

"I'll make you a bargain then," Philip said.

Margo swallowed hard, her expression distressed. Guilt swamped him. He hadn't meant to upset her. His proposal had seemed, in the moment, the most natural thing in the world.

"I won't ask you marry me again," he said, "at least not until you're out of mourning, but"—he held her gaze—"if you find yourself with child, there will be no prevarication or denial, we will wed."

❦ CHAPTER 22 ❦

"Come for a walk," Devere said as Olivia ladled ginger preserves onto the final slice of toast. "Or a ride, if you prefer. Margo won't mind if you borrow one of her horses."

Olivia popped the small piece of toast into her mouth and chewed slowly, regarding him as though he'd asked her to ponder one of the great issues of the day. And he had.

Everyone else had already breakfasted and left. His sister and Lord Arlington had set off in the comtesse's whiskey to pay a call on the Duke of Northumberland and tour the wonder Capability Brown had made of Syon Park. His mother and sister-in-law were already buzzing about the house preparing for the dowager's birthday ball, and his father and brother were closeted with the estate's books. The rest of the guests weren't due to arrive until that evening, for the party itself.

"Let me change my shoes," Olivia said as she wiped her hands on her napkin.

She came back down a scant ten minutes later shod

in a pair of dark green half-boots and with a large, straw portrait bonnet to keep the sun off her face.

"Where shall we begin?" she said as she adjusted the angle of her hat.

"With a call on the dowager," Devere said with a smile that she didn't quite trust. "It never pays to be in her black books. She'll most likely be taking tea in The Orangery at his hour."

He ushered her out of the house via the main landside entrance, and Livy could clearly see why he'd said the house was meant to be seen from the river. This entrance, which surely was the one most visitors saw, was a bland double staircase that met in a large terrace before a tall door.

To their left was the stable block, to their right, a well-scythed lawn split by a flagstone walkway that led unerringly to what could only be the dowager house and its attached orangery.

"It reminds me of the stories I've heard about the Prince de Condé's *Hameau de Chantilly*," Olivia said as they approached it. In direct opposition to the main house's simplicity, the dowager house was a two-story brick cottage built of red, yellow, and black bricks set into an elaborate pattern.

Devere nodded. "It's the finest *cottage orné* in all of England. Don't let the thatched roof fool you. It's merely ornamental."

They were admitted by an ancient, stooped butler who led them ponderously through the house, his wig shedding powder with every step. The ornate entry hall opened to an elegant drawing room. Both were decorated with a profusion of white plasterwork.

"Is the entire house decorated like this?" Livy whispered, staring at what looked like violins set onto the walls flanking the doors.

"You have no idea," Roland said. "I'll have to give you a tour if the dowager is agreeable. Each room has a theme. The entry hall, as you've seen, is dedicated to the bounty of the farm: baskets of fruit, sheaves of wheat, branches of blossom-laden trees. The drawing room is musical. There are violins, horns, even flutes all dipped in plaster and mounted on the walls." He pointed to one of the violins, set beside the door, with trailing ribbons and a curling sheet of music.

The door between the violins was thrown open by the butler, and the sweet, humid air of The Orangery washed over them. "Master Roland, my lady. And Lady Olivia Carlow," the ancient servant said.

"Roland." A small, dark-eyed woman glanced up from perusing the newspaper with the aid of a lorgnette. Her expression wasn't exactly welcoming. In fact, she very much reminded Livy of her first encounter with Devere's father. "Come here, boy." She held out a hand.

Devere made his way to her side in three long strides and bowed over her hand. When he'd kissed the fingers left exposed by her embroidered mitts, he leaned forward and kissed her cheek as well. "Hallo, Grandmamma. I see Booth is still with you."

The dowager didn't bother to acknowledge his observation or return his greeting. Her gaze slid past Devere and locked on Livy. Dark and intense, it was like being assessed by a raven. Devere waved her forward, and Livy sketched the dowager a polite curtsy before strolling across the flagstone floor to join them.

"Good morning, my lady."

Devere's grandmother raked her eyes up and down, studying Livy from head to toe and back again. "She's pretty enough, Roland, dear—takes after her father, who was always a very pretty boy—but I'm not convinced it's a wise match."

Devere winced. "Grandmamma," he said, his tone full of embarrassment and reproach. It was as close to pleading as Livy had ever heard from him.

"What?" the dowager countess said, not looking or sounding at all apologetic. "Would you prefer I coddle you with polite lies?"

Livy caught a burst of laughter behind her teeth, returning the old woman's appraisal. It was hard not to appreciate her position. Livy felt the same way herself. She was a questionable prospect.

"Infinitely," Devere said with feeling.

His grandmother sighed and refreshed her teacup from the pot resting on a tray on a small table. "Unworthy," she said before taking a sip.

"It's what polite society does," he pointed out.

"And it's what I do when dealing with the hoi polloi, but it's not what we do among ourselves." Her tone brooked no challenges. "Lady Olivia, which would you prefer? To be aware of our concerns or to be kept in the dark like an idiot child?"

Livy smiled. "I prefer the world with the skin off."

The dowager shot her grandson a triumphant look. "Well, that's a mark in her favor."

"One of many." Devere met Livy's gaze over his grandmother's head, and Livy bit her lip to keep herself from smiling back at him.

"Face, form, and fortune. Yes, yes, but with a notorious scandal attached as well."

"Fifty thousand pounds not enough marchpane to make the scandal go down easily?" Livy said. If the dowager was going to be brutally—rudely—honest, there was no reason she shouldn't do the same.

The dowager countess gave a cackle of laughter. Her dark eyes flashed like the raven she so resembled. "It's certainly a start. Roland," she commanded, "take Lady Olivia for a ramble about the grounds before she's forced to throw your sister's misadventures in my face."

Roland gave his grandmother another kiss on her papery cheek before taking Olivia by the arm and practically dragging her from The Orangery. If he'd been capable of blushing, his grandmother would surely have pushed him to it.

"I don't know what I was thinking," he said, "exposing you to her without an audience to keep her in line."

As they rushed past a doddering Booth, who was quietly puttering about the hall, Olivia laughed and squeezed his arm. "It's rather hard not to like the dowager countess," she said. "Even if the feeling isn't mutual."

"Oh, it's mutual." Roland waved Booth off as the old man started to rise from his chair. "We'll see ourselves out, Booth."

He yanked the door open and then dragged it shut behind them with a loud, reverberant clang. "If she didn't like you, she'd have let you throw Margo in her teeth and then explained in excruciating—and unintelligible—detail why Margo's many lapses in decorum aren't comparable to your situation."

"Well, they're not, for—barring you, and I'll grant that's a large lapse indeed—I've never had any lapses in decorum."

"I'm honored to be your first," Roland said, the urge to laugh nearly choking him. He had no doubt Olivia and the dowager would have become fast friends if the betrothal were real. The idea was almost enough to make him wish it were.

"As well you should be," Olivia said, every bit as haughtily as his grandmother could have.

"Minx."

Olivia grinned, her eyes sparkling under the wide brim of her hat. "Show me your favorite childhood haunt."

"My favorite?" Roland ran his childhood adventures through his head. They all involved his siblings: boating on the Thames, riding their ponies across the fields after imaginary foxes, swimming in the small tributary that cut through the woods. He eyed her, his brain whirling with ideas. "That would be the stream we played in on hot days."

"You mean like today?" Olivia said, lifting her hair from her neck, trying to capture the nonexistent breeze on her skin.

Roland nodded. It was considerably warmer today than it had been yesterday. Much warmer since the last storm had blown through. It was not yet noon, and he could feel sweat pricking his brow.

"Come along," he said. "The woods should be shady at the very least, and we can cut through them to get to the village, where we can have nuncheon at The Boar's Head, thus avoiding my family for as long as possible."

"A sterling plan, to be sure," Olivia said, linking her arm through his and allowing him to lead her past the stable block and the home farm and into the woods.

"I'm imagining the woods here are different from the forests you're used to. We've very few oaks. It's mostly beech and hawthorn and, as you can see, great quantities of bracken as far as the eye can see."

Olivia nodded as they stepped into the shade and Roland steered her toward an almost invisible bridle trail that cut through the deep sea of ferns.

"Stay out of the bracken as much as you can," he advised as Olivia took a misstep.

"Are there adders?" She shivered visibly and rubbed her arms. "We lost a hound to an adder bite last year. It was horrible."

"Yes, but I was thinking more of the skylarks and the bluebells. In all our romping through the bracken as children, none of us were ever bitten. I can't think of anyone who ever has been. Besides, they'll be sunning themselves on a day like today, not lurking on the bridle path."

Under the tree canopy, it was cooler, and the damp, loamy scent of the woods seemed to filter down with the dappled light. They walked in silence for a good while, Roland leading the way on the narrow path.

"When was the last time you came this way?" Olivia said as she stopped to disentangle her petticoat from a protruding thicket.

"I can't even begin to remember," he said. "Years, certainly."

"As you guessed, it's very different from what we have at Holinshed. Our woods are more oak and ash, and the trees aren't nearly as close together as these." She took two steps and stopped to tug her skirts loose from yet another snag. "Why do I feel as though I've wandered into one of the Grimm brothers' horrible stories?"

"I suppose the dowager does make a rather good witch."

"I have a feeling she was more in the nature of a fairy godmother when it comes to you and your siblings."

Roland pulled his hat from his head and ran his handkerchief over the back of his neck. "Yes, well...I can't say that when I've found myself in the basket she wasn't occasionally the one who rescued me."

Olivia clutched her skirts tightly about her legs. "One should always know whom to turn to in a pinch."

"And for you, that's your father."

Roland took several more steps before he realized Olivia was no longer right upon his heels. He glanced back to find her standing on the path in a beam of sunlight, mouth working as though she couldn't breathe.

"Olivia?"

She cleared her throat, blinking rapidly. "Yes, it was always my father. But that ended when my marriage did."

She stepped toward him, but Roland held his ground. This was something he didn't want to know. He was almost positive. "It doesn't seem that way to me," he said as she pushed past him. From what he'd seen, they appeared to be the best of friends.

She shook her head, but didn't look back. "You're friends with my former husband's brother, and you no doubt were privy to all the sordid details. Perhaps you even know some that I don't. Well, he—my father—refused to take me in when the scandal hit. He made me stand by Souttar, left me marooned with his horrible family."

Anger was clear in the set of her shoulders as she quickened her pace and marched off ahead of him. A sudden burst of horrified guilt flooded through him. She'd been betrayed by every single man who should have taken care of her. It was monstrous, and it made him monstrous, too.

"But you've forgiven him, surely?"

She stopped abruptly and turned to face him. "He meant it for the best, so yes, but I haven't *forgot* that when I needed him, he put propriety first."

"Do you really think that's what it was? Propriety?" Roland caught up to her and reached out with one hand to touch her arm, slowly, softly, as you would with a frightened child. "You don't think, perhaps, that he was playing the odds? Looking to achieve the best outcome possible for you?"

Olivia blew out a long, slow breath as she turned and began to once again make her way down the path. "Of course that's what he was doing, but that's not what I *needed* him to do. Just like I didn't need him to force me back into Society."

"But if he hadn't done so, we never would have met. Or it would have been under circumstances that wouldn't have been at all conducive to your letting me anywhere near your person." Roland gave her his best rakish grin. "And I think that would have been a very great shame."

"Of course you do," she said dryly, clearly having mastered herself again. "Oh—" She stopped abruptly as the bridle path dropped off in front of them. "No wonder you said it was a favorite spot."

Roland stepped carefully past her and then helped her descend the rough patch where the earth had washed away, leaving nothing but exposed rock and tree roots. It was just as he remembered it. The stream cascaded down a small waterfall and into a large, deep bowl. The water was clear, the rocks at the bottom of the pool distinct and easily seen. It was surrounded by large boulders, except where it flowed away toward the Thames, where the boulders gave way to smaller and smaller rocks.

He crouched down and trailed his fingers through the water. It was cool, but not unpleasantly so, especially on a day like today, when even in the shade he could feel sweat beading on his skin.

Olivia wandered slowly up toward the top of the small waterfall, glancing about as she went. Roland shrugged out of his coat and sat down on an outcropping of rock to watch her. She threw out one hand, braced herself on an encroaching tree, and clambered up the last boulder.

She smiled down at him and Roland's breath caught in his chest. She really was ridiculously lovely. That he was growing to like her only made her all the more attractive.

While Olivia picked her way across the stream, Roland attempted to pull off his boots. He hooked the heel of one under the arch of the other and wiggled his foot out. The other one was a bit more trouble, but after a bit of a struggle, it finally slipped off.

He'd stripped down to just his shirt and breeches before Olivia noticed. As he yanked his shirt over his head, he heard her indignant gasp.

"What *are* you doing?"

Roland tossed his shirt aside and thumbed open the

first button on his breeches. "What does it look like I'm doing? I'm going for a swim."

Olivia blinked at him, clearly prepared to protest such a plan but unable to find the right words. Roland grinned at her, shucked off his breeches and drawers in one motion, and leapt into the water. When he surfaced in the middle of the pool, Olivia was shaking droplets of water off her petticoats, laughter bubbling out of her.

"You could join me, you know," Roland said as he moved to lounge on a submerged shelf of stone. Her eyes traced over him, pausing at his groin. His cock began to stiffen, undeterred by the cold water.

"I think not," Livy said before turning to make her way back down to the pool. She kept her gaze carefully averted as she went, her attention given over entirely to the rocks and roots beneath her feet.

"What, no interest in playing naiad to my Hylas?" Roland said from his perch. Livy didn't strike him as the kind of woman to throw herself into an *al fresco* encounter, but that didn't mean he couldn't make a little headway.

"No time," she said, with a dramatically sorrowful expression. "Hylas never left the naiads' spring, and to the best of my recollection, we're due back at the Abbey for your grandmother's birthday celebration this evening. And it would appear from our positions, that it's you who's cast in the role of naiad."

Roland found himself grinning. "You're too well-read for a woman."

Olivia lips twitched as though she were trying to prevent herself from smiling back at him. "Consequence of being the only child of a scholarly father. As well as the fact that there's nothing else to do in the country really. Read and ride. And I spent ample time doing both."

"There's fancy needlework." That earned him a glare from between narrowed eyes. "Or plain if you prefer to make something useful. Margo used to amuse herself decorating boxes and frames with shells. And there's always knotting a fringe or tambour work."

"And there you have it, everything wrong with being a lady of leisure." She sat down on a rock beside the pool and pulled off her gloves. She dangled her fingers in the water and splashed it onto her wrists before patting damp hands on her neck. Droplets raced down her chest, disappearing into the bodice of her gown. Roland swallowed thickly as his erection grew almost painful.

"At least dip your feet in." Roland pushed off his rock and swam back to the center of the pool. "You can't really mean to forgo such a small pleasure?"

Olivia eyed him as he treaded water.

"Shall I promise not to look at your naked feet?"

She burst into laughter, shaking her head as though she herself couldn't believe she was about to give in. "I'm afraid I'll have to allow you to do a great deal more than look."

∽ CHAPTER 23 ∼

Devere stared up at her, clearly not understanding. Yet another privilege of being male. Livy extended one foot and gestured toward it. "My stays don't allow me to unlace my own boots."

He struck out toward her, and Livy simply stood and stared. The water didn't obscure much of his powerful form as it sluiced over him. Wide shoulders, arms as finely muscled as those of the laborers who scythed the lawns at Holinshed, and what she couldn't see now, she remembered all too well from watching him greedily as he disrobed. Long legs, a taut stomach, and a member that even at rest was larger than those she'd seen depicted on ancient statues or pottery. She'd never seen her husband naked in the light as she just had Devere, but she was sure Souttar hadn't looked anything like the man before her.

Devere stopped at the water's edge and reached for her, fingers dripping, skin glistening in the light. When Livy didn't move, he propped his chin on his fist and simply watched her.

"I didn't say I was going to let you play abigail."

"Didn't you?"

Livy let his question hang in the air. This was a mistake. She could feel it. But the excitement pulsing through her urged her closer to the water. Devere's hand snaked out and wrapped around her ankle. He pulled himself partially out of the pool as he unlaced her boot. Rivulets of water ran down his back, defining every line of muscle and bone.

This was what it felt like to be wanton. She was sure of it. Her skin burnt where he touched her. The dull ache that pulsed in her womb intensified until it almost hurt. She'd never anticipated her husband's touch the way she did Devere's, had never wanted him to come to her so badly that her hands shook as they did now.

Devere unhooked her garter with a skillful flick of his thumb and slid her stocking down. She lifted her foot, and he pulled the length of silk free. Livy swallowed hard, ignoring the clamor of alarm that sounded dimly inside her. He might be the predator, but she still held the whip. He'd go only as far as she let him.

The rock was rough and warm beneath her foot. Devere leaned forward and removed her other boot. The stroke of his hand on her thigh as he loosed her remaining garter nearly sent her crashing to the ground.

Devere yanked her stocking free and tossed it atop her boots. Panic fluttered in her stomach, and she pushed it back down as he retreated into the pool, his gaze, hot and full of desire, flitting up to meet hers before returning to her feet. He was waiting to pounce, circling warily as though she might still take flight.

Livy stepped to the edge of the pool and sat down,

careful to keep her skirts dry. Devere moved in again as she dipped her feet into the water. The pool was deep, right from the edge, no wading in. It was all or nothing.

Hands encircled her ankles before sweeping up her calves. Devere hooked his fingers behind her knees and tugged her to the very edge of the pool. Livy held him off, pushing against his chest with her toes. "Don't get ahead of yourself," she warned him. "I won't be bedding you here on this rock."

He chuckled as if he'd known she was going to set terms. One hand, cold from the water, then hot as it met her skin, slid up her leg, and Livy jumped. Devere steadied her. "Today is about nothing but *your* pleasure."

Livy nodded, ignoring the implication that some future date would be about his. He could imagine it, dream of it, but that didn't mean he could bring that want to fruition.

His thumb circled on the inside of her knee, a slow, seductive caress. His head disappeared behind the curtain of her petticoats, and Livy gasped as his mouth trailed up her thigh. A hand slid up the opposite leg and ran aground on her mons. She was slick and swollen with excitement. Fingers explored her, spread her open, and then Devere's thumb found the sensitive peak at the apex of her thighs. Livy bit back a whimper.

The slightest hint of a bite on her inner thigh was followed by Devere pushing her legs wide and replacing his thumb with his mouth. He sucked and lapped, filling her with his fingers. His wet hair was cold as it trailed across her overheated skin, the sensation almost painful.

Livy clutched her skirts, raising them, beyond embarrassment as Devere pushed her toward her climax with his mouth and hands. Her thighs gripped his shoulders, and Livy held on for dear life as he slid a third finger into her and moaned into her flesh. Her body clenched around him in response, the first flutter of her climax singing through her veins.

So damn close. As close as she'd been on the boat when she'd made him stop. Livy arched, scraping herself on the rock beneath her. Devere braced her as she began to slide down toward the water, his shoulders holding her up now, his mouth locked over her, drawing hard.

Livy climaxed with a cry that seemed loud even to her own ears. Devere drew his tongue up the full swollen length of her as she tried to piece herself back together.

He dropped a hot, open-mouthed kiss on her quaking thigh and lifted her, setting her back far enough that she wouldn't spill bonelessly into the water when he let go of her.

"You're not the slightest bit in love with me yet?" Cold water splashed over her exposed legs as he fell back into the pool.

"Do you wish you were dead yet?" Livy closed her eyes and simply lay there, savoring every small pulse and quiver as her body recovered. She heard the slosh of water as Devere climbed out of the pool and opened her eyes when a spray of droplets fell across her chest.

He was standing beside her, looming really as was his typical wont, wringing out his hair. Livy found herself staring up in slightly awed appreciation. He was fully aroused, shaft hard and full, dusky head engorged. It was all she could do not to reach out and touch him.

Devere caught her looking, and his confident smile

widened into a grin. "Like an old dog, he'll go back to sleep as soon as he realizes you're not going to pet him."

"What?" Livy sat up, dizzy for a moment as she did so. The leaves and dappled light swirled, like a painting purposefully smeared before it dried. Livy wiped a hand over her eyes.

A deep somewhat rueful laugh rumbled out of Devere. He turned and retrieved his drawers, long lines of muscle moving under olive skin. He pulled them on and fastened them shut, the clear line of his erection still more than obvious through the linen but thankfully more easily ignored when veiled.

"Let's get your shoes on," he said, still smiling, "and then you can play valet."

Devere helped her up and knelt down before her, hair swinging loose over his shoulder and beginning to curl at the tips as it dried. He carefully pulled her stockings on, fingers lingering as they smoothed the silk into place. He pushed her skirts up and hooked her garters, circling them as though checking that they were properly in place. Livy's blood heated anew. She could feel each beat of her heart repeat between her thighs like a secret entreaty: Appease me, take me, fill me.

Devere held out a boot, and Livy slid her foot into it after he dusted off the bottom of her stocking. He did the same with its mate, holding her foot on his thigh, just below his still-evident erection, as he laced it. When her boot was laced and tied, Devere patted her foot as though she were a horse whose shoe he'd picked before he stood and went to his own pile of discarded clothing. He yanked it on with brutal efficiency: stockings, breeches, shirt, waistcoat.

He sat to pull on his boots, and Livy picked up his coat and began dusting it off. Little bits of dried bracken clung to the heavy linen. Livy brushed them away. His coat smelled like him. Like bergamot and brandy. The heady rush of scent did nothing to distract her from the bulge straining beneath the fall of his breeches or the heavy rush of desire pumping through her veins.

She wasn't sure she'd ever be able to look at Devere in quite the same way again. How could any woman look at a man who'd touched her in such a way and not be drawn back to those moments of intimacy? Shocking enough to have had his hands and mouth on her, to have given herself to him in such a way, but she simply couldn't get the image of him naked and rampant beside the pool out of her head. Couldn't stop imagining what came next.

With a fluid motion, Devere plucked his coat from her grasp and shrugged into it. Livy ran her hands over his shoulders, smoothing it down. He felt good. Better than any man had a right to. It was all she could do not to lean in and bury her nose in his neck. She contented herself with buttoning up his waistcoat.

Devere scooped up his cravat from where it lay draped in surrender over a large frond of bracken. He looped it over her, winding the length around his fists, and dragged her to him. His mouth came down on hers as he trapped her against his chest, but where she'd expected something hard, something punishing, his lips were soft, a gentle exploration.

Livy worked her arms free and wrapped them around Devere's neck. This she could do for hours. No one ever spoke about the simple wonder of a kiss. They were too busy warning where it might lead.

A crackle in the woods brought Devere's head up with a snap. Livy turned to follow his gaze. A small spaniel stood not ten feet away, eyeing them with enormous brown eyes. Devere's grip on his cravat loosened momentarily, and Livy took a step back. At the sound of her shoe scraping across rock, the dog barked once and raced off into the woods.

Devere unwound one hand from his cravat, freeing her. He shook out the crushed length of linen and tied it in a haphazard knot around his throat before thrusting the ends through a buttonhole like a postillion.

His hair was nearly dry already and seemed curlier than ever. She knew women would kill for such hair, for a life free of curling papers and tongs. Livy held out the plain black ribbon he'd used to bind his queue, and Devere scraped his hair back and bound it up. "Nuncheon?"

≈ CHAPTER 24 ≈

The look on Olivia's face as she sampled The Pig and Whistle's homebrew was priceless. Her eyes watered and blinked rapidly, her mouth screwed up with distaste, and she swallowed with obvious reluctance.

"You could have spit it out." Roland took a sip of his own ale. A bitter nut brown, it was perfect on a hot afternoon. As late in the day as it was, they had the inn's small outdoor garden entirely to themselves. It was little more than rough-hewn tables and benches spread out under a cluster of trees, and it usually played host to local laborers and the occasional lost traveler.

"I've never had an ale." Olivia pushed the tankard away from her as though the beverage might leap out and force its way down her throat. "And I don't think I ever shall again."

Roland chuckled and took another sip of his own. "That's probably just as well. Wouldn't want your father thinking I'm corrupting you."

Her eyes widened and color stained her cheeks. He

loved her blushes. They gave away the simple fact that she was out of her depth when it came to flirtation, no matter the front she put up. It was endearing in its own way. She had so many little quirks that he was going to greatly miss when she sent him packing.

Old Thomas, who'd owned and run The Pig and Whistle for as long as Roland had been alive, came out with a large plate loaded down with the same simple fare he served the laborers: apples, sharp cheese, and hearty bread.

Roland reached for an apple. "Thomas, can you bring Lady Olivia a cider? Thank you."

She smiled at the ancient innkeeper apologetically as the man wiped his hands on his apron and nodded. "Of course, Master Roland."

He could see the laughter in her eyes at his being addressed as if he'd yet to be breeched. As Old Thomas disappeared back into his inn, Roland shook his head and made a reproving sound with his tongue. "Don't start," he warned.

"Having always been *Lady Olivia*, how I'm addressed hasn't changed, but yes, there are certainly servants—and tenants—at Holinshed who still treat me as though I were five years old."

Before he could respond, Thomas reappeared with another clay tankard, which he set before Olivia with an expectant air. "It's pear cider, my lady, very sweet and cold from the root cellar."

"Thank you, pear is my favorite," Olivia said before picking up the rough pottery mug and taking a drink.

Thomas beamed, and Roland bit into his apple, letting the sweet juice flood his mouth. He'd bet a monkey she'd never tasted cider before today either, but it was more likely to please a palate used to sweet wines and orgeat punches than ale.

"Coffee?" he said as Thomas left them.

"Coffee?" Olivia cocked her head, her expression uncomprehending.

"Yes, coffee. Do you drink it? Or do you prefer cocoa or tea in the morning?"

"Cocoa and a muffin with ginger preserves."

"Though you had tea and toast this morning."

Olivia took another sip of cider. "It's rude to demand something other than what's offered."

"I feel exactly the same way."

She raised a brow, challenging him. "I find that somewhat surprising given your behavior since our bargain commenced."

Roland nudged the plate at her, and Olivia began to eat. "I'm yours to command, my lady. At any time you may snap your fingers and call me to heel."

"You're no dog." Olivia took a bite of bread and cheese and chewed thoughtfully. "Dogs live to obey. You live in the hope of an opportunity to do as you like."

"Perhaps I am more of a tom," Roland said with a dismissive shrug. "I imagine most men are, but be assured, whatever *opportunities* I might take, I go only as far as you allow."

Olivia nodded and reached for her tankard with an unsteady hand. "That's what frightens me."

When they returned to Croughton, Devere's brother called him into the library, and Livy continued upstairs to her room with a grateful sigh. She had several hours in which to compose herself and dress, and she felt in need of every minute.

Devere had been charming and gentlemanly for the rest of the afternoon, walking her back by a circuitous route that took them down to the Thames and then up through the garden, mimicking their arrival. The roving spaniel, Devere's sister-in-law's pet he'd said, had returned and attached itself to them, scampering off toward the stables when they reached the house.

Her maid appeared with a ewer of hot water, and Livy gratefully stripped down to her shift and washed the sheen of sweat and dirt off her exposed skin. When Frith disappeared into the adjoining closet to shake out her gown, Livy hurriedly washed away the incriminating stickiness between her thighs.

She was still tender to the touch. The fine linen of the towel felt abrasive on her sensitive flesh. Visions of Devere's dark head between her thighs made her pulse waver and her hands shake. Her husband had certainly never done anything like that. She hadn't even known such a thing was possible, let alone that it would bring pleasure a hundred times more intense than simply letting a man get his hand up her skirt.

Livy abandoned the towel beside the ewer and pulled her floral wrapper on over her shift. She ran her hands through her hair, pulling out pins and shaking the curls loose. When the last pin came out, she tossed them all onto the small dressing table where they skittered across the shiny mahogany surface like water bugs skating on a pond.

Frith reappeared, her arms overflowing with pale chine silk. She spread the gown out on the coverlet and began to carefully look it over. "This is the one you wanted, my lady?" She sounded unsure.

"Yes," Livy said as she sank down on the divan. "The countess said tonight was just family and friends, not a formal ball requiring powder and court hoops."

Frith sniffed, apparently not convinced. "The comtesse is wearing a stomacher beaded with jet. I saw her maid reattaching a couple of loose beads just this morning."

Livy eyed the gown she'd selected again. Perhaps it was too plain for even a country ball such as this. Frith had a talent for the subtle, unspoken machinations of dress and precedence. She'd never yet led Livy wrong. "Put it away then and bring out the sea-green spangled gown. That one doesn't need hoops either."

Her maid swept up the offending gown and bustled off with what Livy recognized as her triumphant step. Frith had insisted on packing several gowns more than Livy needed, which meant she'd arrived with a prodigious amount of baggage for a three-day visit. But as usual, Frith had been correct in her instincts.

Livy plucked her book off the table beside the divan and attempted to lose herself in the adventures of Fanny Hill. When she was forced to read the same sentence over for the third time, she rubbed her eyes and set the book back down. She'd read the book more than once—it was a favorite— but amorous, carnal Fanny was the last thing she needed at this exact moment. Fanny saw a handsome man, and Livy couldn't help picturing him as Devere. Fanny did what she wanted, acted the harlot, and Livy felt the burn of indignation low and hot in her chest, and it now excited a far more dangerous heat within her. How far could she push Devere?

~ CHAPTER 25 ~

Roland smiled to himself as he escorted his grandmother into the ballroom and led her to the quartet of chairs set in pride of place before the fireplace. She was quickly joined by her long-standing beau, the equally elderly Duke of Ros. The duke had presented her with a set of bracelets that were already clasped around her wrists.

She waved Roland away imperiously. "Send one of the footmen back with port for His Grace."

"And just for His Grace," Roland said.

The dowager narrowed her eyes at him and pursed her lips. She knew full well her physician had forbidden her to drink port, but she'd never been one to take any man's stricture well.

He was saved from whatever withering reply was at the tip of her tongue by the arrival of his father and a footman bearing a tray with a decanter of sack. Roland bowed and made good his escape. The dowager's harrumph followed him as he searched the stream of guests for Olivia's golden head.

They'd been separated by a long expanse of table and

a great number of people during dinner. And afterward his grandmother had commandeered his support, requiring him to leave Olivia to his brother's care. He'd watched the two of them converse throughout the meal, marveling at what they could possibly have found to talk about with such obvious enjoyment.

After a great deal of searching, he found her within a knot of his male cousins, happily debating the virtues of hunters from Irish stock versus those of Continental origins.

"For a prime hunt like the Quorn, I'll back the bone of an Irish-bred hunter every time," his cousin Gerard said. "But if you're dealing with flatter ground, open country as opposed to walls, a blood horse might be the best choice."

"Thoroughbreds of that kind are too likely to snap a leg over rough ground," Olivia said. A chorus of yeas and nays cut her off, and Olivia laughed.

"I'm afraid Lord Heythrop—a man who knows his horses—doesn't agree with your position, my lady," Gerard's younger brother Stephen said, as though that settled the matter.

Olivia shook her head. Roland couldn't see her face, but he was certain she was giving poor Stephen a look of withering condescension. "Heythrop puts down more horses than any other man I know." She held up her hand when several of the men began to protest her statement. "When we had him to Holinshed, he brought a light-boned gelding more suitable to a ride in Hyde Park than a stag hunt in a forested deer park."

"You sound just like Lord Leonidas, my lady." Roland thrust his oar in.

Olivia turned her head and smiled at him over her

shoulder. She reached for him, welcoming him into the circle of her admirers. Roland displaced a rather grumpy-looking Gerard as he positioned himself beside her, claiming her. His cousins edged back slightly, unconsciously giving ground.

"I'll have to show you the black I bought from him recently," Roland said, deflecting the conversation before his young cousin attempted to begin his argument again.

Stephen perked up. "Is that the enormous beast down in the stable? Saw him when we arrived. Pointed him out to Gerry, didn't I?"

Gerard nodded in assent, rolling his eyes slightly after meeting Roland's gaze. Stephen was a good lad, for all that he was over-eager to be taken seriously as a man. Roland could well remember what it was like to be nineteen and loose upon the town for the first time.

"Yes, that's him. Though Reiver's a simple cover hack, not one of the hunters Lord Leonidas is attempting to perfect at Dyrham."

A footman interrupted them by arriving with a tray laden with glasses of champagne. From across the room, Roland heard his father calling for the guests' attention. He took two glasses from the tray, passed one to Olivia, and led her slightly out of the circle of conversation so that they could see the small group gathered before the marble fireplace that dominated the room almost like a stage.

"If you'd all charge your glasses," the earl said, lifting his own, "I'd like you to join me in a toast to my mother, the dowager Countess of Moubray, on this, her eighty-eighth birthday." A chorus of celebratory huzzahs echoed through the room as people raised their glasses toward the dowager.

"There's other news to celebrate as well, news concerning both my sons, and I'm sure my mother won't begrudge our intruding on her evening with it." Lord Moubray smiled, almost grinning.

Roland's head swam with the momentary sensation that there was no air in the room. He resisted the urge to yank at his cravat, barely. This was it. Once the betrothal was publically announced, there was no backing out of the scheme.

Olivia glanced up at him, a questioning look in her eyes. "Did you discuss—"

He shook his head. No, he hadn't, but his father wouldn't have felt the need for permission. Roland had been expecting Frocester's momentous news to be shared this evening, his brother had as good as said as much this afternoon when he'd called him into the library to share it himself, but he'd had no inkling his own supposed luck in landing an heiress was to be shared.

"Firstly," the earl began, cutting off Roland's opportunity to reply aloud, "Lord and Lady Frocester are to present us with an heir before summer's end."

His sister-in-law smiled shyly, clinging to her husband's arm as the room turned to look at them, but even the dowager's overly loud comment that it was "about time she did" didn't make Caroline's smile waver. Roland smiled back at her when he caught her eye. She had every right to be happy, and it was a relief for him as well. Lord knew he didn't want to spend his entire adult life as "the spare."

"To Lady Frocester," Roland said loudly before draining his glass. Around the room, their friends and family cheered, and several of the cousins moved toward Frocester to offer personal congratulations. Roland knew how very pleased his brother was. Frocester had been almost giddy earlier. He and Caroline had been married for several years now, and the lack of an heir was becoming a sore point with their father. The earl acted as though their inability to fill the nursery was the result of spite.

When the hubbub died down, his father cleared his throat loudly and claimed the room's attention again. "On the heels of my elder son's news comes some for my younger son as well. Roland has become betrothed to Lady Olivia Carlow, and his mother and I would like to congratulate him on his good fortune."

Roland flicked a glance at his mother. She was every inch the elegant matron of the *ton*, but her patently forced smile belied the earl's happy tone and made his stomach twist sourly. False as the betrothal was, the urge to defend both it and Olivia was almost overwhelming.

All his father cared for was the size of Olivia's dowry. The scandal attached to her first marriage meant nothing in light of the fifty thousand pounds she brought to the marriage. Sadly, his mother was harder to appease. At least the countess would be relieved when Olivia put an end to things.

From her place beside their mother, Margo quizzed him with her eyes before saluting him with her glass and drinking. If Lord Arlington was surprised, he didn't show it. He nodded as those nearest him began to speak, no doubt offering their congratulations on the match.

Roland would have been shocked if his father had discussed the timing of the announcement with Arlington. It simply wasn't like him to admit that anyone else deserved to be consulted. And the earl was correct that tonight, among friends and family, was a wise time to make the engagement known. It would filter through the *ton* described in only the most positive terms.

Gerard slapped him heartily on the back, forcing him to cease watching his family and their varied reactions to the news becoming public. "Congratulations, Roland. My very best wishes to you, Lady Olivia. Welcome to the family, and the best of luck in your attempt to domesticate my cousin here."

"Thank you, sir." Olivia finished her champagne and twirled the empty glass between her fingers. "But I've no intention of attempting anything so foolish. Besides, I like him far too much as he is to desire such a change."

⊰ CHAPTER 26 ⊱

"Come out into the garden, my lady."

Margo repressed the urge to grin at the indecent promise in Lord Arlington's eyes. Subtle he was not, in the most glorious, delightful way. She'd feared he would sulk after she'd refused his proposal—or worse, plead his case incessantly. But he'd done neither. He acted as if the conversation had never happened.

He leaned close as they walked. "You're the kind of woman who would have had Charles II and all of England at your feet."

Margo laughed and let him lead her out onto the deserted terrace. "You mean if I'd been brave enough to face Lady Castlemaine's wrath and mean enough to fend off Nell Gwyn?"

Arlington's grin widened. "Have you any doubt of your ability to do so?" he said as he swept her down the stairs.

She shook her head. "Actually, no."

The earl swung her behind one of the large topiaries

and brought his mouth down over hers with an urgency that matched the frenzy she felt pumping through her own veins. Margo clutched his coat and opened her lips. His tongue slipped in, teasing hers. Slick heat and need built until she could barely keep her knees from giving in.

The babble of conversation from the direction of the house brought her to her senses. "Follow me."

Arlington kissed her one last time, hard and fast, before following her down to the next terrace. "Where are we going?"

"Shhh." Margo gave his arm a squeeze. "You'll see. I've been meaning to show you my favorite hideaway, and this seems the perfect moment."

He gave her a perplexed look as they struck out onto the lawn. The thick grass pulled at her shoes, and Margo increased her pace. She pulled the earl into the shadow of a giant yew. He stopped a few steps in. Margo dropped his hand and dove into the shrubbery.

She knew the way as well as she knew the corridors of the house. Had run this same twisting path a thousand times or more. Arlington cursed and then came thundering after her.

"What are you up to?" he said, his voice pitched low, barely discernible.

"This way," Margo urged him on. "Just follow the path. Catch me."

Another muffled curse and then the sound of rapid footsteps resumed. Good. The path was easy enough to follow once you knew where it was. It was even tall enough for him, thanks to the gardeners keeping it trimmed back. Margo lifted her skirts and clutched them tight to her chest to keep them from snagging as she ran. Another turn and the path through the yew opened into a giant, cavernous chamber.

During the day, it was a shady grotto, lit only by the occasional stray sunbeam. At night, it was nearly pitch black inside, moonlight not filtering through with anywhere near the same power of illumination. She could hear Arlington hard upon her heels, the scrape of his shoe, the sound of him drawing breath. The yew's leaves rattled as if stirred by a sudden breeze as she steadied herself on one of the branches.

"Margo?"

His hands were at her waist, spinning her around, holding her fast.

"Yes, my lord?" She wrapped her arms around his neck, kissed his jaw, buried her nose against his neck and inhaled, losing herself in the heady scent of his skin.

"I can't see a damn thing in here." Leaves and twigs snapped loudly beneath their feet as he adjusted his stance.

"Give it a moment," Margo said, dragging him toward the swing she knew to hang from the upper branches of the ancient tree. They bumped up against it and came to a halt. Arlington's hands fisted in her skirts. Margo ran her hand down his chest, fingering the buttons of his waistcoat, dipping into the waistband of his breeches. She spread her hand over the fall, smiling in the dark as his erection flexed in her grasp.

Margo flicked open the buttons. The earl's hands loosened their grip, and she sank down onto the wide wooden seat of the swing as she deftly freed his cock from the confines of breeches and drawers. Arlington's breath shuddered out of him, and he clung to the ropes of the swing. It swung slightly as he braced himself.

Margo eased off her glove with her teeth, wrapped her naked hand around the hard length of him, and bent to flick her tongue over the head of his cock. He made a guttural sound of approval as she took him in her mouth and twirled her tongue around the engorged head. She teased the flared rim before relaxing her mouth and taking him so deeply that her lips met her fingers where they curled about the base.

Arlington groaned and the swing shook. Margo pulled back, dipped down, and stroked upward with her hand, the knuckle of her thumb pushing along the sensitive underside of his cock.

"Damn it all, I can feel you smiling."

Margo worked him with just her hand as she laughed. He sounded as if that were somehow a bad thing. "I enjoy my work," she said before slipping her lips once more over the tip of his cock and licking away the salty precome that had begun to well up.

Some women claimed they didn't like to service a man with their mouth. Margo had never been able to understand why. It was a powerful act, a form of seduction that made you the center of everything. Far more so than simply lifting your skirts and letting him rut between your thighs. Any woman would do that. But from what she'd been told by more than one lover, not any woman could, or would, do this.

Arlington began to pant into the darkness. Margo splayed her free hand over his stomach for balance and urged him on toward his release with the caress of her tongue and the suction of her mouth. He said her name weakly, gave a mumbled exclamation, and then he came.

Margo swallowed, lapped her tongue up the still rigid length of his cock, and then gave it one last lingering suck. The yew creaked overhead as the ropes took his weight. For a moment, Margo thought the earl might sag to the ground, but he righted himself with a sharply indrawn breath.

His voice was as ragged as his breathing as he said, "Castlemaine wouldn't have stood a chance."

The earbobs, given to her by the dowager Countess of Moubray to welcome her to the family, glinted in the candle-light as Livy held them in her palm. A cluster of rubies in the shape of a flower, they were worth a fortune. She'd forced herself to wear them for the entire evening after the dowager had presented them to her, though they'd burnt like shame.

Frith pulled the final pins from Livy's hair and began to brush it out. Livy rubbed her earlobes and stifled a yawn. A light rain had begun to fall. The sound it made on the window would have lulled her to sleep it weren't for the occasional yank on her scalp as her maid worked loose the tangle that her hair had become while she'd danced.

The warm welcome from Devere's extended family was entirely different from the reserved one she'd received from his mother and the amused, yet suspicious, one from his sister. His cousins were genuinely friendly, and his grandmother gruffly approving. It made her feel different, too. Guilty for the deception in a way she hadn't anticipated.

Livy's stomach knotted, and she swallowed thickly,

feeling almost sick. Frith set the brush down and quickly braided Livy's hair. She tied it off with a simple length of ribbon.

"Will there be anything else, my lady?"

Livy shook her head. "No. Good night, Frith."

Frith bobbed a curtsy and gathered up the detritus of Livy's toilette. With her arms overflowing with silk and her hands full of shoes and undergarments, the maid slipped into the closet and closed the adjoining door behind her. There was a cot set up for her within the small room, and by the look of her, Frith was as ready for bed as Livy herself.

Lightning flashed, momentarily throwing the room into sharp relief. A wave of thunder crashed over the house, so loud she could have sworn it rattled the candlesticks on the mantel. Livy grimaced as the intensity of the rain increased to *deluge*. So much for their plans for a morning ride. If it continued like this all night, they'd be lucky if they weren't trapped in the house for the entire day.

Livy snuffed the candles, tossed her nightrail onto the bench before the dressing table, and crawled into bed. The muffled sound of drawers being opened and closed told her Frith was still awake and fussing about. The rest of the house seemed quiet, though it was filled to the rafters with guests. Many of the cousins were doubled up in rooms. Others were sleeping in whatever spare places could be found, such as the library and the countess's sitting room. Even Devere and his sister were sharing their rooms.

Livy stirred restlessly under the coverlet. Devere had

been a perfect gentleman all night. Not so much as a stolen kiss. It should have made the night perfect. Instead it had left her feeling as though she had an itch just below the surface of her skin.

She tugged her nightgown up and slid her hand between her thighs. She'd been thinking about Devere doing the same all night. Remembering not just his hand but his mouth, the slight scrape of his teeth, the slick dexterity of his tongue.

If she used her whole hand, pushed hard with her knuckles, slid her nails across her own flesh, she could almost pretend it was Devere. If she let herself, she could almost imagine that he'd somehow left his cousin Gerard snoring in his room and slipped unnoticed across the house to join her here.

Livy caught her lower lip between her teeth and arched into her fingers. A hand, especially her own hand, simply wasn't the same. It might never be adequate again. Damn him.

❧ CHAPTER 27 ❧

"I hardly see how we could extend you such a sum, Mr. Carlow."

Anger snapped through Henry as he goggled at the moneylender. Damn supercilious bastard. His friend, Lord Frederick, had assured him that Mr. Gideon was only too happy to extend credit to men of expectations who'd landed in the basket. Freddy was into him for more than five thousand pounds. The man's terms might be usurious, but they were no different from those of the rest of his profession, and unlike them, Mr. Gideon was known for his discretion and, more importantly, his patience.

Henry had run through his entire income for the quarter—and then some—since coming home. It was amazing how quickly money disappeared in London. A couple jars of snuff, a few sticks of furniture, a bit of ready for the tables, and he was suddenly reduced to punting on the river tick. But credit wouldn't cover everything, and it wouldn't be extended forever. And if any of his creditors grew impatient, he would find himself clapped into some sponging house until the debt was satisfied.

"I'm sorry, Mr. Gideon." Henry sounded angrier than he intended, angrier than was wise when he was seeking this man's help. He took a deep breath and started again. "Perhaps my situation isn't known to you. I'm heir to Lord Arlington."

The man raised a brow, looking for all the world like an Oxford don ready to give a student a dressing down. "Heir presumptive," he said dismissively. "And here in Bevis Marks, we hear every whisper of gossip that flows through the *ton*. Our business depends upon it."

Henry ground his teeth and swallowed the urge to put the man in his place. Gossip about Arlington and the comtesse was rife. Bets were being laid at White's. He'd borne witness to one himself and been the victim of the bettors' snide jibes. The earl setting up a flirt hadn't worried him at first, but it was fast becoming a very serious concern. Coupled as it was with Olivia's betrothal, the gossip hung over him like the sword of Damocles. Everything his life was based upon was at risk: his station, his fortune, his entire future.

"I don't know what you've heard, but I assure you—"

"You assure me that Lord Arlington will not remarry?" Mr. Gideon cut him off. "That even if he does, he'll not sire a son and leave you and me both whistling for our money? No, sir"—he shook his head, his eyes sharp—"I assure *you*, I'll make no loan upon the slender hope of a presumptive inheritance when the current titleholder is a hale man barely in his forties. And certainly not one of the magnitude you apparently require."

Anger flared into panic, momentarily swamping him. Henry's hands clenched until his knuckles ached. "I have an estate of my own," he said, trying to keep the desperation from his voice. "In Gloucestershire."

Mr. Gideon's expression changed, and he reached for his ledger book, sliding the leather-bound volume across the desk with a sibilant hiss.

"Unentailed?" He flipped the ledger open and began to page through it.

Henry shook his head, feeling as though he were sinking in the Thames. He was going to be sick. He couldn't even afford to return to Italy at this point, let alone to stay in London and pursue his increasingly terrifying prospects.

"Well then, Mr. Carlow." The ledger snapped shut with a finality that rattled through Henry's bones. "I think our conversation is at an end."

❧ CHAPTER 28 ❧

It was just after eleven as Philip made his way briskly down Hill Street. Almack's had closed its doors for the night, and those among the *ton* who were not puffing off a daughter this Season were likely at the theatre, putting in an appearance at the Smythe-Henley musicale, or, like him, preparing to enjoy a more *risqué* evening at the Dorrington masquerade, which was taking place only across the square from his own home.

Philip strode quickly past the long line of waiting carriages and chairs carrying colorfully costumed ladies and gentlemen, rounded the corner, and arrived at the Moubrays' town house only a few minutes after leaving his own door. As he approached, a cloaked figure emerged from the area. He quickened his step as the oily light of the streetlamp revealed it to be a lady clad in scarlet.

Margo grinned at him from behind a simple white mask. The small beak curled over her nose and dipped down toward her full upper lip. The hood of her domino covered what appeared to be heavily powdered hair. The enveloping, sleeved over-gown hid everything but the cheerful red-and-white-striped hem of her petticoat and her delicate kidskin shoes.

She looked like a Meissen chimney piece, every trace of mourning gone. All she needed was a crook and a dainty sheep with a bow about its neck to become an idyllic shepherdess.

Margo had a second domino draped over her arm and a black mask in her hand with a raptor's heavy, jutting beak. She handed them both to Philip and he slid them on, disappearing into the dark folds of silk. He felt wicked. Like a schoolboy on a lark. And it felt good.

Philip's lashes brushed the edges of the eyeholes as he blinked. He adjusted the fit of the mask and clapped his hat back onto his head before offering Margo his arm. Her answering smile cut right through him and set his heart beating as fast as the first time he noticed a maid's bosom. That day had been awkward, exhilarating, tinted with awe and the slight fear of retribution should he be caught. Just as tonight was.

He'd never taken a lover. Never attempted to attend a party to which he'd not been invited. Never slunk around like a tom on the prowl. Margo had changed all of that. She'd changed him.

They rushed past the same line of idle carriages and empty chairs he'd passed on the way to meet her. Margo held firmly to his arm, her free hand raised to keep the hood of her domino in place. Her tinkle of laughter, bubbling forth as she ran beside him, had him feeling nearly omnipotent with joy and anticipation for the night ahead.

There was a long, raucous line of guests all attempting

to enter the Dorringtons' house at once. Many were dressed as he and Margo were, in simple masks and dominos. Others were in full fancy dress. Ahead of them, Neptune was attempting to disentangle his trident from the flowing locks of a man dressed as a pirate. The pirate's wig lifted off his head, and both men began shouting. The crowd parted, and the footmen who'd been manning the door rushed down the steps and dove into the fray.

Margo tugged at his arm, pulling him past the enraptured circle of guests and into the house. "I suppose we shan't need this after all," she said, holding up a small card with neat copperplate crossing it. The "D" in the signature at the bottom was large and distinct.

"Where did you get that?"

The chaos outside died down all at once, and the stream of guests, no longer being entertained by the fisticuffs, pushed them along into the ballroom. Margo shrugged one shoulder in response to his question.

"From a distracted Good Queen Bess."

"So you're a pickpocket as well as a siren?"

Margo caught her lip between her teeth and simply stared up at him. "Nothing so skillful," she said as they made their way deeper into the already crowded ballroom. "She had it in her hand but was completely distracted by the brawl."

"Intrepid of you."

She inclined her head, taking his comment as the compliment it was. "One does like to be prepared." She slid the invitation into his coat pocket, patted it as though assuring herself it was safe, and glanced about the room. "Who shall we be tonight?"

"The Eagle and the Lovebird?"

Margo slanted her eyes at him. The kohl she'd rimmed them with made them appear huge behind the mask. "I should have kept the hawk for myself and come as a harpy."

Philip burst into laughter. "Would you like to swap now?"

She dimpled as she lowered the hood of her domino, revealing artfully curled and arranged hair, carefully dusted with what appeared to be pink hair powder, and generously bedecked with crimson poppies and ribbons.

"No," she said with another smile. "You'd look ridiculous as a turtledove, my lord."

"That I would," Philip conceded, grinning back at her. "Come, the first set is forming, and I know you've been longing to dance."

Margo's smile widened as he led her to the center of the room and they took their places between another couple in dominos and one dressed as a unicorn and what appeared to be an attempt at Persephone, judging by the pomegranate she was awkwardly clutching in one hand and the lengths of wrinkled fabric she had draped about herself in an attempt to create Grecian robes.

As they worked their way up the line of dancers, Philip found himself watching closely for every alteration of expression on Margo's partially hidden face. He'd never noticed quite how full her lips were, or how the single dimple in her right cheek flashed like the evening star just before she smiled.

She licked her lips, and his cock pulsed, ready to rise to attention. Philip looked away from that tempting mouth, thankful as the dance whisked her away and replaced her for the nonce with a veiled Mohammedan princess.

The princess batted her eyelashes above her veil. "Lord Gleeson?" she said, her voice rising with the question.

Philip shook his head.

"Well," she circled, changing spots with him, "you can't be Mr. Craig. You're too tall. And you can't be Lord Steele, as you're too fair."

Philip laughed but didn't answer her.

"Not even a hint?" she said as she slid down the line and Margo returned to him, eyes brimming with mischief.

Margo flicked her glance over the little princess. "You'll have to wait until midnight," Margo said. "Just like everyone else."

The other woman glared and turned back to her own partner with her chin raised high. Margo's burst of laughter only seemed to further antagonize her.

"It's as hot as Hades in here," Margo said, lifting her hair from the back of her neck and fanning herself with one gloved hand. "I need a drink."

Without a word, the earl swept Margo out of the set and shouldered a path out of the ballroom entirely. Margo savored the shiver of excitement his hand at her waist sent racing up her spine. Even without knowing who he was, people gave way. The brutal lines of his mask and the billowing puce-black silk of his domino gave him a menacing air he utterly lacked as the golden Earl of Arlington.

On the terrace, they found a footman circling with wine. Drinks in hand, they retired to perch on the balustrade, withdrawing from the ebb and flow of guests making their way in and out of the overheated ballroom. Margo's damp skin tightened as it dried in the crisp night air. Her cheek itched beneath the layer of rice powder she'd dusted over it.

"So," the earl said, leaning against the stone barrier at the edge of the terrace. "Are the masquerades at Versailles anything like this?"

Margo ran her eye over the crowd, taking in the wide variety of fancy dress the revelers had chosen to attire themselves in. It was a mad, beautiful jumble.

"No." She took a sip of wine, immensely grateful to be outside. As much as she loved to dance, when there were a hundred people packed into a room meant to contain half the number, the heat became oppressive. "At Versailles, they tend to choose a specific theme, or color, for their grand masquerades. The last one I attended required everyone in attendance to dress as an animal."

The earl grinned at her, his eyes almost glowing against the black of his mask. "And what were you?"

Margo found herself sighing as she remembered what she'd worn. "I was a giraffe. With a headpiece that was nearly four feet high." She pantomimed its shape with her empty hand. "I nearly broke my neck attempting the gavotte that night."

"Do you miss it? Life at Versailles?" His voice was soft, as though he were almost afraid to ask the question, or perhaps afraid of the answer.

Margo caught her lips between her teeth and drew a deep breath in through her nose. Arlington needn't have had the slightest trepidation. "No." She shook her head.

"No, I don't. There are things I miss about Paris. The bread alone." She found her mouth watering at the thought. "But Versailles isn't Paris, and my life there, well, it can be hard living up to one's reputation."

"Was yours really so very bad?"

Margo studied the earl. Did he really not know? Did he actually want to? "Wild is more the word I would use, though I'm sure my detractors would have said *mauvaise* with glee. *La Folle Anglaise*. When I married Etienne, I threw myself into my new life, into his life: court intrigues and jockeying for power. And at Versailles, the political and the romantic are all intertwined, inseparable even. You seduce a man because your husband needs his support, because his wife slighted you, because everyone is judging you by your ability to do so."

His lips compressed. A sign of disapproval? Of distress? She couldn't be sure with the mask hiding so much of his face.

"And it was hard for you."

Not a question. A statement of sympathy. Margo felt almost guilty disabusing him of his conviction, of his vision of her, but she'd have felt guiltier still allowing him to go on believing her to be something, someone, she wasn't. That wasn't the kind of relationship they had, or the kind she wanted.

"No." She shook her head, ignoring the flutter of warning in her stomach telling her to stop. "It was easy. That was the problem in the end. It was so very easy. And it would have been easy to stay..."

"But?"

Still hopeful. Still willing to believe the best of her.

Sweet man. "But becoming a widow gave me just enough distance from the day-to-day combat to feel myself suddenly a stranger. I could have reclaimed my place. I could have married a *duc* had I wanted to and flung myself back into the fray with even more power at my back. But I found I had no desire to do so. And so"—she paused, hoping she been clear enough—"and so I came home."

Arlington caught her hand and raised it to his lips. His lips were warm through the thin leather of her glove. "And so you came home."

He said it as though it were some kind of portent, as though it meant something, as though he were willing it to mean something. A part of her even wished he were right.

~ CHAPTER 29 ~

Henry watched from across the street as Devere used the head of his sword stick to knock on the door of a small house on Chapel Street. This was the only interesting thing Devere ever did. The only thing that fell outside the pattern of a young buck on the town. He had come to this house twice this week and three times the week before. Sometimes he stepped inside for only a minute or two; sometimes he stayed longer.

Henry had been convinced Olivia and Devere were using the house for assignations, hard as it was to imagine Olivia being persuaded to do anything so risky. But the blonde who had been watching from an upper window as they approached wasn't Olivia. She was a delicate slip of a girl, with enormous eyes.

Though the knocker was off the door, Devere clearly expected to be admitted, and after a short wait, the door cracked open enough for him to slip inside. Henry didn't wait for him to come back out. He didn't need to. He knew everything he needed to know.

Devere had a ladybird in keeping.

❧ CHAPTER 30 ❧

Roland bit his tongue and damped down his temper as the Arlington butler told him for the third time that week that Olivia was not at home. Unlike when he'd been told the same by the Bence-Jones's butler, Howley was telling the truth. Since the formal announcement of their engagement, Olivia was slowly finding her feet again in Society. It should have been cause for celebration, but he'd grown rather used to having her all to himself. Sharing her, even if it was only with a few of the less-judgmental peeresses, galled.

He checked his watch, giving the naughty painted lady inside the lid the full glare he'd held back from Howley. It was nearly three. He shut the chased gold case with a snap and shoved it back into his pocket. Running her to ground shouldn't be too hard. There were only a couple of at-homes at which she'd likely be welcome, all of them Whiggish granddames.

Roland strode down the street, relishing the tattoo of his cane on the stone of the walk. The Duchess of

Devonshire was also not at home, eliminating his first choice. The duchess's mother, Lady Spencer, had a lively crowd, including his own mother and sister, filling her sitting room. But he quickly ascertained that Olivia was not hidden among the brightly garbed throng.

With a mental curse, Roland greeted Lady Spencer and forced himself to do the pretty for a socially correct quarter of an hour. When he took his leave, Margo claimed his escort and left with him.

"Mother and Lady Spencer are deep amid plans for some charity or other," she said. "Something with a very long name that supports foundlings. I'm famished and well on my way to being drunk. Can you believe Lady Spencer served nothing but sherry today? Take me to Negri's for a cup of tea and a biscuit or two."

"Or three," Roland said, shaking his head at his sister. "Arlington won't chase you with such vigor when you're plump as a nun's hen, and I'm on the hunt for Lady Olivia."

His sister wrinkled up her nose at him and pinched his side, hard. "You missed her at Lady Spencer's by more than a quarter of an hour. She left for an appointment with her mantua-maker. Take me to tea, and I'll tell you where she was going after that."

Roland glared down at her, and she laughed, not even the slightest bit cowed. "You haven't yet perfected father's frown," Margo said, ignoring his attempt to turn toward their own home and cheerfully dragging him onward in the direction of Berkeley Square.

The sign of the pot and pineapple that hung outside Negri's came into view, though it was unnecessary at this point. The street was clogged with carriages. Waiters were busy braving death to deliver tea and cakes and ices to the ladies waiting in them and the gentlemen who stood beside them, while people trying to make their way around the square dashed by them all.

He and Margo turned into the shop itself and wove their way to a small unoccupied table in the far corner. He helped her to a seat and took the one across from her. All attempts to fold himself beneath the table failed, and in the end he twisted to one side and prayed no one would trip over his feet.

A harried waiter appeared, sniffed at Roland's sprawl, and nodded when he ordered tea and iced cakes. "Seed cake or ginger cake, sir? We have both, iced and powdered. Also pound cake."

"Ginger," he and Margo said at the same time.

The waiter nodded and stepped carefully—pointedly—over Roland's booted feet. Margo pressed her lips together, clearly stifling a laugh. "I don't think he likes you."

"If they wouldn't make these tables so damn small—" Roland cut himself off abruptly when he caught the indignant gaze of the women at the next table.

"Now they don't like you either." Margo's glance flicked over the ladies to their left.

"If I wasn't a gentleman..."

"You'd turn me over your knee?" Margo said as their tea arrived. "That would be a grand sight, wouldn't it? Don't forget to sell tickets. You'd make a fortune."

A second waiter appeared with a plate containing four small iced cakes. Small being the operative word. Roland eyed them with an internal sigh. He could smell the ginger and molasses, and the little cakes glistened with the sticky promise of sugary delight, but all four of them wouldn't satisfy Margo, let alone the both of them. He stripped off his gloves and picked one up, eating it in one bite.

"Greedy guts," Margo said as she worked off her own gloves a bit more slowly. "Though I suppose it does take a good deal to keep that great carcass of yours going."

Roland grinned and took a second cake. His sister responded by pulling the plate toward her side of the table, her expression daring him to reach for it.

"We can order more, you know," he said. "In fact, I think we'll have to. These were clearly made for children."

"But they might run out of ginger cakes," she said as she plucked one from the plate.

"And you'd be reduced to pound cake? Or seed cake? Or, God forbid, rout cakes?"

"Precisely," she said with a grin before taking a bite. She chewed slowly, clearly savoring the cake.

"Dare I ask if you and Olivia's father have an understanding?" Roland said.

Margo choked and coughed into her hand. When she stopped, she wiped her mouth with her handkerchief and blinked her watering eyes while still struggling to breathe. People craned their necks and stared. Margo shook her head and reached unsteadily for her tea.

"No," she said after she set her cup back down. "The earl and I..." She shook her head again, dark curls swishing over her shoulder. "We couldn't be further apart when it comes to what we *understand*."

Roland nodded and reached for the last cake. Margo batted his hand away. He flagged the waiter down and gestured at the plate. "There," Roland said. "I've ordered more. And don't think I believe you for so much as a minute when you tell me that Arlington doesn't want to marry you."

"I said we don't agree on the path forward." Margo picked up the last cake and ate it in two bites. Roland bit back a chuckle. So the earl did want to marry her, and Margo was, well, Margo was being Margo. Contrary to the bone. She'd have been equally miffed, perhaps more so, if the man didn't want to marry her.

A new plate of cakes arrived, this one piled high. Roland ate another one while Margo topped off both their cups from the pot. He wanted to tease his sister, rile her up just for the fun of watching her. She'd been happier since meeting Arlington than he'd seen her in years. Maybe happier than he'd ever seen her. She fairly glowed with it, incongruous as that was with her widow's weeds.

"But?" He let the question hang in the air.

She cocked her head. "But I rather imagine that whatever he feels for me now will disappear like fairy gold when you and his daughter put a period to the farce you've been enacting for us all."

Roland opened his mouth to protest, but words suddenly failed him. She was right. He hadn't even thought about it, but she was right.

"Margo?" He reached for her hand, gripping it hard while studying her face.

His sister forced a smile. "Don't look so stricken, Rolly. All good things come to an end. The timing of your own affair will bring mine to a conclusion before the earl and I begin to bore one other."

"What if I didn't put an end to it?"

• • •

"Take me to the fair at Greenwich," Livy said, squeezing hard on Devere's arm as he escorted her through the echoing halls of the British Museum.

His dark eyes narrowed with obvious disapproval. "Charlton's Horn Fair?"

Livy nodded, ignoring his scowl. She'd never been, but she could think of no more outrageous request to make of him, and this Season of theirs could well be her final chance for any and all things of that nature. The idea of spending the afternoon at a fair made famous by its tradition of cross-dressing female attendees was too appealing to pass up.

He shook his head and quickened his pace, practically dragging her past the display of black-and-white Greek vases. "I don't think you'd like the experience."

Up ahead, her father and the comtesse disappeared around the corner, heading for the lecture they'd all come to hear. Livy frowned down at the marble floor. Devere should be jumping at the chance for such an outing.

"Don't want to see me in breeches?" she said. Livy cocked her head so she could see his expression. Devere's eyes went wide for just a moment, their thick, almost girlish lashes making them appear even larger than they were. He glared down at her.

"Want? Lord, yes. You'd put Drury Lane's current queen of the breeches role to shame in a pair of tight buckskins, but if I saw you, so would every other man on the street, and no, that I don't particularly fancy."

A laugh welled up inside her. Livy clapped one kidskin-clad hand over her mouth to dampen it. "What if I agreed not to wear breeches? Would you take me then?"

Devere merely glanced at her again and pulled her into the room where people were milling about, waiting to take their seats. Her father and the comtesse were across the room examining something under a glass dome, while Devere's father was speaking with several of the more prominent members of the Royal Society.

The Duke of Portland nodded to them, and when she smiled, approached. He shook hands with Devere and bent over her hand. "Which of the presentations brought you to us today, my lady?"

"The one about the new species of bird discovered in Denham. Imagine such a thing happening today." Livy shook her head in disbelief.

"New to science," His Grace said, "but not unknown to the people of Denham. It was my mother who sent a specimen to Reverend Lightfoot and urged him to come and see them for himself."

"Her Grace is to be congratulated. Such discoveries in faraway places have become almost commonplace—I seem to see one or two every month in the Royal Society's *Philosophical Transactions*—but here in England?" Devere shook his head. "I guess it's easy to miss what's right before you. Sometimes it just seems too ordinary to be special."

The duke nodded sagely at Devere's pronouncement as he was hailed by Reverend Lightfoot. He sketched a bow and strode away to join his mother's protégée at the front of the room.

"Shall we find a seat?" Devere said. "I think they're about to begin."

Livy took a deep, calming breath and allowed him to

lead her to a seat in the back row. The opening presentation was by Reverend Lightfoot about his new species of wren. Livy listened intently as he spoke, detailing the differences in its nests, eggs, behavior, and coloration from that of the common Willow wren.

"Anyone might see the differences for themselves after this lecture by examining the examples displayed here," the reverend said, gesturing to the line of glass domes at the edge of the room.

Livy craned her neck but could see nothing but a few vaguely brown things within them. The reverend finished, accepted the congratulations of the audience, and retired to a seat at the front with a nod.

The day continued with a Mr. Cavendish's experiments on air. Livy stifled a yawn behind her hand. "Does any of that make sense to you?"

Devere shook his head almost imperceptibly.

"Thank Heaven," Livy said under her breath. She might not have the same level of education as a man who'd gone to Oxford or Cambridge, but she was very well read. Mr. Cavendish's entire presentation made her head swim. The jumps of logic alone were staggering.

"It's rather like listening to some of the speeches in Commons though," he whispered back, his voice colored with humor. "Nonsense mixed with balderdash but said with utter conviction."

"I don't think I can take any more," Livy said, her hand poised on Devere's arm. "Let's go look at ancient, dusty things under glass."

Devere stood, and they practically raced for the door, moving as quietly as they could. Behind them, the response of poor Mr. Cavendish's fellow scientists had become a belligerent rumble. Livy smiled to herself. At least she wasn't the only one who thought he was spouting gibberish.

The heavy wooden door closed silently behind them, and Livy rubbed her temples as they stood poised in the corridor outside. "Headache?" Devere said.

She nodded. "I normally love lectures, but Mr. Cavendish's made my brain feel as though it were turning to jelly."

"Do you want to stroll about the South Sea treasures while your brain solidifies?"

"Don't we need an appointment?"

Devere's smile widened into a knowing grin. "I had a premonition that the lecture might prove a bit"—he glanced at the ceiling as he searched for the proper word—"dry, shall we say? I applied for tickets several days ago. They should be waiting with the porter."

"Brilliant man," Livy said as Devere led her down the corridor. "You're proving far more useful than I ever imagined."

Devere glanced down at her, one brow raised. "I do aim to please."

Heat tinged his voice. Livy's cheeks burnt faintly, and she turned her head away, hoping he wouldn't see the telltale blush. The South Sea treasures would fill the time, but if she were perfectly honest, she'd much rather find a quiet, secret corner where they could be alone for half an hour.

Before she could embarrass herself by making such a suggestion, they were in the entrance hall, and Devere was claiming their tickets from the porter. One of the librarians who served as guides led them through as a private party, no other ticket holders being present and waiting for admission.

Livy was still eagerly perusing the collection that Captain Cook had brought back from his adventures when the snap of Devere's watch opening and closing drew her attention from the most enormous pink shell she'd ever seen.

"Mr. Herschel's lecture on the polar regions of Mars should be at an end. We should repair to the entrance hall to await the rest of our party."

Livy gave the collection one last, longing glance. There was still so much to see. She hadn't prowled about the British Museum since her first year on the marriage mart, and at the time she'd been rather too preoccupied with her suitor to give the collection the attention it deserved. Somehow, even though she was quite achingly aware of Devere as he followed her about, he wasn't the distraction he might have been. The frisson of his presence felt almost comfortable. Like a promise of things to come.

"We can come back. Tomorrow if you like?" Devere said with a chuckle as he followed her gaze to the unexplored half of the room.

Livy slanted a glance at him. "I was hoping tomorrow you'd take me to the Charlton Fair."

"Back to that, are we?" His tone was light, but the grim line about his mouth told her that the answer was still no. He could be amazingly stuffy when he wanted to be.

They arrived in the grand entrance hall of what had once been Montague House, and their guide bowed and left to return to his work. Livy slowly crossed the large expanse of patterned marble to claim one of the small chairs that lined the room. Devere leaned against the wall, looming, as was his wont.

"What if I offered to take you to the races instead?" he said. "That should be suitably outré, as that seems to be your goal. You can drink beer again, and wear one of your enormous hats, and make outrageous bets with all my friends."

"Is there a large party going?" She couldn't keep the eagerness from her voice. She'd never been to any of the races. Her father wasn't addicted to the turf, and her marriage had been too brief for such an outing to occur, if indeed her husband would have thought to take her.

"A very large party." Devere flicked out the skirts of his coat and dropped into the chair beside her. "Mr. Reeves's family has a stud near Staines, and they have a horse running at Windsor next week. I imagine most of us have a great deal of money riding on Spigot. And since his elder brother was injured, the family likes to host events to keep Lord Carteret entertained."

Livy found herself staring at Devere's hand as he spoke about his plans for the upcoming trip to Windsor Great Park. Large, long-fingered, capable of great wickedness. She hadn't been able to stop thinking about how it felt to be touched by him since his grandmother's birthday party. She was consumed by it.

Her stomach fluttered. Lust. That's what this was. Lust and wickedness and all the things the vicar spoke against every Sunday morning in church while she squirmed uncomfortably in her pew. That, too, was new. She'd never fidgeted in church before she'd met Devere. Had never seen herself as the focus of the sermon.

How wrong was it that she was coming to like the sensation?

"Would Lord Arlington be amenable to that?"

"What?" Livy blinked as she realized she'd completely lost track of what Devere was saying.

He laughed and shook his head. "To your joining the party at Bankcroft? Lady Norwich will be there to lend propriety and play duenna, as well as Margo."

"I can't see why he would object."

"Really?" One side of Devere's mouth quirked up. "I certainly can."

❧ CHAPTER 31 ❧

The beat of a dozen hooves smashing down at a thunderous pace echoed through Livy's sternum. The crowd surged around her, swelling and ebbing as people fought for the best view of the race as it swept past. Cheers and screams deafened her for a moment.

Devere and his friends formed a wall, without which she would have surely been carried away or dashed to the ground. Even with them surrounding her on every side, she could feel the jostle of the gathered audience.

One of them, Lord William, the same man who'd snubbed her at the Moubrays' ball, was now eyeing her as though she were a horse for sale. Livy turned her head away, ignoring his laugh at being dismissed. Beside her, the comtesse shouted to be heard. "Did you see Spigot?"

Livy shook her head. Truth be told, she hadn't seen much beyond a jumble of bay and chestnut hides and a flash of the jockeys' colored silks. It was a visual riot, just glimpses from between the shoulders of the men around her.

"He's fighting for the lead with Crimson," Thane said,

his deep voice easily cutting through the babble. "It's going to be close, but that was only to be expected."

"Who owns Crimson?" Livy put a hand up to hold her hat on as the breeze picked up and tugged at it.

"The Duke of Grafton," Devere said into the sudden lull, as the noise died down and the throng once again settled in to wait. "The duke has a large stud and racing is his life. It would be quite something for Norwich if Spigot were to win today."

"Are you telling me I should have bet on Crimson?" Livy said with a laugh. She hadn't bet much in comparison to the men, but the ten pounds she had riding on the outcome had riveted her interest in a way she'd never suspected.

"Never!" Devere's sister said with a reproving shake of her head. "Betting on the favorite brings very little return. Betting on an unknown? Well, I hope to double this quarter's pin money with my modest bet on Spigot."

"Do widows have pin money?" Livy said, surprised. She did, but it was a technicality with her father, who didn't want her to breach her principal, even though she had every legal right to do so.

"Not really," the comtesse said, moving closer as though about to confess a secret. "But I can't get out of the habit of thinking of it that way, especially as I've voluntarily reduced myself to the nursery ranks by coming home to my family."

Sympathy burnt through Livy. She hadn't imagined Devere's sister to feel any of the same constraints she did. "It does feel as though one has somehow been magically transported back in time, doesn't it?"

The comtesse's answering smile said it all. Yes, she felt the sting of it, too, even with the greater freedom Society allowed her.

The rising volume of the crowd announced the approach of the horses long before Livy could sense them. The sound grew, moving toward them like a wave, and broke over them with the return of the pounding hooves. Livy stood on tiptoe to watch as the contestants shot past in a flurry of mud and flying grass.

Spigot, his jockey in the earl's red-and-gold silks clinging to his back like a limpet, was in the lead. Not by much, but it was enough that as they crossed the finish line, there was no doubt as to the winner. The comtesse let loose an unladylike whoop, and Livy found herself joining it, cheering the win.

Devere slung a casual arm about her waist and tugged her toward him. A shiver of awareness raced up her spine, making her pulse flutter unevenly.

"I knew you'd enjoy the races," he said.

"Shall we go collect our winnings?"

Devere threw his head back as a laugh erupted out of him. "I warned your father I might well return you as an inveterate gamester. I don't think the earl believed me."

"Well, it's not as though I can find a race to bet on any night of the week. It's not like becoming addicted to faro, or one of the other games men lose their fortunes playing at while at White's."

"We shall have to work on that, too," the comtesse said as the crowd began to disperse around them. "Or perhaps *Vingt-et-un* is a better choice. Plenty of women play that without causing a stir."

"Not in England they don't," Thane said.

Devere's sister blinked innocently. "Oh?"

Thane shook his head as if in disgust, but the impression was ruined by the slight smile that curled up the corners of his mouth. "Oh, indeed, my lady," he said.

The comtesse shrugged. "I've seen ladies playing it at several parties since returning to England, and I still say we should teach Lady Olivia. Perhaps tonight at Bankcroft? Unless"—she caught Livy's eye and then glanced about in mock horror—"you mean to force us to play silver loo."

Devere's answering laugh became a cough as he attempted to cut it off. "Brat," he said to his sister as the crowd around them finally began to disperse. He offered Livy his arm. "You're utterly failing at the role of chaperone," he threw over his shoulder as they began the short walk to where Reeves's brother had sat in his carriage to watch the race.

"Now, Rolly, really," the comtesse said as they reached the viscount's carriage and Thane handed her in. "I would have thought you of all people would be in favor of such a failing on my part."

Roland shook his head at his sister's teasing salvo as he helped Olivia into the open carriage. Margo was right; he was rather counting on her lax chaperonage. Another house party without Lord Arlington's presence was unlikely to happen again before Olivia attempted to give him his *congé*. Dappled with sunlight and with laughter filling her eyes, Livy was beautiful enough to make him think he would crawl over broken glass for the chance to bed her. The possessive rush that flooded through him at the idea made him think that perhaps simply winning his bet with Leo and Thane wasn't going to be enough.

"I'll leave the two of you in Thane's capable hands while I go and fetch your winnings," he said, sealing off the part of his brain that couldn't stop weighing his chances. "Behave yourself," he added for his sister's benefit.

"What do you think we're going to do," Margo called after him, "kidnap the poor man and run for the border?"

Roland let out a long breath as he walked. The border was starting to sound damn fine to him. How the hell had he got himself into such a mess?

He glanced back over his shoulder. Olivia wasn't watching him. She was turned away, talking to one of Norwich's friends, one hand anchoring her enormous hat to her head. The Season wasn't over. He still had time. Time to see if perhaps he wasn't mad to think she too might be rethinking things.

The crowd gathered around the self-appointed accountants-of-the-turf was large and rowdy, many angry at the upset and the loss of their money. A skirmish broke out between one offended party and the man who held his note. The bookmaker's servant, who rivaled Thane for sheer size and looked to be a prizefighter, judging by his flattened nose and cauliflower ear, stepped in and hauled the man away. A second man, like enough to be a twin, stepped up to take the fighter's place at the bookmaker's shoulder.

This was why he'd left his sister and Olivia behind. He'd seen brawls break out after a few particularly memorable upsets. Spigot's win today was enough of a surprise to those who didn't know the animal that there was likely to be many an angry punter in the crowd. The ladies didn't need their day spoilt by being caught up in such a fracas.

When the crowd of punters settled back down, Roland was able to find the man he'd placed their bets with earlier and present their notes for payment. Mr. Green's expression soured as he stared at the slips of paper and then slid them into his book with a sigh.

"You won't get such odds again," Green said as he counted out their winnings, looking as though each banknote was a knife cut. "But it was a magnificent race, all the same. You congratulate Lord Norwich for me, sir. He's bred a true winner. I look forward to seeing him run again."

Roland promised to do so, tucked the thick pile of banknotes into his pocket, and shouldered his way back through the throng. He kept his hand in his pocket, fingers curled around the wad of paper as he walked. He made an unlikely victim, but there were always pickpockets at large public events. He'd lost his entire pocketbook that way at a mill when he'd been little more than a stripling, and he had no intention of making the same mistake twice.

Roland circled, looking for Reeves. He found him with his father, watching proudly as Spigot was walked in circles, steam still rising off his sweaty back. "Mr. Green sends his compliments, my lord."

The earl grinned, clearly knowing that those compliments were tinged with annoyance. "I'll just bet he does. I must have cost him a mint today."

Reeves shrugged. "He'll recover."

ᵔᵉ CHAPTER 32 ᵔᵉ

The clock on the bedroom mantel chimed softly just as Livy's maid was finishing rearranging her hair. It had taken some doing to work out all the wind-whipped knots.

Frith twisted the last hairpin into place and stepped back so Livy could rise. Livy plucked her gloves from the tabletop and tugged them on as she surveyed herself in the mirror. The simple blue-and-cream-striped gown was perfect for a country house party. She adjusted the van-dyked falling collar, smoothing the dags of blond lace as they fell over her breast.

"Thank you, Frith," she said as she headed out the door.

Bankcroft, like so many grand country manors, was a great block of a house. Nearly all the guest quarters were lumped together in the East Wing. Livy found several of the other guests already in the corridor.

"Prettier than the other one," Lord William was saying to a dark-haired gentleman as they went down the stairs.

"But then Devere always did have a penchant for blondes."
Livy froze in the doorway, waiting for them to descend.
It was inevitable that she should be compared to Devere's
past conquests, but it didn't make overhearing it any more
palatable. A moment later, another door opened and the
comtesse appeared. Livy shook off her annoyance as
Devere's sister took her arm and together they made their
way down the grand staircase.

They reached the drawing room just in time to be led
by the earl and countess into dinner. It rather reminded
Livy of one of the dinners at Holinshed after a hunt—
too many men, and too much wine, accompanied by loud,
raucous conversations where one topic quickly rolled into
another.

When the table was cleared and the port brought in,
Lady Norwich invited Livy and the comtesse to join her
for sherry in the drawing room. "Don't dawdle over the
port," the countess said as they left. "Or if you do, don't
be surprised if the ladies and I go up to bed and leave you
to amuse yourselves."

With that threat hanging over them, the gentlemen
trailed into the drawing room not a quarter of an hour
later, port in hand. Livy finished off her sherry and poured
herself a second glass. Devere met her gaze as he stepped
into the room and the sudden snap of tension between
them made her stomach twist.

She'd felt it all day, the slowly growing *something*,
impossible to define and equally impossible to deny. It felt
as though if she took a step, he'd be drawn along with her,
powerless to resist.

He didn't come directly to her though. He simply

smiled and allowed his friend Reeves to waylay him. Livy
sipped her sherry and tried to pretend she couldn't feel
Devere watching her.

Lady Norwich settled in beside the fireplace with her
eldest son and the viscount's friend, Lord William, who'd
been flirting with Livy after the race. When she'd shown
him no encouragement, he'd transferred his gallantries to
the comtesse without batting an eye. The men set about
giving the countess a moment-by-moment depiction of
the race, right down to the tale of the jockey who'd torn
out the seat of his breeches.

Livy listened with half an ear, nodding and murmur-
ing agreement where it seemed necessary. Devere's sister
held out her empty glass and Lord William immediately
turned his attention to her. He fetched the sherry from the
buffet and refilled both their glasses, and then claimed the
seat closest to her and commenced the same sort of rib-
ald flirtation he'd attempted with Livy at the race course.
The comtesse didn't seem to mind. In fact, she seemed to
enjoy sparring with the man.

When Lord William's innuendo became too lewd to
ignore, Livy broke into the conversation. "Madame la
comtesse was telling me that there was a mill before the
race today. Did you attend, Lord William? I know some
of the party rode out early especially."

Lord William gaped at her. Devere's sister stared at
her with knowing eyes. The comtesse knew Livy was
defending her father's claim on her, and her smile said she
found something amusing about it.

"Um, yes, my lady," Lord William said, still clearly
somewhat bewildered by the sudden change in topic.

"The Irish champion versus Big Jem. A rematch after Jem's loss last month."

Before Lord William could warm to his topic, his friends carried him off to the billiard room. The comtesse turned her attention back to the conversation between Carteret and his mother, which had turned to plans for Spigot's next race.

The tick of cards being shuffled caused Livy to glance across the room. A small group, including Devere, had gathered about a table and was clearly about to begin a game of some sort. Would they really teach her to play *Vingt-et-un*? She'd certainly seen the game played, and she'd heard the stories of men losing fortunes at the table. It seemed a ridiculous thing to do, betting thousands of pounds on the turn of a card. Especially as the men who so often seemed to lose at cards were those who could least afford to do so.

Perhaps she could simply watch?

"Come and see the garden," Devere said, appearing suddenly beside the chaise. "It's not a full moon, but the pond and Doric Temple should be beautiful all the same."

Livy rose, glancing at the comtesse. Her supposed chaperone merely waved her off. "Isn't slipping away with me far worse than teaching me to play faro?" Livy said.

Devere hurried her along with his hand at the small of her back. "Come along before anyone tries to join us."

They made their way out the long windows that adjoined the terrace and then moved quickly down the steps that led out into what appeared to be a vast garden filled with statues and topiary.

"I take it you've been here before?" Livy said as

Devere led her unerringly through the circling walkways that wound between the geometric shrubs.

"Many times," he said with a chuckle. "I've known Reeves since we were at Harrow. And since Carteret's accident, the family holds many events here for his entertainment. Come this way. The reflecting pond, or canal really, is just beyond that hedge. There's a small summer house at one end, built as a Doric ruin. It's quite ridiculous really, a miniature Pantheon, complete with dome, but I've always found it to be a reliable bolt hole."

They stepped through an arched opening in the tall hedge, descended another set of steps, and then Livy found herself gazing at a long, narrow canal filled with blooming water lilies. The portion closest to the summer house was clear of them though, and its glassy surface reflected the pale white light of the waning moon and equally pale stone of the small temple.

Four columns fronted the structure, supporting a frieze whose theme was impossible to make out in the shadowy moonlight. The loud plop of a fish breaking the surface of the pond startled her, and Devere laughed when she clutched at his arm.

"It's not funny. That fish must be big enough to eat a swan by the sound of that splash."

Devere's only response was to laugh all the harder and drag her into the shelter of the summer house. His mouth was on hers almost before they crossed the threshold. Livy sucked in a breath and held it, letting the sensation of his lips, of his tongue coaxing hers to respond, wash over her.

His hand came up to cup her jaw. Impossibly soft

leather, stretched taut over his fingers, whispered across her skin. "You have to breathe, sweetheart."

A shaky laugh got her heart going again, and she inhaled sharply, breathing in the soft scent of the garden and the warm spice of Devere's skin. The hand pinning her to the wall was digging into her ribs so hard she could feel each finger even through her stays. He might well have a penchant for blondes, but at the moment he was hers, and hers alone.

Devere leaned in, warmth radiating off him, and kissed her again. Just a soft exploration this time, lips brushing hers, tongue sliding across her lower lip, inviting her to play. Livy opened her mouth and let him in, returning each caress, savoring the slowly mounting heat building inside her.

His hand slid down her throat, across her chest, and delved into her bodice. He caught her ruched nipple between two fingers and squeezed. Livy's breath hissed out of her as a jolt shot directly from her nipple to the aching spot between her thighs. She wanted his mouth on her, but she couldn't seem to say the words.

He was hard against her belly. In her mind's eye, she could see him rampant and naked, as he had been at the pond. God, how she wanted to touch him. Devere groaned, his mouth hot on the skin just below her ear. The sound vibrated through her. Livy realized with horror that she'd moved to cup him through the fall of his breeches, her fingers tracing the line of his rigid cock.

She yanked her hand away, her cheeks burning fiercely. Devere caught her wrist and moved her hand back, holding it over himself, guiding her.

"Don't stop," Devere said, flexing his hips, rocking into her palm.

He kissed her again, lips impossibly soft against hers. When Livy adjusted the angle of her hand and pushed down, Devere made a low, guttural sound of pleasure that sent heat flooding through her. Her knees began to tremble. It was all she could do not to sink to the ground and drag him down with her.

Devere's breathing grew rough, each exhalation rolling across her skin, making her shiver. His shaft was rock hard in her grip, the head distinct. She pushed the heel of her hand over it, and Devere groaned again. Livy loosed one of his breeches' buttons, her hands trembling, eager to explore.

He kissed her again, his mouth urgent, and then everything shifted as he lifted her and tumbled her down onto the long, low chaise that was pushed against the back wall of the little temple.

He fumbled with her skirts, yanked off his glove with his teeth, and spat it out. His hands roved her thighs, sure and steady. Livy nearly climaxed as his fingers slicked over her, filled her, and Devere's thumb circled on the taut peak at the center of her being.

Livy's breath caught in her throat.

Devere buried his face in her breasts. One nipple slid above the edge of her bodice, and he sucked, hard. The sharp jolt that ran from breast to groin redoubled her pulse between her thighs, echoed it back up into her chest, and sent it zinging to her toes.

He pushed a second finger into her, and Livy found herself arching up to meet his hand, wishing with each stroke that she could risk exchanging that hand for his cock.

"What?" he said against her breast, tonguing her nipple before biting down on it.

"Nothing," she lied, realizing she must have said something utterly incriminating.

"That wasn't nothing." His mouth left her breast, and she whimpered in protest. Devere's fingers curled inside her, finding a spot that reduced her to gasping sobs. "In fact, it sounded very much like you were giving voice to my own thoughts. There isn't much I wouldn't give to be inside you when you come, darling."

"I can't." Her denial sounded impossibly weak even to her own ears. "Can't risk falling pregnant."

"Of course not." His wicked, magical hand stroked and circled. Her thighs began to shake. "But not every pleasure carries the same risk."

His hips eased her thighs apart, the hard length of his shaft lay trapped between their bodies. When he moved, sliding against her, the head of his cock rode over every sensitive valley and peak. Devere set a slow, steady rhythm, each stroke driving her closer to climax.

Livy locked her hands into the fabric of Devere's coat and tipped her head back as his mouth came down on her throat. She whimpered and released him to cover her mouth with the heel of her hand.

"Wet enough to almost make me think I am inside you," he said, nuzzling into her hair.

Livy bit her hand as her climax rolled her. The hollow ache that accompanied it was almost enough to make her reach between them and force him into place.

Devere ground himself into her, his breath coming faster, rougher, then he growled, low and deep in the back of his throat, and she felt the hot spill of his seed on her skin.

Roland pulled his handkerchief from his pocket and shook it out. He offered it to Livy, and when she looked at him blankly, he smiled and slid his hand back up her skirts to wipe away the evidence of their tryst.

He could almost feel the blush that rose on her skin. He helped her up, and she smoothed her petticoats with unsteady hands. Roland buttoned up his breeches and shoved his sullied handkerchief back into his pocket.

She had leaves in her hair. "Come here," he said, reaching for the first one. "You look a nymph. And charming as that is, it's rather a telltale sign that you've been doing something you ought not."

Olivia simply watched as he plucked them from her hair and sent them drifting to the stone floor of the temple. He handed her the last one, and she twirled it between her fingers.

"I think your glove is under the chaise," she said.

Roland stooped to retrieve it and tugged it back on. Olivia took his arm and leaned her head on his shoulder, staring out at the canal. He'd have given his entire day's winnings to know what she was thinking, but at that exact moment, she seemed a thousand miles away.

"Shall we go back inside before my sister is forced in good conscience to come looking for us?"

❦ CHAPTER 33 ❦

I can't say I'm familiar with just how you go about count-ing fawns," Devere said in response to her invitation for him to join her family at Holinshed for the annual event. Livy choked up on Hastings's lead as a squirrel dashed from tree to tree. The dog sighed wistfully but didn't attempt to give chase.

"Really?" Livy said, genuinely surprised that Devere had never been to one. "Every deer park has one. Though some of us take more of an opportunity to turn it into an event than others."

Though they'd had an appointment to go for a drive, Devere had elected to accompany her while she walked Hastings for her father instead. When she'd appeared with the giant hound, she'd thought for a moment he might change his mind, but he took Hastings's gruff greeting in stride and didn't try, as so many men did, to force the dog to submit to him.

"I think you forget what a rarity deer parks have become," Devere said with a chuckle. "A few of the royal dukes have them, of course, and the king, but very few others are so privileged."

Livy bit her lip as she thought about it. Having one had never seemed particularly special. It was just there, as ancient as the castle ruins that made up the outer wall of Holinshed or the forest itself.

"Well then, I expect you'll enjoy the exceptionality of the experience," she said. "Though counting fawns in the park is not nearly as exciting as a hunt, we won't cull the herd until autumn." And he wouldn't be around come autumn, which seemed a pity on so many fronts. "Your sister is invited, too, as are your parents, of course, should they choose to join us. I finished the invitations last night, so I expect they'll receive them today."

They reached the Serpentine and turned to circle the small body of water that was half lake, half canal. A man with a St. John's dog at his heel veered wide to avoid them. Livy didn't pay them any mind. Hastings rarely noticed other dogs; it was children she had to be wary of. He had an unnerving habit of greeting them by jamming his giant nose into their midsection and then sniffing loudly and thoroughly. Most children liked it, but the occasional one shrieked as though they were being eaten.

"Is it going to be a large party?" Devere said.

Livy nodded. "I expect so. Father usually invites a good number of his friends, the same ones who often hunt with us when the fallow deer are in season."

"Squires and rustic country vicars?" He sounded slightly weary at the idea.

Livy made a face at him. "Don't make it sound as if it will be dull. I promise you, it won't. You'll be spending it with me," she added, raising her brows and daring him to contradict her.

Devere flicked his glance over her, as though weighing that in the balance. "I suppose I could be convinced," he said. The slight drawl in his voice sent a spark of awareness flashing through her.

"I thought you might."

They'd returned to town from Bankcroft several days ago. And with that short journey had come a return to normalcy that was both welcome and somewhat unnerving. She didn't quite know how to behave. Part of her was mortified at what they'd done, at what she'd allowed him to do, and even more so by what she'd wanted him to do that night in the summerhouse. But a larger part of her simply wanted to find a way—a chance—to do it again.

"The Season will be over soon," she said, forcing herself to ignore the bubble of panic that welled up inside her at the thought. It wouldn't end abruptly. It would trickle off, dying a little more each week until Parliament adjourned and only those with nowhere else to go remained.

"Yes, my mother is already full of schemes for summer at Croughton Abbey."

Livy's breath caught in her chest. Everything was moving too fast now. Hastings pushed at her hand with his muzzle, and she rubbed his head as they walked.

"What do you mean to do when this is over?" Devere said.

Livy stopped in her tracks and looked up at him. "What do you mean?"

"Your stated goals have all been about avoiding things you fear will be unpleasant." He sounded almost angry. Livy cocked her head and stared. Hastings whined, and Livy shushed him. "What do you want beyond that, Olivia? You must want something."

The small bubble of panic she'd felt earlier expanded in her chest, pushing out until there wasn't room for anything else. Devere looked horrified for a moment before tugging Hastings's leash away from her and propelling them back into motion.

"Never mind," he said as they rounded the corner of the canal and came out at Rotten Row. Hastings's head snapped up at the sight of horses, and Devere checked him without a word. "I shouldn't have asked."

"No." Livy took a deep breath as the panic subsided. "You're right." She felt suddenly lost. As lost as she'd been the day she'd discovered her marriage was invalid. Perhaps more so. At least then she'd had her former husband's family to rail against and an escape to plan. "I hadn't thought beyond surviving the Season and ensuring I'd never have to endure another one."

Devere gave her a lopsided grin. "It seems to me you've rather enjoyed the past couple of months."

Livy narrowed her eyes at him and reclaimed Hastings's lead. "I've certainly made the best of them."

Devere responded with a bark of laughter that earned him a snort from the dog. "Will that beast lie quietly at your feet if we go for a cup of tea?"

"If we bribe him with biscuits, yes."

"Then let's make our way to Berkeley Square and see just how badly we can horrify the ladies at Negri's."

• • •

They'd broached the fourth bottle of claret when one of Lord Leonidas's maids appeared in the doorway of The Red Lion, her woolen bedgown disordered and her cap askew. Roland pushed the full bottle toward the man on his left and shook his head, trying to clear away the cobwebs. After an animated debate with the doorman, the girl made a beeline for their table.

"Begging your pardon, sir," she said. "But Mrs. Draper sent me to fetch you. The lady's brother came and dragged her off. He had a constable with him, and there's been a great hullaballoo." Her hands were shaking. She clutched her gown about her, as though the night was far colder than it felt to him.

"Damnation," Reeves said, standing up quickly enough to send his chair skittering across the floor. He swayed on his feet, and Thane put out a hand to steady him.

"Do you know where he took her?" Roland said. "Did he have any other gentlemen with him, or just the constable?" Would Sir Christopher take his sister home or would he take her to some inn and hand her over to his friend?

"Just—just the constable, sir," she said, her teeth starting to chatter. "She was screaming something awful though. Raised half the street, she did. The constable was shouting the riot act from the steps as I left. There were that many people out in the street to see what was going on."

Devere clapped a hand down on the maid's shoulder, and she jumped. "She can tell us more while we walk," he said, turning the girl toward the door and pushing her along before him.

Thane caught Roland's eye as the two of them followed. "This could cause an unholy scandal."

"Only if they were recognized," Roland said as he pulled on his coat. "A row in the middle of the night? And none of the neighbors knowing who she was to start with? If we act fast, it will be no more than a seven-day wonder that is never explained."

When they reached Lord Leonidas's house, the street was deserted, though there were lights in many of the windows and more than one darkly silhouetted head appeared to watch them. Mrs. Draper glared at them as she waved them inside.

"Do you know where they've gone?" Roland said before the door was even closed.

"I think he's taken her home, sir," Mrs. Draper said, her voice thick with rage. "He said something about her being lucky their mother was still willing to receive her as he dragged her down the stairs."

"Thank you, ma'am," Roland said with a hasty nod. "We should hurry," he added, glancing at Reeves and Thane. Reeves nodded, while Thane merely stood there, looking grim.

"I've fetched his lordship's pistols," Mrs. Draper said, pointing toward a wooden box that sat upon the small table where they usually left their hats and gloves.

Thane flicked the box open and began loading one of the finely crafted dueling pistols. Reeves loaded the second one with the precision of a wholly focused drunk. When he was done, he handed it to Roland.

"I'm sober enough to load," Reeves said, "but I wouldn't trust my aim. Best you take it."

Roland wrapped his fingers around the heavy butt of the pistol and nodded to Mrs. Draper. "Don't wait up, ma'am. We can't risk bringing her back here."

"But you'll send someone to let me know she's safe?"

Roland nodded again before ushering his friends out the door. Together they stalked down the street. When they reached the Bence-Jones's house, Thane didn't even bother to knock. He simply kicked the door in, sending shards of wood flying across the entry hall and startling the footman into something close to hysterics. Roland pointed his pistol at him, and the man fled.

Sir Christopher came rushing down the stairs, loudly protesting their intrusion. Roland shook his head. The man clearly didn't grasp the severity of the situation or the amount of danger he was in. He was also damn lucky Reeves wasn't armed.

Roland cocked his pistol, and the baronet froze. "Is your sister upstairs?"

When the man didn't answer, Reeves took a menacing step forward. Sir Christopher fell back a step before attempting to bar the way. Reeves latched onto the baronet's coat and sent him hurtling down the stairs before storming upward, shouting for Miss Bence-Jones as he went.

When Sir Christopher attempted to right himself, Thane nudged him back with one foot and then pinned him to the floor with it. "I'll have you all arrested," Sir Christopher said. "You can't just do whatever you like with other men's sisters."

Thane cocked his own pistol and leveled it the baronet's head. "I've no intention of hanging over this affair,"

Thane said, his tone disarmingly light. "So don't force me to shoot you."

Abovestairs there was a series of thumps, a howl, and then a peal of somewhat manic laughter. "Got her," Reeves said, appearing on the stairs with Miss Bence-Jones tossed over one shoulder.

Thane continued to hold the baronet down as Reeves carried the man's sister out into the night. "Whatever we want?" Thane said. "No, certainly not. Whatever she wants? I think we can. Can and shall." He took his boot off Sir Christopher's chest and carefully uncocked his gun before turning and exiting through the ruins of the entry portal.

Roland lowered his own pistol. "Don't think for a minute that your sister didn't tell us everything." The baronet blanched. "So if you'd like to be known as a man who arranged his sister's rape, please, attempt to have us arrested. I'm fairly certain my own family can handle the scandal of their son being accused of saving a girl from a brother such as you."

⤳ CHAPTER 34 ⤳

L ivy sat beside the comtesse as the coach rolled swiftly toward Holinshed. Her father was riding alongside, as Hastings took up the entire rear-facing seat. Livy wished she could trade places with her father or that she could have stayed behind and allowed Devere to escort her. With her maid in tow, they could have complied with the proprieties.

She'd been surprised when the comtesse had made her brother's excuses. Surprised, and not a little bit annoyed. She shouldn't allow herself to feel proprietary about him, but she couldn't seem to help it.

The dog sprawled across the coach, his feet dangling off the seat. Devere's sister didn't seem to mind his presence in the least, which was a good thing, as there were twenty more just like him waiting at Holinshed, and her father had never seen the logic behind confining his hounds to a kennel.

Livy shut her book with a thump, and the comtesse looked up from the letter she'd been reading. "Eager to be home?" she said.

Livy nodded and stretched out her legs as much as the coach would allow. "It's been a long time since I was there, almost two years. I'm wondering if it will even feel like home anymore."

"So long?" Devere's sister twisted so she was facing Livy as much as the carriage seat allowed. "The earl speaks as if he spends nearly all his time there."

"He does, at least when parliament is not in session. But I haven't been home since I was married."

The comtesse nodded as though she were piecing everything together. "Where did you go after..." Her voice trailed off as though she suddenly realized there was no polite way to phrase it.

"After I found out I wasn't really married? I went to my maternal grandmother, Lady Heddington. Where I stayed, until she and father decided that it was time to force me back into the world."

"I'm sure they meant it for the best," the comtesse said softly.

Livy resisted the urge to snap at her. "Undoubtedly, but I would still rather they had let me be."

"For how long? Another year? Five? How long would have been enough?" The comtesse folded her letter and tucked it between her skirt and the leather seat. "No matter when you returned, the scandal would have been dredged up. Best to get it out of the way before it became the only thing anyone remembered about you."

Livy nodded. It was impossible not to agree in principle.

"Think of it this way," the comtesse said, obviously sensing that Livy was not entirely in agreement. "Imagine doing only what you did for that year for the rest of your life. Arranging flowers for the church, walking your grandmother's pug, and struggling to escape the condescending visits from the vicar's wife. Add in endless hours of needlework—embroidered slippers for your father or clothes for the poor, makes no difference, a drudgery either way. Or perhaps you've a talent for watercolor or a great love of botany? Tell me that doesn't sound dreary."

"Very," Livy said, horrified by how close to the mark Devere's sister was.

"But now you've escaped such a fate, thanks in no small part to your father dragging you to Town."

The panicked feeling she'd been fighting on and off for days rose again, making Livy's stomach churn. The truth was on the tip of her tongue, and it was hard to swallow it back down. She'd set everything in motion to condemn herself to exactly the life the comtesse had just described. Except now there was Devere, and she was almost certain he was hers for the asking.

❧ CHAPTER 35 ❧

G ood Lord, sir, that can't possibly be where we're going."

Roland glanced out the window of the coach. Through the light drizzle that had begun to fall, he could just make out the ruins of a castle in the distance. One wall had a major breach, and only three of the towers were still standing.

He yawned. It had taken the better part of the day to reach their destination, and they'd traveled for most of the previous night in order to take Miss Bence-Jones to his grandmother. The dowager had pretended to be horrified, but the twinkle of amusement in her dark eyes had been unmistakable as Roland had explained the situation. He had no doubt his grandmother would cosset her new companion to death as they waited for a reply to the letter they'd sent Blakeley.

"You were expecting Windsor, Martin?"

His valet glanced back out the window as though a second look would reveal the mistake. "Or something like, yes, sir."

"Lady Olivia said something about the house incorporating the ruins of the original castle."

Martin shuddered and twitched his coat tighter about himself. Roland bit back a laugh at the man's fastidious horror. He studied the ruins as they loomed larger and larger. He had to admit it was not a promising facade. He couldn't imagine his own father not tearing the entire thing down and beginning anew, but when they rolled across the dry moat and under the gaping threat of the portcullis, they emerged into an immense courtyard with an imposing brick manor house off to one side.

Roland leapt down from the coach when it came to a halt before the house. He turned about, ignoring the rain. There was nothing left of the castle but the walls and partial towers. Immediately encircling the house was a rather formal garden, and from the garden's edge to the castle walls there was nothing but a large expanse of lawn and two enormous oaks.

An unholy baying erupted from beyond the house, and as the front door opened and Olivia appeared, a seething pack of shaggy hounds erupted into sight. "No," Olivia squealed as they frolicked about her, wagging and rubbing up against her. "You're wet. And muddy." She smiled at him and flapped her skirts at the dogs. "Go on with you."

Rather than return to wherever it was they'd come from, the animals turned as one and thundered into the house. "Well," Olivia said, turning to face him, "welcome to Holinshed. Come inside before the rest of the pack joins us."

"The rest of the pack?" Roland said as he followed her inside. "There are more?"

Olivia nodded as he handed his coat and hat over to the footman who came to claim them. "These are the youngsters," she said with a laugh as one of milling hounds rubbed its head across her skirt. "And very naughty they are, too, slipping out to play in the mud. I think the rest are strategically spread throughout the house, sleeping beside whatever fires have been lit."

The half-grown pup's tail wagged wildly as Olivia spoke. Roland stripped off his gloves and held his hand out to the one that approached him. The dog sniffed, nosed his hand, and then snatched a glove and bolted off into the house with its fellows in hot pursuit.

Olivia bit her lip, clearly trying not to laugh. "That's a glove you'll never see again. At least not in a form you'll recognize."

Roland shoved the remaining one into his pocket. "I'll husband this one to sacrifice later then."

"An excellent plan," Olivia said, taking his arm and leading him into the house. "Come and have a drink. And I promise to replace your gloves. It's one of the hazards of visiting us. I should have warned you. Your sister has already lost a shoe as well. Bosworth stole it right off her foot during dinner last night."

"I'm sure Margo was thrilled."

"I'm not sure that's the word I'd have used, but she did get into the spirit of the thing by tossing the other one into the fray."

"So you're warning me to guard my boots?"

"With your life," Lord Arlington said as they entered the drawing room. "I'm sure your valet will be warned by our butler to keep the door to your room tightly shut, but I'll give you the same advice. We've an entire litter of five-month-olds at the moment, and they seem hell-bent on the destruction of every piece of leather they come across, shoes, gloves, bridles, books." He said *books* as though that one particularly pained him.

Roland glanced around the heavily paneled room. "I suppose you should be happy their tastes don't run to wood."

Olivia winced. "We've had that litter, too. Don't look too closely at some of the furniture or the corners of the wainscoting."

Roland accepted a glass of brandy from the earl and strolled over to the fire. It was hard not to laugh. Arlington could more than afford to replace whatever furniture the dogs ate. That he chose not to do so simply meant that on a certain level the destruction didn't bother him.

The fire was walled off by two long, gray bodies. Hastings and a slightly paler bitch were stretched out in front of it. Hastings whined softly and fanned the floor with his tail as Roland approached. Unable to resist, Roland set his glass on the mantel and knelt down to give the dog a scratch.

Olivia's mud-spattered skirts came into view. "That's Rouen sprawled beside Hastings, mother to the horde that greeted you at the gates."

The bitch raised her head, and Roland ran his fingers through the wiry fur that covered her side. "Never a dull moment, eh?" He glanced up at Olivia.

She smiled, clearly happy amid the chaos. "Not with puppies in the house, no." She rubbed at one of the streaks of mud on her skirt with her thumb. "Never a clean one either, though. I'd almost managed to forget that aspect of living here."

Roland stood up and reclaimed his glass. "Is Margo hiding from the dogs?"

Olivia shook her head. "No, I think the comtesse has been adopted into the pack. One of the older dogs is quite taken with her. I don't think Maldon has left her side since she arrived. I think she retired to change for dinner, as should we all. Father, shall I show Mr. Devere to his room? I think Mrs. Hibbert was planning on putting him in The Crusader Room, wasn't she?"

The earl looked at her as if she'd grown a second head. "I haven't the slightest idea where Mrs. Hibbert is planning on putting anyone."

Livy shook her head and motioned for him to follow her. Roland saluted Lord Arlington with his glass and did as he was bid. The main staircase turned back upon itself and led to a long corridor that stretched in both directions.

"Your sister is there." She pointed to the first door on the left. "You're at the very end." She opened the last door on the right, and Roland realized the house wasn't built onto the castle wall; it was built into the castle. The far wall of the room was stone, though a large portion of it was covered with a tapestry depicting a medieval battle of mounted knights.

There was a large bed on one wall, opposite the room's only real window, which looked out on the gate and portcullis. The castle wall had several arrow slits that upon closer inspection were glazed and showed a vista that included the road and the edge of the forest.

Martin was nowhere to be seen, but his shaving case

was lying open on the dressing table, so he was clearly in the correct room. He turned to ask Olivia a question, only to realize she'd slipped away while he'd been exploring. A minute later, Martin appeared through the adjoining door to the closet. He took one look at the still-open door and rushed across the room to shut it. "The dogs are quite predatory, sir," he said before heading back into the closet. "Which coat would you like, the puce silk or the brown camlet with gold braid?"

Philip paced across his drawing room, earning a glare of reproof from Hastings. Sad when the dog was right. There was no reason to be nervous, or rather his being so would do nothing to help convince Margo that she could be happy at Holinshed, happy with him. And that was, after all, the entire purpose of inviting her for the fawn count.

Margo reappeared after changing for dinner with his ancient one-eyed hound still on her heels. The comtesse came to join him near the windows, and Maldon flopped down at her feet rather than join his fellows near the fire.

"Maldon's no easy conquest," Philip said.

"He's just hoping for a shoe," Margo said darkly, though her eyes held a hint of amusement.

Philip chuckled and poured her a sherry. "You don't really mind the dogs, do you?" he said as she took the small glass from him. He couldn't blame her if she did; the dogs were more than he could ask of any sane woman. Either she'd love the house and the dogs as much as he did, or she'd be miserable at Holinshed.

Margo reached up to smooth his brow with her thumb. He didn't realize he'd been frowning. "No," she said, staring up at him, large dark eyes utterly sincere. "I don't mind the dogs."

Philip captured her hand and kissed her palm. Her smile turned sly, and he dipped his head to kiss her. The rattle of the door caught him up short. Margo laughed as he straightened and took a decorous step back from her.

Livy came in with Henry and Devere behind her. His heir went to pour himself a drink, and Maldon growled. The comtesse shushed him, and the hound put his head down with his one eye still on Henry. Philip smiled to himself and sipped his brandy. Margo might not realize it, but she was already behaving as if it were her house, as if shushing an enormous dog was the most natural thing in the world.

Maldon ignored her brother completely as he came to hug her. "Hallo, sister of mine," he said, leaning down to kiss her on the cheek for good measure.

Margo scrunched her nose at him and kissed him back. "Hallo, Rolly dear. Did you arrive early enough to tour the castle? No, well, you'll have to let Lady Olivia show you about tomorrow. It's really rather impressive."

The butler arrived to announce that dinner was ready, and Philip offered Margo his arm. Her brother claimed Livy, as was fitting, and Henry trailed after them, followed by the dogs.

The place settings were grouped at one end of the table as he'd instructed. There was no reason to shout at one another all evening. Philip helped Margo into the seat to his right, while his daughter took the one to his left. Devere claimed the seat next to Livy and Henry resignedly took the only remaining place beside the comtesse.

"Lady Olivia was telling me this house has a history similar to that of Croughton Abbey," Devere said as the first course was served.

Philip smiled. It did indeed. "The third earl, like your own forefather, refused to surrender to Cromwell's forces. So when the roundheads finally battered the walls down, they destroyed what they could and torched the rest. Which I'll admit wasn't all that much, as the earl had wisely sent his family to France when the king was captured."

"Along with the dogs," Livy added, "and every bit of his fortune that was portable."

"Yes, with the dogs. The first pack was a gift from James I, and the family has never been without them. When the monarchy was restored and the earl eventually returned to Holinshed, there was nothing but the ruins of the castle left. Rather than tear it down or remove to another location as so many others did, he built his manor house inside the walls, a testament to his refusal to give ground."

"It's certainly a most unusual house," Devere said.

"It's like a secret world," Margo said a bit dreamily. Her brother shot her a quizzing look, and Philip grinned. Yes, inviting her had been a very wise maneuver. It wasn't that she was mercenary, but ignoring the reality of what he was offering her was harder to do when it was right before her eyes.

"Some parts of the castle are still in use," Henry said, joining the conversation. "The house incorporates parts of it, though it can be hard to tell if you're in the new sections. And there's an intact corridor to the nearest tower where the steward has his office and quarters."

"And the stables were built inside a section of the ruins on the far side of the house," Lady Olivia said. "With the kennels beyond that, and then The Raven Tower at the far end."

"The Raven Tower?" Devere said. "That sounds suitably medieval."

"The birds took up residence while the castle was empty," Philip said as the second course was brought in and laid out on the table. "The third earl said that if they were good enough for the Tower of London, they were good enough for Holinshed. You'll see them out on the lawn taunting the dogs on occasion."

"Yes," his daughter said with a grin. "Several of them can even whistle, and one has learned to call them. You'll hear him croaking out their names and then cackling when they race across the lawn trying to catch him."

When the final course of nuts and sweetmeats was brought in, Henry and the comtesse began to talk of Italy. Philip motioned for the footman to refill his glass. He hadn't been abroad since he'd made the grand tour, but he could still picture it all quite clearly: the ruins of Athens and Rome, the clear water of the Mediterranean, the excitement of the horse races in Siena. He'd spent nearly three years traveling across the Continent; he'd even seen the Levant. It seemed like a lifetime ago.

When his butler appeared with the port, Philip ushered them all back to the drawing room. Henry stayed long enough to down a single glass and talk to Margo a little about her life in France before excusing himself and heading for bed. Philip couldn't help but commend him for the effort to be pleasant. He had to know that his inheritance was at risk.

• • •

Margo shrugged out of her dressing gown and dropped it onto the bench before the dressing table. She was still wide awake, but her candle had burnt down until it guttered in the socket and went out. She'd have to call someone to bring a new one if she wanted to continue to read and that seemed a ridiculous demand in someone else's home. Perhaps if she simply gave in and went to bed, sleep would come. She'd been hoping Arlington would find his way to her room, but for the second night in a row, her hopes appeared to be in vain.

Her one-eyed protector barked softly from his chosen spot upon the chaise longue, clearly chasing rabbits in his sleep. Her maid had tried to shoo him from the room when she herself had left, but Maldon had simply crawled onto the chaise and become an immovable object.

Paxton had finally given up, though she'd offered to find someone from Lord Arlington's staff to come and remove *la Bête du Gévaudan*, as she'd taken to calling it, her loathing apparent in every jaundiced glance.

Margo slid into bed, beat the pillows into shape, and stared up at the dark recesses of the canopy. If she took the plunge and married Arlington, she was almost positive Paxton would decamp to Paris in disgust. London was one thing; Holinshed was clearly something else. And Margo could feel the lure of it working its way under her skin like a barbed hook.

It was so very English. It called to her in a way she hadn't expected. Much like the earl himself. He seemed to have known it would, damn the man.

∼≪ CHAPTER 36 ≫∼

When Roland came down to breakfast, there were many new faces, all male. Olivia was ensconced among them, happily playing hostess. She smiled at him brightly and waved him toward the buffet, which was heavily laden with platters of cold beef, thinly sliced ham and tongue, eggs, steak and kidney pie, and piles of dry toast and muffins. There was also ale, which the elderly Lord Hynde was drinking, as well as an immense silver urn of coffee, which Olivia was presiding over with the skill of someone who'd been doing so since she was a child.

Roland loaded up a plate and took a seat at the breakfast table beside one of the newcomers. The butter was barely soft enough to spread over the cold toasted muffin he claimed from the rack upon the table. Roland stopped trying and ladled marmalade onto it instead. Olivia raised a brow at his greed, and Roland responded by eating it in three bites.

When he'd swallowed the last of it, she poured him a

dish of coffee and introduced him to the two guests he didn't already know. He nodded to Hynde, a friend of his father's, and accepted the baron's congratulations on his engagement.

"Your mother was discussing the wedding with my wife over dinner last week," Hynde said with a sympathetic air. "Seems to have August at Croughton in mind. I'd have thought Lady Olivia would want to be married from her own home."

Olivia busied herself pouring a cup of coffee for Carlow, who had just arrived. "I wouldn't think so, my lord," Carlow said as he took a seat beside the old man. "Bad associations," he added *sotto voce*.

Roland suppressed the urge to eject him physically from the room. The baron looked suddenly embarrassed. "Just so," he said before excusing himself and shuffling off.

"Henry," Olivia said when he was gone. "You shouldn't have said anything."

Carlow shrugged and took a bite of ham. "I wouldn't have thought anyone would need reminding."

"Nor I, but if they don't, I'll take that as a blessing. Mr. Devere," she turned slightly in her seat, "shall I give you the tour you were promised now?"

Roland nodded in agreement. He pushed away from the table, and Olivia rose with him.

"I shall see you all at luncheon before we head out," she said before taking his arm and practically dragging him out of the room. "Get me away before I strangle my cousin."

"Gladly," Roland said. "Though it might be a greater service if I simply strangled him for you."

A smile curled the corner of her lips but she shook her head. "You shouldn't encourage me."

Roland waggled his brows, and Olivia gave in and laughed as they strode purposefully away from the breakfast room. Stealing a bit of time with Olivia was at the top of his agenda for the day. He hadn't thought it would be so easy though. "Where shall we start?"

"With the battlements, I think. The easiest way up is through the tower ruins. That way we don't have to disturb my father, the steward, nor risk our eyes in The Raven Tower."

"Will the birds really attack interlopers?" He'd seen an overly eager visitor to the Tower of London nearly lose a finger when the man had repeatedly poked at one of the half-tame birds.

"I doubt it. Keens is up there all the time to feed them, but it's much pleasanter to give them the go-by."

When they stepped out of the house, several of the puppies heaved themselves up from the ground and joined them. One of them had a shredded bit of leather dangling from its mouth that Roland was all too sure was the remains of his glove.

Olivia took his hand as she led him up the ancient, stone stairs. Each tread was swaybacked like an old horse, worn away by centuries of use. Halfway up, the dogs scrambled past them in a roiling, howling mob, nearly tripping Olivia. Roland caught her and took the opportunity to press her back against the wall and kiss her.

She softened in his arms almost immediately, opening her lips to him, welcoming him in with wicked strokes of her tongue. If he lifted her skirts would she object? He dropped one hand to find out, only to be nearly knocked off his feet by the dogs as they plunged back down the stairs.

"Remind me to show you where the door behind the tapestry in your room leads," Olivia said before turning and racing up the stairs in a flurry of skirts.

When he emerged at the top of the tower ruins, he found that the wide shallow stairs gave way to what would have once been a room of some kind; the bottom of one windowsill was still in evidence and the remains of a doorway led out to the battlements.

Olivia, flanked by the puppy chewing on his glove as though it were cud, was staring out toward the same forest his bedroom looked upon. "Those woods are the deer park," she said, waving one hand out toward them. "This afternoon, we'll be walking the paths in small groups, keeping a tally of the fawns. They can be quite hard to spot, as our herd is mostly black or very dark brown."

"I didn't even know fallow deer came in black." Roland narrowed his eyes and studied the forest intently, trying to see if any of the deer were visible. The tips of the canopy swayed in the breeze, but nothing stirred on the ground.

"They come in a wide range of colors," Olivia said, turning to face him and balancing one hip against the parapet. "The pale ones are easier to spot in the woods though—as you'll soon see—so they tend to get culled at a higher rate than the darker ones."

She wandered away from him, her curls being pulled by the same breeze that wove its way through the forest. She turned to glance back at him as she headed toward the next tower. Roland took a deep breath and started after her. "Wouldn't that be true everywhere?"

He wanted to chase her down, drag her into some dark corner, and do whatever was necessary to convince her that whatever she saw for herself in the future, he should be a part of it. It had begun to feel all too necessary to him that she think so. The question was, was it better to put it to her, or to let her come to that conclusion on her own?

Olivia shook her head, hair tangling with her eyelashes as she did so. She brushed it away. "Very little of the country is as densely forested as it is here. The lighter deer fare better in open country, or that's what grandpapa always said."

She reached the door to the next tower and pushed it open. The room inside was bare except for a large straw pallet covered in a rough blanket. Atop the blanket were three fully gown hounds. None of them bothered to move, not even when the pup who'd been following Olivia blundered right across them.

"This is The Earl's Tower," Olivia said. "It's the only one attached to the house itself. Papa's rooms are just down those stairs."

They went through and out onto the next section of the battlement. "Next is The Steward's Tower." Olivia pointed. "But we should go back the way we came after I show you the view from this side. I don't want to disturb Mr. Lanister."

"What was worth coming to this side for then?" Roland peered out over the wall. It just looked like more forest to him. Stand after stand of gigantic trees. It was like something out of a legend.

Smiling, Olivia took him by the shoulders and turned him about so he was looking inside the walls of the castle. "It has the best view of the house itself and the gardens.

And it's a nice vantage point from which to watch the ravens tease the dogs." She pointed at the far side of the lawn where several of the puppies were running in circles while an enormous black bird swooped and cackled at them. Roland couldn't tell if they were chasing each other or the bird.

A loud caw made Olivia jump, and Roland turned to see a raven hopping toward them like a hunchbacked jester. It paused a few feet away and cocked its head to study them with one black eye.

It leapt closer with an audible rattle of feathers and clacked its beak expectantly. Olivia shook her head. "I should have stolen a bit of meat at breakfast. I forget what beggars they are."

Roland reached into his pocket and pulled out his handkerchief. He unwrapped it and tossed the contents to the bird. It snatched it midair and dove off the battlement as though it feared he might attempt to take the treat back.

"I meant it as a bribe for the dogs."

Olivia smirked, looking for all the world as if she'd caught him attending a committee for the care and feeding of orphans. "Let's go down before the others come calling, demanding their due," she said with a laugh. "They're almost disturbingly prescient."

When Margo failed to see Arlington at breakfast, she went in search of him. Maldon followed her out into the garden, but when she wandered near the stable block, he fell in with several other dogs and disappeared inside.

Judging by the way the dogs were filtering in from all over the castle, it must be time for them to be fed. Her own dogs had always known exactly when they could expect cook to put down their bowl and clearly Arlington's hounds were no different.

Margo turned about slowly, trying to decide where to check next. Carlow had said something about the earl having a study in one of the towers. Though she'd been given a tour of the house the day she'd arrived, the tour had not included Arlington's personal rooms.

The house abutted one of the towers. She could ask one of the servants and risk being told that Arlington didn't want to be disturbed, or she could simply open doors until she found the right one. The beauty of the house being such a maze was that she could always claim to be lost if caught.

As she turned to retrace her steps to the house, she spotted her brother and Lady Olivia atop the battlements. Rolly threw up one hand in a careless gesture of greeting. Margo waved back and quickened her step. If she wasn't careful, she'd end up being waylaid by one of the other guests.

Once inside, she hurried through the hall. A trio of maids were busy spreading sand in one corner while two more slowly worked it across the flagstone floor with small, stiff-bristled brooms. Margo ducked around them to get to the corridor that led to the back of the house. There always seemed to be someone cleaning the floors, which she supposed made sense given the number of dogs traipsing about the house.

The breakfast room was quiet now, but she could hear voices coming from the billiard room. Margo stepped carefully past the door, doing her best to make sure the heels of her shoes didn't clack against the floor. The corridor came to a T. From the sounds of things, one direction led to the kitchens. Margo took the other. The first door led to a servant's thankfully empty room of some sort, with paneled walls and a small, heavily worn baize table. The second opened into what appeared to be a closet for household linens. A large array of irons were neatly arranged before the hearth, and a table with a work basket beneath it sat beside the only window. The final door was larger, heavier, and looked as though it might take several men to open it.

Margo twisted the handle and pushed. It swung easily, the hinges not even making the slightest sound of protest. A set of spiraling stone stairs, exactly like those in the neighboring tower ruins she'd toured yesterday, curved away before her. Margo pushed the door shut behind her.

She was still a few steps from the end of the flight when she was rewarded with the sight of Arlington bent over a ledger book, chewing absently on the end of his quill. He glanced up as she reached the top and stopped.

"There you are," she said as though he should have been expecting her. And indeed he should have, at least in her way of thinking.

The earl gave her a rueful smile and set his quill aside. "I apologize for deserting you this morning, but I've had a series of letters from London that require my immediate attention. It seems that when the fawn count is concluded, I shall have to post back to London at once."

"Lose your fortune on change?"

Arlington laughed and waved her in. Margo stepped forward, looking about the room with interest. It was essentially round, with stairs continuing up on the opposite side of the flight she'd just used. Two windows were cut into the stone walls, with the earl's desk situated between them, facing the center of the room.

"If only it were that simple," he said as he raked his hand through his hair. A few disturbed locks fell into his eyes, and he pushed them back. "There's a movement to oust the prime minister."

Margo nodded. Even though she'd spent most of her adult life in France, gossip about English politics had still reached her in almost every letter she exchanged with her friends and family at home. "Isn't that the major sport in the Lords?"

Arlington's shoulders twitched with silent laughter. "Sadly, yes, and often at the expense of actually governing. So we shall have to make the most of what time we have left."

"Shall we?" Margo said, putting a world of innuendo into the question. She stepped away from the desk, wandering into the center of the chamber. Her shoes slid across the heavy carpet as she spun about to look at him. "I'd been hoping to do so all along."

Arlington stood up fast enough that his chair fell back against the wall with a sound like a shot. He rounded the desk, and Margo took a step backward. "Had you?" he said as his hand closed around her wrist. "And here I thought I was playing the gentleman."

Margo's answering laugh echoed off the stone. "What did I ever do to give you the impression that I wanted a gentleman?"

"Not a damn thing," the earl said. He scooped her up

and carried her up the stairs. "But a lifetime of training is hard to overcome."

A thrill shot through her. This was what she'd wanted since arriving, a display of power, a demonstration of desire, to know the earl wanted her with the same intensity that she wanted him.

The next floor was furnished with little more than a large four-poster bed hung with dark green damask. Arlington tossed her onto it. Margo rolled over and crawled to the center. A hand caught her ankle and dragged her back to the edge.

Her shoe clattered to the floor. Arlington shoved her skirts up, tossing them half over her head. Margo pushed them aside and twisted to look over her shoulder as the earl's hands settled on her hips, sliding over her bare skin. He grinned and yanked her down so that she was bent over the high edge of the bed, feet dangling, scrabbling for purchase.

He lifted her slightly and thrust in with no prelude or warning. Margo arched and gasped, trapped between the earl and the bed. The heady sensation of invasion gave way as her body adjusted and grew wet.

Arlington's weight came down on her. His hands pushed under, grazing her breasts, before curling up over her shoulders so he could pull her back to meet every thrust. He buried his face in her hair, his breath hot on the nape of her neck.

"Ungentlemanly enough?"

Margo could only nod. She'd expected to goad him into action, but this was entirely beyond her expectations. Magnificently so.

Arlington's breathing changed as he found a steady,

pounding rhythm. Margo forced one hand down between herself and the mattress. Her fingers slicked over her clitoris. She brushed the earl's cock as he rocked into her. Margo pressed up, circled, and rode her hand, chasing her own release as surely as the earl chased his.

She came with a muffled scream. Arlington paused as she pulsed around him. "My valet could walk in on us," he said as he began again, driving himself into her with long, hard strokes. "Or a maid. Or any of the guests really. If I made you scream loudly enough, do you think they'd come running?"

Margo bit down on the coverlet as a second climax rolled over her. The earl growled her name into her ear and spilled himself inside her. After a moment, he pulled away to fling himself down beside her on his back.

Margo turned her head so she could see him out of one eye. "I think you like the idea of being caught," she said.

He glanced over at her, handsome, disheveled, and grinning from ear to ear. "I like the results of being caught."

"Scandal?"

"Marriage."

Margo pushed herself up onto an elbow and threw her skirts down to cover herself. Arlington reached out and tucked her hair behind her ear. His fingers traced over her jaw. "Afraid whatever your brother and my daughter are up to will put me off?"

~ CHAPTER 37 ~

Margo didn't answer him immediately. She just stared down at him with a slightly guilty expression. So she suspected something was wrong there, too.

He'd told himself he was being overly cautious, that his daughter knew what she was doing, what she wanted, but he couldn't get past the feeling that she and Devere were playing some sort of game.

Philip sat up and tugged the ribbon from the remains of his queue. He shook it out, raked his fingers over his scalp, scraped his hair back, and tied it up again.

When he was done, Margo let her breath out with a long sigh. "Frankly, yes," she said in a purely matter-of-fact tone.

"I forced her back into society before she was ready, and your brother and whatever scheme they've been playing at are her revenge."

The comtesse climbed down out of his bed and smoothed her hands over her skirts. Philip fought down the urge to toss her back in and keep her there. The room felt suddenly cold.

She looked about for her shoe and wiggled her foot into it. "Revenge might be too strong a word," she said when she was once again fully shod. "I'd say my brother is her foil. Her defense against the *ton*. Or he was at the beginning."

Philip buttoned the fall of his breeches. "And now?"

Margo chewed on her lower lip. He could almost see the cogs turning in her head as she weighed her response. "Now I think he's in earnest. No"—she stood up a little straighter, clearly about to make a confession—"I know he is. I think it's your daughter who still needs convincing."

Philip nodded. He'd come to much the same conclusion watching them over the past few weeks. It was the only reason he'd let the farce continue. "Then I say we leave it in your brother's hands and see if he can bring her round."

Olivia stopped directly in front of him, and Roland nearly bowled her over. "Shhh," she said over her shoulder as she crept forward. "There's a small herd just behind that next stand of trees. I see three does and at least four fawns."

Roland craned his neck. He could just make out the dark bodies of the does. The speckled fawns were harder to find in the shady gloom. "I think I see five fawns."

"Two nursing, one at the base of the tree, and one wandering closer to us," Olivia said, ticking them off on the small square leaf of ivory that hung from a chain at her waist.

"There's another one just there." Roland pointed beyond the does. "You can't see it now because one of the does is in the way."

Olivia shot him a look that said she didn't quite believe him, but she added it to her tally. The bridle trail wound past the small thicket where the does and fawns were grazing. Lord Hynde and several other guests were up ahead, heads bent together as they pointed and counted.

"Let's go this way," she said, turning off the clear, main path and pushing her way through the encroaching underbrush.

"Is this even a path?" Roland watched the ground carefully as he followed in her wake. He'd already snagged his foot on a protruding root once. He'd be damned if he ended up breaking an ankle out here.

"Barely. Mr. Lanister needs to get the paths seen to or there'll be no getting through here by autumn." She stopped to free the skirt of her habit from a trailing branch before marching on.

Roland had wondered at her appearance when she'd come down to luncheon in a well-worn camlet habit of an indeterminate color somewhere between mud and moss. Her choice made complete sense after he'd seen her leave the path and fight her way to any small opening where she thought she might have seen a deer.

His sister must be in a rage by now if her own habit were snagging as often as Olivia's. But Olivia seemed to relish all the effort it took to actually find and count the fawns.

She put up a hand for him to stop. "Two more over there." She ticked them off. "Lots of twins this year. Oh, look." She waved him forward and, when he reached her, directed him to a small cathedral grove. "We've got a white one. Those don't crop up all that often in our herd."

She turned her ivory sheet over and made a tick on the backside. "Papa will want to know about that one."

"Will you cull it?"

"Yes, but not in the autumn hunt. Lord Sykes has a white herd in his park. He's always happy to receive another from elsewhere to strengthen the blood."

"Won't it be hard to catch?"

She tossed him an amused glance. "Haven't you noticed that they don't run, even when they see us? Fallow deer aren't timid."

"Doesn't that make hunting them somewhat awkward?"

"Oh, they run from the dogs quick enough," she said as she continued down the nearly invisible track. "And the hunt is tradition. Our dogs are deerhounds. They'd have no purpose without the hunt."

"You love it, don't you?"

She turned to look at him, framed by towering oaks, hair a tumbled riot. "The hunt?"

"Holinshed."

"Yes," she said simply. The afternoon sun hit her face in tiny beams as it shot through the leaves, sparking off her eyes and hair. She had a streak of mud high on one cheekbone and what looked like a bit of bracken caught in one trailing curl. She'd never looked lovelier, never looked more herself.

Roland took a quick step toward her and kissed her hard and fast. When he broke away, she kept her fingers interlocked at the back of his neck.

"I asked you what you picture for yourself," he said, "and I've yet to receive an answer, but I want to make a simple suggestion: include me in it."

Olivia's brow puckered, and he bent his head and kissed her again. She sagged into him, becoming a heavy weight in his arms. Roland rested his forehead against hers. "I mean it, Livy. I think you should marry me."

A crackling in the brush followed by a loud curse announced the presence of other participants on the narrow track. Livy broke away from him. She picked her way carefully through the brambles, moving swiftly away from whoever was about to intrude upon them. After she'd gone a short distance, she paused and turned back to look at him.

"Is that really what you picture for yourself?" She looked perplexed. The small crease between her inquiring brows made him want to kiss her again until it faded away.

Roland strode after Olivia. When he caught up with her, he pulled her behind the gnarled trunk of an immense oak, putting the tree between them and the path. Olivia ran her fingers along the lapel of his coat as if she were ascertaining that he was real.

"Just think about it, Livy."

"I have been." She leaned back against the tree, her grip firm on his coat. "Believe me, I have been."

Devere's smile widened into a grin and he kissed her again, his mouth hot and urgent as it covered hers. Livy's heart was hammering as though she'd run a long distance, and her legs felt unsteady.

She had been thinking about what she wanted. In fact, she'd thought of little else since their trip to Bankcroft. The comtesse's rather pointed questions on their journey here had merely served to goad Livy into accepting that in any life she pictured for herself, Devere had become an integral part, a necessity.

"Do you love me?" he said.

"Yes, you've won that bet, too, horrid man."

He chuckled, clearly taking her abuse as a compliment. "But just think," he said as his lips traced her ear. "You'll have a lifetime to make me wish I were dead. Surely that alone is a fine inducement to marriage."

"A fine inducement to marriage would be an actual declaration of love on your part," Livy said as she pushed Devere back slightly so she could see his expression. She was certain that he did, but she needed to hear him say the words.

His eyes widened, cocoa brown turning amber in the light. "Livy"—he cupped her face and lowered his head until he was staring directly into her eyes—"let me make myself perfectly clear. I love you. There's no other reason I'd propose in earnest. Not to get you into my bed, not to enrich myself with your dowry, not to pave the way for my sister and your father. And if you don't believe me, I'll just have to work at it until you do."

Livy let the purity of the moment flood through her. She felt certain of herself and her choices for the first time in more than a year. She slipped her arms about his neck and settled a portion of her weight on him. "You'll have to be the one to tell your mother I want to be married from Holinshed, bad omen or not."

❧ CHAPTER 38 ❧

After her father and his cronies departed, the house had slowly sunk into a dark, protracted silence. Livy had never stayed awake to listen to it happen before. First the sounds of the guests preparing for bed died away, followed by the muffled chaos of their maids and valets retiring for the night. Down below, she could hear the faint sounds of footmen moving about the house, checking doors and windows, rousting dogs. Then even that died away. It was as though the house sighed and settled in, not unlike the dogs.

Livy clutched her wrapper around her as she slipped out of her room and sped down the corridor. Her slippers whispered across the floor, the kidskin soles unaccountably loud in the deep silence of the sleeping house.

Her hands shook, and she curled her fingers into the light fabric of her wrapper. The night had turned sultry, making every layer of clothing feel like a burden. A distant rattle in the depths of the house made her jump and she froze in place before taking a shaky breath and running lightly to the end of the corridor. She turned the handle, relieved to find the door unlocked.

Devere was sitting beside the cold grate, a tumbler of what she suspected was brandy in one hand and a book in the other. He glanced up as she eased the door shut. He didn't look shocked at her arrival, but one brow rose appraisingly as he studied her. One of the candles on the mantel guttered in its socket, the hissing sizzle of its demise causing him to glance away from her.

Livy caught her breath. Her heartbeat expanded to fill her entire chest. Heat flooded through her, pushing back the last bit of uncertainty. Devere stood up and set the book on the mantel. His hair was loose, and he was wearing a frogged dressing gown of striped silk, the combination making him look like a foreign potentate.

Devere studied her, one side of his mouth sliding up into a ghost of a smile, and Livy realized she was still clutching the doorknob, as if she wasn't entirely sure she was staying.

"Lost?" he said, stepping forward so that the brace of candles lit him from behind, turning his dark hair into a halo.

Livy shook her head. "I was hoping you'd still be awake."

Devere's half-smile blossomed into a grin. "I was going to give the house another half an hour to settle in for the night before attempting to storm your room."

His glance flicked over her, appraising and possessive. Livy's pulse stuttered before redoubling. She crossed the short distance between them and plucked the glass of brandy from his hand. She drank it down in one swallow and set the empty tumbler on the mantel beside the book.

Devere tugged her into his arms, his mouth coming down over hers, lips soft but powerfully insistent. He pushed her wrapper off her shoulders and she let it slide down off her arms and onto the floor. Her maid would be horrified at such casual abuse. Livy smiled at the thought and put her energy into returning Devere's kiss. What she was doing tonight would horrify Frith far more than the abuse of her wardrobe.

Devere's mouth slanted over hers and nipped along her jaw. His breath was hot on her, already damp on her skin. Livy fought with the frogs that held his dressing gown closed, her fingers stiff and clumsy.

His hand covered her breast, cupping it, weighing it, rolling the nipple between his thumb and forefinger. Livy's breath whooshed out in a gasp as she yanked the final closure free.

Her encroaching hands met an expanse of fine linen rather than the naked flesh she'd expected. There was something about the idea of a rake in a nightshirt that seemed absurd. Devere chuckled and shed his dressing gown before yanking his nightshirt over his head.

Livy took a step back and flicked an appreciative glace over him. She'd seen him naked at the pond, had covertly inspected every angle, trying to memorize the details. But this was different. He was hers.

He was a big man, but lean like a working animal. Livy ran a finger along the sweep of his collarbone and over his shoulder. He felt like warm stone. Unyielding. Candlelight painted shadows across his skin, the hollows of muscle and bone were starkly beautiful in a way she hadn't anticipated.

Deft fingers loosed the tie that gathered her night-gown at the throat, and he dragged it down, exposing her breasts. Livy's breath hitched as Devere tipped her into one of the large wingback chairs and sank down to his knees before her.

His mouth found her nipple and he sucked hard, teeth rough against her skin. His tongue flicked and circled. A jolt of pure pleasure shot from breast to groin, painful and exciting at the same time.

Her nightgown rose in a frothy wave as she spread her thighs so she could draw him in closer. She wrapped her hand about his rising shaft, and Devere tugged her to the edge of the seat. The dull ache of unfilled desire blos-somed into something far more acute.

Too impatient to go slowly, Livy slid the engorged head of his cock along her already slick folds, guiding him to where she wanted him. Devere paused, and Livy hooked a leg behind him, trapping him in place. She caught his earlobe between her teeth. "One of the few perquisites of my situation is that I'm not a virgin you have to go slowly with."

Devere's grip on her tightened as he thrust in. Livy gasped with pleasure as he filled her and dug her nails into his back. She'd forgot what it felt like, the momen-tarily alien sensation of her body stretching to accommo-date a man. And a cock was utterly different than a finger or two; there was something about it that made her feel complete in the moment.

Livy raised her other knee, and wrapped both legs around Devere as she arched to meet him. Her husband had been decorous, had handled her gently, almost with reverence, but he'd never once made her quake with need as she did now.

"I can't wait," she said against his neck, inhaling the scent of his skin, letting it flood over her and run through her like a drug. "Don't make me wait."

Devere gave a throaty chuckle that echoed through her as he shifted, deepening the angle of their joining. Livy sobbed into his shoulder.

"Stay with me," he said, his body driving into hers, each hard stroke pushing her closer to her climax. Her thighs began to quake and her toes tingled. Devere clapped his hand over her mouth at the first hint of a scream and then rode the flickering pulse of her release all the way down to his own. His head dropped into the hollow of her shoulder, and Livy hugged him. She could feel the faint throb of his cock inside her. Her body constricted in response, and Devere moaned into her neck, the sound vibrating through them both.

He lifted his head to kiss her. His tongue traced her lips and then pushed inside as he cupped her face with one hand. He glanced from her to the bed. "Give me a moment and we'll do that again."

~ CHAPTER 39 ~

A soft, insistent whine woke Margo before it was even light. Maldon. She slipped out of bed and padded across the room to let the dog in before he raised the entire house. She found herself smiling dumbly at the one-eyed beast's shaggy countenance, even as she shivered and shifted her weight from foot to foot on the cold wooden floor.

The hound's happy whine of greeting changed into a low growl as he pushed past her and stepped into the room. His shoulders bunched as he hackled and his growl erupted into a series of barks so loud Margo felt momentarily deafened.

"Maldon, no. There's nothing—" Her correction died in her throat as she saw the man standing behind one of the chairs near the fireplace. Fury swamped the flicker of panic as she recognized him.

"Call that damn thing off," Carlow shouted as Maldon continued to bark. The hound squared off between her and the intruder. The man kept the solid wingbacked chair between himself and the dog.

Margo backed slowly out of the room, the horrible

import hitting her just as the other guests appeared at her back, crowding into the corridor until it seemed like there must be dozens of them rather than only a handful.

Margo glanced from the bleary, startled face of Lord Hynde back to Carlow. She was going to be sick. "It would serve you right if Maldon ate you," she said, meaning every word. Not that it would do her any good. A mauling would simply add to the splendor of the gossip.

The circle of witnesses moved back as though she were a burning ember. She could see Rolly at the end of the corridor, just emerging from his room, still pulling on his dressing gown. A confused-looking Lady Olivia stood behind him. None of the other guests even noticed the real scandal taking place behind them. Everyone's attention was riveted to her own unfolding drama.

"Maldon, come!" Margo eased the door wider. The great hound still stood in the middle of the room, a growl like thunder emanating from its throat. She called the hound again, and it slunk over to join her in the hall, casting a warning eye back at Carlow as it did so.

"What's going on?" Roland said as he glanced into the room and Carlow emerged from behind the chair.

The murmur of conversation grew. Lady Olivia pushed her way forward. Would anyone but Margo register her tousled appearance? No, not with Carlow, equally tousled, standing in her room like an actor ready to make his debut.

"I can't seem to find my other slipper," Carlow said.

Rage whipped through Margo. Nothing she said or did would outweigh the simple fact of his presence. "I can only assume you left it in your room before invading mine," she said.

"Invading?" Carlow made a show of buttoning up his dressing gown and pushing back his hair. "You and I both know I was invited. How did you put it? *The tedium of country life is only surpassed by the tedium of the attentions of gentlemen who aspire to the squirearchy.* I think I have that right."

"You're a liar," Roland said as he put a steadying hand on her shoulder.

"Am I?" Carlow didn't even bother to look at her brother but kept his triumphant gaze locked with Margo's.

"You are," Margo said, refusing to flinch or back down. "And I'm fairly certain the earl will think so, too."

"What I think, Madame la comtesse, is that you're little better than a titled whore. And I think Arlington will realize that once he hears about last night. Can you even name all of your past lovers—"

Carlow's denouncement was cut off as her brother's fist sent him crashing to the floor. The dog leapt to its feet with a growl, clearly ready to join in, and Margo caught it by the collar and hauled it back. Maldon strained in her grip as Carlow scrambled up. He swiped at the blood trickling from his nose with the sleeve of his dressing gown.

"Say it again, Carlow," Roland said. Margo knew full well that her brother, much like Maldon, was more than prepared to tear Carlow limb from limb.

"Your sister's a whore. And it's bad enough that she's playing my cousin for a fool, but you're doing the same to Olivia. Did you know he has a mistress, Livy? She's blond like you. A timid little thing. So frightened of her own shadow she never leaves the house where he keeps her."

• • •

Livy felt the focus of the room shift from the comtesse to her. A gaggle of mostly elderly men, absent their wigs and wearing nothing but their nightshirts and the occasional banyan, all turned to goggle at her. She looked at Devere, who stood flexing his hand as if he'd like nothing better than to hit Henry again.

"He wouldn't." Her throat seemed to swell shut on the words. Devere wouldn't do that to her. He'd promised.

Henry gave a disparaging snort and dabbed at his still-bleeding nose. "Ask him why he couldn't accompany you to Holinshed. Go ahead. Ask. He and I both know why. Because he was too busy at number five Chapel Street. She must be quite something, eh, Devere?"

Devere's hands clenched into fists but he didn't say anything. Something like horror crashed through her. Her hands were icy cold, and her blood felt sluggish in her veins. This couldn't be happening.

"Say something," his sister said, her hands still locked on Maldon's collar even though the dog had stilled.

Devere glared at Henry and then turned his back on him. "Come downstairs and let me explain."

"Explain that you aren't keeping a woman in a house on Chapel Street? I don't see what would prevent you from doing that here and now." Devere was a masterful liar, but at the moment the ability seemed to have entirely deserted him. His expression was bleak as he glanced at their audience and then back to her.

"Livy?" His tone was almost desperate.

Livy nodded as she sucked in a shaky breath. He wasn't denying it because he couldn't. Several people, including Lord William, had hinted at just such a thing, but she'd brushed it aside as mere gossip. "I don't want an *excuse*. There should be no need for one." She took a step back from him, skirted around the knot of stupefied-looking men, and strode to her own bedroom door as quickly as she could.

How could everything have seemed perfect only a few minutes ago? She'd been tucked into his bed, putting off yet again the decision to return to her own room, too happy and content to force herself out of his arms. He'd said he loved her. He'd seduced her into loving him, just as he'd said he would.

Devere caught her as she was turning the knob. No one else had moved. They were all rooted in place like the chorus of a Greek tragedy. "She's not my mistress," he said, keeping his voice low.

"No? And Henry is lying about your sister seducing him as well? Look at them"—she pointed down the corridor to the men outside the comtesse's room—"not a one of them believes you. And why not? Because they all know you. Both of you."

Devere's brows drew down into a frown. "I thought you liked Margo?"

"So did I. And I thought you loved me, that you understood that I've had my fill of public humiliation. But I was clearly wrong." The lump in her throat was making it hard to breathe. She pushed open the door and stepped inside, turning to prevent Devere from following her.

"You've won your bet, so let's have an end to it. I love you, or I did last night, as fantastical as that seems at the moment. And you've certainly ensured my father won't try to force me back into society, so you've fulfilled your part of our bargain as well."

"Does it comfort you to know you've won yours too then?" he said as he rested his head against the door frame. He looked sick, his usually olive skin as pale as new plaster.

"Making you wish you were dead?" Livy said, a sudden spurt of anger causing tears to well up hotly behind her eyes. "Good. That makes two of us."

❧ CHAPTER 40 ❧

Olivia slammed the door shut, and Roland heard the sound of the lock being turned followed by what he was almost certain was a sob. Damnation. He was going to throttle Henry Carlow.

He spun about and marched back down the hall. The remaining guests were milling about outside Margo's room uncertainly. Not a one of them would look him in the eye. Margo was leaning against the wall, slowly stroking the ugly brute of a dog that had adopted her as mistress.

Carlow was nowhere to be seen.

"Whichever of you sees Carlow first can tell him, if I ever so much as set eyes on him, he's a dead man," Roland said as he strode toward them. He stopped beside his sister. "Get dressed, darling." He tucked a stray curl behind her ear and whisked away the start of a tear with his thumb. "We'll leave as soon as the coach can be made ready."

She nodded and slipped back into her room, taking the dog with her. Roland glared at his fellow guests until they broke apart and scattered toward their rooms. It wasn't their fault he and Margo had the reputations they did, but it was infuriating to have been stitched up by them when, for once, neither of them was actually guilty.

He was in the process of yanking on his coat when his valet appeared with a basin of hot water and a towel over one arm. The only sign that Martin had been hastily rousted from his bed was the burr of whiskers on his jaw and the slight disorder of his neckcloth. Martin moved at once to help him with the coat.

"The coach will be ready in a nonce, sir."

Roland allowed Martin to shave him and then haphazardly knotted his own neckcloth while Martin put up his shaving things. Roland paced across the room. Anger was giving way to something that left him feeling hollow. He didn't want to leave, though that was best for Margo, so he would. He wanted to track Carlow down and feed him to the ravens.

He pulled his purse from his coat pocket and handed Martin a wad of bills and coins. "Pay the servants their vails and bring the comtesse's maid and our baggage back to town."

His valet nodded and turned to pick up Roland's hat. He fidgeted with the cockade before handing it over along with a pair of gloves. When Roland stepped out of his room, there wasn't a soul to be seen. Good. There wasn't any chance of his being able to take leave of them with even common civility. He knocked on Margo's door, and it was opened by her furious-faced maid.

He stepped into the room, and Margo gave him a wavering smile. "Shall we shake the dirt of Norfolk from our heels?" she asked.

Roland held out his hand to her. The skin beneath her eyes looked bruised. She didn't deserve this. She was in Carlow's way, just as he was, and the man had quite masterfully disposed of them both. There had to be a way to turn the tables on him, but at the moment, Roland couldn't see it. He felt as though his brain had been addled. He couldn't seem to form a coherent thought that went beyond murdering Carlow.

There was no one but the butler downstairs to see them on their way. The man's face was carefully blank of all expression as he ushered them out of the house to their waiting carriage. The earl's one-eyed hound trailed along behind them, glancing from side to side as if he too was looking for something to slake his bloodlust on.

Roland glanced back at the house. There were curious faces in several windows, but not in Livy's. The curtains were drawn across them still, shutting the world out.

He handed Margo up into the coach, and the dog scrambled in after her. Roland didn't even bother to try and remove it.

"If his lordship wants the beast back, he can come and claim him himself," he told the two startled servants before climbing in and shutting the door with a snap.

The hound sat on the floor of the coach, pressing as close to Margo as it could, its massive head in her lap. Roland squeezed in beside her and tossed his hat onto the opposite seat. "Mamma is going to have fits when she sees your new pet."

Margo stroked the dog's head and it burrowed into her skirts. "I was thinking it's time to go home anyway."

"To Paris? What about Arlington?"

His sister shook her head, her lower lip caught between her teeth. "I'm sure I could convince the earl that Carlow is lying, but I don't see the point. Not when the scandal of his daughter's broken engagement would be hanging over us and you'd be barred from the house. As things stand, I have no desire to remain in London. And since you have no more reason to stay than I have, you can escort me home and spend a few months licking your wounds."

Roland draped an arm around Margo, and she settled into his side, her head propped on his shoulder. He hated to admit she was right, but she was. "I've my own reasons for needing to go to Paris," he said, "and your making the trip alleviates one of the major obstacles."

Margo shifted her head and glanced up at him. "Your supposed mistress?"

Roland nodded. Of course Margo could put two and two together and come up with the proper answer. "Miss Bence-Jones. She's engaged to John Blakely, but her brother's been trying to make her break things off since their father died. A few weeks ago the matter came to a head, and the girl fled the house."

"And you've been hiding her ever since?"

"Not just me, it's a conspiracy. Lord Leonidas isn't using his house at the moment so we've secreted her there. Carlow must have seen me delivering one of Blakely's letters."

"You're a fool, you know that, Rolly? A good-intentioned one, but a fool all the same."

Philip's first inkling that something was awry came when his daughter failed to appear as they'd arranged.

Though it wasn't unusual for a delay to be met on the road, and it was always possible that she'd stayed behind at Holinshed for one reason or another.

The realization that something was deeply wrong became full-blown when he attempted to pay a call on Margo later the next day and was informed by the Moubrays' butler that the comtesse had left for Paris that morning. Disquiet flared into anger. What the hell could have gone so wrong in a single night? It should have been impossible for Margo to leave him in such a fashion.

When he returned home, an ominously large stack of mail awaited him. The usual invitations and business correspondence were intermixed with three letters that looked to be of a more personal nature. One was clearly from his daughter. Another was from Henry. At the bottom of the stack was a letter sealed with a blob of plain blue wax. He didn't recognize the handwriting, but it was an elegant, clearly feminine hand. Margo.

Philip poured himself a glass of brandy. He had a feeling he was going to need the fortification. Whatever disaster had befallen them all, it was no doubt summed up inside those three sheets of paper.

Livy's missive was short and to the point. With no explanation at all, she stated that her engagement was at an end and made clear her intention to remain at Holinshed for the remainder of the Season. She was angry. He could see it in every hard stroke of her quill.

His heir's letter shed a bit more light on the situation. Philip crumpled the letter in one fist. He'd be more inclined to believe Margo had seduced Lord Hynde than Henry. She didn't even like Henry, and Hynde, for all that he was old enough to be her grandfather, was still spry and charming.

He turned the final letter slowly about on the surface of his desk, using two fingers to keep it in motion. He was oddly reluctant to open it. Would it be a collection of polite lies, or would it be filled with blunt truths that would leave him wishing for prevarications?

He cracked the wax with his thumb and spread the folded sheet of foolscap open. It began with *My dear Lord Arlington, I'm afraid I've stolen your dog and taken it to Paris. Please forgive me.*

He assumed she meant Maldon. He couldn't help but smile at the image of the comtesse and his giant one-eyed hound on the prowl through the streets and gardens of Paris. Was it an invitation for him to follow? It certainly felt like one.

Like his daughter, she danced around the events that had led to her decision. There was a passing mention of an unfortunate misunderstanding; her assurance that whatever was said, the gossip was unfounded; and then the letter ended with her begging to be remembered as his friend.

Philip picked at the wax seal with his thumbnail, shaving tiny bits off while he plotted. Livy had to be dealt with first. He drained his glass. The women in his life were going to drive him to an early grave.

❧ CHAPTER 41 ❧

Livy's coach reached the outskirts of London just on the edge of a storm. It was hard to imagine that only the day before it had been a glorious late-spring day. The formerly vivid blue sky was nothing but gray, roiling clouds that threatened rain at any moment.

She hadn't meant to leave Holinshed, but the more she'd thought about what had happened, the more she'd realized that she couldn't allow Henry to be the one to explain the events that had taken place to her father. There was no doubt that Henry would have reached town at least a day ahead of her, but she was praying he had been delayed in confronting the earl.

Though battered and bruised, Henry had been entirely too keen to demonstrate his support. There was something about his solicitude that made the hair on the back of her neck stand up. For all his solemn expressions and concerned looks, Henry was pleased with what had happened.

Livy had a sinking feeling that she'd made a mistake in

not hearing Devere out. Her damn temper. She'd let shock and an overwhelming sense of hurt outweigh her common sense. If nothing else, she could have broken things off quietly as she'd always intended to do.

When she reached her father's house in Mayfair, she discovered that the earl was out and not expected back even to dine. If the servants were surprised to see her, they hid it well. Livy hurriedly changed her dusty carriage gown and set out for the Moubrays' residence. She couldn't call on Devere, but she could call on the countess and the comtesse.

The square was full of nursery maids and children eking out a last bit of play before the clouds broke. A footman, with a pug straining on a long, leather lead, was leaning against the fence, clearly flirting with a maid in a striped red gown. She had a sturdy apron tied about her waist, which one small charge was clinging to. The first drops of rain began to fall, and the maid hurriedly scooped the child up.

Livy quickened her step. Devere had asked what it was she wanted, and there it was. Or at least there was a part of it. She wanted a quiet, normal life, perhaps with a child or two. It shouldn't have been too much to ask, though it felt as out of reach in that moment as it ever had.

She knocked at the Moubrays' front door and was admitted by a somewhat befuddled-looking butler. "Good afternoon, Emerson. Is the comtesse receiving?"

"The comtesse is not here."

"Lady Moubray?" Livy said hopefully.

Emerson nodded as though it pained him to admit it. "Her ladyship is in the drawing room." He crossed the marble hall and opened the door. The women inside went silent when she was announced. A teacup rattled loudly in its saucer, the sound sharp like the ringing of a small bell.

Livy glanced warily around the room. Just Lady Moubray, Lady Jersey, and Mrs. Verney. The countess blinked rapidly as Emerson shut the door behind her.

"I was hoping to speak with your daughter," Livy said into the awful silence. "But I hear she's out."

"Margaret has returned to Paris," Lady Moubray said, her brows pinched together with confusion and concern. "Roland went with her. Didn't your father tell you?"

Livy shook her head, tasting bile at the back of her throat. "I just returned to town myself. I haven't had a chance to see the earl yet. I was—I was hoping the comtesse might be able to clear something up for me for before I did."

"I'm sure you were," Mrs. Verney said a with hard stare. Obviously some version of events was already making the rounds, and just as obviously, Livy was not faring well in the telling.

"I apologize for disturbing you, my lady," Livy said. She turned to go, only to be caught by the countess in the hall.

Lady Moubray stopped her with a hand on her arm. "Neither of them will tell me what actually happened." The countess sounded bereft.

Livy's eyes burnt, tears threatening to spill over. She blinked them away. "My cousin happened, and I was too angry to think until it was too late."

The countess nodded, her powdered curls bouncing about her face. "Do you think"—she hesitated, as if afraid to ask—"do you think the earl might go after her?"

"I don't know," Livy said truthfully. "Do you think he should?"

The countess nodded again. "But tell him to go quickly. I know my daughter. It won't be long before she does something thoroughly outrageous, just to prove to the world that she's still whole. It looks like it's begun to rain in earnest, my dear. You'd best hurry home." The countess glanced about the hall. "Did you come without a footman?"

Livy nodded. There hadn't been one available, and she'd been in a hurry. It wasn't as if she really needed one to go a couple of streets in Mayfair. "Emerson," the countess said, clearly horrified. "Get one of the footmen to escort Lady Olivia home. And bring her an umbrella. She seems to have come away without one of those as well."

Emerson disappeared momentarily, returning with a large black umbrella in one hand and a liveried footman at his heels. Livy put up the hood of her cloak before stepping outside and allowing the footman to open the umbrella for her. With the umbrella clutched in both hands, she set off into the downpour.

At the end of the street, Livy glanced out from under the edge of the umbrella. The walk was nearly deserted, just a miserable-looking boy waiting to sweep the crossing and a gentleman in a leather greatcoat with his hat drawn down low to keep the rain off. She put the umbrella back at an angle to fend off the worst of it and stepped out into the street.

As the man in the greatcoat passed her, she felt something hit her side. It skittered along her stays and struck her hip sharply. The next blow took her hard in the ribs. The Moubrays' footman shouted and crashed into the man. Livy swung the umbrella. The spokes shattered, and the fabric tangled about the knife in the man's hand.

She yanked it free, and the knife went flying. The man in the greatcoat scrambled out from under the footman and went pelting off down the street.

The urchin was staring at her with wide, round eyes. "You're bleeding, miss."

Livy looked down. Her bodice and petticoat both had slowly growing red stains. The Moubray footman looked as shocked as the boy. "I'd best take you back to her ladyship."

"My house is closer," Livy said as her hands started to shake. "It's just around the corner."

The footman got his arm around her and, with a mumbled apology, half carried her to her father's front door. Parsons opened it, and they both stumbled into the hall, water pouring off them to pool on the marble floor.

~≈ CHAPTER 42 ≈~

Philip came home from a long, discordant day in the House of Lords to find his house in an uproar. "What do you mean Lady Olivia's been stabbed? By whom?"

His butler blanched. "We don't know, my lord. She's still with the doctor, and the Moubrays' footman was not very forthcoming on the matter. He said only that a gentleman in a greatcoat stepped out into the street and attacked Lady Olivia as he was escorting her home."

Philip didn't bother to ask why his daughter was being escorted by someone else's servant. He could easily guess, and it was pointless to remonstrate with her or Parsons now. Livy had never seen the sense in dragging a servant everywhere with her, even when she'd been a girl.

When he reached her bedroom, he found her draped in a sheet while her maid held a candle and Dr. Kingston carefully cleaned a long gash in her side. The doctor looked up as Philip entered the room.

"I've given her laudanum," the doctor said, before turning back to his work. "She's not seriously hurt, just a couple of scratches thanks to her stays, but if we don't get all the fabric out, the wounds will fester."

Philip rounded the bed and bent over her. Livy gritted her teeth as the doctor worked. Her eyes were cloudy with the drug, but she was clearly still conscious of what was going on around her. "Met a random madman in the street," she said. "It seems like there ought to be a nursery rhyme in there somewhere."

He nodded and brushed her hair back from her face before drawing a chair up and taking her hand. She squeezed it hard, flinching as the doctor smeared something all along the wound and began to bandage her up.

The doctor finished and waved Philip over to the basin where he began washing his hands. "As I said, not badly hurt. The wounds should scab over in a day or two, and if they don't become infected, they should heal cleanly. She's a lucky girl from what the footman described."

Philip nodded, and Kingston gathered his things and left. Livy's maid scooped up all the dirtied linens and remains of her gown and swept out of the room behind him.

"I needed to see Madame de Corbeville," his daughter said.

He turned to find Livy watching him with feverish eyes. "For which you'd need to go to Paris," he said as he reclaimed the chair beside her bed.

"I think you should, Papa."

"Go chasing after her, begging her to take me back?"

"Don't be flippant," she said drowsily, using one of her grandmother's favorite rejoinders. "You weren't actually engaged, so she can't take you back."

"I suppose not," he said with mock seriousness as he

tucked the sheet over her shoulder. "We can talk about it tomorrow." He stood up, snuffed out the candle, and walked to the door.

As he shut it behind him, Livy said, "Besides, she has your dog."

❧ CHAPTER 43 ❧

Livy forced her way out of bed in the morning, much to her maid's horror. After Frith changed her bandage, smearing the wound with more of the vile-smelling ointment the doctor had left behind, Livy put a pair of loosely laced half-stays on over her shift and went down to breakfast in her wrapper.

The earl looked every bit as horrified as Frith to see her up and about. "Your maid could have brought you breakfast," he said.

"Of course she could. And then you could have slipped out to attend today's session of the Lords, and I wouldn't have seen you again until tonight." She covered a slice of toast with ginger preserves and ate it greedily. She'd had nothing since a hurried luncheon at The Starry Plow the day before. She was surprised her stomach hadn't woken her with its growls.

"Did you already speak with the constable?" she asked.

"Yes, for all the good it did." The stiff snap of his newspaper told her how very upset he was.

"I was serious about Paris," she said, changing the subject as she reached for a second piece of toast.

Her father set the paper aside, filled a cup with coffee, and slid it across the table to her. He looked older than she remembered, like the light had gone out of him. Livy knew bone deep that his state wasn't due solely to her being attacked because she felt the same dead weight of soured love inside her own chest.

"I never doubted you were," he said.

Livy made a face at the coffee but drank it anyway. It was too much trouble to call for cocoa. "Just because I've no intention of marrying Devere doesn't mean you shouldn't marry his sister, Papa. In fact, I rather think you should."

"And what makes you think the comtesse has any desire to marry me?" He fiddled with his empty coffee cup, not meeting her eye as she studied him.

"I'm not blind," she said finally. "And I'm not selfish enough to want the both of you to be unhappy simply because there might be some initial awkwardness or gossip."

Her father refilled his cup. Dark brown liquid sloshed over the edge and down into the saucer. "Can't forgive him?"

Livy shook her head. "I think Henry was lying about the comtesse, but he wasn't lying about the woman Devere was keeping here in London."

Her father looked honestly startled. "Devere admitted to keeping a mistress?"

Livy shook her head again, not wanting to explain, even to him. The earl's expression hardened.

"I don't think I should go to Paris," he said.

Livy opened her mouth to protest, but he held up a
hand to silence her. He was making a mistake, and worst
of all, it was a mistake that meant Henry had won.

"I think *we* should go to Paris. You may not want to
listen to him, but Devere deserves a chance to explain
himself. And you owe it to yourself to listen, Livy."

Philip paused outside the imposing gate that led to the
courtyard of Margo's Paris home. It was two stories high,
with several doors of various sizes spaced across it. Her
mother had given him the directions easily enough when
he'd asked. All that was left to do was to actually see her.

The trip to Paris had proved entirely uneventful. There
was a short delay in Calais while they worked out the
details of their passports, and the roads were so rutted
and rough that he'd been worried Livy's wounds would
reopen, but now that they'd finally reached Paris, it all
seemed worth it.

He'd left Livy napping at their hotel. She still wasn't
entirely sure she wanted to see Devere, and he didn't want
to force the issue the moment they arrived.

The narrow, cobbled street was filled with carriages,
and the walk was equally clogged with people. Philip took
a deep breath and knocked on the smallest of the doors set
into the gate. After a moment, the sound of the lock being
turned became evident and then the door swung inward.

Philip held out his card. "Is Madame de Corbeville at
home?" he asked in French.

The liveried footman waved him inside. "I shall go
and see, monsieur. Beware the dog."

Philip chuckled. He might be the only man on earth

who didn't need to beware of Margo's new pet. While he stood waiting, he saw Devere pass through the inner courtyard. When Devere spotted him, he stopped and turned to come and greet him.

"We weren't expecting to see you, my lord."

"And yet, here I am," Philip said.

Devere eyed him warily. "Come in and have a drink. Margo's in the bath, but I'm sure she'll want to see you."

"I'd rather bribe you to tell me exactly which room she's in and then to leave the house."

"I'm not sure Margo would take that very well."

"I'm sure she'll take it about as well as Livy will your showing up at the Hôtel Maubourg and letting yourself into room ten." He fished about in his pocket for the key to their suite of rooms and held it out. It wasn't a large hotel, but he never stayed anywhere else when he came to Paris. The proprietor had been only too happy to accommodate him when they'd arrived that morning, sending away another party with an excuse about a misunderstanding of dates.

Devere reached for the key, and Philip pulled it back, wrapping his hand securely around it. He wanted those directions first.

"Through the main door, up the stairs, third door on the left," Devere said, a conspiratorial grin spreading across his face. "Don't blame me if she sets the dog on you, my lord."

Philip smiled back at him and tossed him the key.

Roland paused long enough to direct the servants to stay out of the earl's way before pulling on his greatcoat and hat. He couldn't do much else to smooth the way for Arlington, but at least the man would have an undisturbed reunion.

At first, he thought Paxton might bridle when told to make herself scarce, but she merely nodded and headed back toward the kitchens with her armful of towels. Margo's footmen were gathered in a tight knot in the courtyard. All three of them watched him as he crossed the yard. He flipped them a silver *écu* and told them to go and get a drink.

The hotel the earl had named was within easy walking distance. Roland ploughed his way through the afternoon crowds, earning dirty looks and rude hand gestures with nearly every step. Once inside, no one moved to stop his progress. The proprietor barely even glanced his way as Roland strode past him and disappeared up the stairs.

He let himself into the left-hand suite as the earl had directed. Frith gave him a startled look before shutting the lid on Livy's trunk with an audible thump, pointing to the adjoining door and whisking herself out of the room.

Roland smiled to himself. He conspired in Margo's best interest, and Livy's father and maid conspired in hers. Lord Arlington must believe he had at least some chance of bringing Livy round or he would never have brought her to Paris, let alone set him on her like a hound loosed to hunt.

He cracked open the door. No sign of her. Stepping into the room, Roland could just make out that there was someone in the bed. He toed off his shoes and quietly crossed the room. He should wake her, but he wasn't going to. If he woke her up, she might tell him to leave.

If he just waited, at least he'd have the time between now and then.

She was fully clothed except for her shoes. Her feet looked small and oddly vulnerable in nothing but stockings. The clocks disappeared under the hem of her skirt, their points seeming to urge him to follow.

He shrugged out of his greatcoat and the silk one he wore beneath it and climbed carefully into the bed in his shirtsleeves. Livy mumbled in her sleep and fit herself to him as though his presence were the most natural thing in the world.

Roland wrapped an arm around her waist and pushed his nose into her hair, content to simply lie beside her and breathe in the scent of warm skin and lemon.

❧ CHAPTER 44 ❧

Livy came awake with a start. There was a large, masculine arm draped over her and a hand she recognized cupping her breast as though it belonged there. She hadn't meant to fall asleep in the first place, and she certainly hadn't thought to wake up with Devere curled around her.

Where was her father? Where was Frith?

Devere kissed the back of her neck, and Livy rolled hastily away. She sat up carefully, her breath hissing out of her. Her side always seemed to stiffen up when she slept.

"I suppose sending you here was my father's way of forcing me to talk to you." Livy slid out of the bed and opened the doors that led onto a small Juliet balcony that overlooked the street. She needed air. And space between them in which to think.

The coverlet rustled as he climbed out of the bed, and the floors creaked as he followed her. Livy turned to watch him as he approached, but she stayed outside where she could breathe. The sun was hot on her shoulders. Below her, she could hear the rumble of the city, similar to London, but somehow softer.

"She really wasn't—isn't—my mistress." Roland stood just in front of her, leaning one shoulder against the doorway. "If you want to hear it from her own lips, I can take you to the ambassador's house right now."

"You brought her to Paris with you?" The idea stung. It was a poor way to begin an explanation, let alone an apology.

Devere paused, clearly considering his words. He took a deep breath and let it out slowly. "Along with my sister as chaperone, yes. Miss Bence-Jones, now Mrs. John Blakely, is the woman Carlow saw. She came of age two days ago and was married out of His Grace's private chapel on the very same day."

Livy felt the knot in her chest loosen so fast her knees wobbled. There was no denying that he was telling the truth. He could hardly have made up so fantastical a story, especially not when he offered his sister and the ambassador as witnesses.

She leaned against the low railing for support. Devere didn't move. "You should have told me."

He blew out a long breath. "It wasn't my secret to tell, but if the need should ever arise again, I promise to tell you."

"That's the best you can do?"

"I'm afraid so."

Livy pushed away from the railing and stepped up to put her hand on his chest. Her fingers curled over the edge of his waistcoat of their own accord. "I think you should promise that the need *will* never arise again. Married

gentlemen have no business being involved in such peril-
ous subterfuges. Let it fall to Thane, or Reeves, or one of
your other friends who has no wife to embarrass or upset."

"Shall we make it part of the vows?" One arm slipped
around her waist. "Do you hereby solemnly swear to give
all potentially embarrassing schemes the go-by?" Livy
narrowed her eyes at him, and Devere grinned, wholly
unrepentant. "So I'm forgiven?" he said.

Livy's hand tightened on his waistcoat. "You're forgiven if I am."

He bent his head and kissed her, lips coaxing her to
respond. The door rattled behind them, and he dropped a
last, swift kiss on the tip of her nose. Livy peeked around
Devere's shoulder, expecting to see her father. Her greeting died on her lips as Henry strode into the room, his
boots dusty, as though he'd just alighted from a long trip.

Livy's skin flushed with anger at the sight of him.
Her throat tightened, and a sharp ache built inside her
chest. She opened her mouth to command him to leave,
but was cut off by his blustery, "What the hell is *he* doing
here?"

Devere, clearly the "he" in question, turned slowly
about, and put one arm out to keep her on the balcony. "I
could ask the same of you, Carlow. Does Lord Arlington
have any idea you're in Paris?"

"Not as yet. I was coming to try and reason with him."

"Reason with him?" Livy said. "I think we're well
beyond that."

Henry reached into his pocket and pulled out a letter.
"You don't think I know that?" He waved the crumpled
paper at her. "Have you seen this? Disinherited. Nothing

but the title when he dies. And not even that if he manages to get himself an heir on his new wife." The word *wife* came out as though it were the most vile word in the English language.

Devere took a menacing step forward, and Livy went with him, clinging to the back of his waistcoat. Henry's tirade continued, his voice rising until he was shouting. "He didn't even write me himself. He had his damn solicitor do it. Sent it to me with a stack of banknotes and his best wishes for a safe journey back to Italy. I'm not some whore he can give her *congé*. I'm his heir."

Henry paused for a breath. The letter crackled in his fist. "I never meant for you to be hurt," Henry said, his tone suddenly cajoling. "Lewis wasn't supposed to touch you. You understand, though, don't you, Livy? I have to defend what's mine."

Livy suddenly understood all too well. She was going to be sick in a moment. Her stomach churned and she swallowed hard. Her jumps felt as tight as a full set of stays.

"What the hell is he talking about?" Devere looked like Hephaestus himself, his brows drawn down into a tight solid line across the bridge of his nose.

"Oh, Henry." Livy shook her head slowly as she stared at him. "You should go now. Before my father gets back and finds you here."

"I can't," Henry said, his eyes wild and his jaw tight. "I have to make him understand. He can't do this to me."

"Livy," Devere said, the one word drowning out Henry, cutting him off. "What does your cousin mean, *you* were never supposed to be hurt?"

• • •

Roland felt Livy's hands loosen their grip on his waist-coat. She smoothed them across his back until they rested at his waist, then dropped her head, letting it press against his shoulder blade. Her cousin paced, as though tightly enclosed, his agitation palpable.

"He means," Livy said finally, her voice so soft the words were barely discernible, "that the man who attacked me last week in London was after your sister. But the comtesse had already left for Paris, only Henry didn't know that."

Roland's curse echoed through the room. Carlow stopped in his tracks, his shoulders hunching as if waiting for a blow. With a last glance at Livy, the man turned and raced for the door. Roland lunged after him, seized him by the trailing hem of his coat, and hauled him back.

The sound of threads popping was loud and distinct as Henry's coat split up the back. Roland heaved again, yanking Carlow off his feet, and sending him flailing to the floor. A spur sliced across Roland's leg, a bright burst of pain that colored his vision red.

Carlow scrambled to his feet, backing away. "It's not my fault."

"Sending someone after my sister isn't your fault?" Roland circled, putting himself between Carlow and door. Livy was clinging to one of the great carved legs of the bed, her face white. Roland forced himself to breathe. Killing Carlow would only make things worse, and he was angry enough to beat him bloody. "Whose fault is it? Mine?"

"Yes, if you like," Carlow said as he bumped up against

the carved caryatid that supported the mantel. His hand closed over the fire poker and his lips curled into a ghost of a smile. "It was you who introduced them after all, so you're as much to blame for my predicament as anyone."

"You should put that down, Carlow," Roland said. Though he sincerely hoped that the man didn't.

Livy's sharp intake of breath caused her cousin to flinch. He glanced past Roland, gaze fastening on Livy, and his face hardened. Carlow flexed his arm, testing the weight of the poker. Without a word, he leapt forward like a fencer, swinging the poker in a high arc.

Roland ducked and raised one arm to block the blow. The heavy length of iron caught him hard across the forearm, pain radiating down into the bone. Roland grabbed hold of the poker with his other hand, twisted aside, and yanked it out of Carlow's grip.

Livy dashed across the room, a flash of white and gold at the edge of Roland's vision. She flung open the door, screaming for help. "*Au secours! Au secours!*"

Carlow's expression changed to pure panic, and he fought to regain the poker, fingers digging into Roland's flesh, spittle flying as he cursed Roland and Livy both. They slid across the floor, the leather soles of their shoes offering no traction on the polished wood. Roland dropped the poker and spun away, striking Carlow hard in the face with his fist as he did so.

Carlow fell back a step, wiping blood from his mouth with the back of his hand.

The distinct rumble of running feet sounded through the outer room. Livy stormed toward them, hair flying, her father's walking stick raised like a cricket bat. Roland waved her back. He didn't want her anywhere near her cousin. Not even in the guise of avenging angel.

The only weapon at hand was a small gilt chair. A fantasy suited only for a lady's boudoir. Roland caught it one-handed and, turning with his full weight behind it, hit Carlow broadside. The chair splintered into pieces with a thunderous crack and Carlow collapsed onto the floor in a heap.

Roland brought his foot down on the man's wrist, pinning it. When Carlow's hand went limp, Roland kicked the poker away from him. It skittered across the room and disappeared under the bed. Livy's cousin moaned and covered his head with his free arm.

The room was suddenly overflowing with the hotel's staff and the earl's own servants, everyone looking somewhat stunned by the tableau of destruction before them. Nearly every bit of furniture except the bed had been overturned. The mantel ornaments lay smashed on the hearth, nothing but tiny bits of broken porcelain and scattered, trampled flowers.

"Are you all right?" Livy set her father's walking stick aside. She tugged her fichu free and pressed it to his cheek to stanch the blood he could feel dripping down his face. There was more blood oozing down his leg from where Henry had caught him with his spur and a nasty red stain was growing beneath the large rent in his shirt sleeve.

"What on earth are we going to tell them?" Livy glanced over her shoulder at the ever-growing cadre of people flowing into the room.

"As little as possible," Roland said, pushing her hand gently aside. "Unless you want to see Carlow hang."

Livy glanced at her cousin and drew a shaky, uneven breath. "What I want is to never see Henry again."

Roland nodded and firmly escorted their audience out of the suite. He sent Livy out to the sitting room while he and Lord Arlington's valet attempted to get her cousin back on his feet. Roland righted one of the wingback chairs and together they tipped a groaning Carlow into it.

Raised voices from the antechamber made it clear that the hotel's owner was incensed about the damages. Roland ground his teeth.

"Go and see if you can calm the proprietor," Roland said to the earl's man. "The last thing we need is someone summoning the *maréchaussée*." The man nodded, looking relieved, and left the room.

Carlow moaned again and opened his eyes. He put one hand up to grip his head as though he were checking to see that it was still whole. Roland glared and considered his options. The French constabulary weren't likely to concern themselves with a brawl between two Englishmen, at least not so long as the hotel's owner was compensated. The real concern was what to do with Carlow himself. Pitching him over the balcony was probably not the best plan, though it held an appeal Roland couldn't deny.

Roland leaned against the mantel, the shattered remains of a vase crackled underfoot. "I want to make one thing perfectly clear." Carlow looked up, his eyes bleary. "You'd better hope that nothing *ever* happens to my sister or to Livy. Because if anything unfortunate does befall them— a violent footpad, a dangerous highwayman, a deadly house breaker—I'll see that you're held responsible."

Carlow sat up a bit straighter and pushed his hair back from his face. His split lip was already starting to swell. "You and I both know that there's no way you can prove I did anything."

"Prove? No. A failing of our system of justice, to be sure. But you needn't concern yourself with what I can prove, because believe me, I won't. I'll kill you myself if you leave me no other option. As for today, I'd advise you to run for Italy as quickly as you can, and I'd recommend you stay there, for you won't find yourself welcome in England ever again."

❦ CHAPTER 45 ❦

Roland sat still while Livy dabbed at the cut on his cheek with a salve her maid swore by. It smelled like turpentine and she knew from personal experience that it stung like fire. She clucked her tongue as he wrinkled his nose. "I don't think it needs a plaster," she said, standing back to survey him. "But you won't be the handsomest man in Paris for a good while."

He rolled his eyes at her and stood up. "I doubt I was the handsomest man in Paris before Carlow slashed my cheek open."

Livy bit her lip and raised her brows provokingly. Roland grinned back at her. He still looked like a pirate after a battle, for all that he'd changed out of his torn and bloody clothing and tamed his hair. She ran a finger over the scrape on his chest that was already blooming into an ugly bruise. Roland caught her hand and brought it to his mouth. He kissed her palm and she smoothed her thumb across his cheek.

When he let her hand go, Livy sighed and set the salve

container back into the traveling medicine chest. It was simply impossible that the desperate scoundrel Henry had become was also the beloved cousin she'd known her entire life. Her head ached from trying to make sense of the day.

The earl's valet had fetched Lord Arlington back to the hotel as quickly as he could, but Roland had already seen Henry off the property with his tail between his legs. Once Livy's father had finished swearing a blue streak, he had summarily packed both Roland and Livy off to Margo's house, leaving the proprietor of the Hôtel Maubourg to sift through the rubble and prepare an accounting of the damages.

Dusk was setting in as Livy shut the lid on the medicine chest and Roland pulled his dressing gown on. He hissed as it slid over his bandaged biceps. That ragged tear in his flesh had required a plaster, as had the one on his leg. While Livy was helping him with the closures, one of the comtesse's maids appeared to light the candles. The girl glanced at them a curiously, but didn't linger.

"Papa is in a rage," Livy said. She dropped her head onto his shoulder, rubbing her cheek against the heavy silk.

"With me?" Roland said, sounding surprised.

Livy raised her head and met his gaze. His eyes were black in the gathering dark. "You've deprived him of his true target," she said. "He wasn't at all happy with your solution. He's still mulling over pursuing Henry to Italy, though I hope you'll convince him to let things be."

"If that's how your father chooses to spend his honeymoon, that's his business." Roland twisted one of Livy's curls around his finger. "But I expect Margo will talk him out of it."

Livy turned her head and her curl spiraled off his finger. "Just take me home," she said with shiver. "Tomorrow wouldn't be soon enough for me, but I suppose your sister will need time to settle her affairs here before we can return to England."

Roland bent his head to capture her mouth. Livy pressed herself tightly against his side, burrowing into him as though the night were freezing cold. "We could have the duke's chaplain marry us tomorrow," he said, "and then I could carry you home with perfect propriety, regardless of what Margo and your father might have planned for themselves."

Livy blinked, trying to make sense of what he'd just said. "We could, couldn't we? Though I shudder to think what your mother will say..." Her voice trailed off.

Roland smiled and kissed her again. "Leave my mother to me."

❧ EPILOGUE ❧

Holinshed, October 1789

From the battlements, Livy had a clear view of the chaos that had overtaken the great lawn within the walls of Holinshed Castle. She supposed she should feel guilty for stealing a quiet moment away from the tumult, but she couldn't seem to summon up even a smidgin of remorse.

Two sides of the perimeter were lined with large white tents, adding to the decidedly medieval air of the courtyard. All they needed were pennants to complete the effect, and perhaps a rack for jousting poles and armor. With the addition of the Devere siblings' friends and family to the guest list, there was simply no other way to house the number of people who now flocked to the hunt.

The lawn itself was awash in children and puppies and harried-looking nurses. Boys in nankeen suits whizzed across the grass, trailed by younger children of both sexes in colorful gowns and the occasional pudding cap. It was something Livy had never pictured, certainly not at Holinshed. That her father would be at the center of it all, laughing while digging his twins out from beneath a wriggling mass of ten-week-old hounds seemed odder yet. The eldest boy grimaced at their father and set off running to catch up with the older children as soon as the earl set him back on his feet.

Livy smiled to herself and leaned back against the hard stone of the embattlement. Stephen, Lord Errol, not only had his mother's coloring, but her temperament. No need to worry that Henry, or anyone else, would ever take advantage of the boy. And there was very little need for her to worry that Henry would ever inherit, as Stephen and his twin brother were both hearty and hale.

Under one of the giant oaks, she could see Dominic de Moulines demonstrating a fencing maneuver while two of the older boys looked on with rapt attention, their own blunted foils dangling from their hands. Holinshed's annual stag hunt had transformed over the past several years from a sennight of gentlemen sleeping in every nook and cranny of the house into a whirlwind of pique-niques, balls, several hunts, and many days of shooting.

This year, quite suddenly it seemed, there were children everywhere. It was as though the nursery had simply disgorged them all at once. Even Roland's friend Sandison had been convinced to join them, after Livy had made an explicit point of assuring her former brother-in-law that they were more than welcome. Sandison's pale head among the crowd might bring up unwelcome memories of her first marriage, but the sting had gone out of them long ago.

Her own son, Edmund, six months younger than his

uncles, had just been released from the constraints of leading strings. From her position atop the wall, she could see him, with one undoubtedly grubby hand clutching tight to the skirts of his father's coat. Roland spotted her and threw her a casual salute. One of the pups frolicked in a circle about Roland and Edmund. It leapt up onto Roland, and he knelt down to scratch its head.

The door to The Earl's Tower creaked softly, jerking Livy's attention away from the party on the lawn. Margo smiled at her conspiratorially.

"When I saw you up here, I knew you had made a very wise decision to escape," the countess said as she adjusted the voluminous cap she wore perched upon her curls. Margo shielded her eyes with one hand as she studied the hive of activity taking place down on the lawn. "Your poor father. Do you think he had any idea what he was letting himself in for when he welcomed Rolly and me into the family?"

"You, yes," Livy said with a laugh, "but no one is prepared for Roland."

Margo cocked her head. "Isn't that the truth," she said, her smile widening. "And what a marvelous truth it is."

London's most sensual former courtesan, Viola Whedon, is incapable of being seduced—she does the seducing. Until she meets Leonidas Vaughn...

Please turn this page for an excerpt from

Ripe for Pleasure.

❧ CHAPTER 1 ❧

London, May 1783

There was someone in her room.

The floorboards creaked, the wood protesting in its shrill way. Muffled footsteps sounded across the room, the tread far too heavy to be that of her maid. Viola Whedon froze beneath the covers, holding her breath. A faint line of candlelight licked through a crack in the bed curtains. Her heartbeat surged in time with the ticking of the mantel clock, a thready, sickeningly fast vibrato.

"It's got to be here." A man's voice, thick, angry, and entirely unknown to her.

"May'hap we missed it in the last room?" Another man, no more familiar than the first.

Viola carefully folded the covers back, the slight rustle of feathers and linen as loud as the clatter of iron-shod hooves on cobbles to her ears. She peered carefully out, not disturbing the curtains. Two men stood by the mantel, both squat and solid. The kind of men one passed near the docks or saw emerging from the slum of Seven Dials.

Just the sort of ruffians she'd have expected Sir Hugo to hire. They'd had such an enormous row when Sir Hugo discovered that he was to be included in the second volume of her memoir. It wouldn't surprise her at all if he were to attempt to steal. Or perhaps one of her other former lovers had hired them? Several who had refused to buy their way out of her memoir had made threats about taking more drastic actions to prevent publication. Despite the warm May night, Viola shivered. Did they know she was here? That this was her room?

One of the men held a candle while the other explored the mantel, clumsy fingers roughly caressing the wood. He made a disgusted sound in the back of his throat and spat. Viola clenched her jaw, revulsion pulsing through her. If only she were the heroine of a novel with a pistol under her pillow... If only she weren't alone in her bed.

Whoever had hired them, they weren't going to find her manuscript—not where she'd hidden it—and she wasn't going to simply wait for them to beat its location out of her. She needed the money that the manuscript would bring. Couldn't live without it, in fact, thanks in no small part to Sir Hugo. And she planned on living to spend that money as extravagantly as possible.

Viola took a deep breath, the familiar scent of her perfume and hair powder and crisp, clean linen not at all comforting, and steeled herself for a mad dash across the room. She was closer to the door than they were, and she had surprise on her side, because they'd left the door wide open.

She slid her feet over the side of the bed, eased the curtain back, and sprinted for the door. A startled oath burst from both men. Within seconds, they were pounding down the corridor after her, heels loud upon the uncarpeted floors, clearly not afraid to raise the whole house. One of them caught her hair and pulled, hard. She yanked her head free, vision blurring as she lost a chunk of hair.

Viola swung around the corner and half fell down the stairs, bouncing off the wall at the landing and skidding down the last flight, clutching at the banister to keep from falling. Her only footman lay facedown on the floor in the entry hall.

Viola vaulted over him. Her hands shook as she fought with the latch and wrenched the front door open. Please let there be someone on the street. Please.

One of her pursuers grabbed hold of her nightgown; threads popped and the gossamer nettle fabric tore. Viola screamed and struck him in the face with her elbow. He went staggering back, cursing. Warm air rushed over her as she ran down the front steps, searching the street for any sign of life, for any chance of rescue.

His cousin was a fool.

Leonidas Vaughn ran his fingers lightly over the cold hilt of his sword as two lumbering shapes slipped over the gate and into the small garden of number twelve Chapel Street. A horse blew its breath loudly through its nose in the stable behind him. A cat slunk by and disappeared into the dark recesses of the mews.

It was so like Charles to make a brash, frontal assault when the situation plainly called for subterfuge. For subtlety. For seduction. But nothing he'd said had changed his cousin's mind. Charles saw only what he wanted to see: a fortune waiting to be claimed.

It had been only a few months since they'd buried their grandfather. A bare week since they'd marveled at the cache of letters discovered among the mountains of papers at Leo's newly inherited estate. And in the days since Leo had followed his cousin back to town, Charles had already set the wheels of the hunt in motion...just as Leo had known he would. The fevered gleam in Charles's eyes had been all too clear as letter after letter revealed the details of the King of France's attempt to support Bonnie Prince Charlie's bid for the English throne.

They'd always dismissed their grandfather's tales of hidden treasure and tragedy as the stuff of legends, no different from the stories of Shellycoats and Kelpies Leo's mother had told them when they were boys. But the tragedy of Charles's family was real enough, and it seemed the treasure was, too. The small packet of treasonous letters left no other conclusion. Though the assumption that it was still waiting to be found—like a princess in a tower waiting for the first kiss of love—was questionable.

True or not, two villains from the stews weren't going to find it. But their intrusion would give him the opening that he needed, a chance to make the lady of the house beholden to him. And all he'd had to do to earn that opportunity was spend a few nights lurking outside her house waiting for his cousin to strike.

The night watchman had just turned the corner, his halloa of "all's well" echoing back faintly. Leo smiled into the dark. Any minute hell would break loose in number twelve. All he had to do was wait. Charles's men would deliver Mrs. Whedon directly into his hands.

A scream rent the humid darkness, bringing every detail sharply into focus as his pulse raced to meet it. A woman in nothing but her nightclothes erupted from the house. Her hair flamed in the lamplight as though it were afire, red-gold curls tumbling down to her hips. Mrs. Whedon. With that hair, it could be no other. Not a maid or a housekeeper but the lady herself. His luck was in.

Her eyes met his, and the night seemed to stretch. He could see terror there, a layer of anger below it, all the more intense for its impotence. Curses raced after her, low and guttural, intermixed with the sound of heavy, booted feet coming down a flight of stairs.

Leo shot out one hand and caught a flailing wrist, hauled her around, and held her fast. A scent that was pure summer—grass on a warm day, flowers drowsing in their beds—washed over him.

"Men. In my house." Her words were clipped, laced with fury. Her hand trembled, and she balled it into a fist, twisting in an attempt to free herself.

Leo thrust her behind him as a man in a dark coat came flying down the steps, a knife clutched in one hand. Leo drew his sword, using his left hand to hold Viola in place. It was only a dress sword, and though razor sharp, the rippled facets of the pastes covering the hilt were less than reassuring in the moment. Mrs. Whedon clutched the back of his coat, hampering him. A breath shuttered out of her, and her hand tightened, pulling him back.

"Where is it, bitch—" The man choked off as he hit the walk and his gaze locked on Leo's sword. He fell back a step, clearly assessing things, eyes darting about the empty street.

Leo shifted his stance, leveling his blade. "Wake the neighbors," he said over his shoulder.

His coat swung free. A flash of white and gold moved past the edge of his vision. Thank God. Mrs. Whedon wasn't famous for doing as she was told, but then what woman was? An unholy pounding resounded down the street as she beat against her neighbor's door, marking time as the seconds ticked by.

His cousin's gutter rat stared him down. The man's head sat upon his shoulders like a rock set on a stump. His jaw was heavy and his mouth hung open as though it were too small to contain his tongue. Not large enough to be a prizefighter, he had a menacing air all the same. A mad butcher's dog on the loose, capable of violence far in excess of his size. He hefted the blade, shifted his weight. Then with almost lazy disinterest, he thrust his knife into his boot and sauntered away, whistling. He turned into the entry of the mews down the block, nothing but the sharp notes of his ditty marking his presence, until that too dissipated into the gloom.

Leo glanced back over his shoulder. His quarry stood on her neighbor's porch, watching him. His hand shook as the rush of confrontation left him. He lowered his sword to hide it. He couldn't afford even the slightest sign of weakness. Not now. Not when Mrs. Whedon stood not four feet away.

"The knocker's off the door," she said matter-of-factly, one pale hand clutching the torn neckline of her gown. "No help there."

"Finally drive one of your protectors to murder, ma'am?"

A small smile curled the corner of her mouth as she descended the stairs, one slow, deliberate step at a time. Naked feet appeared and disappeared below her hem. Her toes gripped the ground. Her arches flexed, slim ankle-bones leading up to a flash of calf with every step. Her wisp of a gown slid from her grip, exposing one pale shoulder and a great deal of pale décolletage.

A deliberate maneuver. It could be nothing else. Like all women who rose to the top of their particular trade, Mrs. Whedon was a consummate performer. She had to be. Even under circumstances such as these. Gone was the fleeing victim, replaced by a feral Venus. Leo swallowed hard, wanting to touch, to reach out and grab. To possess that startling beauty, if only for a moment.

What man wouldn't?

"Possibly, my lord." Her reply jerked his attention away from her breasts. He'd been reduced to staring like a green boy by that damn wisp of a nightgown. "There were two of them, by the way." Her voice dropped, becoming an intimate, throaty entreaty of its own. "Intruders I mean, not protectors."

Leo smiled in appreciation. She'd certainly had more than two protectors. And based on that "my lord," she clearly knew exactly who he was, though their paths had never formally crossed. Paying for a bedmate was both repugnant and utterly unnecessary when the world was brimming with willing widows and unsatisfied wives. Besides, younger son that he was, he didn't command anywhere near the kind of fortune it took to secure a highflier like the one standing before him, even had he desired to do so.

A rivulet of sweat slid down his spine, like the ghostly touch of a past lover. He forced himself to ignore it, shifting his attention instead to the house. Armed intruders were far safer opponents than Mrs. Whedon. Especially when she was only a thin layer of cloth away from being naked. Even in the dim light, he could clearly make out the teasing circles of her nipples and the shadow at the apex of her thighs.

Lust grabbed disdain by the throat and shoved it down. Leo held his breath for a moment, searching for the control that seemed to have deserted him. Yes, he wanted her. And he meant to have her before all this was done. It was integral to the entire plan. But it would be on his terms, not because he allowed himself to be swept up in the drama and illusion of this not-so-chance rescue. And certainly not because he'd paid whatever price she might have in mind.

Leo turned away from her and strode into her house, making a vague gesture for her to follow. Inside, hysterical sobs greeted him. Two maids sat at the bottom of the stairs in a sea of flannel wrappers. A much older, harassed-looking housekeeper stood over them, nightcap askew, a large kitchen knife clutched in her hand.

One of the maids looked up and hiccupped, her face red in the candlelight. "He's dead. We came down when we heard you scream and found Ned like–like..."

Mrs. Whedon pushed past him, her hand perfectly steady as she shoved him aside. "Is there anyone else in the house, Nance? Did you see another man?" The sobbing girl shook her head from side to side, her hand covering her mouth.

"Back door was open though, ma'am," the housekeeper said.

"Then it's likely your other intruder has also left the premises." All four women turned to look at him as though he'd sprung from the ground like a fairy toadstool. The little maid sucked back another hiccup.

He picked up one of the candles and set his foot on the first tread of the staircase. "Stay here while I check the house. No, one of you had best wait out on the steps for the nightwatch."

The housekeeper nodded her grizzled head and turned toward the door. Leo put her, the sobbing maid, and the dazzling Mrs. Whedon firmly out of his mind as he crept up the stairs.

The house was utterly quiet. Soft, dark room after soft, dark room greeted him. The mantels had been swept clean, pictures ripped from the walls. A clumsy attempt to be sure. The treasure had to be better hidden than that. A porcelain figurine lay smashed on the floor of what appeared to be the only occupied room—Mrs. Whedon's, judging by the faint hint of *Eau de Cologne* that permeated the space.

Leo set the candle down and sheathed his sword. The men were gone, and his cousin had never been inside the house in the first place. A personal assault wasn't at all Charles's style. There was no point in roaming about armed like a buccaneer on the deck of a ship.

Her room was surprisingly simple. Plainer, in fact, than his own. It was hardly the lair of a woman famed for wanton indulgence.

No paintings or prints adorned the walls. The curtains surrounding the bed were a deep, solid blue. No embroidery to enliven them. No trim to soften them. The bed-clothes spilling from between them were nothing but crisp, white linen. No silver brush sat atop the dressing table. No profusion of scent bottles lay scattered atop its surface. Just a few serviceable dishes and boxes, such as any woman might have for her powder and patches and pins. In fact, the only decoration appeared to be a mirror, a bit tarnished about the rim, and the smashed figurine.

Leo crouched down and scooped up a few of the larger, opalescent shards. Two legs ending in cloven hooves. A delicate head, ears pricked. A white deer. A symbol of good fortune in Scotland. A sign to the knights of old that it was time to begin a quest. A creature straight out of legend. Something not unlike Mrs. Whedon herself.

One of the Second Sons is after an

heiress's heart...

Her brothers are after *him*.

Please turn this page for an

excerpt from

Ripe for Scandal.

❧ CHAPTER 1 ❧

London, October 1784

He had the saddest eyebrows in the world.

They were straight and well defined, but they dipped from the center downward to their end, leaving him with a melancholy expression that didn't entirely dissipate even when he smiled. Every time Lady Boudicea Vaughn saw him, she found herself wanting to cup his cheeks, smooth those brows with her thumbs, and kiss away whatever it was that haunted him.

Not that he'd ever noticed...

Gareth Sandison, second son of the Earl of Roxwell, still thought of her as his friend Leonidas's scrubby little sister. He treated her more as a boy than a woman, when he bothered to acknowledge her existence at all. Mostly he seemed to do his best to avoid her.

As the Season progressed, Lady Boudicea had found herself missing his taunts. Missing his scathing wit and withering set-downs. Fighting with Sandison was far more invigorating than flirting with her London suitors. He might not like her, but he saw her. Truly saw her and sparred with her as an equal, or he had until she'd grown up and made her curtsey to the king.

Their roles had changed seemingly overnight. Instead of being her brother's friend, he was a rake to be avoided. Instead of being simply Beau, his friend's baby sister, she was Lady Boudicea, marriageable daughter of a duke. It was maddening.

The dance reunited her with her partner, Mr. Nowlin, and she dragged her attention away from Sandison. Nowlin smiled at her, brown eyes teasing her for missing her step. Beau smiled back. He might be an Irishman with a penchant for too much scent, but he was certainly handsome enough, and the lilt in his voice was charming. Half the ladies in London were enamored with their newest addition with his pretty coats, gleaming buckles, and fulsome compliments.

Sandison's pale head caught her attention again, and she jerked her eyes away from him. He was standing against the wall, flirting none too slyly with the very married Lady Cook. Her husband was, no doubt, in the card room oblivious to the set of horns sprouting from his head.

The lady and Sandison were rumored to be lovers, but gossip made such allegations about people on a regular basis. According to the scandalmongers, Beau herself always seemed to be on the cusp of contracting some grand alliance or on the verge of covering her family in mortification.

The scandals she'd nearly caused—or that had nearly

been inflicted upon her by various overeager suitors—didn't bear thinking about. Better by far that the *ton*'s gossips distract themselves with rumors of unsuitable engagements and heartless flirtations. The truth would ruin her.

A trickle of hot wax fell in a drizzle onto her chest and splattered across the silk of her gown. Her skin stung and she bit back an oath, missing the next series of steps. She sucked in a sharp breath and pulled the wax from her breast, flicking it to the floor with disgust. This was the second time tonight. Beau glanced up at the offending candles and stepped carefully back into the dance. Getting it out of her hair was going to be pure hell.

Beau glanced over her partner's shoulder, meeting Sandison's gaze for the briefest of moments. A smile hovered about his lips. Whether it was for her or Lady Cook she couldn't say, but given the way his companion was thrusting her ample bosom at him, it was likely the latter.

Light glittered off Sandison's hair. He'd been silver-haired as long as she'd known him, as were all the men in his family by the time they finished their teens. He never bothered to wear a wig, just his own pale locks, clean and immaculately dressed.

His family was reputed to be the illegitimate descendants of the disreputable second Earl of Rochester himself. A rumor that lent him a certain air of titillation, a deliciously illicit cachet. It drew women like moths to a flame... or maybe it was just his eyebrows.

She couldn't be the only woman undone by them. Could she?

•   •   •

She was watching him again.

Gareth could feel her gaze upon him as distinctly as if she'd reached out and run her hand down his arm. Lady Boudicea Vaughn: possessor of two gigantic brothers, a father who was legend with the small sword, and a mother who was herself distractingly entrancing even as fifty became a distant memory.

Lady Cook reclaimed his attention, her lovely face pulled into a pout. She wasn't used to being ignored, nor was she likely to be forgiving about such a breech. Especially over Beau. They were of an age, and she'd married one of the many suitors that Lady Boudicea had declined.

Gareth traced one finger along the exposed skin between the sleeve of Lady Cook's gown and the top of her kidskin glove. The tiny tassels dangling from the edge of her ruffle swayed. She shivered and stretched her neck out like a languid vixen. He circled his finger over the pulse point at her elbow, and she let out a small, indiscreet moan.

If their host's garden wasn't so well lit and filled to overflowing with guests, he'd have steered the oh-so-willing Lady Cook outside and satisfied them both. As it was, he'd have to wait and see if her husband accompanied her home.

Lady Boudicea disapproved of his dallying with married ladies. Hell, she disapproved of *him*. She always had. She'd been scathingly disapproving as a girl, more haughtily so since she'd left off playing with dolls and taken her place among the *ton* in London. Even muddied from head to toe and only twelve years old, she'd already had the ability to make him feel like an impudent fool. A decade later, he still couldn't say that he'd ever come out on top when they'd clashed.

And clash they did. It seemed inevitable at this point. Unavoidable. Was it wrong of him to enjoy it? To look forward to their little skirmishes? Probably so, but it was too delicious an entertainment to give up. Or it had been. He'd made a concerted effort to avoid such interactions of late.

He schooled his expression, concentrating on Lady Cook's breasts, the creamy flesh overflowing her bodice, begging for admiration. Anything to keep from glancing across the room, from meeting Beau's frosty gaze, from crossing the room to see if he could tease a smile out of her, make her rap him with her fan, provoke her into some small indiscretion...

Lady Cook inhaled, holding her breath for a moment, breasts rising until the edge of her areolas peeked out of the fabric. Full, soft, ripe. But somehow not as tempting tonight as they'd been previously. Tonight her smile was brittle, and the powder obscuring her skin was too heavy, making her corpse-like rather than luminous. The small taffeta beauty mark she'd placed beside her mouth was half-obscured in a frown line.

Beau's laugh caught his attention like a whip. He clenched his jaw and forced himself not to follow it back to its source. She was haunting him this season. Her brother Leonidas had asked him to keep an eye on her while he was absent from town. It hadn't seemed much of a burden at the time, but now that March was giving way to April and the Season was well and truly underway, a mild irritant had become outright torture.

Why was she was still unmarried? Were his fellow Englishmen blind, deaf, and utterly stupid?

She'd been out for several years, and while rumor had

her engaged a dozen times over, nothing had ever come of any of it. It was maddening. *She* was maddening.

She was the daughter of a duke, with a dowry that was likely to be immense, and she was far from being an antidote. Her one fault—aside from that temper—was her height. At nearly six foot, few men outside her own family were tall enough not to appear ridiculous beside her.

Look at the poor fop she was dancing with now. Gareth blew his breath out in a disgusted huff. Even in his evening pumps, the man was barely her match. If not for the poof of his wig he might even have appeared shorter than she. But still, somewhere there must be a man who was suitable? They didn't call the *ton* the top ten thousand for nothing. Even if you discounted those who were too short, too old, too young, and female, that had to leave a score or more who would suit? Didn't it?

Life would be so much simpler if she were married and happily domesticated somewhere far away like York or Dublin or Edinburgh. She was Scottish, after all. That should have expanded the pool of suitors. And everyone knew Scots tended to be great tall fellows. Surely there was a Highland laird or two in need of a wife.

Yes, life would be simpler if only she were somewhere else. Somewhere where she couldn't spend her evenings glaring at him and making him wish that he were something other than a penniless younger son.

That fact was like a flea biting deep below the layers of his clothing, niggling and occasionally sharply painful. He had more than enough for a life of elegant leisure for one, but it wouldn't stretch to supporting a wife. Certainly not one of Beau's quality and station.

They had a term for men like him who married girls like her: fortune hunter. Her father would shoot him before he'd give permission for such a match. Her brother Leo wouldn't bother with the gun. He'd use his bare hands.

No, men of his sort didn't marry, unless they took orders or found themselves a wealthy widow. There was no reason to do so, and every reason not to. And they certainly didn't marry girls with Lady Boudicea's pedigree and prospects. Not since Hardwick's Marriage Act went through anyway. Damn the old blighter.

Gareth forced a smile as Lady Cook pressed herself against his arm suggestively. She leaned in, close enough that he could almost feel her lips on his skin.

"I feel faint." Lady Cook opened her fan with a flick of her wrist, the sound causing heads to swivel toward them.

"Of course you do, my lady. Perhaps some air?"

Lady Cook smiled in response. Gareth propelled her through the thick of the crowd, circumventing the dancers. Her fingers slid possessively over his biceps.

A lady with the heart and soul of a whore from the gutter. She was everything a man such as he needed in life. Beau passed them in the whirl of the dance, so close her skirts struck his leg, silk and wool clinging to each other. Gareth ground his teeth and swallowed hard, ignoring the way his pulse leapt.

He'd known since the first time that he'd seen Beau with her hair up that he was done for. She'd come down the stairs in her father's house in a spangled silk gown, hair dressed and powdered, eyes glittering with excitement, and his lungs had seized.

Gone was the muddy child. Replaced, as if by fairy

magic, with a startling young woman whose vivid green eyes had a secret dancing behind them. A devilish, teasing secret.

If he'd thought for a moment that he had any chance at all, he'd have made himself miserable over her. As it was, he simply avoided her when possible and picked fights with her when avoidance wasn't an option.

Tonight, Lady Cook was going to be all that he needed to keep Beau at bay. They cordially loathed one another. Had done since their very first encounter. Beau would never seek him out so long as Lady Cook was on his arm. Lady Cook glanced unhappily around the garden. It was brightly lit with colored lanterns, and revelers had spilled forth from the house to choke its narrow walkways.

"My husband will be here all night playing cards and drinking too much port. Escort me home, Sandison. It will take hours simply to extricate my carriage from the mess outside...I'll need something to keep me amused."

Gareth nodded, tucking her hand securely into the crook of his arm. Lady Cook's idea of entertainment would no doubt prove entirely unimaginative, but it was better than spending half the night watching the unattainable Lady Boudicea Vaughn dance with other men, one of whom might someday actually get to call her wife.

His chest felt empty, soulless, as he hurried Lady Cook toward the door. This was his lot: unchaste wives and widows with an itch to scratch.

There'd been a time when he thought his life perfect.

～ CHAPTER 2 ～

Rush off to Firle Hill? Now?" Gareth's friend Roland Devere stared at him across the table. Sunlight streamed in through the window, casting half of Devere's face into shadow. Gareth squinted and slid his seat so that he wasn't staring directly into the light.

The taproom at The Red Lion was nearly empty. Most of his fellow League members had taken themselves off to a mill and the rest must still have been abed, exhausted from their exertions the night before.

Gareth blew out his breath in a disgruntled sigh and nodded. "Got a letter from Souttar this morning demanding my presence in no uncertain terms."

"How much trouble could your brother possibly have got himself into? He's only been married three months. Perhaps he needs advice of a very delicate nature?" Devere grinned wickedly.

"More likely he's bored, mired in the country, and simply wants Sandison at his beck and call," Lord Peter Wallace said with a shake of his head. "Someone to order about, someone to go shooting with, someone to play cards and chess with. You know what Souttar's like."

"Likes to have a fag. Always did," Devere said with a hint of disgust. "Never happier than when ordering someone about. I remember that much clearly. You'd think his new wife would fulfill that role admirably."

Gareth wrinkled his nose. The summation was perfectly accurate when viewed from the outside. He'd always been his brother's favorite subject, but it had also always been the two of them against their father. They might treat each other dreadfully, but when it came to dealing with the earl, he could always count on Souttar to have his back. He'd been close to refusing when he'd first read Souttar's summons, but truth be told, there was a hint of desperation in the wording, and a week or so away from town and Lady Boudicea would be a welcome relief.

He'd very nearly called out her name while fucking Lady Cook in her plush carriage. Whatever his brother wanted—and it was sure to be petty; it always was—it would still be better than causing a scandal of epic proportions because his mind was endlessly bent on a single subject. He'd come so very close to disaster with Lady Cook...

Gareth shuddered as the implication of his near slip worked its way down his spine: death, dismemberment, scandal, ruin. One simple word, one mistake, and he could have destroyed both their lives. Lady Cook wouldn't have taken the mistake lightly, and she wouldn't have spared either him or her former rival. The gossip would have lit up London like the Great Fire of 1666.

Not a soul would have believed either of them innocent. He was a rake, known for dallying with other men's wives. The leap to seducing virgins wasn't all that far... and when the girl in question was the outrageous Lady Boudicea Vaughn? Well, very few would want to believe her innocent. Seduction and ruin were her just deserts. Her entire family was considered either mad or depraved, and her brother marrying a courtesan had only added to that image.

Gareth shook off the sensation of doom. Better to put up with his family's decidedly feudal ideas for a few days or weeks. He'd be happy to see his mother, at least. His father's idea of her rights and prerogatives was nearly as ancient and restrictive as what he thought the dues of an elder son. Everyone was there to serve the earl first and the heir second. No one else really mattered.

Gareth could only be thankful he had no sisters. Their lot would have undoubtedly been worse than his, mere pawns for his father's machinations. At least he, as a man, could escape the greater part of his father's control now that he was grown.

The small independence that his maternal grandfather had left him had helped immensely. His father hadn't even bothered to threaten to stop his allowance for the past year or so. The earl took no pleasure in making empty threats, but Gareth knew with a cold certainty that his father would eventually attempt some new method of bringing him to heel. The earl simply couldn't help himself.

Devere waved his cup high, and the landlord's daughter appeared scant seconds later with a pot of steaming coffee. He heaped lump after lump of sugar into his cup until Gareth nearly gagged at the thought of drinking it.

"How long do you think you'll be gone?" Devere asked. "You'll be back for our cricket match, won't you?"

"Cricket's a sacred trust, especially when it's us versus the chuffs from Eton. Even my father wouldn't seek to prevent my returning for that." Gareth grinned and topped off his own cup.

"Bloody Etonians." Devere blew on his coffee, steam curling up and obscuring his eyes for a moment. "It's Harrow forever, and we'll show them this year as we have for the past ten."

"Now, now," a deep voice scolded from the door, and Anthony Thane crossed to join them. "League first; school second."

Gareth watched as the largest of his friends settled onto a chair that appeared far too small to hold him. Thane was certainly tall enough to be in the running for Beau's hand, but like himself, Thane was hobbled by his status as a second son. That and his position as an MP.

If Thane ever did marry, it would be to someone who could be a brilliant political hostess, not to a girl who preferred hunts to the balls that followed them and hobnobbing with dusty squires to playing games of political intrigue with the king's courtiers.

"League first, now and always," Devere agreed. "But all such bets are off when it comes to cricket. You shall be on one side, and we shall be on the other."

Thane chuckled, showing an expanse of teeth that seemed almost predatory. "Enemies on the field; friends off it. You should be aware that we have a new man. A bowler of unusual skill. Crawley's youngest brother. He's seventeen and preparing to take orders. But for now"—his smile grew—"he's all ours."

Devere grinned in return. "I wish you luck with your Crawleys, but I doubt one green boy will make the difference."

Thane nodded sagely, but a confident smile lurked in the corner of his mouth. "We shall see. Our luck has to turn eventually."

Gareth sipped his coffee, letting the bitter liquid linger on his tongue, and settled in to watch his friends bicker. It was likely to be the last amusing conversation in his life for several weeks, knowing Souttar.

Beau stepped out of the circulating library on Pall Mall and was nearly bowled over by a mob of running boys. Curses flew between them as they dodged around her in a swirling mass. The ball they were kicking bounced off the window of a passing carriage, earning them a rebuke from the driver, who pulled to, the axles groaning in protest at the sudden change in speed.

"My lady?" Beau's footman eyed the roving pack of boys with distrust.

"I'm fine, Boaz. Just apprentices on the loose."

"Yes, my lady." As he spoke, his eyes widened, and he dropped the carefully wrapped stack of books that he was carrying and lunged for her.

Hands grabbed her from behind, dragging her into the stopped coach. Boaz was shouting furiously; she could hear him even after the door shut behind her. He hit the side of the coach hard enough to rock it, but the coach rolled into motion all the same, leaving him and his tirade behind.

Beau flailed, hands fisted, feet lashing out. Her foot connected with some part of her abductor. He yelped, and then she was being crushed into the seat, the man's weight bearing down on her. Further struggle became impossible. Futile.

Musk flooded her nostrils, the man's cologne so strong that it choked her. Nowlin. Her eyes watered, and she held her breath, trying to clear her head. This close, inside the small coach, the scent was overwhelming.

"Get. Off. Me." Beau lay still, heart beating madly, as though it might claw its way out of her chest. The seat creaked and sagged as Nowlin finally clambered off her.

"Oh, my darling, tell me I've not hurt you."

Beau clenched her jaw until her teeth ached. His Irish lilt didn't make his preposterous blandishments one jot less ridiculous. Her pulse dropped so suddenly she felt dizzy. She blinked, eyes adjusting to the dark interior of the coach. He sat poised near the door, a patently false smile lifting the corner of his lips.

"Mr. Nowlin. What do you think you're doing?"

"Isn't it obvious? We're eloping, my sweet love."

Beau's throat tightened. She'd been abducted before. Her fortune almost guaranteed such rough-and-ready attempts to acquire it, and she seemed cursed to inspire acts of deluded romance. But neither of the men who'd attempted to gain her hand and dowry had been a mere acquaintance as this one was. "Mr. Nowlin." She laced her voice with steel, doing her best impression of her father. "Stop this coach and put me down at once."

"Can't do that." His smile grew, cocking up on one side. "Can't, my sweet love. We must make haste."

"Do stop calling me that. You sound like a moonling." She struggled with her hat, which seemed to have been irrevocably crushed and was now drooping over her eyes.

A hearty laugh answered her, and she felt the first flush of real concern. She freed the ribbon that held her hat and stared down at the broken circle of straw.

Her father and brothers would catch them long before they reached Scotland—of that she had no doubt— but she'd been warned not to get herself into any more scrapes. A wave of panic radiated through her limbs.

Her brother had suggested that perhaps they should have left her to Granby. But this was entirely different. Granby had admittedly been one of her flirts. One of her favorites. A man who might, in his wildest imaginations, have convinced himself that she would welcome his advances, even if her father wouldn't. Nowlin was very nearly a stranger. She'd only ever danced with him the once, for heaven's sake.

Leo couldn't be so cruel. He wouldn't. She forced herself to breathe and watched Nowlin for any hint that he might be creeping toward her. If he touched her, she couldn't possibly be held responsible for what she might do.

Her stomach threatened to turn itself inside out as he turned to look at her, but her glare kept him pinned firmly in place. He didn't look like a man inflamed by love—or even lust—and there was something grim about his eyes. Something serious that belied his smile.

Beau swallowed and hunched into the corner, refusing to give in. Panic and terror wouldn't serve her at all. At some point, they'd have to stop. They'd have to change horses, and he'd have to let her out of the coach. It was six days or more to Scotland. She simply had to be ready to seize whatever opportunity for escape presented itself. She'd done it before, and she could do it again.

When they stopped for the first change, Nowlin sat with his foot propped up on the opposite seat and his leg pressed hard against the door, barring the only exit. At the sound of a knock, he dropped the window. A cool breeze, promising rain, washed over her. Beau found herself inhaling deeply, as though there'd been not enough air inside the coach.

Nowlin took a parcel wrapped in brown paper from his servant and shut the window up with a loud bang the moment that the coachman's hand disappeared. Beau sagged back into the squabs. Tension drained out of her. This stop offered her nothing, no chance of escape, no opportunity to bolt.

Once the coach was back in motion, Nowlin unwrapped the paper and offered her a small loaf of brown bread and a chunk of grayish cheese. Beau took the bread and gnawed on it in silence, shuddering at the thought of even touching the cheese. The stench alone was enough to set her stomach roiling.

Her abductor shrugged one elegantly clad shoulder. "There's scant time for hot meals taken in taprooms, so you'd best learn to make do. No? Have it your way." He ate her portion in two healthy bites and washed it all down with the contents of his flask.

Beau methodically chewed the leathery crust of the bread. She was certainly hungry, but not hungry enough to eat that cheese. Not yet, anyway. A few more missed meals and she might be regretting her choice.

A few miles on Nowlin tapped the roof and the carriage rolled to a halt. He flicked his gaze over her and climbed out. The scrape and a *thunk* told her that he'd latched the door shut from the outside. Beau eyed the small window in the door. If she took off the pads that held out her petticoats, she *might* be able to squeeze through... but her bright, floral jacket would be all too visible if she was forced to run. She might as well be waving a flag.

Beau peeled off her gloves and took her purse from her pocket. She hurriedly counted the coins. Nearly a pound. Plenty of pocket money for an afternoon's shopping, but not nearly enough to get her home even if she could somehow manage to slip away from Nowlin.

Beau cursed under her breath and shoved the purse back into her pocket. Even with her brothers both out of town and her father likely ensconced at his club, the wheels of her rescue must already be in motion. Boaz would have seen to it.

Leo might have threatened to leave her to her fate in a fit of anger, but surely he wouldn't actually do so. Beau worried the seam of her glove with her teeth. No, even if Leo wouldn't come for her, her father would.

Of that she was sure.

Shadows lengthened as they rolled swiftly northward. Shivering, Beau rummaged through the small storage spaces under the seats: empty wine bottles, a single woman's shoe, a scanty wool blanket, slightly moth-eaten, and smelling oddly of dog and mold. What was more telling was what was missing. There was no gun. Either there never had been one, or Nowlin knew better than to leave her alone with one. Aside from the bottles, there was nothing to arm herself with, not even a traveling set with a dull knife.

Still shivering, she curled up under the blanket, the sturdiest of the bottles clutched in her hand.

THE DISH

Where authors give you the inside scoop!

From the desk of Katie Lane

Dear Reader,

Have you ever pulled up to a stoplight and looked over to see the person in the car next to you singing like they're auditioning for *American Idol*? They're boppin' their head and thumpin' the steering wheel like some crazy loon. Well, I'm one of those crazy loons. I love to sing. I'm not any good at it, but that doesn't stop me. I sing in the shower. I sing while cooking dinner and cleaning house. And I sing along with the car radio at the top of my lungs. Singing calms my nerves, boosts my energy, and inspires me, which is exactly how my new Deep in the Heart of Texas novel came about.

One morning, I woke up with the theme song to the musical *The Best Little Whorehouse in Texas* rolling around in my head. You know the one I'm talking about: "It's just a little bitty pissant country place…" The song stayed with me for the rest of the day, along with the image of a bunch of fun-loving women singing and dancing about "nothin' dirty going on." A hundred verses later, about the time my husband was ready to pull out the duct tape, I had an exciting idea for my new novel.

My editor wasn't quite as excited.

"A what?" she asked, and she stared at me exactly like the people who catch me singing at a stoplight.

She relaxed when I explained that it wasn't a functioning house of ill repute. The last rooster flew the coop years ago. Now Miss Hattie's Henhouse is nothing more than a dilapidated old mansion with three old women living in it. Three old women who have big plans to bring Miss Hattie's back to its former glory. The only thing that stands in their way is a virginal librarian who holds the deed to the house and a smokin' hot cowboy who is bent on revenge for his great-grandfather's murder.

Yes, there will be singing, dancing, and just a wee bit of "dirty going on." And of course, all the folks of Bramble, Texas, will be back to make sure their librarian gets a happy ending.

I hope you'll join me there!

Best wishes,

Katie Lane

♥ ♥ ♥ ♥ ♥ ♥ ♥ ♥ ♥ ♥ ♥ ♥ ♥ ♥ ♥

From the desk of Amanda Scott

Dear Reader,

What happens when a self-reliant Highland lass possessing extraordinary "gifts" meets a huge, shaggy warrior wounded in body and spirit, to whom she is strongly attracted, until she learns that he is immune to her gifts and that her father believes the man is the perfect husband for her?

What if the warrior is a prisoner of her father's worst enemy, who escaped after learning of a dire threat to the young King of Scots, recently returned from years of English captivity and struggling to take command of his unruly realm?

Lady Andrena MacFarlan, heroine of THE LAIRD'S CHOICE, the first book in my Lairds of the Loch trilogy, is just such a lass; and escaped Highland-galley slave and warrior Magnus "Mag" Galbraith is such a man. He is also dutiful and believes that his first duty is to the King.

I decided to set the trilogy in the Highlands west of Loch Lomond and soon realized that I wanted a mythological theme and three heroines with mysterious gifts, none of which was Second Sight. We authors have exploited the Sight for years. In doing so, many of us have endowed our characters with gifts far beyond the original meaning, which to Highlanders was the rare ability of a person to "see" an event while it was happening (usually the death of a loved one in distant battle).

It occurred to me, however, that many of us today possess mysterious "gifts." We can set a time in our heads to waken, and we wake right on time. Others enjoy flawless memories or hearing so acute that they hear sounds above and/or below normal ranges—bats' cries, for example. How about those who, without reason, dream of dangers to loved ones, then learn that such things have happened? Or those who sense in the midst of an event that they have dreamed the whole thing before and know what will happen?

Why do some people seem to communicate easily with animals when others cannot? Many can time baking without a timer, but what about those truly spooky types who walk to the oven door just *before* the timer goes—every time—as if the thing had whispered that it was about to go off?

Warriors develop extraordinary abilities. Their hearing becomes more acute; their sense of smell grows stronger. Prisoners of war find that all their senses increase. Their peripheral vision even widens.

In days of old, certain phenomena that we do not understand today might well have been more common and more closely heeded.

Lady Andrena reads (most) people with uncanny ease and communicates with the birds and beasts of her family's remaining estate. That estate itself holds secrets and seems to protect her family.

Her younger sisters have their own gifts.

And as for Mag Galbraith… Well, let's just say he has "gifts" of his own that make the sparks fly.

I hope you'll enjoy THE LAIRD'S CHOICE. Meantime, *suas Alba!*

Amanda Scott

www.amandascottauthor.com

♥ ♥ ♥ ♥ ♥ ♥ ♥ ♥ ♥ ♥ ♥ ♥ ♥ ♥

From the desk of Dee Davis

Dear Reader,

Sometimes we meet someone and there is an instant connection, that indefinable something that creates sparks between two people. And sometimes that leads almost immediately to a happily ever after. Or at least the path taken seems to be straight and true. But sometimes life intervenes. Mistakes are made, secrets are kept, and that light is extinguished. But we rarely ever forget. That magical moment is too rare to dismiss out of turn, and, if given the right opportunity, it always has the potential to spring back to life again.

That's the basis of Simon and Jillian's story. Two people separated by pride and circumstance. Mistakes made that aren't easily undone. But the two of them have been given a second chance. And this time, just maybe they'll get it right. Of course to do that, they'll have to overcome their fears. And they'll have to find a way to confront their past with honesty and compassion. Easily said—not so easily done. But part of reading romance, I think, is the chance to see that in the end, no matter what has happened, it all can come right again.

And at least as far as I'm concerned, Jillian and Simon deserve their happy ending. It's just that they'll have to work together to actually get it.

As always, this book is filled with places that actually exist. I love the Fulton Seaport and have always been fascinated with the helipads along the East River. The buildings along the river that span the FDR highway have always been a pull. How much fun to know that people are whizzing along underneath you as you stare out your window and watch the barges roll by. The brownstone that members of A-Tac use during their investigation is based on a real one near the corner of Sutton Place and 57th Street.

The busy area around Union Square is also one of my favorite hang-outs in the city. And so it seemed appropriate to put Lester's apartment there. His gallery, too, is based on reality—specifically, the old wrought-iron clad buildings in SoHo. As to the harbor warehouses, while I confess to never having actually been in one, I have passed them several times when out on a boat, and they always intrigue me. So it isn't surprising that one should show up in a book.

And I must confess to being an avid Yankees fan. So it wasn't much of a hardship to send the team off to the stadium during a fictional World Series win. I was lucky enough to be there for the ticker-tape parade when they won in 2009. And Boone Logan is indeed a relief pitcher for the Yankees.

I also gave my love of roses to Michael Brecht, deadheading being a very satisfying way to spend a morning. And finally, the train tunnel that the young Jillian and Simon dare to cross in the middle of the night truly does exist, near Hendrix College in Arkansas. (And it was, in fact, great sport to try and make it all the way through!)

Hopefully you'll enjoy reading Jillian and Simon's story as much as I enjoyed writing it.

For insight into both of them, here are some songs I listened to while writing DOUBLE DANGER:

"Stronger," by Kelly Clarkson
"All the Rowboats," by Regina Spektor
"Take My Hand," by Simple Plan

And as always, check out www.deedavis.com for more inside info about my writing and my books.

Happy Reading!

Dee Davis

♥ ♥ ♥ ♥ ♥ ♥ ♥ ♥ ♥ ♥ ♥ ♥ ♥ ♥ ♥ ♥ ♥

From the desk of Isobel Carr

Dear Reader,

I have an obsession with history. And as a re-enactor, that obsession frequently comes down to a delight in the minutia of day-to-day life and a deep love of true events that seem stranger than fiction. And we all know that real life is stranger than fiction, don't we?

RIPE FOR SEDUCTION grew out of just such a real-life story. Lady Mary, daughter of the Duke of Argyll, married Edward, Viscount Coke (heir to the Earl of Leicester). It was not a happy marriage. He left her alone on their wedding night, imprisoned her at his family estate, and in the end she refused him his marital rights and went to live with her mother again. Lucky for her, the viscount died three years later when she was twenty-six. And while I can see how wonderful it might be to rewrite that story, letting the viscount live and making him come groveling back, it was not the story that inspired me. No, it was what happened after her husband's death. Upon returning to town after her mourning period was over, Lady Mary received a most indecent proposal...and the man who made it was fool enough to put it in writing. Lady Mary's revenge was swift, brutal, and brilliant. I stole it for my heroine, Lady Olivia, who like Lady Mary had suffered a great and public humiliation at the hands of her husband, and who, also like Lady Mary, eventually found herself a widow.

And don't try finding out just what the poor man did or what Lady Mary's response was by Googling it. That story isn't on Wikipedia (though maybe I should add it). You'll have to come let Roland show you what it means to be RIPE FOR SEDUCTION if you want to find out.

Isobel Carr

www.isobelcarr.com

Find out more about Forever Romance!

Visit us at
www.hachettebookgroup.com/publishing_forever.aspx

Find us on Facebook
http://www.facebook.com/ForeverRomance

Follow us on Twitter
http://twitter.com/ForeverRomance

NEW AND UPCOMING TITLES

Each month we feature our new titles
and reader favorites.

CONTESTS AND GIVEAWAYS

We give away galleys, autographed copies,
and all kinds of exclusive items.

AUTHOR INFO

You'll find bios, articles, and links to personal websites
for all your favorite authors—and so much more.

GET SOCIAL

Connect with your favorite authors, editors, and
other Forever fans, and share what's important to you.

THE BUZZ

Sign up for our monthly romance newsletter,
and be the first to read all about it.